The
Girl
Who
Escaped
from
Auschwitz

BOOKS BY ELLIE MIDWOOD

The Violinist of Auschwitz

ELLIE MIDWOOD

The Girl Who Escaped from Auschwitz

bookouture

Published by Bookouture in 2021

An imprint of Storyfire Ltd.
Carmelite House
50 Victoria Embankment
London EC4Y 0DZ

www.bookouture.com

ISBN: 978-1-80019-498-4
eBook ISBN: 978-1-80019-497-7

Dedicated to all the freedom fighters, past and present; to everyone who has ever spoken against oppression, persecution, and inequality. Keep speaking your truth and fighting your battles. Your bravery won't be forgotten.

Prologue

Żywiec Mountains, Poland. July 6, 1944

The road before them, framed by towering mountains and emerald valleys, stretched long and empty in the early-morning sunlight. Under the dome of a pale blue sky, the air was fresh with the promise of freedom in it. Her blue overalls dusty and wrinkled after yet another night spent in a forest, Mala chewed contentedly on the blade of sweet grass, unbothered in the slightest by the rumbling of her stomach. Next to her, Edek was whistling a joyful tune, his arm draped around her shoulders, his SS tunic unbuttoned and smelling faintly of moss and smoke.

"Hungry, Mally?" His whistling stopped abruptly at the particularly loud noise her belly had produced.

Brave and in love, she tossed her head, gazing at his unshaven, tanned face with infinite affection.

"We can go off the road and try to find some more mushrooms," he suggested, searching her face.

Long before they had escaped Auschwitz, he'd promised to take care of her, to guard her life with his own, to do his utmost to make her forget the horrors of the death camp, but instead, he made her troop along the endless ribbons of half-trodden roads and survive on mushrooms and berries and sleep under the open sky, with only his embrace protecting against the elements.

Little did he know, that was all Mala needed: his arms around her and the air that didn't carry the stench of crematoriums with it. Hunger was the least of her concerns—Auschwitz had trained her well for surviving on a crust of bread.

"No, I don't want to stop just yet," Mala said. "Let's keep going. The sooner we reach the village, the better. We'll buy some food, together with civilian clothes for you." She gave her lover a mischievous once-over. "Else, the partisans will shoot you on sight if you appear before them in such an attire."

Feeling the molten dental gold rolling under his fingers in his pocket—a ghastly present from the *Sonderkommando*, the inmates manning the furnaces, to aid their escape—Edek nodded and hastened his step, as though spurred forward by their inaudible, powerful voices: *get yourselves to safety, tell the partisans your story, lead them, along with the victorious Red Army, toward this blasted place and avenge all the innocent souls we've been forced to burn by those SS beasts.*

The SS beasts, whose uniform he was presently wearing.

Passing his hand over the stiff gray-green wool, Edek thought of the moment he'd finally tear the hateful thing off of himself and burn it until nothing was left of it but ash.

Mala stopped to re-tie her boot. Just a few steps ahead of her, Edek gazed at the mountains longingly.

Lost in his thoughts, he didn't catch the deathly undertone to Mala's voice when she called his name.

"Edek."

It came from behind, a doomed half-a-gasp cracking with horror.

He turned, smiling—*What it is, my love?*—and felt his smile faltering, slipping at the sight of her ashen face, her eyes staring ahead. It seemed that all the pain in the world was reflected in their golden irises that had suddenly lost all of their shine.

Standing perfectly still, Edek slowly followed her gaze and felt himself sinking into a black abyss at the sight of two uniformed figures walking purposely and deliberately toward them.

They must have appeared from behind the bend of the road, heavens only knew why. The Germans hardly ever patrolled this area; Edek and Mala had been assured of this much by the Soviet prisoner of war inmates who had conducted several successful escapes themselves and the sympathetic Polish civilians who worked in the camp and were only too glad to stick it to the Nazis by helping another couple of inmates escape.

A dreadful, sickening shiver rising the heckles on his neck, Edek looked with infinite longing at the forest looming to their right, then shifted his gaze back to the approaching German border patrol. The muzzles of their submachine guns shone brightly in the golden rays of July sun. He stared at the weapons with bitter disappointment, angry tears already pricking his eyes. He'd seen far too many comrades mowed down by those guns to nurse a hope that the woods were within reach, that the border patrol men would somehow miss from such close distance, that at least Mala would escape the hail of the German bullets…

As though reading his mind, she picked up his hand and pressed it tightly, shaking her head with a small smile.

He had always been a dreamer. She had always been the voice of reality and, now, that reality stared into his soul with those black muzzles and there was suddenly no escape from it.

"Forgive me, please, Mala… I love you."

They were the very last words he uttered before the Germans leveled with them, saluted crisply and politely demanded, "Your papers, please, Herr Unterscharführer."

Chapter 1

Auschwitz, autumn 1943

Edek had had enough. The grim realization of it dawned on him along with the first slanting rays of the sunset bleeding red atop the barracks' roofs as he watched SS Officer Brück stomp repeatedly on an inmate's head with the steel-lined sole of his tall jackboot. The guard had been at it for quite some time now; his victim had long ceased not only resisting but moving altogether, and yet, the SS man kept crushing his skull with a disgusted viciousness of a farmer crushing a rodent with his shovel.

After all, that's precisely what they, the inmates, were to the SS—vermin. The Nazis had made their sentiments known to the new arrivals on their first day. Edek was among the very first political prisoners to receive such a "welcoming address" after their transport spilled them, dazed and sun-blinded, onto the infamous Auschwitz ramp in June of 1940. Seven hundred and twenty-eight people arrived in what used to be Polish barracks that day. It was on that day that Edward Galiński, the maritime school cadet, had ceased to exist. From that moment on, he became *Häftling*—inmate—531, sentenced to hard labor for…

What was it precisely that the Polish section of the Gestapo had stuck him with? So much time had passed since he was forced to sign his confession, the details of it kept slipping Edek's mind. A suspiciously sweet-talking, bespectacled German official had courteously explained to him that in order to leave the Gestapo cellar alive, Herr Galiński had better put his signature under the unreadable text in German and admit that he was plotting against the Reich along with other members of the Polish intelligentsia. Edek had tried to explain that he was a simple plumber's son and had never even dreamt of classing himself with the intellectual elite, let alone enter into any conspiracies as part of their circle. The German official had nodded sympathetically, slammed his fist into Edek's temple a few times, cleaned his hand thoroughly with a handkerchief, and advised him to think again.

By the end of the week, Edek had signed the paper.

Everyone eventually did, the Gestapo officer had explained to him amiably as he put Edek's case among rows and rows of similar dull-gray, swastika-bearing folders lining the walls of his newly established office in Tarnov prison. Behind the barred window, instead of Polish national flags that had all been taken down after the German invasion in 1939, crimson *Hakenkreuz* banners slapped against the façade. In the courtyard, crimson pools of blood sat next to the pockmarked wall. Enemies of the German Reich were shot there—journalists and liberals mostly, who agitated the regular folk and confused their minds against the official state propaganda. The Gestapo did away with such outspoken types first. They spoke the truth far too loudly for the Nazis' liking.

The Nazi didn't lie, as Edek learned from the men who shared the same transport to Auschwitz with him. They all were there on the same charges. "We're guilty of being young, healthy men capable of picking up weapons and organizing a revolt against those Nazi sods," one of them had said as he pulled on his cigarette, his eyes staring apathetically into the void. At his feet was a small bundle of personal possessions each inmate was permitted to take with him to their new destination, the name of which their escort kept like some sinister secret. He spoke in an undertone, for the abovementioned *Nazi sods* had replaced Polish policemen at the station and were presently sitting on a bench in the same train car, glaring at the Poles with beady eyes and barking abuse at them each time someone turned their gaze toward the window. "That's enough for them to ship us all someplace away from the general population on conspiracy charges," the man had carried on. "Women with children and the elderly don't represent any threat to them. That's why they're the only ones whom the Germans have left in peace, for now at any rate."

The young man's name was Wiesław.

Now, three and a half years later, he stood next to Edek and watched the SS guard stomp an inmate to death, and just one stolen glance at his friend's face told Edek that he had also had enough.

"We have to get out of here," Edek murmured in Polish.

It was sheer bad luck that Brück, the SS officer, heard him. At once, he whipped around, forgetting all about his victim buried in the mud.

"Using your swine language again?!" He was breathing heavily. In his neck, the vein was bulging under the tight collar with SS markings on it. "Do you wish to spend a few days in the *Strafblock* to freshen up your principles?"

Eyes downcast, Edek apologized promptly. He'd already spent more days in the punishment cell than he cared to remember. The size of a doghouse, the cell was a concrete sack with no windows or even standing room; only a filthy bucket in the corner to do one's business and a food bowl placed before him once a day. Though the physical discomfort was not the punishment; the real punishment was the complete and total isolation in that all-consuming darkness that slowly but surely drove one mad. After a mere few hours, a paralyzing sensation of having been buried alive began to creep up and even howling at the top of one's lungs didn't help in the slightest. Whoever designed those ghastly affairs went through the pains to ensure that his punishment inventions were almost entirely soundproof. One could scream themselves into consumption; there were only four walls and the echo of your own hoarse voice to reply to the desperate pleas.

No, Edek didn't fancy going back there at all.

The SS man, hands shoved in pockets, strolled up to the pair. He was a young fellow like them, hardly older than twenty-five, with the same smooth face and bright eyes, only, his body was all flesh and muscle and his head wasn't shaved but cut according to the fashion—short on the sides and the back, with a long, silky forelock falling onto one eye. The Aryan master of the world, solely on blood principle. A wry smile was playing on his lips.

"What was he saying to you?" He stood nose to nose with Wiesław, his pale blue eyes staring at the inmate without blinking.

But Edek's friend was not to be deceived by the suddenly friendly tone.

"He was admiring your wristwatch, Herr Scharführer," he explained in a grave tone in his halting German. "Said he's never seen such beautiful work."

Edek began to breathe again. Wiesław could be relied on in such matters—the man's ability to think on his feet had long ago earned him respect among the camp population.

The SS guard lifted his hand languidly. The red of the sunset glinted softly on the golden face of the watch. *Stolen from one Jew or the other,* Edek thought to himself but, naturally, said nothing, only apologized for speaking in his native language once again.

Scharführer Brück noticed the short prisoner number on Edek's chest, recognized a camp veteran and waved him off generously.

It wasn't the first time that his inmate number, or the red triangle of a political prisoner, had saved him from a beating or a bullet. Ever since the SS brought the first Jews to Auschwitz, it was commonly decided that all of their Nazi ideological hatred would be directed at them. The Poles suddenly found themselves to be elevated to the positions of the *Kapos*—inmate functionaries—along with the German criminals who proudly wore their civilian clothes with green triangles sewn onto them. Not that Edek minded such a welcome change, but he couldn't help but feel for the poor devils who were being slaughtered solely for belonging to the wrong race.

"Where are you two heading?" the SS officer asked.

"Birkenau, Herr Scharführer," Edek replied promptly. "On Rottenführer Lubusch's orders."

"Lubusch? The *Kommandoführer* in the locksmith shop?"

"*Jawohl*, Herr Scharführer. We're helping the carpenters on his orders whenever he tells us."

Edek was about to explain further, but Brück had already lost all interest.

"Take this stinking carcass to the cart—" with a lazy sweep of the hand, Brück indicated to what the inmates called the death cart that stood by the barrack's wall, a small mountain of corpses piled on it, "and off with you. You were sent here to work, not ogle people's watches."

But despite the guard's grumbling and his smirk, Edek saw how much the compliment had pleased him. The wristwatch must have been expensive indeed. Edek wondered about the man who had parted with it prior to parting with his life and felt sick to his stomach.

We have to get out of here, he had told Wiesław and he meant it. He'd had enough of the SS men trampling their innocent victims to death; he'd had enough of them appropriating the murdered men's riches. But, more than anything, he'd had enough of showing deference to all of these uniformed bastards, of apologizing for speaking Polish, of having to tear his cap off his shaved head each time one of them was near, of being called a subhuman and having to act like one.

Chapter 2

Birkenau, women's camp

The processing block was in wild confusion, as it always was when a fresh batch of new arrivals was chased through the block's stations with cracks of the horsewhip and crude insults. On the ramp, many of the unsuspecting women had their hopes high, still. It was in this block that they ordinarily parted with the last of their illusions, aided by the blows of the *Kapos* and mocking shouts of the SS.

Haunted by the memories of her own blood-chilling experience in the processing block, Mala stood beside the main SS warden's desk, patiently waiting for the warden to finish her paperwork, and watched the terrified crowd before her with eyes full of inner torment.

A camp runner in charge of delivering SS orders and official documents from one block to another when she wasn't busy aiding the women's camp's leader Maria Mandl with office work, Mala no longer had anything to fear from the wardens or the *Kapos*. An official armband with an insignia of a *Läuferin* on her left bicep, civilian clothes and dark-blond hair pulled into a bun instantly distinguished her from the general camp population. And still, she loathed the processing block the most; it was the place where the last fragments of hope were clubbed to death, where former lives were cut short and swept away along with lumps of shorn hair, where names were abolished and replaced by numbers, forever branded into women's forearms with a crude tattooing tool.

"Lose all of your clothes, you filthy sows! *Schnell, schnell, schnell,* move it, move it, quick! Everything off; yes, your dirty undergarments also, my gentle piglets." A harsh snap of the whip was followed by someone's startled cry. "Quit your stalling and get the line moving before something happens."

Still, some tried to protest; usually, the matrons from the Orthodox families. Their tearful pleas weren't about themselves, either; it was their young daughters' modesty they were concerned about the most: *Do with us as you please, but spare the girls, Frau Aufseherin!* The sheltered, wide-eyed, petrified girls who trembled in their mothers' protective embraces before being torn from the loving arms. The girls who were shoved toward the nearest male inmate on duty, who questioned "if they wished to undress themselves or required assistance? Because they were all too glad to deliver."

Loud guffaws came from the inmate functionary's comrades. They worked at the next station—a vast room where chairs had been set up in the usual German orderly manner and where the naked, humiliated, crying girls' hair was shorn by the industrial shaving machines.

It was the shaving that would remain Mala's worst memory of her own first day at Auschwitz, for as long as she would live. A year and a half had passed since a Red Triangle prisoner ran his coarse fingers through her dark-blond locks—*like gold! A shame, really*—and tutted in apparent disapproval as Mala's beautiful hair fell in clumps over her bare shoulders, into her lap and open palms.

As though in defiance, or out of some desire to preserve at least something of her former self, she had clasped one of the locks in her palm and refused to part with it, even when they were being chased through the disinfection block. She held onto it when they were dunked into a tub of some green and atrociously smelling chemical solution; she didn't let go of it when powder was thrown on her nicked and already-burning scalp, armpits, and pubic area; she kept it clasped in her fist when they were shoved into the dingy room with showerheads glaring at them ominously from the ceiling. Later, Mala had learned that the gas chamber looked precisely the same. Fortunately for her, the receiving SS doctor on the ramp was looking for persons with knowledge of languages and she fluently spoke six. No gas for Mala that day; a regular shower only. Essential inmates were in short supply; she learned it quickly enough.

The Orthodox girls parted with their hair with a sort of a resigned apathy. They would have to part with it soon regardless; it was a custom for a Jewish bride to shave her head on the night of her wedding and keep it shaved for the rest of her life, wearing turbans or wigs in public, and remaining as bald as the day she was born until her death. But Mala wasn't raised in a religious Jewish household. Her father positively refused the idea of the commune, of a woman's sole role being a mother and homemaker, of having to consult religious leaders on just about any major decision, and so, he had moved his entire family from the Polish city of Brzesko to a much more cosmopolitan Antwerp in Belgium and raised his daughter to be an independent and self-sufficient young woman.

Against Orthodox rules, Pinkus Zimetbaum encouraged Mala to get the best education he could provide and, when the family business fell on hard times due to his rapidly progressing blindness, he would not stop expressing his gratitude to Mala for picking up the role of the breadwinner. To be sure, their old conservative Polish community's rabbis would have never approved of a young woman working in the well-known fashion store Maison Lilian, but Pinkus did, and not only did he approve, he actively encouraged his daughter to make her own living so that she wouldn't have to be dependent on anyone's goodwill.

"This way, if something happens to me, you shall be able to support yourself, Mally. I brought you here, to Antwerp, so you would live your own life, the way you want and not the way the commune sees fit. So you would discover love all on your own, instead of marrying someone a commune's matchmaker found for you. I couldn't bear the thought of it—you, being unhappy. I want you to be as free as you wish and enjoy everything the world has to offer. You're such a brilliant girl, Mally. A brilliant girl and a free spirit, of which I'm immensely proud. Do not allow anyone to take your freedom away."

But the Nazis came to Belgium after they swallowed up the other European countries just as effortlessly and, unlike Mala's father, they didn't care one whit whether she was Orthodox or assimilated. A Jew was a Jew and the only good Jew was a dead one, or at least one working for the prosperity of the Reich—such was the latest psychology among the Germans. Next, the familiar business came—the holding camp in Malines, the cattle train, Auschwitz, number 19880 tattooed into her skin.

First, they took her freedom. Then, they took her hair. The latter Mala had already managed to get back. One day, she would regain the former; she swore it to herself.

Now, a camp veteran, she watched these new girls being shorn like sheep with somber, pitying eyes and couldn't help but run her fingers through her own hair, as though to ensure that it was still there, that she had pulled through, that she had clawed her way to the very top of the local totem pole and was safe from abuse and obliteration. And yet, she still carried that lock of shorn hair neatly tucked in the small cloth bag she kept in her skirt's pocket. It was a reminder of her freedom lost and her promise to regain it one day.

"This is the abuse of human rights that goes beyond any comprehension!" cried out one woman now. "We aren't criminals; what reason do you have for putting us here and treating us as such?"

Instantly alarmed, Mala glanced up sharply at the woman who dared to speak up. She was still dressed, very smartly at that, in a tweed suit and patent leather shoes. Mala noticed one of the inmate functionaries already ogling them with unhealthy interest.

Pushing herself off the wall against which she was leaning, Mala made a move toward the vocal lady, who hadn't, apparently, grasped the fact that there was no such notion as human rights in this death factory.

Refusing to be silenced by the terrified crowd around her, her voice was gathering volume and conviction along with it. "I studied international law. There has never been a precedent such as this in the civilized nations' history that free people were rounded up and herded like sheep for slaughter into camps against their will. I demand to speak to the representatives of the international—"

A blow from a *Kapo*'s baton put an abrupt end to her complaint. He had administered it atop her scalp with the impersonal cruelty of a butcher who had long grown used to the job and performed it mechanically and exemplarily well. Like a puppet, from which someone had just cut a string, the woman fell in a heap at the *Kapo*'s feet.

"Is the big-mouthed bitch dead?" the SS warden inquired from behind the desk. She had not once raised her elegantly coiffured head from the list, onto which she was writing the names and numbers.

The *Kapo* dealt a sharp kick into the woman's midsection. The entire block could hear the air escape her lungs; yet, the *Kapo*'s most recent victim had not budged.

"*Jawohl*, Frau Aufseherin," the *Kapo* confirmed, undisturbed. "Process her." He gestured to two of his underlings. He didn't need any more direct orders from the uniformed woman. He was a well-oiled killing machine, with a wooden baton at his hip as a sign of the SS-granted authorization to reduce the numbers of the undesirables, with empty eyes devoid of any emotion.

The corpse was stripped bare without further ceremony. In the corner, by the tall sacks already filled with the discarded clothing, two women from the *Kanada*—the sorting *Kommando* where the prisoners' belongings were confiscated and redistributed—were arguing over the dead woman's jacket. Mala watched on as another inmate was already shaving the former lawyer's curled hair, while his *Kommando* mate was probing her orifices for hidden valuables.

"Just two golden fillings in her mouth," he announced the result of his search.

An inmate dentist was already waiting nearby with the pliers at the ready.

The SS warden gasped suddenly. "That blasted cow! Does anyone know her name?"

"Helga Schwarz," the *Kapo* supplied his victim's name after consulting the documents that the *Kanada Kommando* left lying on the floor—their only interest was in the clothing, not yet another dead Jew's identity.

"*Dr.* Helga Schwarz," Mala corrected him very softly. "She was a Doctor of Law."

It was oddly pleasing to see that the warden added "doctor" before the woman's name in the list that she handed to Mala, allowing the murdered woman that last dignity at least in death.

As Mala carried the processing block paperwork to the camp office to be filed, she kept whispering Dr. Schwarz's name under her breath, committing it to her memory. The Nazis and their subordinates may have slaughtered and already forgotten her, one of their countless victims, but Mala wouldn't. She would carry her memory out of the camp and tell the world that Dr. Schwarz had died a hero, fighting for her fellow sufferers' rights till the end.

Chapter 3

Auschwitz

As it always was in the middle of the afternoon, the camp locksmith shop was abuzz with activity. The machines roared and hummed; now and then, sparks descended upon the concrete floor in a shimmering waterfall. Metal shavings crunched under the boots of the *Kapos*, who strolled about with an air of importance, their coarse fingers caressing the handles of their batons, while their hard, piercing eyes searched for the slightest excuse to apply their clubs to one's back. The strong smell of iron and grease hung in the air.

After a rather superficial inspection, Edek hurled a metal part he'd just produced into a wooden box. It was his two hundred and seventy seventh for today, he realized with a sort of grim self-loathing. He didn't mind making the locks, but then, one day, Karl, one of their *Kapos*—a short, mean-spirited German whose mouth was permanently twisted into a malicious smirk—had informed them of their products' ultimate destination. Suddenly, everyone's stomach had contracted with revulsion for contributing to the successful functioning of the Nazi terror machine.

"The Gestapo jails, my gentle lambs," Karl had declared in a singsong, jeering voice. It was obvious from his hateful smile the diabolical pleasure he was drawing from their communal look of mute, stunned disbelief. "You're helping lock up your own people. They shall thank you, I'm sure, when they arrive here. *If,* they make it this far."

Karl was a professional criminal, sent to Auschwitz for re-educational purposes. Edek always found it perplexing, the fact that the German justice system placed murderers, rapists, and thieves above them, former ordinary civilians who had never broken the law, solely on blood principle. According to the Nazis' warped logic, *Reichsdeutsche* criminals could be re-educated; in contrast, Polish nationals, Soviet prisoners of war and Jews belonged in concentration camps.

In the midnight silence of his barrack, Edek often lay wide awake and searched his memory to pinpoint the exact day when the world had turned upside down, when the criminals began to be hailed as heroes, when free press had turned into a propaganda machine, when a narcissistic, cruel dictator started to be looked upon with reverence as a savior of the nation—and could not. Soon, he ceased thinking about it altogether. It outraged his sense of justice far too much; it made him tremble with righteous indignation and, in Auschwitz, wasting one's nerves on empty illusions was a sure ticket to the gas.

"Whatever are you getting yourself wound up for?" Wiesław had demanded one night, his voice thick with sleep. They shared a bunk and all of Edek's tossing must have gotten to him after all. "You're wasting precious energy for nothing. Will your perfect logic about the world order persuade the SS to release you? Fat chance. So quit your stirring and exasperated sighing and off to sleep with you. In a place like this, one ought to forget about such matters in order to survive. Now, what you need to remember is who from the SS kitchen trades bread for cigarettes and which *Kapo* won't bash your head in for spending more than a minute in the latrine. Those are the matters of paramount importance. All else is irrelevant."

Two hundred and seventy-eight. Now, Edek marked the number on the sheet and thought about the extra ration of turnip soup he would receive if he produced five hundred of such details—the reward for over-completing the daily quota, according to the new *Kommandant*'s orders. The old one had operated slightly differently: he simply sent the prisoners who couldn't keep up to the crematoriums.

Two hundred and seventy-eight details to produce two hundred and seventy-eight locks to lock two hundred and seventy-eight people up in the dingy Gestapo cellars that stunk of blood and death. It was beyond comprehension, the fact that such numbers could exist in the first place, that there were so many people for the Nazis to lock up. But then Edek roved his gaze around and saw that the numbers added up after all. The Auschwitz crematoriums had swallowed up hundreds of thousands—perhaps millions—up until now and it was Edek's profound conviction that Auschwitz was far from being the only such place where people were murdered for nothing more than the wrong nationality charges.

A runner's shout—"Mail for Rottenführer Lubusch!"—brought Edek out of his bleak reverie. He wiped his grease-smudged hands on a rag and took the letter from the boy, almost grateful for the distraction.

"Run along, I'll give it to him," Edek promised the boy. "Herr Rottenführer is in his office. I was just heading there anyway."

Near the entrance of the *Kommandoführer*'s office, two *Kapos* were smoking. At the sight of someone turning the corner, they froze stiff with fear, but then, seeing that it was only an inmate, relaxed their shoulders and continued to gossip about recent Auschwitz affairs.

Edek paused in front of the door, pulled the striped cap off his shaved head, adjusted his uniform and knocked.

"Enter."

Rottenführer Lubusch, their work detail's direct supervisor, was writing something at his desk. He was a young man who appeared older than his years due to the pensive, somewhat forlorn look in his pale eyes; a type that belonged in the dusty libraries of the old world's universities instead of the oil-slicked locksmith workshop in Auschwitz. Everything about him—his sensitive hands with long, slender fingers, the air of quiet sophistication that wasn't acquired and cultivated but rather inherited, even the manner in which his dark hair was parted on the right, sharp as though slashed with a razor—stroke a false note with the SS uniform that he was wearing. It was form-fitting and elegant, but it suited him just as poorly as a striped uniform suited Polish intelligentsia. Perhaps that was the reason why Lubusch constantly scratched under his collar and winced uncomfortably, complaining about the coarse material or the soap the laundry *Kommando* used. His very skin rejected it, or at least, such was Edek's conviction.

Edek saluted sharply—he didn't mind saluting this particular SS man—and approached Lubusch's desk.

"A letter for you, Herr Rottenführer. And the production numbers for the first half of the day. I'm in charge of the lunch distribution today—"

But Lubusch was no longer listening. Having recognized the small, careful handwriting on the envelope, he snatched it eagerly from Edek's hand and tore into it, a warm smile growing on his face, instantly transforming it.

"You know where to put it." Without looking up, he waved Edek toward the filing cabinet, seemingly forgetting that it was his duty to sign and stamp the list first.

Concealing a knowing grin, Edek retreated to the cabinet and pulled out the drawer with the current month's files, shuffling through them with purposeful slowness to give his superior his privacy. Lubusch had always been a decent fellow, but after he went on leave about a year ago and returned with a slim golden band around his finger, his treatment of the inmates had mellowed and he even began to actively help them behind his own *Kapo*'s backs.

Edek stalled for as long as he thought was appropriate, cleared his throat as softly as possible and opened his mouth as he turned to face Lubusch. *What a scatterbrain I am today, Herr Rottenführer!* he planned to say. *Your signature and the stamp—*

But he was stopped in his tracks, paralyzed by what he had seen. The letter still clenched in his hand, Lubusch was lying face down on his folded arms, looking like a man who had just been shot. He was perfectly motionless; only the fingers of his free hand were clenching and unclenching in impotent desperation.

Frightened and unsure of himself, Edek made a move toward the door; opened and closed his mouth, unable to produce a single sound, and began to search the office frantically for anything, literally anything—

A water carafe! He rushed across the room, grasped it by the neck, and nearly spilled the water onto the doily—a present from Lubusch's wife, he was sure of it. While filling the glass, he tiptoed toward the desk and put the glass near the SS officer's hand as quietly as possible.

"Water, Herr Rottenführer?" he asked gently.

Whether it was the genuine concern in Edek's voice or the gesture itself, Lubusch finally broke. His shoulders began to quiver with silent, pitiful sobs that, for some reason, tore at Edek's heart as though it was he who was suffering.

Remembering the *Kapos* in the corridor, Edek rushed to the door and promptly turned the key in the lock. He brought it to Lubusch and, just as he did with the glass of water, nudged it delicately toward the *Kommandoführer's* pale hand, under his fingers. After that, he straightened next to the SS man's desk and remained as still as a statue, guarding his master with grave, silent dignity.

An entire minute must have passed before Lubusch raised his head and slowly wiped his face with the back of his hand. To Edek's surprise, he didn't seem embarrassed in the slightest with his tears and didn't bother hiding his vulnerability. He simply sat gazing vacantly ahead with his bright, wet eyes—astonishingly human, almost noble in his sudden fragility.

In search of at least some clue, Edek stole a sideways glance at the letter and regretted it almost instantly.

"…if you only knew how deeply it hurts, being looked upon like a second-class citizen at all times. Just yesterday, a grocer—grocer!—had the insolence to question me solely because of my accent. While I was

arguing with him, someone whistled a policeman; the policeman fetched a Gestapo official. Had I not had your photograph and all of my identification on me, including our marriage certificate, God only knows where they would have taken me. The grocer apologized afterward; explained that he was only doing his civic duty. Thought I was an escaped foreign worker. And that was just one of my recent adventures. And you say it's safer for me to be in Germany. I should never have left Poland! I'm hated here, hated solely for—"

Edek averted his eyes. He needn't read any further, everything was clear as day.

"What's your first name, Galiński?"

Edek glanced up, startled. Not at the term of address—Lubusch only called the men in his workshop by their last names, never by their numbers—but at the unexpected intimacy of the question.

"Edek—Edward," he quickly corrected himself.

A small smile appeared on Lubusch's face. "Really?"

Edek nodded his affirmation, somewhat surprised.

"So is mine. How do you spell it? With a W?"

"Yes, with a W." Edek discovered that he was smiling as well.

"My wife is Polish." His namesake confessed what Edek had deduced himself by now.

Edek nodded, unsure of what he ought to say. Neither "that's wonderful" nor "I'm sorry" appeared to be a suitable reply and so he blurted out the only thing that came to his mind: "I didn't know you were allowed to marry Polish women."

"Officially, we aren't."

"But you still did."

Lubusch shrugged his shoulders evasively. It was evidently a painful subject he wasn't particularly fond of discussing. "Frankly speaking, I always thought all the racial laws were ridiculous."

Edek blinked in astonishment. That was something new entirely, coming from an SS man, no matter how lenient.

"Are you married, Edek?—Do you mind if I call you Edek? Or do you reserve this right for your friends only?"

"Not at all, Herr Rottenführer. Edek is much better than *Häftling* 531."

"That much is true, I suppose."

"And no, I'm not married."

"Have a girl waiting for you at home?"

Who would wait for so long? Edek wanted to say.

"No, Herr Rottenführer," he replied instead.

For some time, Lubusch stared pensively ahead.

"Who is considered inferior in your country?" he said eventually.

"Jews, I suppose. A lot of people don't like them."

"What about you?" Lubusch asked.

"I like and dislike people based on their character, not race or religion."

"So, if you fell in love with a Jewish girl, would you have married her?"

"I would have."

"All right. So, say, you did marry her. But now your compatriots are treating her horribly because—as you said it yourself—many people don't like them in your country and she grew terribly unhappy…" He paused, as though tasting the words before uttering them, "What would you do?"

"I would have taken her someplace where she would be happy," Edek replied without hesitation.

"And say, if you were in the army?"

"I would have run away." He didn't even blink.

Lubusch looked at him closely. "You would have deserted then?"

"For the woman I love—yes."

"They would have shot you if they caught you."

From Edek, a shrug. "It would have been worth it. At least my beloved would have remembered me as a hero who risked everything for her and not a coward who—" He bit his tongue, stopping himself mid-word, but it was much too late.

Too terrified to even think, Edek risked a glance at Lubusch and saw, to his relief, that the SS man was chuckling. That was the last thing he had expected.

"Don't fret, I won't take you to the wall and shoot you for speaking the truth. I needed to hear that, I suppose."

"I wasn't talking about you." Edek desperately tried to save the situation. "I was talking hypothetically…"

"Naturally, hypothetically." Lubusch looked as though he found Edek positively amusing just then. "I said, don't fret. I'm not mad. Have you ever seen me mad?"

"No, Herr Rottenführer."

"You truly would have run then?" Lubusch narrowed his eyes slightly, turning serious again.

"Yes, Herr Rottenführer."

"And to where?"

For a few moments, Edek considered. "Holland, I suppose," he ventured eventually. "I heard they treat all immigrants the best."

"And what if Holland was occupied?"

"Then England, I guess."

"And how would you get there?"

"There must be someone who would have smuggled us for a certain sum. Isn't that why some French Resistance fellows are serving their terms here?"

Lubusch nodded. His eyes had grown brighter; the haunted look was gone out of them. A faint blush colored his usually pale cheeks. Edek could tell that something profoundly important was at war within him, some ideological battle in which his uniform and his duty was slowly losing to a Polish girl who crocheted doilies for him and signed her letters, *with infinite love, always yours, A.*

"You go ahead and fetch lunch for your *Kommando*," Lubusch said at last, as though just now remembering himself. "And give everyone double rations. The numbers are exceedingly good today."

Picking up the key, Edek hid a smile at the thought that Lubusch had not once looked at the production list. He was already on his way when he heard a soft "thank you" behind his back.

"Thank *you,* Herr Rottenführer," Edek replied.

Thank you for keeping your humanity in a world that prides itself in ruthlessness.

Chapter 4

Birkenau

Mala's hand, with a stub of a pencil in it, hesitated over the official form. Despite the small iron stove in the nurses' cubicle, on particularly cold days, Mala could see her own breath coming out in translucent clouds. The *Revier*—the complex of sickbay barracks for the inmates—was a far cry from the comfort offered by the camp office where Mala ordinarily worked, but she never complained. The thought of helping her fellow inmates warmed her better than any central heating system would.

Maria Mandl, the head of the women's camp and Mala's immediate superior, had regarded Mala in amazement when the latter had asked to be appointed to that particular duty in addition to the ones she was already carrying out.

"You wish to be put in charge of assigning discharged inmates to different details? Whatever for? You'll have to spend hours in an unheated barracks crawling with lice and disease."

"It's quite all right, Lagerführerin. I know the camp better than anyone and I know the inmates. I believe I shall do a much better job of matching them to different roles according to their qualifications and abilities than some *Kapo* who simply puts their names next to details without bothering to ensure that they're up for a job."

"They have to be up for any job," Mandl had countered, unimpressed. "That's the sole reason they are allowed to live, so they can work and contribute to the final victory. If they don't wish to work—or claim that they can't—we have a special place for such duty shirkers."

The gas chamber. Mala's face had grown very still.

"You are correct as always, Lagerführerin," Mala had replied, "but what I meant to say was that it would be wiser to assign seamstresses to sewing details rather than sending them to gravel raking. Former construction workers would do a much better job producing rubber at the Buna factories at the Monowitz subcamp than French salesgirls. And, naturally, doctors and nurses would apply their talents with much greater use taking care of the sick rather than emptying latrines with the *Scheisskommando*. Do you not agree with me?"

The question was rhetorical, of course, but Mala had long grown used to the fact that even the most irrefutable logic had no place in the dark shadow of Auschwitz. The camp wasn't organized with the purpose of putting enemies of the state to work; it was designed as a death factory, where such "enemies" would be exterminated through work, starvation, or disease. That was why the *Kapos* in charge of such assignments took great pleasure in competing with one another in matching the most unsuitable candidates to work that was simply beyond their victims' intellectual or physical powers. Cosmopolitan girls who used to work for fashion magazines found themselves peeling potatoes in the kitchen; jewelers' apprentices, with their fine hands, were sent to the laundry detail; musicians were appointed as truck drivers and former truck drivers discovered themselves assisting SS physicians without having the faintest idea of what they were doing.

It had been idiotic to hope that Mandl would see reason, but much to Mala's surprise, the women's camp leader had approved of the idea.

On her first day as an appointed official, Mala had marched into the sickbay with a radiant smile full of hope; now, she sat examining the list in front of her with her eyes dark with anguish and cursed for burdening herself with the responsibility of choosing who was to live—and who to die. There were only two available positions in the *Kanada* work detail, where clothes were in abundance, where food could be found in countless suitcases, where gold and precious gemstones could be concealed in one's mouth to be exchanged for something edible later. The rest of the positions were all in the outside work gangs. To be assigned to an *Aussenarbeit* was essentially a death sentence to an inmate, and particularly in the harsh Polish winter.

Mala shuddered each time, when delivering messages to the wardens, she saw skeletal women in their threadbare robes lifting stones that must have weighed as much as the women themselves, carrying them across the field, where another outside work detail was breaking them up for road building. If they didn't trot fast enough for the *Kapo*'s liking, they were lashed and cursed at. If they dropped their load or collapsed under its weight, they were shot or mauled by the SS wardens' dogs. Even the strongest prisoners lasted mere weeks doing back-breaking work for the Reich; the weaker ones dropped like flies within days, and sometimes even hours. Their *Kommando* mates carried them back into the camp each evening—a grotesque parade of the dead and soon-to-be dead, marching through the gates to the cheerful sounds of the camp orchestra.

Mala threw a gaze full of agony at the small window behind which the wind was howling viciously and almost thought of putting her own name onto the list instead of one of the condemned women. Only, it would be of no use; Mandl had grown much too dependent on Mala's services. Even the camp leader Hössler, Mandl's superior, held her in high esteem, sneaking French cigars into her pockets whenever she brought documents into his office—"*Trade them for some cheese and butter; in winter, those are two items of the most paramount importance to keep warm.*" They would never let her go. She was chained to them good and fast.

Stasia, an inmate physician, stuck her head through the door, pulling Mala out of her dark musings. "Still working, Mally?"

Mala's glare was eloquent; compiling these death lists was the last thing she wished she were doing.

Sliding into the room, Stasia pulled the door after herself noiselessly. A Polish doctor, she wore the red triangle of a political prisoner on her chest with visible pride and was notorious among the camp population for getting into arguments with SS physicians. Oddly enough, her outspoken manner and sharp, analytical mind had earned her the respect of her German "colleagues." More often than not, they authorized her demands for proper medical supplies, which undoubtedly had saved many lives. She had a severe face that seemed to be permanently set into a grimace and thin, bloodless lips that rarely smiled; however, it was her eyes that betrayed her true nature. Warm-brown and brilliant, they radiated compassion and a desire to help that went beyond one's official obligations. Her job was never done once she shed her off-white coat. Stasia was constantly on duty, ready to trade her own last ration in exchange for a life-saving roll of pills, never complaining about doing double shifts whenever an influx of patients overwhelmed the sickbay doctors.

"Listen, Mally," she began in an urgent whisper. "Rita, the Soviet girl who I asked you to smuggle some Cardiazol for, has to go to the *Kanada*. I just learned she has a boyfriend in the *Sonderkommando*."

"Ah, the corpse carrier detail."

It was both tragic and strange, the fact that the *Sonderkommando* was considered the camp elite due to their privileged position, and yet, no one willingly volunteered to join their ghoulish detail. And who could blame them in all good conscience? Just one look at the haunted faces of those hulky inmates, who trooped around the crematoriums in their tall rubber boots, was enough to frighten away even the most desperate types. It was a damnable business, escorting entire families to the gas chambers every single day, listening to the screams and frantic banging on the airtight door that grew weaker, gradually dying out completely, and then dragging those bodies out by sticks with long hooks on them—for some couples clung to each other with such force, it was impossible to separate them otherwise. Piling them up onto the industrial elevator; laying them out on the floor for the dentists to extract their golden crowns and search their orifices for hidden treasures; stacking them onto the gurney in a certain fashion and shoving them into the raging inferno; hosing the foam, blood, excrement and urine off the floor of the gas chamber and waiting for it to dry before admitting another batch inside. Zyklon-B, a cyanide-based poisonous gas used by the SS for mass murder, didn't dissolve well in the humid conditions.

The *Sonderkommando* smoked while they waited, mostly in silence. Such work inspired the desire to throw oneself onto the electric wire, not to partake in small talk. In exchange for their grisly services, the SS kept them warm and snug in their two-bunk beds inside the crematorium itself; kept them well-supplied with food and, most importantly, alcohol; and rewarded them with visits to the Auschwitz brothel. Though that last privilege was reserved for the non-Jewish inmates only. Not that it mattered; according to the working girls themselves, the *Sonderkommando* men mostly wanted to lay their heads on a warm woman's lap and cry softly while the girl gently stroked their shaved heads. *The corpse carrier detail.* It had the highest rate of suicides among the entire camp complex.

"The very same." Stasia perched on the edge of the flimsy desk, which didn't even squeak in protest. How thin they all had grown, Mala mused, focusing on the physician's sharp eyes in which thoughts were constantly at work. She had befriended Mala before anyone else did; only later did Mala discover the reason for such friendliness: Stasia belonged to what was called "an organization" in the camp's terms. The local resistance that refused to submit to the SS-imposed order. "At any rate," she continued, "now that Rita's almost recovered, you ought to assign her to the *Kanada*. She'll be able to get certain things out, to exchange them later for whatever's needed. And don't fret, she's as reliable as they come.

I spoke with her countless times while I was treating her; she's a Red Army girl, very ideological, so you can imagine how much she loathes the Nazis after they captured her and her comrades. First-rate resistance material."

Half-glancing at her, Mala couldn't help but grin. Speaking in riddles and undertones had long become Stasia's second nature due to her clandestine activities.

"You'll be getting your cut for it; it's all already arranged," the inmate doctor continued. Only her lips moved with great urgency, the rest of her face remaining perfectly still. She hadn't blinked once, her eyes delivering the message that she didn't wish to put into words: *We need this, Mala. This is a question of life and death for all of us, not just one inmate.*

Mala understood everything. Though not a member of "the organization" herself, she assisted them with whatever she could.

Stasia's face positively transformed when she saw Mala write Rita's name on the official form. At once, she extracted sulfa drugs, five pieces of bread, a few loose cigarettes and a golden ring out of her pocket. "For your troubles. I know it will be difficult to explain why a Soviet Jew got the most kosher position in the entire camp and not a *Volksdeutsche.*"

"Lagerführerin Mandl doesn't question me all that much. I don't think she wants to be bothered." Mala pocketed the goods, already mentally distributing them among the inmates she would see later.

Stasia's fellow underground members were also on Mala's to-visit list. The people who were still plotting, against all good reason, simply because they wouldn't be able to live with themselves otherwise. Neither would Mala. They all said she fit right in with them and, to Mala, that was the highest praise there was.

In front of one of the barracks in the men's camp, Mala slowed down her steps and came to a gradual halt. Leaning against the splintered wall, she lit a cigarette, her eyes never leaving the wide, open space in front of her. In Auschwitz-Birkenau, one could never be too vigilant. Danger was virtually everywhere; the air stank of it just like it stank of burnt flesh and singed hair.

In moments like these, she was grateful for the militaristic training she had received in Hanoar Hatzioni—one of the Antwerp Jewish youth organizations. The local Zionists saw the writing on the wall when Hitler was still promising peace to the world. While the rest of the world ate those promises up, Hanoar Hatzioni members were marching in formation and crawling in trenches on their bellies, boys and girls indistinguishable from each other in their jodhpurs and heavy boots—children preparing for the war which the adults blindly denied. During the day, Mala studied hard to be smart; during the evenings and weekends, she trained even harder to be strong, so that when the Nazis came, she would face them as a soldier, not a trembling lamb heading for slaughter. It was Mala's profound conviction that it was that training that had ultimately helped her survive a death camp so far; that had taught her how to draw strength from one's hatred, how to identify goals and follow through with the most audacious plans. How to outwit the SS in their own lair, as she was presently doing.

The ladder leading to the roof began to quiver faintly under someone's weight. Before long, a carpenter's boots appeared in Mala's view, then the dark blue overalls, followed by the carpenter himself—a tall, sly-faced fellow from Slovakia with the red triangle of a political prisoner sewn over his heart. Pavol got himself into Auschwitz for trading in fake passports, though he, himself, took great offense whenever anyone dared to doubt the legitimacy of his merchandise. According to him, the passports were very much real, purchased with his hard-earned money from the deceased person's family members who had no use for them at any rate, just like the deceased themselves.

"Just whom was I harming with my innocent actions?" Pavol would inquire with a look of the frankest self-pity. "Mr. Jew needs a passport to flee the country; the family that had just lost their father needs money; it's a simple matter of demand and supply, with myself acting as a mediator between the two parties. The Gestapo agent accused me of falsifying the documents! Pfft! I never falsified anything in my entire life. All I did was put a new photo in the passport. Wouldn't even alter the name. Well, just the part of the stamp that goes over the photograph, a very tiny bit of it. But the passport itself, just like the name in it, was real!"

It appeared that Auschwitz's re-educational program had failed in his particular case, as Pavol had not only refused to abandon his old "mediator's" ways but turned the local trading into quite a profitable business. The slight paunch he had managed to develop in a place where people dropped from starvation like flies attested to that.

At once, he opened his arms in a welcoming gesture. "Mala! You're a sight for sore eyes!"

Her gaze never leaving the compound, Mala pressed herself against the man's chest and coiled her arm around his neck. To any curious eyes, they presented an innocent enough picture—a pair of lovers, both from privileged details, stealing a hug and a swift kiss in between their errands. The punishment for that, in the severest of cases, would be a whip against one's buttocks, but Mala had already established herself as Mandl's protégé. No *Kapo* was stupid enough to report her. That was a useful position, indeed.

"Right pocket of my jacket," she whispered into his ear by way of greeting. "Sulfa drugs, like you asked."

It was Mala's suspicion that the Slovak was not only a forger but a former pickpocket; she hardly ever felt his touch whenever he extracted the goods. A pickpocket with a moral code—he never took anything besides what she had indicated.

"Most obliged, Mally," Pavol spoke just as quietly into her ear, the stubble on his cheek scratching at her skin, tender in the frost. "The scabies fellow sends his best regards."

She felt her pocket sag significantly when he lowered his portion of merchandise into it.

"And these are from me, personally," he added, demonstrating a few long nails before dropping them quickly into her pocket. "Pinched them just this very morning." With the wryest of smiles, he tossed his head at the roof he was supposed to be fixing.

Mala grinned, genuine gratitude shining in her eyes. The nails were in great demand with the *Sonderkommando*, whatever they were stowing them away for. Just like empty sardine tins that the Slovak luckily had access to.

"Thank you. And this is for you. For your trouble," Mala repeated Stasia's words, dipped into her pocket and produced two pieces of bread and a few loose cigarettes. They instantly disappeared into the pocket of Pavol's overalls.

After another quick hug—purely fictitious, for the Slovak had a moral code concerning that too and never took advantage of the situation—the two conspirators went on their respective ways. The carpenter, up the ladder; Mala, toward the crematorium, her steps heavy with dread.

It was these trips that she loathed the worst. Not even the suffering of the sickbay could compare to the morbid atmosphere of these death factories. And yet, she trooped forward, her hand clutching the nails inside her pocket. She had seen far too many people vanish into their maws to remain a silent bystander and wait for her turn to ascend those steps into the purgatory quietly and decently, like the SS hoped they all would do.

In front of the imposing rectangular building, Oberscharführer Voss was smoking, elegant and tall in his form-fitting gray overcoat.

"Mala." He coughed into his gloved fist. "What brings you to our forsaken parts?"

She was a Birkenau runner, an inmate in charge of filling women's working details; the *Sonderkommando* was an all-male one. Perfectly aware that she had no business there, Mala grinned amiably at the crematorium's *Kommandoführer*. "The laundry detail *Kapo* sent me. She wanted me to ask the *Sonderkommando*'s *Kapo* when he wanted their bedsheets to be disinfected."

"Didn't they just disinfect them?" Taking another deep pull on his cigarette, Voss narrowed his eyes in suspicion. He was lenient enough, and particularly when drunk, which was more often than not, but he was no idiot.

"New *Kommandant*'s orders, Herr Oberscharführer. The bedsheets ought to be disinfected every week due to the typhus outbreak. Another guard has just caught it. Herr Kommandant says he doesn't wish to lose any more of his men to that blasted plague." Mala made a suitably regretful grimace.

At those words, Voss saw reason at once. Even though he had his own separate quarters in the crematorium, he slept under one roof with his *Sonderkommando* men. Judging by his expression, he had no desire to become yet another statistic. He was already motioning Mala inside.

"Put that headscarf of yours over your face," he advised when she was almost through the doors. "They're still sorting those stiffs. It stinks to high heaven in there."

Voss's reluctance to directly supervise his men's macabre duties explained the *Sonderkommando*'s privileged position better than any words would. The SS preferred to accommodate their forced conscripts the best they could just so they, themselves, wouldn't have to do the dirty work. They wanted the Jews and other undesirables dead without their direct involvement.

Quietly, Mala snorted with chill disdain as soon as her back was to Voss and made the first resolute step into the Auschwitz inferno.

Inside the vast antechamber, the *Kanada Kommando* inmates were pulling the clothes off their hooks and hurling them into big industrial sacks. Mala's eyes slid along the walls adorned with signs in nearly all European languages—Bath and Disinfection, Proceed

Straight Ahead, Leave Your Valuables Here for Disinfection. She averted her gaze in disgust.

The faint trace of chemicals in the air scratched at her throat as she advanced further along the corridor and toward the opened, airtight door. A *Sonderkommando* man in a respirator stomped out in his rubber boots, pulling two corpses by their ankles. By the elevator, two of his comrades were waiting for him with a small gurney that was already piled with bodies.

Even the headscarf covering her nose didn't mask the stench of death that made Mala's eyes water. The bodies were still soft, pliable; their arms moved when the man in rubber boots stacked two last bodies atop the sizeable mound. Their eyes hadn't glazed over yet; the tears were still visible on their unnaturally ruddy cheeks with a net of burst blood vessels around their noses and mouths. From their lips, pinkish-white froth still dropped, mixing with blood that had run from their noses.

The inmate in a respirator pulled it off his face, wiped his wet forehead with the back of his hand and then, to Mala's amazement, produced a handkerchief and began to clean the corpses' faces. The other two men waited patiently for him to finish and only after he stepped away, satisfied with the result, did they push their heavy load inside the industrial elevator. Its doors closed with a loud clang that reverberated through the entire building, it seemed. Mala felt a shiver run through her at that sound, full of desolate finality.

"Are you looking for someone?" the *Sonderkommando* man asked her, regarding the bloody handkerchief in his hands with eyes full of torment.

"Konstantinos. Your Polish friends call him Kostek."

"The Greek fellow?"

"Yes."

"He's upstairs, manning the ovens."

"Could you fetch him, please? It's important."

"It must be." The man's grin resembled a painful grimace. "Else, why would anyone willingly come here?"

He called the elevator and remained in the same position—eyes downcast, shoulders slumped—until the doors opened to swallow him, much like they swallowed everything in that hell. The *Krema*, as the crematorium was called among the local population, was the SS's Moloch, the god of death they had created and worshipped with due diligence.

Left alone in an overpowering silence, Mala advanced, step by tentative step, into the chamber where a thousand voices had screamed not even an hour ago. Inside, the soft humming of air ventilators was audible. Through the small vents in the roof, pale sunlight seeped into the ghastly dungeon. Several hollow columns wrapped in metallic mesh protruded from the ground and disappeared into the torn squares of blue sky just visible through the hatches. Mala approached one of them, searched for electric wires and, not finding any, carefully touched the mesh. Here, the chemical smell was even stronger.

"Are you mad, lingering around those things?" A hand grasped her shoulder and pulled her away, back toward the heavy metal door.

Mala recognized Kostek, wearing the *Sonderkommando* "uniform" of civilian clothes and rubber boots. In his hand, he held a hose from which water was dripping. Incredibly tall, he towered not only over his fellow *Kommando* mates, but most of the SS men as well. His olive skin invariably displayed a permanent five o'clock shadow no matter how closely he shaved. Across one of his green eyes, a long scar stretched, cutting his right brow in two—a present from the Greek Gestapo in reward for his resistance activities, according to Kostek himself. Whenever he spoke of those "glorious days," his face always creased into a dark sneer. Caught, tortured, assigned to the detail that broke men stronger than him, he not only hadn't relented but swore revenge, even if it came at the cost of his own life. A perfect fighter in Auschwitz's underground army.

"The SS lower gas pellets inside through those columns," he explained, hosing down the floor. "It's mostly dispersed by now, but it can still do damage to your lungs."

"I'm sorry. I didn't know. I though the gas was just that—gas."

"No. Pellets. Light blue and very deadly."

There was a long pause. Mala looked down at the gray concrete emerging from under the layer of blood and grime, at the water shimmering in the pallid light seeping from the hatches, at Kostek's face that hadn't betrayed a single emotion aside from the haunted glaze in his eyes that made it difficult to look into them without flinching. She wondered if he had nightmares.

"Do you dream much?" Mala probed carefully.

The solitary ray of sun broke through the nearest hatch and, all at once, the mist from Kostek's hose burst into a myriad of lights. Offensive and grotesque, a rainbow hung over the death chamber like a demented decoration. His face twisting into a grimace of utter distaste, Kostek threw the hose down, staring through the hatch at the torn piece of blue sky with accusation.

"No," he spoke at length. "I don't dream at all. Too tired to dream."

"I sometimes do," Mala confessed, watching the water colored faintly with pink pool around her boots. "But I never remember my dreams in the morning."

"Perhaps it's for the best."

Mala didn't argue. Perhaps it was.

Then, as though remembering herself, she reached into her pocket. "Your tins, as promised. And even some nails today."

"Nails!" Kostek brightened at once and reached for the items the way most inmates reached for bread. The *Sonderkommando* men were well fed by the SS—they had other priorities. "Thank you. You have no idea how helpful these are."

"I don't, that much is true." Mala paused before giving Kostek a curious look. "Whatever do you need these for? I can still see how the nails may be used as a sort of weapon, but sardine tins? Are you planning to cut your supervisors' throats with them or something of the sort?"

"Something of the sort." He was laughing. It was strange to hear laughter in that chamber, strange but oddly hopeful at the same time. Kostek leaned very close to her. "We're making bombs out of them."

"Bombs?" Mala regarded him with great skepticism.

He moved his shoulder slightly. It was a *you-don't-have-to-believe-me-if-you-don't-want-to* shrug.

"A Soviet prisoner of war taught us how. Two weeks before camp leader Hössler shot him."

Mala mentally calculated the number of tins she had passed to Kostek and his comrades by now and looked at him with alarm this time. "Just how many do you have?"

"Enough to make things hot for the SS," he gave a vague reply in tow with a conspirator's wink. "We just have to wait for the Allies to come close enough. As it is, Africa is already lost to the Nazis; Italy has switched sides and is fighting against them now; the Red Army has been chasing them west ever since Germany lost Stalingrad and is fighting already in Ukraine from what we last heard—take my word for it, it's only a matter of time till the reinforcements are here. Then, we'll stage such a revolt, they shall remember us for a long time."

It was a local fantasy, just like inmates' dreaming of the things they would do once they were liberated, the food they would eat, the torture they would inflict on their former tormentors. Everyone indulged in it now and then and no one really took it seriously. But, that day, Mala looked into Kostek's eyes and, for some reason, believed him.

Chapter 5

Auschwitz

Edek and Wiesław were insulating a guard's booth. It stood near the very gates with their infamous slogan—*Arbeit macht frei*—work makes you free; a small black and white doghouse with its SS chain-hound inside guarding its morbid kingdom. Not a single person would slip by that watching SS without proper authorization. The gates of Auschwitz Hades were sealed good and fast under his watch. Though, presently, the chain-hound was smoking as he wound circles in front of the gate to keep warm. Apparently, having to be stuck with two inmates inside such a small booth was beyond his desire.

"Have you ever seen a sunset like this one?" Edek spoke in an undertone, his gaze riveted to the sky. The whipped butter of golden clouds was slowly melting around the glowing disk, reddening the tops of the trees tucked in snow. "As though someone spilled pure honey atop the reddest apple one can find."

"You're hungry then?" Wiesław chortled softly, throwing a quick glance at the pacing guard.

Edek, too, saw that the German was growing impatient.

"You're just a damned romantic, aren't you?" Edek snapped in sudden, senseless anger.

Wiesław shrugged, not offended in the slightest by his friend's outburst. They were all prone to those now and then. He had long grown used to ignoring them. "Is that why you pleaded with Lubusch to let us come here? So you can ogle clouds or some such?"

This time, Edek ignored the jab. "No, you miserable mutton-head," he explained amiably, lowering his voice to a whisper.

"I pleaded with Lubusch to let us come here so we could find out how one walks out of here without raising any suspicion."

For an instant, Wiesław froze with a hammer in his hand, blinking at his friend in stunned wonder. An uncertain smile twitched on his face for a fleeting moment, while he waited for a punchline to the joke. When it didn't follow, he grew serious at once and gave Edek a warning shove with his hammer. "Why would you talk such rot? Have you forgotten what they do to the others when someone goes under the wire? Mass executions in reprisal, to prevent more adventure-seekers from following suit. Is that what you want? Innocent men's lives on your conscience?"

Edek shook his head impatiently. "That was before."

"Before what?"

"Before the new *Kommandant* arrived. Remember what happened to the man who had escaped because he missed his mother? Herr Kommandant not only didn't execute him but returned him to the block perfectly unharmed and prohibited the *Kapos* to punish him in any way."

Wiesław remembered. The entire affair was so inconceivable, it had become the talk of the camp for the next two weeks. The old *Kommandant*, Höss, would have shot the bastard himself. The new one, Obersturmführer Liebehenschel, forgave the man out of pure sympathy. In Liebehenschel's eyes, running away simply to hug his mother was a selfless act of love, not a crime for which one ought to have been shot.

"Kommandant Liebehenschel is a sentimentalist," Wiesław conceded. "I wonder how he ended up here, in Auschwitz."

"Lubusch says in punishment."

"For what?"

"Lubusch doesn't know himself. He heard the new *Kommandant* was under house arrest prior to his arrival here. Supposedly for hurling a glass of champagne at Hitler's portrait during one of their SS soirees."

"Is that a fact?" Wiesław's expression betrayed his mistrust.

"How would I know? I lost my invitation that day and didn't make it to the party," Edek hissed back with great sarcasm.

From the direction where the swamps lay, the wind had picked up and brought with it the stench of rotten water. Dark clouds crowded overhead, bulging with heavy, wet snow. With the sun almost gone, the forest loomed ahead, full of shadows and something vague and threatening.

Partisans and freedom, Edek realized just then. Freedom, which he could almost taste if he licked his wind-bitten lips; which he could almost see if he just looked closely and long enough—

"What's taking so long?"

Both men jumped at the harsh shout in German.

"Beg your forgiveness, Herr Rottenführer," Edek muttered, injecting as much humility into his voice as possible. "We don't want to make a quick job out of it. Winters are brutal here; we want to make sure we insulate it properly, so you stay snug and warm in there until spring." At once, he began padding out the walls with a renewed vigor, Wiesław hammering eagerly after him.

With an annoyed sigh, the guard turned away and began stomping his feet louder than before.

"We'd better hurry," Wiesław whispered in Polish. "That sod will catch a cold, but it'll be us thrown into the *Strafblock* after he reports us."

"Let him freeze himself into pneumonia," Edek replied with a sneer. "Lubusch will cover for us. And now, with the new *Kommandant* in charge—"

He didn't finish his thought. The guard had just shouted *Halt* at someone approaching and raised his arm, his left hand resting on his submachine gun that hung over his shoulder.

"Heil Hitler," a muffled voice greeted him half-heartedly.

Out of the corner of his eye, Edek saw an SS man, his face nearly invisible in all the layers of scarf he was wearing, greeting his comrade with an arm bent at his elbow. Next to him, an inmate stood shivering. Unlike his SS escort in his warm long overcoat, all the prisoner was wearing was an old Soviet tunic with bullet holes in it and striped pants that were so short they left his ankles entirely exposed to the harsh elements. Edek saw that the skin on his face and above his mended short boots had already turned a dangerous shade of beet-red—the first warning sign of frostbite.

"He's a piano tuner," the newly arrived guard mumbled from under the layers of his scarf, gesturing toward the trembling man. "I'm taking him to Höss's house. Frau Höss has been complaining about the piano for weeks now; says she can't entertain her guests properly." He accompanied his words with an expressive roll of the eyes.

Edek found it puzzling, the fact that the old *Kommandant*'s wife voluntarily chose to stay in Auschwitz instead of following her husband to wherever he had been transferred to. Rumor had it, her life here was so comfortable, she didn't mind one bit the constant gut-churning, nauseatingly sweet smoke from the crematorium chimneys, as long as she had her personal slaves tending to her garden and *Kanada* detail supplying her with the latest fashion and precious stones brazenly confiscated from freshly murdered victims.

"I'll need an *Ausweis* for him," the guard announced, tossing his head in the trembling inmate's direction. "You know the rules—no pass, no strolls outside for his kind."

His SS comrade released an annoyed sigh. "Will you make me go all the way to the *Kommandantur* and go through the pain of authorizing a pass for one miserable Jew? Where's your brotherly understanding?"

"Oh, quit your moaning," the guard countered, unimpressed. "It's a safe bet this is the first time you ventured outside your work detail this winter and I have to stand here every other day. Where's brotherly understanding in that?"

A particularly harsh gust of wind picked up a handful of snow flurries and threw them with violence in the men's faces. Even Edek, who was somewhat concealed by the walls of the booth, gulped a mouthful of icy air and felt his breath catching in his throat. The SS man swiftly swung round, pulling the scarf even higher over his face as he waited for nature's attack to pass. The piano tuner next to him shifted fearfully from one foot to another and shut his eyes, with tears in them, against the elements.

"Are you cold, my tender children?" the SS guard laughed mockingly. "Say your thanks you're not on the Eastern front, freezing your fat tails off in one dugout or another while the Russkies are showering you with their new Katusha rockets."

"What do you know about that?" his comrade snapped back, turning around.

"Enough to last me a lifetime." The guard patted his thigh affectionately. "Still carrying splinters from that Soviet bitch in my leg."

"Declared unfit for frontline duty?" There was a measure of respect in the other's voice now.

"What can I say? At least I left that hell with all of my limbs still about me. The rest of my company wasn't so fortunate."

The SS man with the scarf over his face stepped closer, speaking in a low, confidential tone while gesturing occasionally toward the inmate and the administrative building. After a pack of cigarettes traded hands, the two SS men appeared to have come to an understanding.

Holding his breath, Edek watched the guard motion his comrade and the inmate through the gates. Soon, the two disappeared into the whitewashed day.

At once, Edek dealt Wiesław a blow in the ribs.

"Did you see that?" Edek whispered excitedly in Polish. "They just walked out of here. *Heil Hitler* and off they go, not even a proper paper check. Nothing!"

"An SS uniform and German speech will do the trick." Wiesław chuckled soundlessly.

"So?" Edek refused to surrender.

"So, we don't have the first one and neither can we speak the second without our outrageous Polish accents."

"Some SS men here are *Volksdeutsche* Poles, Romanians, and Hungarians," Edek argued. "From German settlements, but not quite perfect German speakers themselves. Could we not pass for such?"

"With our Slavic mugs?"

"They aren't so Aryan either, if you saw them."

"You truly have it all worked out already, don't you?" Wiesław demanded mockingly. "Where are you planning to get a uniform?"

Edek didn't reply straight away. He stared with infinite longing into the pristine white expanse that lay just outside the gates and into which the inmate and his SS escort had disappeared.

"Lubusch," he whispered at last.

Wiesław nearly dropped his hammer with astonishment. "Our Lubusch? Kommandoführer Lubusch? SS Rottenführer Lubusch?"

Edek shook his head. An uncertain grin began to spread on his face. "No. *Edward* Lubusch. A man who is married to a very nice Polish girl."

Wiesław may have been staring at him in confusion, but Edek was already working things feverishly in his mind, ridiculously hopeful and, once again, believing in miracles against his better judgement.

The evening roll call was mercifully swift. Inside their barracks, an iron stove was cracking merrily. Needless to say, it wasn't enough to warm the entire block, but it made men huddled around it feel somewhat human again, and that was already an achievement.

"What a fireplace we had in our house in Lublin!" a former textile merchant said reminiscently, holding his calloused palms against the fire. "All green marble adorned with gold, wide and tall

enough for a man to stand inside, when it wasn't lit, of course…
A dream!"

Edek remembered him from the transport they had shared,
as an imposing man in a three-piece suit, with a polished pin in
his silk tie and a handsome watch with a golden face. The watch
was the first item he had parted with; he had traded it for a mug
of tepid water during one of their stops on the way to Auschwitz,
handed to him through the narrow window by a local station
worker. He could have never suspected that the stop was the first
among many; by the time their transport pulled to the infamous
Auschwitz ramp, he was no longer the man who had boarded it.

But what truly broke him was a letter from his wife, in which she
informed him in rather cool and formal tones that due to his racial
status she had obtained a divorce to which his consent, as a Jew,
was not needed, and assured him that his business was well-taken
care of by her new fiancé, an Aryan businessman from Posen. The
merchant received it only six weeks after his arrival. Something
snapped in him and, soon, he had refused to accept reality, choosing
to lose himself in the memories of the past, where his young wife,
adorned with fragrant furs and drowning in diamonds, showered
him with unrestrained affection, and where he was still the rightful
owner of his house, in which the fireplace was so wide and tall a
man could stand in it.

"What use do we have in that mythical fireplace?" It was the
historian from a university, the name of which kept eluding Edek.

"Let the man gossip about old times. What harm is it to you?"
Edek said.

"He's exciting everyone else with empty illusions. As if we'll
ever come out of here." The historian released a derisive snort and
pushed his steel-rimmed glasses back onto the bridge of his nose.

One of the men turned to stare at him, a young fellow from
a good family who toyed with communist ideas far too much for
the Germans' liking. "Do you not think we will?" He searched the

historian's face. "What about the Soviets? People say they're fighting already in Ukraine. Poland is next. Surely, as soon as they reach us, they shall liberate us and reinstate our rights—"

From the historian, another burst of scornful laughter. "And you assume the SS shall just hand us all over to the Soviets?" He shook his head at such naiveté.

"No. I assume they shall just leave us all here."

"*Just leave us?* Just leave all the witnesses to the crimes they have committed?" The historian gave him a pointed look. "Now, that would be the most inconceivably idiotic thing of them to do; do you not agree?"

The young communist's brow furrowed. "But then… What else would they…"

It had then dawned on him; Edek could tell by the ashen-gray shade the young communist's face had taken.

"Surely, they won't kill us all. I mean… the entire camp?"

For a time, the historian gazed silently into the flames. Without his habitual scornful façade, he was an esteemed intellectual once again.

"I have studied far too many wars and conflicts to nurse any illusions on the account of the Nazis," he said at last. "Retreating armies have a tendency to annihilate everything in their wake. Stalin's Scorched Land policy—I've learned this personally from the captured Red Army POWs—was the last example of this. Back in 1941, when the Red Army was still retreating, Stalin ordered his Commissars to raze every last village to the ground, contaminate every single water source, slaughter all livestock they couldn't take with them. He didn't do it to cover any crimes; he only ordered it so the enemy wouldn't have any shelter or an evening meal. Now, imagine what the SS shall do when the Soviets approach our forsaken parts. Do you honestly believe that Hitler won't give his men the same order? They'll slaughter us all; mark my words. No one wants us to walk out of here and start telling our stories."

The young communist stared at him in mute horror, the silence of the barracks only confirming the grim prediction. Not a single person said anything against it. Everyone knew precisely it would be their fate.

Later that night, Edek once again couldn't sleep. The historian's prophetic words wouldn't let him.

"He's right," Edek spoke into the darkness, knowing that Wiesław couldn't sleep either. "They'll off us all and raze the entire campsite to the ground."

"Thanks for more nightmares," came Wiesław's voice from the shadows.

"I'm only saying, we don't really have anything to lose." Edek lifted himself on one elbow, his eyes gleaming about in the night. "If our fate is sealed regardless, we should try to at least do something about it. So we don't die like meek sheep, but as men, who stood up for something."

"And what precisely is it we're trying to stand up for?"

"The most important thing there is. Freedom."

"I always thought the most important thing there was, was love."

Edek laughed, but then saw that his friend wasn't joking.

"You *are* a damned romantic after all," he shook his head at Wiesław.

For some time, they lay side by side amid soft snores and the howling of the wind outside the barracks walls.

When Wiesław spoke again, it was the last thing Edek had expected: "Do you know anyone who could get us an empty *Ausweis* from the camp office?"

Edek turned his head to look at him. Wiesław was staring at the bunk above, chewing on a strand of straw he'd pulled out of his pallet, his face pensive and earnest.

"You're with me then?" Edek whispered, still not quite believing it.

"I can't abandon you in your reckless enterprise, can I? What kind of a friend would that make me?"

A head appeared then from the second-tier bunk. It was the historian.

"You ought to get to Birkenau and ask for Mala. Mala Zimetbaum, *Läuferin*. She goes into the office all the time and, rumor has it, she's the person to seek if you need something *organized*. She'll get you your *Ausweis*, if you ask nicely."

He disappeared before they could thank him properly. Soon, Wiesław fell asleep and only Edek stayed wide awake, repeating the name to himself like a prayer.

Mala.

Mala Zimetbaum.

His ticket to freedom.

Chapter 6

Birkenau

Mala was sitting at the desk in the *Schreibstube*—the camp office—typing up Mandl's handwritten orders. From time to time, a painful grimace creased her brow: the sheer number of grammatical errors was beyond belief. On her very first day here, Mala made the mistake of approaching the women's camp leader to inquire if Lagerführerin wished for Mala to type up the orders as they were or to correct the misspellings first, and received a resounding slap for her insolence.

"Which one of us is a native German speaker, you insolent sow?" Mandl had roared, thoroughly enraged. "Which one of us wears a uniform and gives orders here? I should have you shot for your long tongue where you stand!"

Only Obersturmführer Hössler's timely interference had saved Mala's life. Mandl's immediate superior had entered the office to investigate what the row was about, laughed heartily when Mandl tried to pour her grievances on him, and dismissed the matter with a negligent wave of his hand.

"Everyone knows you can't spell to save your life, *Liebling*." The term of endearment seemed to appease Mandl. To Mala's amazement, the leader of all wardens even blushed. "The girl is an interpreter and a secretary; let her do her job. That's what she's here for." And, before Mandl remembered herself, he grabbed hold of Mala's elbow and steered her, gently but firmly, out of the room, away from the SS woman's wrath.

Later that day, Zippy, a Slovak inmate who had arrived with one of the first transports and was much more camp-savvy than

Mala, instructed her on the local rules: "Never, and I cannot stress it enough, *never* tell an SS woman, let alone Mandl, that she's wrong in any way. Yes, they're uneducated and barely literate for the most part, but if you know what's good for you, you'll keep your mouth shut and act as though they're God's gift to humankind."

"But these orders…" Mala had regarded the handwritten sheet, mortified. After she had left her position at Maison Lilian fashion house for a better paid and more prestigious one of linguist-secretary at a diamond company, she took particular pride in her superiors' praise of her meticulous work. The more the administration commended her efforts, the longer she stayed after work, double- and triple-checking every single document as though the satisfaction of the international clients depended on her translation solely. The more foreign business newspapers and magazines she consumed, underlining and memorizing expressions she wasn't familiar with and which would be useful for the company's correspondence; the more business lunches she attended as her immediate boss's interpreter, sacrificing days off and holidays simply because she wanted the company to be as successful as possible. Never in her life could she imagine that she would be slapped for her efforts, but that was the grim Auschwitz reality now. "If one official or the other reads them and sees this mess, they shall think it's the inmate who typed them who's at fault." She'd looked at Zippy. "They'll order me to the gas for not doing my job properly. Surely, Mandl won't acknowledge that these are her mistakes?"

"Naturally, she won't. So you correct everything and clean it up as much as you can; insert a few fancy words here and there to make her sound intelligent and enjoy a Red Cross parcel she may throw at you in gratitude when she gets a commendation from her higher-ups. Just don't open your silly mouth and shove it into her face next time." Zippy gave her a conspirator's wink.

Since then, endless months had followed one another in one bleak parade. Under Zippy's guidance, Mala had become just as camp-savvy, and soon, Mandl began to approve of her and even openly praise her before her superiors. Before long, *Mally* was one of Mandl's personal favorites, with her own room in the camp office, good clothes, decent food, and a number of privileges the rest of the inmates could only dream of. The necessity to show deference to someone she so thoroughly despised was sickening to Mala, but Zippy explained how such a position could be beneficial, not only for her personally but for *people who could use some help*—with an expressive look that Mala instantly understood—and soon, Mala joined forces with the brave men and women who refused to be turned into slaves and swore to die fighting instead.

Lost in her memories, Mala gazed vacantly at the opposite wall, where Zippy ordinarily sat, and suddenly, such a deep longing for home, for freedom, came over her, she thought she would howl with grief.

A commotion outside pulled her out of her dreary thoughts. Craning her neck, Mala recognized SS Rapportführerin Drexler—*a right bitch, if she'd ever seen one,* according to Zippy—shouting abuse at the women she had just chased out of the barracks and made to kneel in the snow. Her warm cape flying after her, the report overseer stalked along the rows of women—five abreast, the usual camp formation—and slashed her horsewhip at the faces of seemingly random victims. She was one of the most ruthless SS wardens in the entire Birkenau, known to shoot inmates just for "having the insolence" to look her in the eyes.

Inside the camp office building, the windows were closed and thoroughly insulated and the radiators hissed loudly, pumping heat into the SS quarters, and yet, Mala still caught snatches of Drexler's usual phrases. They didn't change much throughout the years: "Dirty Israelite tramps… disgusting, filthy swine… I shall teach you how to… how many times have I warned you… ought to have cleaned out that pigsty the first time…"

Mala guessed that the order of someone's block wasn't up to Rapportführerin's high standards. As punishment, the inhabitants of the offending barracks would kneel in the snow, holding rocks in their hands stretched over their heads for at least two hours. Whoever lowered their arms received a bullet from Drexler's service gun. She had a reputation to mind, after all; Mandl herself praised her for being the best disciplinarian in the camp. *A barracks full of Jews who couldn't keep it sparkling enough wouldn't ruin it for her*, the warden's stiff back seemed to say as she dealt blows with true SS generosity. The fact that her victims had no access to fresh water and had to use their morning ration of so-called coffee to wash their faces at least to some extent, let alone washing their clothes or barracks, didn't matter to Drexler.

Disgusted, Mala turned back to her typewriter.

The door swung open and in walked Obersturmführer Hössler. His overcoat was open and, in his hand, he held his swagger stick and uniform cap. At once, he greeted Mala with a warm smile as she rushed to take the items from him.

"How goes it, Mally?"

She was *Mally* to all of them now; not quite an inmate, more of a civilian subordinate they genuinely liked.

"It goes, Herr Obersturmführer."

"Mandl's not in?"

"She's at the selections with Dr. Mengele."

"Ah, that's right. I was supposed to go to that too." He bent his knees slightly so that she could remove the overcoat from his shoulders. "But then I decided not to. It gets too depressing after a while. All of those naked skeletons running about like some grotesque circus." He grimaced.

Mala's well-practiced face betrayed nothing. She went to hang his heavy coat onto the rack by the door.

"What's with the ruckus outside?" Perching on the edge of her desk, Hössler tossed his head in the direction of the window.

"Rapportführerin Drexler is administering the punishment."

"For what?"

Mala shrugged her shoulders. Birkenau wardens didn't need a reason to bash someone's head in. "Would you like some coffee, Herr Obersturmführer?"

She was accustomed to his ways by now. Whenever he came over, found that Mandl was absent, and installed himself in that precise position on her desk, Mala knew to expect "a talk."

"If it's not too much trouble." Once again, Hössler smiled warmly at her.

"Not at all. Lagerführerin Mandl has just left. The carafe in her room is still hot."

When Mala returned with a tray, he moved from the top of the desk to the chair and helped her assemble the tray before him.

"Where's your friend?" He glanced at Zippy's empty desk over his shoulder.

"She's at the rehearsals with the camp orchestra. They're preparing something special for Christmas, she told me."

"That's right. I keep forgetting she plays her little mandolin in addition to her secretarial duties." A fond smile appeared on his face. "Frau Alma turned those girls into a real orchestra, didn't she?"

Mala glanced up at him. Zippy had told her about the fascination the local SS had developed for Alma Rosé, the famous Viennese violinist and conductor, but the almost deferential *Frau*, particularly coming from Hössler, still astounded her. No one was called *Frau* here. The most privileged inmates were addressed by their first names; the lower castes considered themselves fortunate if they were called by their number. Most of the times, though, it was, *come here, shit-Jew* or *pick that up before I get annoyed, you quivering hog.*

"I'm afraid I didn't get a chance to visit the new Music Block yet, Herr Obersturmführer."

"It's not new," Hössler protested. "They installed it in August, I think."

Mala offered him another apologetic smile as she poured cream into his porcelain cup.

"Is Mandl slave-driving you so much that you can't find the time for some music?" he teased, stirring his coffee with a silver spoon that looked ridiculously tiny in his large hands.

"I'm not complaining, Herr Obersturmführer. I like to keep busy. I shall find the time to visit the Music Block. Helen—" Mala purposely used Zippy's official name, not the one under which she was known to the underground, "won't stop singing the praises of Frau Alma. She says she's a true violin virtuoso."

"She is," Hössler confirmed, with unexpected affection.

Mala suspected that his interest in the violinist wasn't purely musical.

"Is she Jewish?"

He started, stiffened somewhat at the seemingly innocent question. "She's Viennese," he grumbled back, almost defensively, as if it was a crime to like a Jew.

Mala wisely refrained from further interrogation. Viennese it was, if that satisfied him.

After picking up the cup, he then lowered it again. "Bring one for yourself. You know how much I loathe drinking coffee on my own."

"I can't, Herr Obersturmführer." Mala shot an expressive glance at the door.

It was closed but not locked. Anyone could march in.

"Mandl isn't coming back any time soon."

"I'd rather not risk it, Herr Obersturmführer. Naturally, they won't say anything to you, but they'll put me on the next truck to the gas chamber."

His brown eyes instantly darkened and the pleasant smile slipped off his face. "I'm in charge of the extermination here!" His usually smooth tone with which he lured the new arrivals into the gas chambers—the very reason why his nickname was Moshe Liar by the Jewish members of the *Sonderkommando*—changed as though by magic. "No one puts anyone on any truck without my direct authorization!"

Mala bit her tongue, regretting saying anything at all. "Forgive me, please, Herr Obersturmführer. You're correct, as always." Lowering her head in response to such shouts had long transcended into a natural, dog-like instinct.

Hössler raked both hands through his dark, thick mane, taking a long, calming breath. Among the SS, he was the most unpredictable one. No one could ever tell what would set him off in the next instant, and when that happened, even his own subordinates knew to make themselves scarce.

A shot rang out. Startled, Mala turned to the window just in time to see a woman prisoner fall into the muddy snow, a halo of ruby red slowly growing around her shaved head. Her skeletal hands still held onto a stone, even in death. Drexler must have shot her simply because she didn't like her face.

"No, you forgive me, Mala." When she looked at Hössler in surprise, he shook his head with a dejected sigh. He, too, was gazing at the scene out the window. "You're right. It's an extermination camp. We were put here to exterminate. Not even the new *Kommandant* with his humanistic policies can change that."

He sounded as though he was genuinely upset by the fact. He brought a cup to his lips but didn't take a sip and his dark eyes stared somewhere past Mala.

"You know, I studied to become a photographer when I was young," he said in an odd, somewhat surprised tone, as though he, himself, didn't quite believe it.

"What happened?"

He didn't answer at once, lost in the past where he wasn't praised by the Berlin higher-ups for his *exceptional talent at establishing an exemplary operation of the crematoriums and demonstrating innovative techniques and work ethic that ought to be used as a model in all other similar facilities.* Mala had read the commendation when it had just arrived from the WVHA—the SS Main Economic and Administrative Office in charge of concentration camps. In her opinion, work ethic and gas chambers didn't belong in the same sentence, but Gruppenführer Glücks, the highest-ranking concentration camp inspector who had signed the document, appeared to have a different view on the matter.

Hössler began to talk, softly and with infinite longing, about the studio in which he worked as an apprentice, about the magic of the darkroom and the secrets of saving underexposed or overexposed pictures. He was entirely transformed now; in his eyes, usually extinguished and black, a light had ignited; he was smiling genuinely, immersed in a world that no longer existed; his pale, sunken cheeks acquired a soft blush as he talked and talked, having completely forgotten about the coffee that was growing cold, about Mala, about the camp around him.

"...filthy pigs!" Drexler's shrill shout penetrated through the walls of the camp office.

Mala saw Hössler's shoulders jerk slightly at the shout. He stopped abruptly. When the realization dawned on him that it was the camp that was real and not his career as a photographer which had come to an abrupt end due to the raging inflation as he had explained, his face turned to stone once again. He rose from his chair with difficulty, his brows knitting tighter and tighter together. Hard, bitter lines once again framed a slash of his mouth. He turned the lock on the window and shoved it open with such force, the glass nearly shattered.

"Shut your trap, you dumb fucking bitch!" he bellowed at the warden with sudden savage hatred that had sent his entire body shaking. "I can't hear myself thinking behind all your shrieking!"

Mala saw Drexler's head swivel toward the window. The warden blinked a few times, her face slowly growing red after such an unexpected, vicious rebuke.

"Have you swallowed your tongue?" Hössler roared, still not satisfied.

Mala had never seen him speak to his female colleagues in such a manner. He was considered one of the most refined gentlemen among the coarse SS lot, and yet, she understood him just then. Mala's office was a safe refuge for him, a place to come to when no one was around and just talk, talk for as long as it was possible about the life he had ruined for himself, to reminisce about the man he had never become, to lose himself in a daydream where he wasn't burning humanity by thousands. And now, Drexler and her crude curses had brought him back to the harsh reality, reminding him of what he wished so desperately to forget; showing him, in a distorted mirror, what he, himself, had turned into.

Drexler tried to explain something, but Hössler had already slammed the window shut. His day was evidently ruined, and he went to fetch his overcoat.

"I'm sorry, Herr Obersturmführer," Mala said.

He nodded, already in the door. "Me too."

Through the window, Mala watched him stalk past Drexler moments later, throwing something spiteful and even more insulting in her face. As soon as he was out of view, the warden took out her horsewhip and began slashing at the faces of her victims with doubled energy. Averting her gaze from the gruesome scene, squeezing her eyes closed, Mala pressed her ears shut, but even through the shield of her own palms, she heard the sickening sound of skin splitting under Drexler's blows.

It wasn't the day they'd agreed on, but that very instant, Mala decided that she would go and see Pavol-the-carpenter, schedule or not. She had food stored in her room—good stuff, the cheese from the Red Cross parcel and even half of the salami; he'd take it as a payment. Going hungry was a small price in exchange for the knowledge that the *Sonderkommando* would get their supplies, that they would stage their revolt sooner rather than later, blowing all four crematoriums to hell—and exact revenge on all the SS who would come to fight them.

Chapter 7

Auschwitz-Birkenau

After much deliberation, the details of the plan began to take shape.

"The Auschwitz guard on gate duty may know other Auschwitz guards," Edek speculated, whenever Wiesław and he had a minute to themselves. "It would be much less of a risk for me to pose as a Birkenau guard. My German is good enough to pass for a Polish *Volksdeutsche* SS volunteer; there's plenty of them in the camp. It shouldn't raise any suspicions."

"I'll never pass even for a Polish German," Wiesław argued, shaking his head. "I can barely string two words together in German. They'll never buy it."

"And that's why you'll remain who you are—a regular inmate whom I shall be leading to work outside camp grounds. Just like that SS man we saw, with the piano tuner. It's a perfect cover. No one shall suspect anything."

"Yes, but the trouble is, we're not part of the Birkenau crew. How are we going to get ourselves transferred?"

"Leave it to me," Edek promised.

Rather to Wiesław's surprise, just a week later, an order came for his transfer to Birkenau women's camp, where he was to join a carpenters' detail.

"However did you pull that off?" Wiesław asked Edek as he stared at his transfer card in astonishment.

From Edek, a nonchalant shrug and a wry grin. "How do you think? A few strategically placed bribes did the trick."

"What about you though?"

"There was only one position open. But don't fret." Edek gave his friend a reassuring clap on his back. "I'll talk to Lubusch about my own transfer. I'm sure he'll come through. For now, I'll just keep volunteering for the temporary carpenters' *Kommando* that he sometimes sends to Birkenau to assist their local ones. First things first: we need to make contact with that Mala girl. As soon as we have an *Ausweis*, we'll start planning the rest."

"How are you planning to find one girl among hundreds of thousands?" Wiesław regarded him with great skepticism.

"Pavol, the carpenter who assisted your transfer, has a set day and place where she usually meets him. For a price of two pinched lemons and my promise to delegate certain goods to her, he traded places with me."

A few days later, attired in the *Kommando*'s blue overalls, Edek and Wiesław were fixing the pipes in Birkenau's Sauna—a tremendous affair through which all new arrivals were processed and where the privileged inmates could have their daily showers. At once, Edek realized that it was a local black market of sorts; just in the past half-hour, during which the Sauna stood still, having processed its usual daily quota, a rather impressive number of deals was carried out between the inmates who had something to trade.

Even the local *Kapos* and block elders were in business. Noticing new faces, a busty German with a blue bow in her long braid pounced on Edek and his comrade, offering them, in the most seductive of tones, "a very pretty girl—or a boy, if that's what you're after—for a very reasonable price, too." Racial status didn't matter, as long as they had bread or cheese.

"That's our Puff-Mutti or just Mutti, as she insists to be addressed as. She used to be a brothel madam in her native Bavaria," a fellow maintenance worker informed them, steering both men away from the German block elder and advising the woman to leave off. "Old habits die hard."

By the row of sinks stained with rust and general grime, a round-faced inmate in a warm padded jacket was caressing the cheek of a handsome boy, who, Edek guessed, couldn't have been older than sixteen. The boy's beautiful amber eyes were fixed on the inmate's other hand, in which he was holding a whole pack of cigarettes—a fortune in camp terms. Passing the couple by, Mutti reminded the inmate that half of the pack was hers. He scarcely heard her, already whispering something into the boy's ear and nudging him gently towards one of the stalls.

A well-nourished girl with her hair curled and pulled into a fashionable do which was in vogue in the pre-war years walked with purpose across the vast room, the sound of her low heels echoing off the tiled walls. From under her coat, she extracted a bottle of liquor and held it before another Sauna worker, a woman of around forty with red hair and a pale, freckled face. The lady inspected the label, nodded in satisfaction, and produced something wrapped in waxed paper, tied with a string. When the girl passed by Edek on her way back, he caught a tantalizing whiff of smoked meat—the fresh type, not the usual Auschwitz rot. At once, he caught himself swallowing mouthfuls of saliva as he stared after her with feverish eyes.

"Wherever are they getting the goods from?" In genuine amazement, Edek turned to look at the local maintenance fellow.

"The sorting detail—the *Kanada*." The man shrugged. "The new arrivals come here with suitcases packed with all sorts of goods, food and valuables. Inmates who work in the *Kanada* have regular feasts every other day. Whatever they cannot eat, drink, or use themselves, they trade, or bribe the *Kapos* and the guards with. It's not like the goods' rightful owners will need them anytime soon. Most of them are gassed upon arrival anyway."

He spoke of death with such nonchalance, as if he were making small talk about the latest weather forecast.

"Does Mala come here often?" Edek tried to ask as innocently as possible, without lifting his gaze off the pipe he was presently working on. "Mala Zimet—"

"You don't have to specify." The man grinned knowingly. "There's only one Mala."

"Could you point her out to me when she comes in?"

"I won't have to. You'll recognize her right away."

At first, Edek didn't quite understand. The Sauna was over-crowded with beautiful young women who looked like they belonged on the streets of cosmopolitan Warsaw and not among the pitiful camp lot. Unlike the genderless, skeletal creatures he'd seen on his way here, hunting for scraps of anything edible on the frozen ground—a rotten potato peel, if one was fortunate—these girls were well-dressed and well-fed. All of them looked as though they worked at the camp office; how was he to distinguish Mala among them?

"She will be wearing her *Läuferin's*—runner's—armband." Wiesław gave Edek a certain look. "And quit your fidgeting. We're here to conduct business; you're not waiting for your blind date to arrive."

Edek tried to laugh carelessly in response, but for some reason he couldn't. It was idiotic, of course, but he discovered that he was nervous. His stomach kept contracting, not in the freefall, sicken-ing manner when one sees an enraged SS approaching him with a raised club, but in a long-forgotten, breath-catching way, like it did when he longed to kiss a girl for the very first time—intoxicating, heady, and slightly terrifying.

The maintenance fellow was right. Edek did recognize her, but not by her armband or the description given to him by the historian. It was the steps that gave her away, purposeful and hurried, belong-ing to someone who had no time to lose on empty gossip and the exchange of pleasantries. Listening to them approach, Edek froze with a pipe wrench in his hand, suddenly unable to turn his head.

It must have been all the fantasies he had filled his head with. By extension, he now associated this woman with freedom, homeland, and everything he so dearly loved. It was difficult to look at her just now, as though in fear of disappointment.

A narrow palm fell on his shoulder, and he ceased breathing altogether. She was already turning him toward herself with surprising insistence; he could see her tall boots, not unlike the ones the wardens wore, the hem of her brown overcoat, the warm, woolen skirt peeking from under it. And then, a sudden and unexpectedly wrathful, "You're not Pavol!"

Her German was harsh and unforgiving, just like her gaze.

Edek glanced up and scrunched his face, as if expecting a slap.

Mala looked like she was ready to award him with one, for wasting her time and demanding a meeting in someone else's name.

"No. I'm Edek." That was all he could come up with as he stared, as one enchanted, at her face.

It was set; she was obviously mad. Her light-brown eyes, narrowed like those of a cat, dissected him into pieces, and yet it occurred to him that he had never seen anyone so beautiful. Against the dim light of the overhead lamps, her hair shone like liquid gold. Crystal droplets of melted snow shimmered in the dark lashes—

Edek's ogling ended abruptly. She was already turning away, uttering a curse under her breath—his ticket to freedom, homeland, everything he so dearly loved.

"Mala, wait!" At once, he was on his feet, trying to catch her sleeve.

She freed her arm and gave him a withering glare.

In spite of himself, Edek made a step toward her. "I brought Pavol's goods for you."

She regarded him with mistrust.

"Please." He gestured toward one of the shower stalls, where they could talk in private.

Whether it was the wild appeal for mercy that she saw in his eyes or the miserable tone of his voice, her features softened a bit. She motioned for him to follow her.

The stalls were the German madam's domain. Mala paid the woman her fare—a cigarette—and marched to the very end of the dingy corridor. Edek kept his gaze trained on the floor as he trailed after her. Whatever was happening in some of the stalls, he didn't wish to witness.

"Well?" Mala demanded in Polish, as soon as they reached the furthest stall. "Get on with it. I don't have much time." She switched between languages with such natural ease, Edek regarded her with a newfound admiration.

Remembering himself, he extracted three sardine tins out of the pockets of his overalls. "I didn't eat the sardines. The tins were already empty when he gave them to me," he rushed to assure her.

Rather to his surprise, Mala grinned. It was dark in the stall, but Edek could swear that the expression in her eyes turned from cold to coy.

"You don't know what these are for, do you?" she asked, inspecting the tins in her hand.

Edek shook his head, watching her pocket the tins in puzzlement.

"All the better for you," Mala said. "The Russians here have a saying, *the less you know, the better you sleep.*"

"You speak Russian too?"

"Why? You need something from the Soviets?"

"No." He wetted his lips. "I need an *Ausweis*. The real one, from the camp office."

"What else, then? A new Mercedes with a personal driver to drive you out of here?" she asked with a mocking grin.

"Why, can you organize that too?"

In the darkness, her teeth shone dazzling white. Edek discovered that he was smiling as well.

"It depends. What can you offer in exchange?"

"My life in your eternal servitude?" Edek suggested.

Mala made a face. "Your life, with its eternal servitude, belongs to the SS."

"That's why there's the need for the *Ausweis*. I don't quite fancy such a life."

Her smile slipped. For some time, she studied his face closely.

"How do I know you're not a Political Department's agitator?"

"Do I look like one?"

After a very long moment, during which Edek was holding his breath, Mala finally smiled again. "I suppose not. Your eyes are too honest. What are you in here for, anyway?"

"For nothing."

"You're not a Jew to be here for nothing."

"I'm a Pole who can hold a weapon in his hands. In the eyes of the Nazis, it's a crime, too."

Mala nodded sagely. That much was true.

"I know it's not enough—" Edek dug into his pocket and extracted a handful of sharp metal shavings and broken details from his workshop, "but Pavol said—"

"Oh, that's just grand!" Mala interrupted him, going after what seemed like regular junk to Edek with impressive enthusiasm. "Could you possibly get more?" Now it was her turn to give him a pleading look.

"I'm working on a permanent transfer here, but while I belong to the locksmith *Kommando*, I'll certainly bring you as much as I can."

Mala was positively beaming now. "What sort of an *Ausweis* do you need?"

"The type that an SS man would demonstrate to the guard at the gates, good for one inmate accompanying the guard, for work outside the camp territory. Is there such an *Ausweis*?"

For a moment, Mala considered his question. "I suppose. But what are you trying to bribe an SS escort with, at any rate? No one will be mad enough to go through with your enterprise. They'll be thrown into the local Gestapo jail for aiding the escape at once."

"Let me worry about the SS man. The less you know, the better you sleep," he said, repeating the saying he'd just learned.

Mala chuckled softly. "Do you, at least, have some sort of a plan for when you're outside?"

"Yes." It wasn't entirely true, but it wasn't an outright lie either.

In the few short days that he'd spent among the Birkenau carpenters, Wiesław came to know about Antoni Szymlak, a civilian tiler who did odd jobs around the camp and who smuggled mail and parcels for local inmates. Most of the civilian Polish workers who lived in nearby villages and were hired by the camp administration to do specialized work around the camp that the inmates weren't qualified to do preferred to stay as far away from the inmates as possible. After all, fraternizing with the prisoners could land them in Auschwitz after the first denunciation to the camp Gestapo. However, there were a few civilians who risked their freedom and lives to aid those in need. Fortunately for Wiesław and Edek, Szymlak belonged to the latter category.

As soon as Edek heard about the man, he latched onto the idea that if Szymlak was indeed as sympathetic as the carpenters claimed, he could be persuaded to provide them with temporary shelter once they escaped. After that, they would make it across the Beskidy mountains and to Zakopane, a town where Wiesław's sister lived and the Germans didn't show their noses all that much. It was a land of the partisans—freedom fighters, former soldiers who narrowly escaped the clutches of the Nazis, and ordinary Polish patriots who lurked in the forests and attacked the Germans at every opportunity that presented itself, just to disappear after a successful raid back to the shadows to which they now belonged. For quite some time now, Edek had nursed hopes of joining them.

"All right then." Mala's voice brought him back to reality. "I'll get you a pass. But it may take some time. Best to do it at the end of the month, right before they close all the books. That's the only time the SS get careless and may overlook the disappearance of an *Ausweis*."

Edek nodded. He trusted her judgement. Mala looked like she knew precisely what she was doing.

"I'll meet you the day after tomorrow then?" He looked at her expectantly. "To bring you more shavings and parts," he clarified.

Suddenly, Mala reached out and pressed his hand. A warm smile once again played on her full, soft lips. "That'll be most helpful. I'll be waiting."

Then, she was gone, and he stood, dumbfounded and strangely lightheaded, in the dingy stall.

Chapter 8

Auschwitz

It was another pale, winter day, with a sky so low and leaden, it made one forget that the sun ever existed. In front of the locksmith's shop, Lubusch was smoking. Past his eyes, columns upon columns of inmates were trudging toward the gates—*Aussenkommando* prisoners, conscripted to work outside in the subzero temperatures all day. Whenever they leveled with the SS man, one of their *Kapos* shouted the usual "caps off" command and viciously clubbed whoever wasn't quick enough to tear the striped prisoner's hat off his shaved head in time.

Edek had been sent to fetch Lubusch. An illustrator, who used to work for a liberal newspaper in Warsaw and who made a grave mistake of drawing anti-Nazi political sketches for the publication, had once again jammed one of the machines in front of Edek's eyes and gave him a conspirator's grin when Edek didn't betray him. After poking and prodding at the machine for a few minutes, Kapo Vasek told Edek to fetch Herr Kommandoführer to sort it out. However, seeing the SS man's face just then, Edek didn't wish to disturb him and so, he stood by the wall of the block and, just like Lubusch, followed the columns of the gray skeletons as they marched to their deaths to the cheery sound of the camp orchestra.

Suddenly, one of the skeletons stumbled a step, staggered out of the column so as not to break the rest of the men's marching order, and slowly sank to his knees, keeling over. A *Kapo* pounced on him at once and began working on the man's sides and legs with his wooden club, shouting at him to "get your fat behind up, you stinker, you duty shirker, I'll show you yet how to lay about, you lazy Jew-pig—"

"Hit him about the face a little harder!" another *Kapo*, also a Green Triangle, brayed with laughter as he passed by. "Maybe you'll conjure up a miracle and make him rise from the dead."

"He's not dead," the first *Kapo* protested.

"Sure, he is. Look at him!" The second one made a show of walking up to the corpse and kicking him demonstratively in the genitals. "See? Dead as a doorknob."

The first *Kapo* grumbled at his comrade's retreating back and yanked two of the inmates out of the column. "Get that filthy carcass out of my sight and be quick about it before I get annoyed."

When they were passing by Lubusch and Edek, Edek saw a young inmate wiping his face on his shoulder. His breath was coming out in harsh, silent sobs. Lubusch made a step toward him, inquiring if he knew the old man.

"My father," the young inmate managed between tears, his face twisting into a painful grimace once again.

"I have to write his number down," Lubusch said.

With purposeful slowness, he extracted his black notebook and wrote down the dead inmate's name and number. Ensuring that the young man's *Kapo* was far ahead of them, the SS guard slipped a pack of cigarettes into the boy's pocket. Edek heard Lubusch whisper some words of sympathy very softly to the young inmate, in response to which he cried even harder. Kindness produced odd effects on people here. They had simply lost all habit for it.

"Now, off you go," Lubusch said with intentional loudness. "There's a death cart; march to it at the double. Duty shirkers, the lot of you."

Turning back to the locksmith shop barracks, he finally noticed Edek.

"Is something the matter?"

"One of the machines seems to be jammed again, Herr Rottenführer."

"*Unterscharführer*," Lubusch corrected him, staring vacantly after the couple of prisoners he'd just dismissed. With as much respect as it was possible, they were laying out the young inmate's father's corpse atop a small mountain of other bodies. "I'm officially a non-commissioned officer now; not a simple soldier anymore. Christmas promotion for a job well done." His voice was hollow, bitter.

"Congratulations, Herr Unterscharführer," Edek said mechanically and bit his tongue at the glare that Lubusch threw him.

"What's wrong with the machine? Did one of you jam it on purpose, to sabotage the production again?"

Edek started, not quite knowing what to say in response to the truthful accusation. So, Lubusch knew all about their machinations. Knew, and never said anything, not once, let alone punish anyone for ruining the numbers of his detail.

A faint smile appeared on Edek's face. "Does it matter what precisely caused it, Herr Unterscharführer?"

"It does, if I discover some alien part jammed into it right in front of a *Kapo*'s eyes. If he sees it, there will be no way for me to conceal it and it will be the *Strafblock* for the ones responsible." Lubusch looked at Edek closely. "Well? Will I find anything?"

"It's a very strong possibility, Herr Unterscharführer." Edek lowered his eyes.

Lubusch released a sigh and passed his hand over his forehead as if it all was too much for one day.

"I can try and distract the *Kapo* from putting his nose where it doesn't belong." Edek gave Lubusch a probing glance.

"Are you looking to earn Vasek's baton?" Lubusch chuckled mirthlessly.

"I'll be careful, Herr Unterscharführer."

"Did you jam it then?"

"No. I never jam any machines."

"Why not?"

Edek searched for the right words. "Because even though I should love to sabotage production, I never wish to cause any trouble for you. You have your own superiors before whom you are responsible. I'd never want you to get into hot water because of me."

"Why take responsibility for what you haven't done then?"

Edek gave a shrug, purposely avoiding Lubusch's inquisitive eyes. This was even more difficult to explain, but after Lubusch surprised him with a discreet clap on his shoulder, Edek realized that the SS man understood everything perfectly.

"Come on then, Galiński. Duty calls and all that rot."

Edek stepped before him, hardly breathing. This was his only chance, the perfect timing, and he would be damned if he missed it. "Herr Unterscharführer, may I ask you for a small favor?"

"What sort of a favor?"

"May I be transferred to the fitters' *Kommando* in Birkenau? Permanently?"

The SS officer scowled slightly. "Why Birkenau? The living—and working—conditions are much better here, in Auschwitz."

"It has nothing to do with living or working conditions, Herr Unterscharführer."

"What then? Are you not treated well here?" He sounded slightly offended.

Edek quickly shook his head. "No, of course not; I'm treated here exceptionally well, Herr Unterscharführer..." He hadn't quite thought the whole affair through before opening his mouth and now he was feverishly trying to come up with a suitable excuse. Instead, he stood before his *Kommandoführer* opening and closing his mouth like a fish thrown out of water.

All of a sudden, a knowing grin appeared on Lubusch's face. "Is it a girl, then?"

Startled, Edek glanced up. Mala's face appeared before his eyes and, suddenly, he was terrified at the thought of being uncovered.

"Look at you, you've gone quite red in the face," Lubusch continued his good-natured teasing. "A girl! Who would have thought? You first-rate Romeo!" He was laughing now, a genuine, carefree laugh that Edek had never heard from him before.

Edek had just begun to protest, but then thought better of it. Why not a girl, after all? A suitable enough explanation, one Lubusch would sympathize with, to be sure. He hung his head, silently admitting his defeat.

"What's her name?"

"Mala," Edek whispered, in spite of himself.

"Polish?"

"Jewish. Jewish-political," he quickly corrected himself. "She wears a red triangle over the yellow one."

"I'll be damned." Lubusch was positively beaming now. "It's what we spoke about. A hypothetical Jewish girl for you to fall in love with. What do you say to that? I ought to join the gypsy camp and work part-time predicting the future. Very well, Galiński. You'll get your transfer. It'll be my Christmas present to you."

Following him into the shop, Edek was overcome with the feeling of the most profound gratitude. *Saved,* he thought in his excitement, scarcely suppressing a huge grin growing on his face.

Inside, Kapo Vasek's enraged shouts could be heard through the entire work detail. He had lined up all of the inmates along the wall and had already conducted his own interrogation concerning the jammed machine, judging by their split lips and bloodied noses. He appeared to be so consumed by clubbing his victims, he failed to notice his own superior as he entered the shop.

"Do you think I don't know what you sly apes are up to? Do you think you shall keep getting away with your tricks? The same machine, jamming the third time this month. Do you think I don't know it's one of you who is doing it? I swear, the moment I

find out the pig who did it, I shall break every bone in his hands!"
Like a true servant of the Nazi regime, Vasek followed up every
sentence with a blow of a baton to an inmate's midsection or head.

"Attention!"

Edek felt his shoulders jerk at Lubusch bellowing next to him.
He looked thoroughly incensed.

The *Kapo* swung round and tore his hat off at once.

In a few long steps, Lubusch closed the distance between the
entrance and Vasek.

"On whose orders?!" Lubusch shouted in the *Kapo*'s face. "I'm
asking you, on whose orders are you mutilating my workers?"

When Vasek failed to explain himself, Lubusch continued his
dressing-down with even greater enthusiasm.

"If you put half of them out of commission, who shall finish the
quota for the month? Or do you plan to volunteer for the entire
detail, what?" He backhanded the man with such force, Vasek
stumbled a step back despite his powerful physique.

Edek saw a few inmates quickly hide satisfied grins.

"I said, what?!" Lubusch looked positively homicidal just
then.

Vasek mumbled something about sabotage and promised to
produce evidence, if Herr Unterscharführer just helped him take
the blasted thing apart.

"You haven't the faintest idea how the machine works and yet
you're ready to state, with such absolute certainty too, that's it's
the case of sabotage?" Lubusch drawled mockingly.

It occurred to Edek that it was Lubusch's idea to keep the *Kapo*
away from the machine by instilling the fear of God into him,
but, oddly enough, it produced quite the contrary effect on Vasek.
He began to dig through the parts like a man possessed and, just
as Lubusch had feared, discovered a small part jammed into the
construction after all. He held it before his superior's eyes with the
look of a child desperately seeking an adult's approval.

Now, not even their *Kommandoführer* could save them. Having joined the line of his *Kommando* mates, Edek saw the illustrator regard his hands with tragic eyes. They were all well acquainted with Vasek's punishment methods. They all knew he would go through with his threat.

"Now." The *Kapo* turned to face them, victorious. The sound his wooden baton made when he slapped it into his palm made Edek nauseous. He already anticipated it smashing into his bones. "Will the guilty party show some decency and step forward voluntarily, so I can freshen up his principles or shall we do it the hard way? Twenty-five lashes to every second person? It's all the same to me. Makes no difference how many of you, conniving stinkers, shall suffer for an idea."

No one budged. All eyes were directed at the concrete floor. In perfect silence, Lubusch's steps echoed loudly as he left the work detail, disgusted. With the *Kapo*, of course, not the inmates. Edek didn't blame him one bit. If he were in Lubusch's place, he wouldn't want to witness what was about to follow either.

To be sure, Lubusch could have stopped Vasek. Could have told him not to punish the men. Vasek would look at him, wondering if Herr Kommandoführer was off his rocker, obey as he should, but then quietly report him to the Political Department and it would be the end of Unterscharführer Lubusch for them. They had already shipped off such sympathetic guards to the Eastern front to teach them how to love their enemy. Whoever still wore a uniform and possessed at least some sort of conscience was very careful in displaying their humanity from that point on.

"Each second one it is," Vasek concluded amiably when no one spoke up, gesturing for the first "second" man in line to step forward.

Edek saw that it was the historian. The man walked over to the worktable with a resigned look about him and placed both forearms on the surface, exposing his thighs for Kapo Vasek's whip—the prescribed position for an inmate about to be lashed. There was a commotion in the line, as inmates began to demand for the guilty one to identify himself.

Out of the corner of his eye, Edek noticed the illustrator clench and unclench his fingers in utter desperation. He was in great demand among the local SS population; they commissioned portraits of themselves or their beloved ones from him with envious regularity. Quite often he dreamt out loud of opening his own gallery when he finally left Auschwitz. He would do well, everyone agreed, with such talent…

Just when the illustrator made the slightest move forward, Edek rushed toward the *Kapo* and positioned himself firmly before the burly man.

"It was me. I jammed the machine."

A malicious, dark grin spread slowly over the *Kapo*'s face. He advised the historian to get lost before anything happened, all of his attention on Edek now.

"Well, well, my brave little sailor. Twenty-five lashes it is, to tender you up a bit, and then we'll get to the real business."

Bracing himself, Edek placed his forearms where the historian's had just been. The *Kapo* was already brandishing his whip with twenty-five separate strands.

"You know the deal. Count each strike. If you lose count, I shall start from the beginning."

Aware of the agonized eyes of his *Kommando* mates on him, Edek took a deep breath and instantly felt it being knocked out of him after the very first vicious blow.

"One," he called out, struggling to keep his voice under control when all he wanted was to howl as the whip's strands sliced at his legs, one blow equaling twenty-five.

Hot, searing pain began to radiate from the back of his thighs.

Another blow. He winced, his eyes pooling with tears in spite of himself.

"Two."

The hissing of the whip slashing first through the air; then through his skin.

"Three."

His knees began to tremble, threatening to buckle. Cold sweat broke on Edek's face; he could no longer tell whether it was perspiration that was running down his cheeks, or tears.

Another blow.

"Four!" he cried out. It was impossible to keep his dignity anymore.

Hissing. Another skin-splitting strike. Blood running down Edek's legs; through the mist of his own tears, he saw the crimson droplets land on the worktable as the *Kapo* raised his whip once again.

"Five…" It took tremendous effort to keep himself up when all he wanted was to surrender to the black abyss.

"That's enough!"

Lubusch. His image swam in Edek's eyes and, through the searing pain, he smiled at the man, who had come to his rescue. Lubusch could have stayed in the comfort of his office and closed his eyes to the entire business; pretended that it didn't concern him, the fact that the *Kapo* decided to skin one of his workers alive. After all, Lubusch's superiors had already shipped him off once to the Stutthof-Matzkau concentration camp's penalty unit precisely for that sympathetic attitude of his. The second time, they could very well throw him to Auschwitz—and this time as a regular inmate, for the Political Department wasn't famous for giving second chances for re-education. And still, there he stood, noble and stern-faced, Edek's savior in the flesh.

The *Kapo's* hand, with the whip in it, froze mid-air. He regarded his superior questioningly.

"Lashing is too nice of a punishment for him. I'll take him to the *Strafblock* for the stunt he pulled," Lubusch said, motioning Edek to follow him.

Summoning every last ounce of energy, Edek could barely drag his feet, but he did, like a dying sheepdog following its master.

"They'll sort him out there; it's their specialty, after all."

Seemingly satisfied with such an arrangement, Kapo Vasek smiled broadly, tucking the whip back under his belt. It was Edek's conviction that it wouldn't remain there idle for long.

"Don't fret," Lubusch told Edek as soon as they stepped outside. "You'll rest there for a couple days and then they'll let you out. I'll tell them you're one of my best workers. They won't harm you; you have my word."

"Thank you, Herr Unterscharführer," Edek whispered, inhaling greedily the sharp, frosty air.

As they trooped along the icy road, he kept throwing glances at his namesake, unsure of what had revived him more—the biting chill of the wind or Lubusch's words that had once again restored Edek's faith in humanity.

Chapter 9

Birkenau

Mala gave a pause when, instead of Edek, she saw his friend waiting for her in the Sauna. He was a handsome young man with darker coloring than Edek's, a high forehead and sensitive deep-brown eyes. His face brightened when he saw her; he even waved, but Mala had seen far too many people belonging to the local resistance swinging from the gallows for trusting whom they shouldn't have to keep suspicion out of her voice.

"Whatever happened to your friend?" she demanded by way of greeting.

"Got himself into the *Strafblock* according to the note the Punishment Block *Kapo* smuggled for me," he explained almost cheerfully and offered her his hand. "I'm Wiesław."

At the *Strafblock* announcement, Mala felt beads of perspiration break on her temples. The blood drained from her extremities, leaving her cold with fear, but her face betrayed nothing.

She shook his outstretched hand. "Mala." Aware of every breath she drew, she managed to keep her voice cool and controlled. "What precisely did he get himself into the *Strafblock* for?"

"Oh, nothing to do with our business," Wiesław rushed to assure her, lowering his voice despite no one paying any attention to them. "Stepped up for a fellow who had sabotaged one of the working stations."

"Why?" Mala asked in genuine surprise. Such noble, selfless acts were a rarity in Auschwitz. Here, it was everyone for himself, a true dog-eat-dog world.

Wiesław gave a shrug. "He is like that, our Edek. Can't stand the sight of other people suffering. We are from the same town, but I only properly befriended him on the transport; we were in the same car. Out of us all, he was the only one with military training, so as soon as they put us all there, he instantly began to organize us with at least some sort of order. When we arrived in Auschwitz, he announced that the elderly ought to have better bunks and double rations. There were a few elderly men among us, doctors, clerics, and professors mostly—the real Polish intelligentsia—unlike us, who got arrested for being young and able-bodied. Naturally, someone—there are argumentative types like him everywhere—had a problem. To be honest, he'd been spoiling for a fight from the moment we'd got off the train; but it was when he'd refused to give his bunk to an elderly professor that Edek swiped him a couple on his snout. That put an end to the discussion at once." He chuckled fondly at the memory. "We've become good friends since. He's a first-rate man, our Edek."

Mala discovered that she was smiling as well. "He was in the Army then?"

"Not exactly. He was a maritime school cadet when the war started. He always joked that the Gestapo arrested him for his handsome sailor's uniform."

Mala smiled wider. One had to have a sense of humor to make jests about one's arrest and particularly if they had to deal with the secret German police.

"Did they beat him?"

"Naturally." Wiesław looked at her as though it was obvious. "All of us got slapped about the face for a good few weeks before they shipped us all here."

"I was rounded up by regular SS." Mala's eyes had a faraway look in them.

From the shadows, the past arose once again; the past, too painful to remember and impossible to forget. Mala always found it strange that her memories had a smell to them—railway steam and machine oil, her own French perfume, Chesterfields the traveling salesman who shared a bench with her chain-smoked, and the stale, sour sweat of the SS man's woolen uniform approaching her with his hand on his holster. He had singled her out as soon as she stepped off the train at the Antwerp Central Station, and no wonder—the yellow star all Belgian Jews had been forced to wear as of the recent occupying forces' order was enough of a giveaway. Her parents had implored her not to risk it, but Mala still went to Brussels, where, rumor had it, hiding places for the local Jews could be organized. Not for herself; Mala was certainly not the hiding type, but for her blind father and her gentle mother, who, Mala knew, wouldn't last a day in the Gestapo's captivity. As for Mala, she had planned to go underground with her old contacts from the Hanoar Hatzioni youth organization and fight the Nazis till the victorious end—or her own death, whichever came first. But the SS guard in his sweat-soaked tunic put a swift end to her plans with his, "Papers, please." Instead of joining the resistance, Mala found herself working in the registry at the Dossin Barracks at Mechelen—a collection, holding, and deportation point for Jews. And when there weren't any more Jews to process, they shipped her, along with the other registry workers, to Auschwitz—*thank you kindly for your services; unfortunately, they're no longer needed; you shall find the gas chambers to your right.*

A story too personal and too painful to relate to someone she'd just met. Instead, Mala released a sigh and said only, "They didn't beat us and didn't charge us with anything. Simply put us all on the train for being Jewish scum that contaminated their Aryan air with our foul breathing. That's a direct quote."

Wiesław averted his gaze, visibly uncomfortable. "I'm sorry," he mumbled, hiding his hands in his pockets.

Mala shrugged indifferently. *It's life.*

"Could we go someplace private?" he asked, glancing up at her. "I have something for you. From Edek."

Mala retreated into the darkest corner of the Sauna, where the yellow glare of the lamp scarcely reached, and turned to face him.

"Step closer." She caught his sleeve and pulled him toward herself. "I don't want anyone to see."

The deep blush that crept over Wiesław's face betrayed the fact that he wasn't used to the amorous business most inmates came here for. Mala found it almost endearing.

"Don't fret. I'm not going to kiss you," she teased him good-naturedly. "Now, what is it that you have for me?"

Wiesław wetted his lips nervously before fumbling with something in his pocket. "We made an agreement the day after he first met you that if something happened to him, I'd keep coming here and bringing you this." He extracted a full palm of metal parts and shavings.

For a moment, Mala stared at it, speechless. Then, as if remembering herself, she quickly opened her pocket for him.

"I personally don't understand the joke—" Wiesław chuckled in embarrassment, transferring the goods from his pockets to Mala's, "I would expect for him to ask me to bring you something edible, but he said, 'metal parts are what she wants. Must be something terribly important.'"

"It is," Mala confirmed very softly, feeling her cheeks grow warm. She still couldn't believe that it was her little contraband Edek was so concerned about instead of his own affairs.

"What do you need these for?" Wiesław regarded her with curiosity.

"Same as what you need that *Ausweis* for," Mala explained calmly. "To stick it to the Nazis one day."

The same steel that was in her pockets now shone in her eyes. Wiesław nodded his acknowledgement with respect and offered her his hand once again with a solemn look about him. "One day."

"One day," Mala repeated, grinning, sliding past him and disappearing into the crowd.

Chapter 10

Auschwitz

At first, it was darkness and intolerable pain. Then, the pain dulled, and soon, it was just darkness, cold and impenetrable and smelling frighteningly of wet earth and Edek's own body. The punishing cells were so narrow that when Edek straightened completely, his heels and the top of his head were pressed firmly against the floor and the ceiling, and then, the eerie, disturbing illusion of being buried alive was complete.

Three times a day, an inmate functionary slid the hatch in the door open, placing a bowl with turnip soup or a piece of bread with some moldy cheese in Edek's cell. It was by those feeding times that Edek could tell the time of the day and could count the days themselves.

He was grateful for the miniscule portions just then. He scarcely produced any body waste and, therefore, the bucket in the corner that served as his personal toilet didn't emanate too much of a stench. The sympathetic inmate emptied it each evening so that Edek could at least sleep for a few hours without being tormented not only by the obliterating darkness, but by the sickening smell. It was the same inmate who shoved some old newspapers through the hatch so that Edek could insulate his clothes and feet with them. In addition, a straw pallet and a blanket soon made their way into his cell. Edek regarded the unexpected gifts with the utmost gratitude: at night, when the frost settled in, the walls of his cell were like ice to the touch.

"Your lady friend sends her regards." The *Strafblock Kapo*, the same one who passed a note to Wiesław on Edek's request, patted the blanket affectionately before passing it to Edek.

"My lady friend?" He blinked at the man in confusion.

"Of course. Do you think I'm giving all this stuff to you out of the goodness of my heart?" The *Kapo* snorted with laughter. "You must be really something in the sack. She gave me a whole smoked sausage in exchange for accommodating you."

He was about to slam the hatch shut when Edek thrust his hands out of it pleadingly, risking getting his bones crushed.

"Wait! Herr Kapo, what was her name?"

It was the *Kapo*'s turn to stare at him with a mixture of amazement and respect. "Why, you have several of them, you dog?" His belly was shaking with laughter. "I don't know her name. She didn't introduce herself, much to my disappointment."

"What did she look like?"

"Like Goldilocks from the fairytale. Pretty as a picture. A regular princess," the *Kapo* responded with a wry grin before signing to Edek to get his hands away from the hatch so he could lock it.

Mala. Just the thought of her name warmed him better than any blanket would. *The angel. The savior.* It was his profound conviction that without the newspapers and a woolen blanket wrapped around him, he would freeze to death on one particularly cold night.

Left to his own devices, Edek had plenty of time to think. He thought a lot of his past and dreamt even more about his future. Whenever he contemplated his past, he always saw his father first—a simple plumber with big dreams of his son becoming an officer, and paying all his meager savings toward Edek's new uniform. The old man had teared up when he saw Edek wearing it for the first time. The very memory of it, of his father's warm embrace and his selfless parental love, made Edek wipe his own tears with the back of his hand. Confined to that concrete sack, beaten and starved, more than anything, he longed for his home. He longed for his mother's homemade meals and kisses on the forehead, for his dog's wet tongue on his cheeks and the warmth of its body pressed against his legs at night. Only, Auschwitz was now his home, and instead of his father's loving arms, he had Vasek's fists to contend with.

When reminiscing about his familial home became too painful, Edek turned his thoughts to the future. In it, there was always a dense forest, his partisan squad and the Nazis he and his new comrades would ambush, eventually freeing their land from the Reich's yoke once and for all. Edek dreamt of heroics, but each time, his thoughts veered off course and it was always Mala's face that ended up before his eyes. That hauntingly beautiful face and those mocking lips of hers: *What else then? Do you need a Mercedes too, with a personal driver?*

Invariably, Edek ended up chuckling at the memory of that single encounter and was astounded at the fact that he still could laugh in the first place; buried alive in that frost-covered coffin, it was Mala's words that kept him sane and counting the days till their next meeting. It would come, he was sure of it, just as he was sure that she would go through with her promise and get the *Ausweis* for him—and then, with Lubusch's aid… For some reason, Edek would always lose his train of thought at that precise point.

On the sixth day, at breakfast—it was just a mug of bromide-infused water the SS had the nerve to call coffee—Edek realized that he could no longer see his imaginary comrades' faces from the partisan squad. Mala's image replaced them once and for all and there was suddenly no going back for Edek. The realization of it both excited and terrified him. All at once, the *Strafblock* had lost its power over him.

I'll be waiting, she had told him without quite meaning what he wanted it to mean; yet never before had Edek been so determined to come out of there alive.

*

When the guard opened the door on the ninth day, Edek realized that he couldn't walk. Only crawl, on all fours, like an animal, for his muscles had grown much too weak after his solitary confinement in a cell that didn't permit any movement. That was precisely how the SS wanted them—humiliated, beaten into submission, reduced to an animalistic state—but Edek refused to give the guard the pleasure of seeing him on his knees longer than needed. Using the wall for support and trying not to cry out in pain at his muscles strained to the utmost, he pulled himself up and squared his shoulders in defiance. His legs were trembling something frightful; his eyes, no longer accustomed to the bright light, were brimming with tears, but he stood all the same.

In the room reserved for interrogations and dealing out punishment, a small delegation stood. Through the film of tears, Edek recognized Lubusch and, next to him, the new *Kommandant*, Arthur Liebehenschel, surrounded by a few of his adjutants. Edek's hand flew to his head instinctually and lowered slowly, as soon as he remembered that he no longer possessed an inmate's striped hat to take off as a sign of respect before the SS.

An officer from the Political Department addressed Edek, reading out a sentence about sabotaging the detail's production: "…a grave offense against war effort and German Reich… a crime that must not go unpunished… requested by Unterscharführer Lubusch and approved by camp Kommandant Obersturmbannführer Liebehenschel…"

His words scarcely registered with Edek; his eyes were trained on Lubusch and Lubusch only, expectant and pleading. To his great relief, his *Kommandoführer* gave him a brief encouraging nod in tow with a smile. It touched his mouth for an instant only and was gone before anyone could notice, but suddenly, the panic slipped away from Edek. He began to breathe again.

From what Edek had grasped, he was to be lashed again, in the presence of the camp *Kommandant*—on Unterscharführer Lubusch's request.

Kommandant Liebehenschel, a handsome man in his early forties, cleared his throat for the umpteenth time. Edek saw him clasp and unclasp his hands and look around as though desperately searching for an exit, as if it was him who was about to get his buttocks skinned by the executioner's lash.

In the meantime, the executioner, a brawny man with a red, pockmarked face resembling a bulldog's, was instructing Edek on how to stand correctly to receive his punishment.

"Take your pants off," he growled, indicating where Edek was to place his forearms. Suddenly, his face was right next to Edek's, who could smell chewing tobacco on the executioner's breath. "I won't hit you hard," the man whispered through his barely moving lips, "but you scream as loudly as you can manage, if you know what's good for you. It'll be over before you know it."

It was an odd request, but Edek had spent enough time in Auschwitz to follow such advice.

The executioner fussed some more over his victim, then turned to his distinguished guests waiting for permission to start. It was the political officer who gave it.

From his place, Edek saw how pale the *Kommandant* had grown as he stared in great alarm at the whip, with several beaded ends, in the executioner's hands. To his credit, the latter made a big show of rising it slowly and dramatically over his shoulder.

The blow stung, not half as badly as Vasek's, but Edek screamed so wildly that Kommandant Liebehenschel shouted for the executioner to stop it at once.

"His legs," Liebehenschel muttered, white as chalk. "He's already been lashed. And that affair counts for ten lashes at once." He pointed at the executioner's whip and Edek saw his hand trembling. "That's enough. You'll maim him for life. He won't be committing any more such sabotage. Will you?" This time Liebehenschel stared directly at Edek. In his tragic, black eyes was a wild appeal for confirmation.

In a shaking voice, Edek promised that he wouldn't.

The *Kommandant* breathed out in relief. "It's all settled then. Release him back to his barracks. No! Wait. Send him to the sickbay. He needs to have his wounds tended to before he can return to his duties."

After the *Kommandant* and his escort were gone, it was Lubusch who volunteered to take Edek to the camp hospital barrack.

"I hope you won't hold it against me," Lubusch said, dealing him a friendly clap on his back as the two were making their way out of the punishment block's dungeon. "The Political Department wanted to keep you there for a month. But I suggested an alternative they couldn't refuse—a demonstrative punishment before the *Kommandant*'s eyes. Liebehenschel is a sentimentalist," Lubusch explained with a confidential grin. "He can't bear the sight of inmates suffering. The gas chamber, he won't even go near. He nearly worked himself up into a nervous breakdown after he saw women and children heading into Hössler's domain in Birkenau. I knew that if I got him to watch over your execution, he would stop it at once."

"Thank you, Herr Unterscharführer." Edek actually meant it.

For a time, they walked silently side by side, Lubusch matching his strides to Edek's much slower ones.

"Is it true that he hurled a glass of champagne at Hitler's portrait?" Edek finally asked.

Lubusch moved his shoulder. "That's one version of events."

"May I ask what's the other?"

"He left his wife for a young woman of an unreliable political status," Lubusch replied vaguely. "And refused to break it off with her when his superiors demanded he did so." He paused for a while and then added in a voice that was full of romantic finality, "She followed him, to Auschwitz, after they shipped him off here as a punishment."

It occurred to Edek that Lubusch was thinking of his own wife who had followed him to Germany despite her racial status. Edek desperately tried to stop his train of thought, but he couldn't help himself: all of a sudden, he was wondering too. He was wondering if Mala would follow him if he offered her the chance to run.

Chapter 11

Birkenau

Mala was passing her most recent haul to Kostek, her *Sonderkommando* connection, when the siren began to blare over the crematorium. Instinctively, their eyes darted to the ceiling. *Could it be?* They exchanged hopeful looks. *An air attack?* The civilian Polish workers, who did odd jobs around the camp, never missed a chance to impart "the war news" to the local population, to raise their spirits. The Auschwitzers were aware that the Allies had bombed German cities, but not once had they seen an allied plane flying over their forsaken parts. It was everyone's conviction that the Soviets would reach them sooner than the Western Allies, but even the Red Army was still too far away, fighting somewhere in Western Ukraine, from what they had last heard.

As the sirens wailed, they were hoping for a miracle; but then familiar German shouts filled the crisp winter air outside, along with frenzied dog barking, and their hope died, much like everything did in Auschwitz.

Sensing danger, Kostek grasped Mala's hand and pulled her toward the elevator, but it appeared to have been locked. Issuing a curse in his native language—only the SS had the keys to the blasted thing, he explained as they ran—he made toward the exit with Mala in tow, but a frightened crowd of the *Sonderkommando* men were already pushing toward them, sweeping them back toward the gas chamber.

"Everyone inside, now! *Schnell, schnell, schnell!* Quick, quick!" the SS man bellowed, accompanying his words with the cracking of his horsewhip.

Mala only caught a glimpse of the guard's face, but she instantly recognized him. It was Hauptscharführer Moll, one of the officers in charge of the *Sonderkommando* and their ghastly detail. His brutal face was red with fury; his strawberry-blond hair was in disarray, which was highly unusual for him; the veins in his neck bulged as he shouted his commands at the stupefied men; his good eye rolled like mad, while his glass one remained unblinking and dead. The contrast was truly petrifying.

"Inside the chamber and stay there, you bloody oafs!"

A few SS men advanced toward the crowd, their submachine guns leaving the *Kommando* no chance for a revolt. In the general commotion, Mala lost Kostek.

"Damn this rat trap!" someone said beside Mala, his voice cracking with bitter tragedy. "They cheated us again."

Her back pressed against the column with its metal mesh, Mala was frantically twisting her head around, trying to make sense of the situation. Inside her chest, her heart was beating wildly.

"What's happening?" she asked no one in particular.

A few faces turned to her, regarding her with genuine sympathy.

"Every six months or so, they liquidate the entire *Sonderkommando*," a man near her explained. "After they liquidated our predecessors, we swore that we wouldn't go down without a fight. That we would foresee it happening—"

"Our time is not up yet!" someone shouted wildly. "It hasn't been six months yet. We have four more weeks to live!"

"It's almost Christmas, you SS swine!" another man cried. "Have you not the heart at all? Killing us all before the holy day?"

Painfully aware of a sense of dread creeping over her, Mala felt her entire body trembling. The SS were already herding more men into the chamber; these new ones brought with them the stench of singed hair and burnt flesh from minding the ovens upstairs. Their cries and curses mixed with the wails of the air-raid siren, deafening and terrifying.

By some miracle, Kostek found her again; and for an instant, his face reflected immense relief. In another moment, he was elbowing his way toward the airtight door in which the SS men were brandishing their whips and submachine guns.

"Herr Hauptscharführer!" There was desperation in Kostek's voice as he called for Moll's attention. His fingers clutching Mala's wrist were like iron. "There is an outsider among us. Mala Zimetbaum, the runner from the camp office." He was gasping by the time they reached the group of the guards.

At once, two muzzles of submachine guns were aimed directly at their stomachs.

"Back!" Moll shouted, his face twisting with rage.

"But she doesn't belong—" Eyeing the weapons in alarm, Kostek was groping for the right words. "Lagerführerin Mandl and Obersturmführer Hössler would never approve—"

Moll struck out at him with the speed of a venomous snake. His fist caught Kostek square in his jaw and made him stumble back a step despite his solid build. Moll was already upon him, pummeling him with his fists, until Kostek surrendered and fell to the floor, only covering his head with both arms to protect it from further assault. After dealing him a few swift kicks in the stomach and legs, only then, breathing heavily and sweating bullets, did Moll step back. The entire chamber heard the clang as the airtight door locked after him with an ominous sound.

Enveloped in semi-darkness, all eyes were directed at the hatches in the ceiling. The siren kept blaring, but so far, the hatches remained closed.

Mala crouched by Kostek. He was still dazed but was already working his way up, holding onto one of his comrades' elbows for support. Using her headscarf, Mala set to cleaning his face.

"Why bother?" He managed a bloodied smile. One of his eyes was already swelling. "We shall all be dead in a few minutes."

Mala considered saying that she was a human and that's what humans did, but then found fault in that logic. No; humans could no longer claim that their humanism was what separated them from the animals. Even animals helped each other; Mala herself had witnessed a hen warming orphaned ducks under her wings on an old farm in Poland. Humans were the biggest hypocrites among all species, for they banned abortions for Aryan women and yet they had no qualms about throwing Jewish children into gas chambers. They talked about helping fellow men and yet turned entire ships full of refugees away from their shores, condemning them to death. They spoke at length of their Christian values, but when it came to offering shelter to the persecuted, they shut their doors and chased the invaders off their property with guns and curses.

"Because your face is bloody and the right thing to do is to clean it," Mala said instead.

Kostek grinned with his broken lips. "How much better the world would have been if everyone did the right thing."

"Hopefully, future generations will learn from our mistakes."

"You think so?" He arched a skeptical brow. "You know, after thousands of years filled with bloodshed and conflicts, I have long lost all faith in humankind."

"So did I. But I still have faith in a fellow human. Now, I have faith in you." Mala looked at him. "You knew they were about to kill you all and yet you risked your life to save mine."

"And you risked your life coming here in the first place." He averted his gaze, suddenly unable to meet her eyes. "Forgive me, please, Mala."

"I have nothing to forgive you for." She smiled gently. "It was the right thing to do."

His shoulders quivered in the twilight of the chamber and Mala couldn't tell whether it was from tears or mirthless laughter.

*

The sun was descending, but the siren was still roaring its demented song above the camp compound. Now the searchlights had joined it, blinding the inmates lined next to their work details and barracks. They'd been standing to attention for hours now; scarcely feeling their own extremities, which felt as though they were frozen solid to the ground. At first, they had shivered violently; next, they had grown apathetic and sleepy and had to be nudged by their barrack mates to reply their *Jawohl—present*—whenever the SS man called out their number. Now, a good number of them were lying on the snow—it was their comrades who shouted their numbers for them and propped them up for the guards to see their ash-gray, dead faces.

The patients of the sickbay, whoever could walk that is, had also been chased outside by the SS doctors, while their inmate orderlies were checking the numbers of the bedridden ones inside the hospital barracks.

He could no longer feel his lips and yet Edek was certain he was smiling as he stood for the interminable roll call in the glacial cold. For he knew what the incessant wailing of the siren meant.

Someone had attempted the impossible and succeeded.

Someone had escaped from Auschwitz.

"Whatever are you grinning at?" Roman's purple lips barely moved. He was Edek's bunkmate, also sent to the sickbay to recover from a *Kapo*'s beating that had left him with painful welts on his buttocks that required surgery. "They can get him, still."

"They won't get him." Edek's feverish eyes stared wildly into the night, ignited by hope. "He's gone far, far away by now."

"They have the dogs."

"There are marshes all around here. He'll lose them there in no time."

"He's probably drowned in one of those swamps, the hot-headed idiot."

"No, he didn't."

"How do you know?"

"I just do." Edek tried to shrug but wasn't sure if he actually managed to do so. He had long lost all feeling in his extremities. "He has to be alive. If he's dead, I may as well go to the wire right now."

This time, Roman didn't argue. He understood.

*

Mala had never thought she would be so relieved to hear camp leader Hössler's voice. He spoke to them through the airtight door and yet, the crowd inside was so anxiously breathless, they heard each one of his words perfectly.

"Listen up, men. There has been an escape. So far, only one inmate is presumed missing, but we can't exclude that he had an accomplice or accomplices."

Mala's breath caught in her throat. *Edek?* But it couldn't be. Wiesław said he was locked in the *Strafblock*. The *Kapo* had confirmed it too, when she bribed him to supply Edek with a straw pallet and a warm blanket.

She listened closer.

"We're going to open this door to conduct a roll call among you lot," Hössler continued in his well-regulated voice. "There are machine guns mounted in the corridor; if you try to run or do anything idiotic, we won't have much choice but to shoot you all. Now, we don't want that and, surely, you don't want that." A pause, to drive his point home. "May I, as your leader, count on your good reason and behavior?"

Hössler wasn't called a sweet-talker by the *Sonderkommando* for nothing, it occurred to Mala. Where Moll bellowed and raged, Hössler spoke in measured tones and appealed to their logic. Mala understood only too well how he could persuade Auschwitz's new arrivals to walk straight into the gas chamber without suspecting a damned thing. It was difficult not to fall for his lies; it was even harder to separate them from the truth.

"I don't think they're planning to gas us," she whispered to Kostek. "I mean, they've already locked us inside. All they have to do is drop the gas. Why all this song and dance about an escapee?"

A few heads turned to her. The last thing she wanted was to give them hope when they could be annihilated in the next instant, but Hössler lying to them simply didn't make sense.

"Well?" She nudged a man with a *Kapo*'s armband in the ribs. "Go on. Tell him we'll comply before they change their minds and gas us all on principle. It is, after all, easier to count dead bodies than living humans."

That last argument propelled them to action. Several voices at once identified themselves as *Sonderkommando* leaders and promised their full cooperation.

After a torturously long minute, the sound of the door handle turning on the opposite side broke the tense silence. When the heavy metal door opened—slowly and cautiously—the first thing the inmates saw were the muzzles of three machine guns blocking the narrow corridor. Behind the guards manning them stood the top crematorium SS brass, guns drawn as well.

Only Hössler wasn't armed. Perfectly undisturbed, he held a clipboard in his hand with a mechanical pencil attached to it by a string.

"Everyone, try to stand as closely to that wall as possible." He indicated the left side of the gas chamber. After the prisoners moved obediently to one side, he nodded in satisfaction. "Good. We'll have a roll call now. After we establish that everyone is present, you shall all be released."

The men exchanged anxious looks; then, all heads turned expectantly to Hössler once more.

"When I call your number, you shall step forward, say *Jawohl*, and after I acknowledge you, you will move to stand on the opposite side."

"So that no sly apes call 'present' for their absent comrades," Moll inserted, a smirk visible on his face.

Hössler turned to him, annoyed at the interruption, and obliterated him with such a withering look that Moll retreated back into shadows at once—away from his superior's ire.

The first one to cross the vast room was one of the Poles with a low number—a camp veteran, just like Edek. Soon, more and more inmates joined him on the opposite side. Hössler started when he noticed Mala in the thinning crowd of prisoners.

"Mala? What are you doing here?"

"I brought a message to Kostek, from the *Kanada* detail," Mala explained hurriedly. "Their *Kommandoführer* is on leave and they're working out the new schedule for trucks to pick up the clothes from the crematoriums."

Technically, it wasn't a lie. Mala was camp-savvy enough to have a good excuse to be where she had no business being each time she ventured on resistance business.

"Why hasn't anyone reported this to me?" Hössler turned to his underlings, glowering. As though on command, all of them riveted their gaze to their boots, suddenly finding them positively fascinating. "I asked you a question." Hössler didn't raise his voice one bit, but everyone, the inmates and the SS included, ceased breathing at once. "Why is my *Läuferin* locked here, along with the *Sonderkommando*, and no one has reported this to me?"

"Herr Obersturmführer, allow me—" Mala stepped forward, wetting her lips. "Kostek tried to alert Hauptscharführer Moll to my presence here, but…" She purposely let the words hang in a strained silence.

Hössler had seen Kostek's bruised face. She needn't finish her explanation.

His face blotched red with anger, Moll stared at Mala in silent fury, his hand clasping the butt of his gun as though itching to put it to action. *You insolent Jew-bitch,* his twisted expression read, *I won't forget this.*

"Come here." Hössler signed to her with his clipboard. "Stand next to me. I'm going to the office anyway. You'll walk with me."

"*Jawohl,* Herr Obersturmführer."

Mala made her way among the machine guns and only resumed her normal breathing once she was standing by Hössler's side.

"With you—" the camp leader threw another annihilating glare in Moll's direction, "I shall deal later. It's a punishable offence, the failure to report such things to one's superior."

Mala stood with her back to Moll, but she could feel his good eye drilling holes in the back of her head the entire time that Hössler conducted his roll call. The satisfaction from making things hot for Moll as a revenge for his treatment of Kostek was short-lived. She had just made an enemy that would jump on the first chance to slaughter her in the manner of which only he was capable. In spite of herself, Mala inched closer to Hössler.

If only there was a way out of this all. But it was Auschwitz, the Grim Reaper's abode, with SS harvesting souls at will and hopes going up in smoke from the industrial chimneys. Here, death had many faces. Moll was only one of them.

Chapter 12

Edek kept running his hand over his new blue overalls—the official uniform of the Birkenau fitters' *Kommando*. He hadn't grown used to it yet, just like he hadn't grown used to the fact that he was now one step closer to freedom. It was Lubusch who made his transfer possible to the sector D of Birkenau men's camp after Edek had been released from the sickbay. Edek made a solemn promise to himself that when he was out of this place, when the war was over, he would find his namesake, shake his hand and have a drink with him—to freedom and to brotherhood. And to such wars never taking place for centuries to come.

"I suppose congratulations are in order."

He jumped at the voice and banged his head on the sink the pipe under which he was presently fixing. Lubusch's recommendations must have been glowing indeed since the local SS put him to work in their own quarters, where the tiles were shining and clean, the toilets porcelain and white, where Zarah Leander sang about love through the loudspeakers on the radio, and mirrors lined the walls and in which Edek didn't particularly like to look.

"Mala." Still holding his head—he would have a nice-looking bump on top of it tomorrow—Edek straightened before the young woman. He was beaming at her like a fool, but with the best will in the world, he couldn't wipe that grin off his face.

"No need to break your head on my account." Her caramel eyes were shining with mirth. "The SS shall see to it for you."

"That much is true." Edek rubbed the sore spot in embarrassment. "One can always count on them in such matters."

She watched him for a time with apparent interest and Edek watched her back, suddenly self-conscious and thankful for the *Kanada Kommando* outfitting him with freshly disinfected overalls that didn't stink of stale sweat and hardened grease. As he studied Mala's face, Edek discovered that oddly enough, instead of bringing out imperfections, the harsh artificial light of the SS latrine brought some luminous quality to her pallid, radiant skin instead. Under the bright lamps, her golden hair burst into color, shining and healthy, as though in defiance of all the illness and death surrounding her. But it was her eyes that riveted him with some inexplicable, magnetic force. Such steely, rebellious power was concentrated in them and yet such warmth radiated from their amber specks, and Edek felt all the layers of horror he'd lived through fall off him gradually like dried plaster. For a few precious moments, he felt free of the camp. She stood in front of him, hands in pockets, beaming, her cheeks fresh with frost, and time itself didn't dare to move forward.

"I almost couldn't believe it when I was processing your transfer order in the camp office," Mala broke the pregnant pause. "I thought it was you who deserted our little paradise last Tuesday."

"Without bidding goodbye to you? I wouldn't dare."

She arched a lively brow. "Your friend Wiesław was speaking the truth then. You must have been quite a ladies' man back home."

Edek stared at her in mute horror.

"He said that?" He finally managed the words. In his mind, he was ready to slaughter his so-called friend.

Mala tormented him with her face, devoid of any expression for a few moments, but then suddenly burst into laughter. Edek thought he'd never heard anything so beautiful. Its notes echoed around the washroom and, suddenly, the camp indeed seemed like a paradise to him.

"No, he didn't. I was pulling your leg."

Edek breathed out in relief. "I never thanked you for the *Strafblock*," he spoke at length, fumbling with pliers. "For the blanket and for the straw pallet."

"I never thanked you for sending Wiesław with goods for me."

"I wanted to make sure that you'd still have them if…" He desperately scrambled for words. Saying "if I died" seemed wrong somehow; not when she stood before him with her golden crown of hair and those death-defying eyes. He couldn't bring himself to even mention death in her presence. "If something happened to me," Edek finished carefully instead.

"I couldn't let anything happen to you."

Her tone was conversational and yet there was some hidden message behind those simple words that made Edek's heart stumble in his chest and miss a beat.

"Thank you," he repeated and instantly cursed his own stupidity inwardly for not saying what he truly wanted to say to her.

"You're welcome."

The moment was lost. *Idiot*, Edek closed his eyes, his cheeks burning with frustration.

All business once again, Mala glanced over her shoulder. "I found a blank for your *Ausweis*. There's a problem though."

It took him great effort, but Edek managed to recover himself. "What problem?"

"It requires a photograph."

"A photograph?" he repeated after her like a demented parrot.

"Yes, a picture of the inmate, whom an SS guard accompanies. Now, I know you don't want to give away much of your plan—who am I to you, after all?—but I have to ask you out of sheer necessity: can you get a photo? I won't even ask whether it's for you or Wiesław or both; you'll glue it inside yourself. But you need the photo."

"It's for Wiesław. The plan is, we walk through the gates together, I dressed as an SS man and Wiesław as an inmate I'm taking for a job outside the camp. You were right before when you said that no SS guard would agree to go through with such a dangerous enterprise. But he might risk giving us his old uniform, and that's precisely what we're counting on."

Edek hadn't the faintest idea why he'd just blurted out the entire scheme to the woman he scarcely knew; he only knew that he trusted her. Trusted her with a secret that could get him and his best friend executed and yet, there he stood, pouring his most sacred thoughts to her without a shade of doubt in his mind that she would rather take the plan to her grave than betray it to the Nazis.

Something changed in Mala's expression. The wry grin was gone and in its place was a look of wonder and disbelief at the fact that he was so open with her, and something else that Edek couldn't quite detect.

She didn't ask for any more details, merely nodded and murmured, "Wiesław's photo then," under her breath, solemn and already working things out in her mind.

"Can a camera be had in Birkenau?" Edek asked, already knowing the answer.

"Mhm. And the film to go with it. And a darkroom hidden in the back of a barracks." She gave him a look full of scorn and, instead of crying out in desperation, he laughed in embarrassment. She even managed to lighten such a tragic situation.

For a time, Mala paced the washroom, her brows drawn tightly in concentration. Edek watched her in silence and didn't dare move in order not to disturb her. Suddenly, she came to an abrupt halt and turned to face him.

"Wiesław arrived with the same transport as you, didn't he?"

Edek nodded.

"So, he's a low number, too?"

"He is." He held his breath, feeling that she was onto something, and yet, much too afraid to believe it.

"Back in 1940 and 1941, the SS were still taking photos of the new arrivals. They stopped the practice when the Jewish *Aktion* went into full swing and they simply didn't have the time to process all of them." A dark shadow passed over Mala's face at the mention of the mass deportation and extermination of the European Jews, most of whom ended up in the Auschwitz gas chambers. "So, his photo must be attached to his file. I only received your transfer orders but not files themselves. They must be still kept in the main office in Auschwitz." Mala tapped her forearm with one of her long fingers, staring through Edek as she was planning something feverishly in her mind. "I could get that from their office."

"Will they give it to you?"

"If I tell them that the camp leader Hössler wants it, they will."

"And if they call for a confirmation?"

"My good friend and colleague, Zippy, shall pick up the phone and confirm it for them."

"What if they insist on speaking to Hössler directly?"

Mala grinned darkly. "No one insists on speaking to Hössler if they can help it. Trust me."

"I trust you," Edek said, meaning something quite different.

There was a long pause, the hail ticking on the window like a clock, Zarah Leander's song pouring out of the loudspeakers that carried long and far above the camp. Edek hoped that it would take Mala a few weeks to procure the file, the photo and the blasted *Ausweis*, and he wasn't even sure he wanted it any longer. He found that, the closer he was getting to freedom, the less he wanted it. It had suddenly dawned on him that without her, it didn't amount to much.

*

Auschwitz's concrete road was a welcome change from the hardened-mud road in Birkenau. It was spotless, freshly cleared of snow by the special *Kommando*; only by Block 11, the infamous punishment and execution block, there was a fresh puddle of blood and a trail of it heading in the direction of the old crematorium. Mala walked around it carefully, inwardly relieved that she hadn't caught sight of the death cart itself.

Among many Auschwitz horrors, the death cart and the grisly *Kommando* manning it was one of the worst as far as Mala was concerned. The wooden wagon piled high with corpses and pulled by four grotesque inmates' "horses" had been one of her first impressions of Auschwitz that had annihilated all of her hopes of getting out of that place alive. Still a fresh arrival, deceived, like many, by the camp's gates' slogan that work would set them free, Mala had stood riveted to her spot, staring at the inmates pitching the bodies straight out of the barracks' window and into the awaiting arms of the prisoners in the cart.

At the sight, her brain had refused to process the mortifying truth. She had wondered if it was a sewing detail of some sort, and whether they were about to transport the mannequins somewhere. But, gradually, her eyes began to absorb it all—the gray flesh stretched over the bones; the genitals, on the account of which the cart *Kommando* was making crude jokes—*I'll be, look at that fellow's asset! Must have served him well back home*—the caved-in skulls from which the brain matter was leaking through the boards of the cart and onto the spotless concrete; the sightless eyes and toothless mouths opened in their last silent screams.

To this day, Mala couldn't tell what terrified her more: the sight of it, the sickening sound of the bodies hitting the boards that grew progressively duller as flesh was piled upon flesh, the meticulous efficiency with which the *Kommando* was stacking the day's "harvest" as they jokingly called it… or the cheerful whistle of the *Kapo* as he accompanied the cart pulled by the inmates who looked like they'd end up in it within a day or two.

Lost in the nightmare of her memories, Mala didn't realize that she had stopped altogether in the middle of the street. Only when two inmates hustled by her with water buckets and brushes, bending down to clean the blood off the road, did she emerge from its dark spell, forcing her legs to move again.

She walked along familiar streets with strangely civilian names to them—Cherry Street and Camp Street and, naturally, Adolf Hitler Street—the nameplates announcing them accompanied by carvings depicting daily camp life. Under one such nameplate was an inmate being beaten by a *Kapo*, under a second, an SS man's dog biting a prisoner in the buttocks—comical stuff that the guards must have found perfectly delightful. She walked past the two-story, red-brick barracks with their numbers highlighted by bright lanterns, and past the trees, now bare and skeletal and oddly befitting the place, much more appropriate than when they stood proud and green and in full bloom as though mocking the local population, just like the crude street name carvings that mocked them as well.

At last, the *Kommandantur* building came into view. In front of the entrance, a guard was smoking. Mala recognized him from her previous visits to the main camp office. He was a somewhat permanent fixture there, a young man with a known weakness for sweets that inmates in need of a favor used to their advantage, and a gun slung over his shoulder that he must have only fired during the obligatory training. Unlike most of the SS in Auschwitz, he never shouted, never hit anyone, and generally preferred to carry out shifts as a *Kommandantur* sentry instead of dealing with the inmates. Mala had a strong suspicion that he wasn't too ideologically inclined; merely didn't fancy freezing his bones in some dugout on the Eastern front under heavy Soviet artillery fire.

"Good morning, Herr Rottenführer."

He waved her off even before she had a chance to present him her *Ausweis*. Almost everyone in Auschwitz-Birkenau knew Mala and her runner's armband by now.

"Good morning, Mala. Herr Kommandant is not in."

"It's all right. I just need a recently transferred inmate's file from the office. They forgot to send it in and you know how Obersturmführer Hössler gets when the paperwork isn't in order."

"Go on then." He stepped aside and motioned her in with a somewhat theatrical urgency about him. "I wouldn't want to get you in trouble."

Walking along the well-heated corridor, Mala wondered how many such guards were scattered around the occupied territories, perfectly harmless and yet aiding Hitler's extermination program like a well-oiled machine. How many doctors, teachers, civil servants, and journalists cringed and yet abided by the new rules because the pay was good and the life not so bad. To be sure, their Führer was a hateful bastard they couldn't stand, but he did go through with his promise and turned their country into a superpower. And if they kept their eyes and ears shut, they wouldn't really hear the screams of little Jewish children being torn from their mothers' arms; they wouldn't see the Party's vicious Brownshirts beating "the anarchists" in the street, and if they allowed themselves not to think and rely on their leader's propaganda only, they would almost believe his outrageous statement that the last rebels who dared to speak against the regime and all of their Führer's vileness were the enemies of the state who would spoil it all for them, the law-abiding citizens, and therefore, needed to be annihilated or locked up. Or shipped to a concentration camp for re-education purposes.

The Führer was kind, indeed. He even gave such anti-fascist, leftist thugs a second chance to change their minds.

Shaking her head in disgust, Mala raised her hand and knocked on the familiar door. Inside the vast file room, several inmates were typing with impressive speed. The only SS officer supposedly supervising them was far too immersed in a British spy thriller he was reading—*Kanada* loot, Mala guessed, hiding a knowing grin; such literature had been long banned in the Reich—to bother himself with Mala's explanations. He merely waved her toward the filing cabinet and turned another page, his brows drawn tightly in concentration. The book must have been good, indeed. Making use of such outright negligence, Mala quickly recovered the needed file and tiptoed out of the room, shutting the door silently after herself.

Only when she was a few blocks away from the *Kommandantur* did she finally open it, releasing a breath of relief at the familiar face looking back at her from all three directions—right, left, and center.

Wiesław Kielar, inmate number 290.

Shutting the file closed, Mala hastened her steps, a bright smile playing on her lips. She had long ago made it a point of honor to help anyone she could possibly help, but if it was within her powers to aid these two men's escape, it would be an entirely different matter altogether. They were running away to fight. She would be aiding the future partisans, the future freedom fighters—perhaps, the future liberators. And then, who knew, maybe one day they'd walk through these gates once again, shake her hand and tell her, "Mala, you're free; we're liberating you after you liberated us," and they would leave this place behind and—

Mala turned the corner, stumbling when she saw the same inmates still polishing the concrete road with their brushes. The surface of it was no longer rusty-crimson, but tender pink.

Happy endings were only possible in spy thrillers. All future partisans who dreamt too much for their own good ended up on the death cart.

And yet, she trooped forward, for she was an obstinate little soldier and surrendering was simply not an option. Perhaps, that was the reason she felt such kinship with Edek. He, too, was a dreamer. He, too, refused to submit.

Chapter 13

"Have they caught the man yet?" Edek asked.

The inmate in charge of the warehouse with supplies didn't need any clarification. The escaped prisoner had been the subject of camp gossip for quite some time now.

"No. The lucky devil must be drinking champagne in some Polish restaurant as we speak," the inmate speculated with a good-natured smirk, handing Edek a document of some sort. "Sign here for the sink."

"Some bureaucracy you've got going here," Edek murmured, mildly surprised and bursting out laughing when Wiesław appeared from the depth of the warehouse carrying a sink on top of his head so it concealed him entirely up to his shoulders. "Just what are you doing, you miserable bonehead?" He knocked on the metal, causing a shout of protest from his friend.

"Quit it! You'll give me a headache. And besides, how else do you suggest I carry it? It's enormous! Carry it yourself if you don't like my method." His voice, amplified by the iron, sent even the warehouse inmate chuckling.

"We drew sticks; you lost," Edek countered, unperturbed, and returned the warehouse fellow his clipboard.

"Now, this business—" the inmate pointed at the sink with the stub of his pencil, "goes into the Music Block latrine and the Music Block only. Understood?"

"Where else would it go?" Edek blinked at him uncomprehendingly.

The man made a sly face. "You're new here, I take it."

Edek scowled.

"Birkenau is not Auschwitz," the inmate went on to explain with an air of a lecturer about him. "Here, black market is everything. Everything that can be pinched, shall be pinched. Everything that can be traded, will be traded. Nothing is off limits. Hence the bureaucracy, as you called it. The SS are trying to stop the widespread stealing. That's why I warned you about the sink; don't even consider putting it to use in any other place or selling it to the local Poles. The SS shall come and check; if it's not inside the Music Block latrine, you'll make an acquaintance with Kapo Jupp's lash, and he's infamous for his heavy hand."

"I've made my acquaintance with Kapo Vasek's whip already," Edek grumbled, rubbing his thighs instinctively. It had been a few weeks and they still hurt.

Outside, the wind was howling. Wet mist coming from the swamps penetrated both friends' overalls and the two sweaters they concealed under their uniforms. Moisture froze in their noses, gluing their nostrils together with every breath they took. They had just left the comfort of the warehouse and the tears caused by the biting frost were already beginning to freeze atop their eyelashes. Pulling the collar of his sweater over his mouth, Edek almost wished that he was carrying the sink to protect him from the elements.

"The Music Block has its own latrine, imagine that?" Wiesław said appreciatively.

"They're considered privileged prisoners." Edek gulped a particularly harsh gust of wind and turned his head away to catch his breath. "Remember the orchestra in Auschwitz? White jackets with red cords—even as a civilian I haven't had such a nice outfit!"

"We didn't have the women's orchestra though."

"We didn't have women in the first place."

"That much is true. Do you think they'll talk to us? The Music Block girls?"

"Of course." Edek laughed cuttingly, his breath coming out in clouds of white mist. "How can they pass on such a catch as yourself? As long as you keep that ugly mug covered, you'll be able to arrange yourself a date."

He was about to add something else, but a swift kick that he'd received quickly put an end to another string of friendly insults.

"What? Attacking the maritime troops?" He dealt Wiesław a playful blow in the stomach.

"Is that how you fight, pitiful veteran of the seas? My mother hit me harder."

Edek promptly shoved him, causing Wiesław to miss a step and nearly fall with his load.

"Quit it! If I stumble into the electric wire, you'll miss the date I'm trying to arrange with our civilian friend from Kozy."

"Not that Szymlak fellow you mentioned?" Edek regarded him incredulously. "The tiler? The one who smuggles all sorts of contraband in and out of the camp?"

"The very same," Wiesław replied with a smug satisfaction about him. "It's costing me a fortune in rations, but it will be worth it if he agrees to help us with our plan. Now, we just need a *Kapo* who knows him to come through with his promise and put us in touch with the man."

"Wiesław, you sly devil! Why didn't you tell me anything?"

"Didn't want to get your hopes high in case the *Kapo* considers it better business to eat my rations and tell me to piss off."

"You should have told me… I would have split mine with yours."

Wiesław waved him off generously, lost his balance and almost dropped the sink. "Don't worry your head about that. I work in the women's camp's sickbay sometimes, in case you forgot. Those ladies feed me plenty of rations, so I won't go hungry any time soon."

"In exchange just for your fitter's services or…?" Edek arched his brow and let the insinuation hang in the frosty air.

Stealing a glance from under the sink, Wiesław delivered another well-aimed kick at his friend's calf, nearly tripping him.

They began to laugh, feeling the warmth creeping back into their extremities that had been frozen nearly stiff, but then suddenly went silent. The women's camp came into view and, along with it, its inhabitants. This army of apparitions barely resembled women.

Upon noticing the two fitters and their blue overalls, they pulled themselves off the frozen ground with great difficulty and followed them along the barbed wire with their gray, skeletal arms outstretched in pleading gestures.

"Bread…"

"Anything to eat…"

Even their hoarse whispers had a frightening, ghostlike quality to them. Edek felt himself shuddering and, this time, it wasn't due to the cold. He shook his head, apologized, and tried to avert his gaze, but still saw it all—infected sores covering bare, shaved skulls; bones protruding under discolored, scaly skin; hollows in place of eyes, as though the visage of death itself stared back at him from each face he dared to look at; and bloodless lips already pulling away from the gums with a few loose teeth still visible in them. Prematurely dead, all of them, these infinitely old women who used to be young, pretty girls just a few months ago.

"Let's bring them something next time," Wiesław suggested quietly. "Surely, we can spare a couple of pieces of bread each."

Edek threw a glance at him. Wiesław didn't have to look; he could have kept that metal sink on top of his head the entire time, pretending that this suffering didn't exist and continue to horse around with Edek to drown out the soft pleas—"just a crust, my mother is dying"—but instead, he pulled the sink away from his face so now only its edge rested on his inmate's cap. He looked, purposely and closely, as if in some perverse desire to imprint it all in his mind, to never forget the horrors he'd witnessed.

"Let's not throw it through the wire though," Edek replied just as quietly. "Remember how the *Muselmänner*," he winced involuntarily, using the camp slang term for the inmates who resembled walking skeletons more than people; it was too painful to even mention them without feeling a dull ache in one's chest, "acted whenever we threw a piece of food at them in Auschwitz? They would hurl themselves on it in one big pile and fight for it like jackals until the strongest one made away with it or a *Kapo* noticed it, produced his wooden stick and let them all have it across their backs. Let's give it to Mala instead. She brings them food as it is; she knows how to go about it delicately."

Wiesław said nothing at Edek's mentioning the girl's name, but his knowing grin did.

Edek released a relieved breath once they approached the Music Block. It stood on the very edge of the camp and, despite the fact that it was facing the crematorium, it was surrounded by a few trees, albeit bare, and didn't emanate the unbearable stench of hundreds of unwashed bodies that most of the regular barracks did. As soon as they stepped inside, Edek understood why: there were only about forty girls in the entire block, all neatly dressed in blue uniforms of sorts and with kerchiefs covering their hair.

Hair, he marveled, standing, astounded, in the door of the warm barracks with his mouth slightly agape. *Girls, with hair... Just like Mala.*

He couldn't see their faces yet; they all sat in a semicircle with their backs to him, but he knew instinctively that they looked nothing like the poor creatures they had just encountered in the women's camp. He would, no doubt, have continued to observe them like some miracle, if their conductor hadn't rapped her baton on the music stand, stopping the music abruptly. Judging by the displeasure visible on her face—more striking than beautiful, with two huge dark eyes that now regarded him wrathfully—he must have interrupted their rehearsal.

"In or out?" the conductor demanded with a strong Viennese accent, in a perfectly no-nonsense tone.

"I beg your pardon?" Edek mumbled, feeling like a school student before a headmaster.

"In or out?" she repeated impatiently. "Did you come here to listen to us rehearse or do you need anything?"

"We brought a sink to install in place of the old one," Edek explained, jerking his thumb over his shoulder, where Wiesław was shifting from one leg to another. "For the latrine."

"The latrine is behind the block." In an elegant, effortless motion, the conductor waved her baton, indicating the direction.

Edek mumbled his thanks, apologized once again, and was about to turn around when a thought suddenly struck him.

"Forgive me, please, Frau…"

"Frau Alma," she supplied. Her first name, not last, for some reason.

"Frau Alma." Edek nodded. "Did you say we're allowed to listen to you rehearse?"

"Well, yes." She gave an indifferent shrug. "It's not prohibited by the camp administration. As long as you're quiet, you're more than welcome in the auditorium."

She resumed her rehearsals before he had a chance to thank her. Respectfully, Edek closed the door after exiting the barracks, but instead of heading straight to the latrine, he lingered by the entrance as one enchanted, drinking in the sounds of the music. It swept over him in warm, comforting waves, almost caressing him with its feathery touch, and all at once, for a few stolen moments, the camp was forgotten.

"How come they have their own latrine?" Wiesław mused out loud, helping Edek uninstall the old, rust-covered sink from its place.

"The *Kapo* said it used to be the SS wardens' block. Before they built special accommodations for them outside the camp, so the Aryan highnesses wouldn't mix with our criminal types." The sarcasm in Edek's voice was palpable.

Wiesław snorted softly under his breath. "You know, before they shipped us all here, I thought that only men were capable of such unspeakable cruelty. I never suspected that women could be just as ruthless. And do you know what bothers me the most about this entire rotten business? They don't think they're doing anything wrong. They refuse to acknowledge themselves as perpetrators. They think they serve their country's best interests and they hide behind that mock-patriotism, which is, in fact, naked nationalism generously spiced with hatred, and wield their guns and whips in the name of their glorious leader and beat and maim and kill in his name and feel not a single pinch of conscience about it. And Hitler, what a cunning bastard he is! How well he brainwashed that herd."

Wiesław's voice gained force, his eyes narrowed, his words—sharp barbs, cutting to the bone with their truths.

"'It's us against them,' he told them, and they believed him, the brainless herd, 'Only I shall bring law and order to Germany and it matters not that I shall do it with the help of the secret police. Only I shall rid you of all the enemy elements—the communists and the pacifists and just general leftists who don't embrace our ideology, and it matters not that I shall imprison them or slaughter them outright. They're the enemy. They shall ruin Germany. We'll strip them of their citizenship and throw them into the concentration camps with Jews and communists—that's where they belong. Only the good Germans shall remain in Germany. Only the ones who kneel and obey and keep their mouths shut. Or, better yet, spew their hatred openly and kick their fellow countrymen as they're being herded onto the cattle trains.' Those are the Germans he wants. And those are the Germans he got. All those with conscience are here. Whoever is left deserve what is coming to them."

Emerging from under the sink, Edek regarded his friend in silent amazement for some time. "Whatever brought that on?"

Edek tried to smile, but the grin came out uncertain, wavering. The words had hit him too hard; he felt them painfully in his chest, as though from a physical blow.

Releasing a breath, Wiesław passed the back of his hand over his forehead. All at once, he looked exhausted, as if that passionate speech took all the strength from him. And yet, in his eyes, Edek saw something close to relief. He understood it, too; it all surged up in them from time to time, that pent-up anger at the injustice of the world, producing such outbursts.

"Those women begging for bread," Wiesław explained, his voice suddenly robbed of all force. "The wardens in their warm capes. The very fact that we're here, messing about with this blasted sink, when we ought to be doing things that we dreamt of doing back home. You would have been giving orders on one ship or the other now and I—" He stopped himself abruptly and shook his head, his mouth pressed into a bitter line. What good was dreaming of the things that would never happen? They only made reality more difficult to cope with.

"You never did tell me what it was you wanted to do," Edek still pressed. For some reason, he felt it was important for Wiesław to tell him all about it.

"It's stupid and it will never happen."

"Of course it will. That's the sole reason we're running away from here." He stepped closer to his friend, who stubbornly avoided his eyes. "So that we can fight for our right to do what we want. So that we destroy all that hatred and replace it with love. So that in place of battlefields, we plant trees and flowers and crops. So that in place of army marches, we will all listen to this." He motioned toward the back wall, from behind which the tender notes of the Viennese waltz could be heard. They echoed around the dingy latrine like precious stones scattered around the sand, lighting up the very air with their reviving, old-Empire breath—intoxicating, going straight to one's head.

"I always wanted to be a writer," Wiesław spoke after a long pause, still refusing to meet Edek's gaze. "Or work on motion pictures. I love motion pictures."

For a few moments, Edek was silent too. "I think you'll make a great writer and a great cinematographer one day," he said, giving Wiesław a friendly clap on his shoulder. "You observe everything very closely. You memorize things. And it's good. Keep doing it, so when we're out of here, you can tell our story to the world, so none of these horrors repeat themselves again."

Wiesław glanced up in surprise.

"What?" Edek grinned knowingly. "You expected me to tease you about it, like we tease each other about everything else?"

"To be frank with you, yes. I did."

"I considered it but couldn't come up with a good joke."

They picked up the old sink and were already heading out when Edek suddenly stopped in the door and spoke again, his expression as grave as ever.

"Promise me, Wiesław."

"What?"

"To write about it."

"How about we co-write it?"

"I'm not good with words."

"Yes, you are. With all the right words."

Chapter 14

"So, you made your acquaintance with Frau Alma?" Mala asked with a playful grin.

They met at their usual place, the Sauna. Inside, it was business as usual, with all sorts of transactions taking place. As he had promised, Edek brought a full pocket of nails and screws, pinched from his new fitters' *Kommando*. This time, instead of taking the contraband from him, Mala stepped very close to Edek and opened her pocket, so he could lower the goods into it himself. In spite of himself, Edek held his breath as he dipped a fistful of contraband into Mala's pocket, feeling heat rising in his cheeks as he sensed the warmth of her body through the thin lining of her coat.

She didn't move away at once, but stood there, still much too close, studying his face with an enigmatic smile on her face. It took Edek great effort to recall what it was precisely she had asked him.

"Frau Alma? Yes." He swallowed, recovering himself with difficulty. "I did. She seems… A bit intimidating."

Rather to his surprise, Mala chuckled. "You're not the only one with that impression. Some of the SS are quite fearful of her. Well, I suppose, that's to be expected." She paused before adding unexpectedly, "Hössler is in love with her. All of his inferiors know she's under his direct protection."

"Hössler?" Edek stared at her, astounded. "Camp leader Hössler?"

"The very same. To be sure, he would never admit to it openly, but…" For a few moments, Mala searched for the right words with her head tilted slightly to one side. "He talks about her constantly and goes to listen to her play her violin nearly every day. The wardens hate her."

"Why?"

"She's from a prominent Austrian family. Her father used to be the concertmaster of the Vienna Philharmonic. Her uncle was a composer. Her brother and she are both celebrated musicians. Their only trouble was they happened to be Jews, assimilated like me, but that doesn't matter to the Nazis." Mala gave an indifferent shrug. "That's why the wardens hate her. Their SS bosses could have thrown Frau Alma into Auschwitz, but they couldn't change her nature. She's a refined, high-society lady and an accomplished violinist and even the local SS elite like Hössler understand it and admire it. The wardens may wear the uniform and imagine themselves the masters of this little camp universe, but deep down, even they understand the difference between them and Frau Alma. She's everything they aspire to be but will never become. And so, they hate her for it."

"I still can't believe what you said about Hössler."

"He's only a man. And love doesn't care for such trifles as race, skin color, or religion."

"My former Kommandoführer Lubusch married a Polish girl."

"See?" Mala gave him a triumphant grin.

Edek didn't tell her how much he, a Pole, liked a certain Jewish girl as well.

"Naturally, Hössler's situation is a little different," Mala continued, as he reddened further. "He'll never act upon his feelings. Instead, he'll keep admiring Frau Alma from afar, continue doing favors for her and never betray himself with a single word. Us women, we see the little things men in love do for us. But, outwardly, he keeps his appearances, supervises gassings at the crematoria, shoots a few prisoners now and then. An exemplary SS man, in his superiors' eyes. Only to me he will talk about her, and only when he knows that no one else will hear." Her face turned pensive. "Sometimes I pity him. He could have been a decent man had he not fallen under his Führer's indoctrination. Free to live his life the way he wanted. Free to love whoever he wanted. He was studying photography, you know. And now…" Mala shook her head.

Us women, we see these little things men in love do for us. Edek stole a glance at Mala's pocket and wondered whether she knew as well, the reason for all of these visits, all of the risks he was taking just to get precious contraband for her. And then her eyes met his and he saw that she knew. Of course, she did. They, women, always did.

He cleared his throat. "And what about her?"

"What about her? She uses him for her own purposes, for privileges for her girls and that sort of thing, and good for her. She's a highly intelligent woman. Zippy positively adores her."

"Zippy is your colleague from the camp office?"

"Yes. She also plays the mandolin in the orchestra. Sometimes, they play here, in the Sauna, on Sundays. You should come along."

Edek searched her face. "Will you be here?"

"Does it make a difference?" Mala asked, her smile turning coy.

"All the difference in the world. I'm not very educated musically. I need someone to explain it all to me," he said, a tad embarrassed.

Mala laughed. "You don't explain music, silly. You enjoy it and dance to it."

"Will you dance with me then?"

Mala didn't answer. Instead, she suddenly cupped his cheek, pecked him on the other one and said, "Thank you for the goods. I shall have your *Ausweis* before Christmas, as promised."

For a long time after Mala had disappeared into the crowd, Edek stood and gazed after her, his palm over the very place where she had kissed him.

*

It poured something unmerciful that afternoon—a rare midwinter rain, icy and sharp like needles against one's face. Soaked to the bone, for the wardens didn't much care whether their runners wore anything suitable for such weather, Mala trooped along the barbed wire fence separating the men's and women's camps, holding a folder wrapped in several layers of cellophane against her chest. Keeping paperwork dry was the priority of the SS. The inmates carrying them were expendable.

On the very edge of the men's camp, one selection or the other was taking place. Accompanied by hoarse shouts and the occasional flicking of the whip, hundreds of gray, cadaverous creatures ran in front of the SS men, inspecting them from a distance, so that *the filthy Jewish scum* wouldn't splatter their tailored military raincoats with mud. From time to time, on an SS guard's signal, a *Kapo* grabbed hold of his newest victim and shoved him toward a growing group of prisoners. With a doomed, tormented look in their sunken eyes, the men clung to each other, razor-sharp shoulders touching under the glistening skin that was gradually turning blue; bony hands covering their private parts in a last attempt to protect their modesty.

Passing them by behind the SS men's backs, Mala swiftly averted her gaze so as not to embarrass them any further. They were already sentenced to death solely because the SS found them to be too frail to keep working for the glory of the Reich. The last thing they needed was some runner ogling them in their misery.

Before long, a deep construction ditch crept into view, from which, Mala knew, the local inmates got their water. It was muddy, crawled with vermin and stunk to high heaven, but since only the privileged prisoners got access to drinking water, the rest of the camp population had to choose between drinking from the ditch or dying from thirst. For the majority, the choice was obvious, judging by the countless outbreaks of dysentery that landed them in the sickbay and sometimes straight in the gas chambers.

Her rain-soaked woolen coat weighing a ton on her shoulders, Mala soldiered on, head held high and mouth pursed into a hard, resolute line. From behind, shrill, scornful laughter reached her, turning her gut with pure, savage hatred. She would recognize that madman's laughter out of a thousand. Only Hauptscharführer Moll, the one-eyed beast, could laugh with such maniacal glee at the suffering of the others. She hastened her step, but the sound of it followed her, growing louder and louder in her mind until it drowned out her own thoughts.

There were plenty of SS men to detest in the camp, but not a single one's behavior caused such revulsion and loathing in Mala as this glass-eyed crematorium supervisor. Unlike most of his colleagues who went through their gruesome jobs with an indifferent attitude of "orders are orders" and "someone has to do this work," Moll took cruel, sadistic pleasure in torturing and murdering his victims in the most callous of ways. Sometimes, when the camp overwhelmed her to the point of delirium, Mala dreamt of revenge—on all of them, really—but it was Moll's freckled face with his glass eye that invariably stood out from the uniformed, faceless crowd.

She ought to do something to make him suffer, Mala uttered a silent oath to herself that dark, winter day. She ought to give him a taste of his own medicine. Hopefully, with Edek's help, someday…

Through the wall of the rain, the immense Mexico compound unfolded before her. It was still in the first stages of construction, with unfinished barracks and the semblance of a road leading to where the *Kommando* was disassembling the downed allied and German planes transported to Birkenau from all parts of Poland where they'd met their untimely end. A few inmates roamed around restlessly, pulling the scraps of their colorful blankets around their bony, shivering frames. It was them and their ridiculous, pitiful attires that had given the compound its name. Unlike the *Kanada* work detail named after the land of riches, the Mexico one was the poorest and the dirtiest in the eyes of the camp administration—a third-world part of the camp, even by Auschwitz measures.

With her trained eye, Mala instantly spotted Polish civilians trading goods with the local inmates on the sly, away from the guards' eyes. The guards, it appeared, couldn't be bothered with guarding anyone in such weather; their commander, to whom Mala was to deliver the written orders and blueprints, preferred to lounge in one of the barracks, where she discovered him engaged in a game of Skat with one of his subordinates. Without taking his eyes off his cards, he interrupted Mala's report mid-word and waved her toward the overturned crate, on which she was to leave the cellophane-swaddled folder amid the bottles of schnapps and half-eaten ham and cheese sandwiches. It was Mala's profound conviction that he wouldn't open it for the next few hours at the least.

On her way back, the rain only intensified. It slashed at Mala's face with each gust of wind and washed away what had remained of the well-trodden path, turning it into a swampy river of mud. With each new step, her feet were sinking into it deeper and deeper as though invisible hands of the dead grabbed at her ankles, firmly set on pulling her under the ground where they had found their last resting place.

Once again, the construction ditch materialized through the curtain of the rain, only this time with Moll staring with curiosity into it, his head tilted slightly to one side. Next to him, his colleague Voss was standing. With his hands clasped behind his back, he scowled deeply at something inside the ditch. The selection, Mala realized, was thankfully over.

Yanking her feet out of the slushy ground, Mala tried to steer as far away from the two SS men as possible, but came to an abrupt halt in spite of herself when a pair of pale hands appeared over the edge of the ditch. Squinting through the rain, Mala stared at the trench with purpose this time and felt her throat constrict with primal horror: it was filled with corpses of the recently murdered men, the men she had seen clinging to each other on the way to the Mexico not even an hour ago.

"Look at this stinking carcass!" Moll brayed with laughter as he pointed with his gloved hand at the man desperately groping his way out. "He's a resilient one. It's the fifth time he's climbed out of there." With deliberate cruelty, Moll moved toward his victim and kicked at the man's hands with his steel-lined boots, sending him sliding in the mud and tumbling back into the ditch. Delighted, Moll turned to Voss. "How much do you want to bet he'll crawl out of there ten times?" Without waiting for a response, he extracted a wad of bills out of his pocket. "I'll bet you fifty Reichsmarks he'll make it to ten."

Voss, who had always been half-drunk and cracking jokes with the *Sonderkommando* men, appeared oddly sober to Mala just then. He didn't budge, even when Moll kept waving the money before his face, which was somber and stern and betraying just a slight hint of distaste in the curve of his mouth.

"What for did you order them to be thrown into the ditch in the first place?" he uttered at last, without looking at his colleague.

Moll only shrugged, unperturbed. "Wanted to see if that desperate scum from the local barracks will keep drinking from the ditch with corpses swimming in it. They didn't mind the mud and the rats; I bet you another twenty they'll hesitate before slurping from the open mass grave, ha-ha!" Once again, he threw his head back, apparently finding the situation positively hilarious. "Don't fret, we'll send someone to fish them out after a few days. I don't fancy dealing with the stench the Mexico construction *Kommando* commander will raise once he finds out we're using his ditch as an underwater cemetery."

Her entire body trembling, Mala stood riveted to her place and stared at him with all the hatred she felt coursing through her veins like acid. But then the two hands miraculously materialized on the very edge of the trench and Mala felt a breath hitch in her throat as she caught sight of the man for the first time. His hair was shorn, and the sharp cheekbones streaked with filth, but how painfully familiar he looked. If only it wasn't for his eyes that stared pleadingly at the SS guards above him, she would have taken him for her father.

"That's six," Moll announced almost admiringly and shoved the helpless man back into the rotten, freezing water.

After releasing a devastated cry, the inmate pleaded in French, promising that he could work, that he was very strong, that he would crawl out twenty times if needed, just to be allowed back into his work detail. But Moll only mocked him with heartless mirth, screaming nonsensical French words over the man's tearful pleas.

"We don't understand your gibberish. Speak German, if you wish to be understood!"

"Stop resisting! Pretend that you're dead or they'll kill you!" Mala screamed in French at the man, possessed by the sudden need to save at least him from Moll's clutches.

Both SS men swung round at once, Moll fixing a withering glare of his only good eye on Mala's slight frame. She held his gaze without flinching, without lowering her own, suddenly brave to a suicidal extent and ready for a fight.

"Ah, Mally," Moll drawled in a singsong voice, a dark sneer spreading over his face. "Come here, pet. Stand right before me; there's a good girl. And now, report to me, as you should, what you just said to that filthy washrag trashing about in the mud?"

With all the defiance she felt burning in her chest, Mala smiled viciously at him and spat, "If you spoke French, you wouldn't need an interpreter for that."

She was aware of the nothingness behind her back, of the edge of the ditch he'd strategically positioned her at just moments before, of Moll stepping closer, nose to nose now, his nostrils flaring with ire, and yet, she took not a single step to avoid the unavoidable.

"You think you're smarter than me, you Jew-bitch? You haven't the faintest idea how long I've been waiting for this moment." He hissed and shoved her hard in her chest, knocking the breath out of her for one short instant.

With a resounding splash, Mala landed on top of the soft mound of flesh and shuddered with primal terror as she groped about to regain her footing. The trembling Frenchman crouched by the trench's wall, searching her face with wild eyes appealing silently for mercy. On top of the trench, Moll was already towering, his hand unbuckling the holster languidly, as though savoring the moment.

With a tremendous effort, on shaking knees, Mala rose from the water and straightened to full height. Without taking her eyes off her executioner, she squared her shoulders and sneered at him with icy scorn, ruining his pleasure.

He was thoroughly incensed now at her prideful stance, at her unflinching glare full of challenge; he lost his temper and began to curse at her crudely, like only the SS could, tearing his gun out and aiming it at her head.

But suddenly, Voss installed himself before him and even though Mala couldn't see his face, she could hear precisely what he said: "If you shoot her, I'll have to report to Hössler precisely what happened."

Voss's voice was cool and collected, but the veiled threat in it was audible. The gun wavering in his hand, Moll regarded him in stunned surprise. In another instant, his face reddened at such a betrayal of the SS brotherhood.

"She's just a dirty Jew…"

"She's Hössler's Jew," Voss corrected him evenly, his hand on his comrade's wrist, pulling it forcefully down. "You don't need any more problems with him."

"All my troubles with him began precisely because of her, after that day at the *Krema,* when that bastard escaped—"

"And as I said, you don't need to make matters even worse for yourself."

"But she's just a Jew… a worthless Jew…" Moll seemed genuinely puzzled to comprehend how the loss of one such Jew could be upsetting to anyone, let alone camp leader Hössler.

"Come." Voss was already steering him away from the ditch. "You've had your fun. Perhaps, they won't be able to climb out of there after all," he offered as a consolation. "Then, we'll report that she fell there herself. Look at this weather. Dreadful, eh?"

When their voices receded in the distance, Mala grabbed hold of the man's ice-cold forearm. "They're gone. Come, I'll help you out."

For the next half an hour, as the darkness was gathering force, they found themselves in a nightmare of slippery mud and pliable, still-soft limbs on which they kept falling. Mala wanted to scream each time her hand felt cold, clammy flesh that shifted and parted under her feet as she attempted to rise, but she only pressed her jaws tighter together, resolved to get herself and the man who looked just like her father in the falling night out of that open grave. They clawed their way through the washed-out, slippery surface, and whenever one fell, the second one followed back to the bottom to prop the other one up again, because it was both of them or nothing—an unspoken agreement of the survivors that was stronger than blood.

At last, after they made it onto the firm surface and simultaneously turned onto their backs, gasping for air from the effort, the man turned to Mala. It was a relief to see that the terror was gone out of his eyes, replaced by warmth and gratitude.

"Thank you," he rasped, his bony chest rising and falling rhythmically, ghostly-pale against the darkening sky.

"Thank you for not giving up," Mala replied, managing a smile.

"May I ask why you risked your life for me?" he asked after a pause. "Please, take no offense, I'm immensely grateful… It's just… You don't even know me."

Mala looked into his eyes, saw the loved and unseeing ones in their place and hardly restrained herself from putting her palm against his cheek. "You look just like my father. Only, he went blind a few years ago. But he's just as resilient as you are." She shifted her gaze toward the sky which kept weeping above them, mourning the humanity under its eye. "I don't know whether he's dead or alive. But you were still alive, and I just had to make sure that you stay so. Sounds idiotic, I know," she tossed her head, annoyed. "Sentimental rubbish—"

"No, no," the man rushed to interrupt her. "Not at all." He paused and then suddenly added, "It's the best rubbish I've heard."

Exhausted mentally and physically to the point of collapse, Mala found enough strength to smile at his words.

When they regained breath, Mala escorted him to the men's camp sickbay and gave her own woolen coat to the doctor in charge as a payment. "He's an essential inmate. Treat him as you would treat your own father."

The doctor grabbed the coat at once but scowled at the man's undressed state. "It looks like he was chosen to die at the recent selection. There may be a problem with him, if his number is on the camp office's list—"

"I work at the camp office. There will be no problem."

Whether it was the tone of her voice or the look she gave him, the inmate doctor nodded his understanding and promised to have Mala's new charge in the best shape possible by the end of the week.

It was pitch-dark when Mala reached the camp administration office, scarcely dragging her feet but infinitely relieved.

"Good God, Mally!" Zippy's eyes widened at the sight of her begrimed friend. "You look like something the cat dragged in. In which muddy ditch did you roll about?"

At those words, Mala released a harsh, one-syllable snort and then burst into mirthless, hysterical laughter. "A ditch with corpses in it." Tears were streaming down her face, but with the best will in the world, she couldn't stop herself from laughing. Her nerves had finally snapped and everything had suddenly come loose. "Moll threw me in it. But I saved him, Zippy… In spite of it all, I saved him. He's alive."

She fell asleep by the radiator in Zippy's private room, wrapped in several layers of blanket. That night, she dreamt of her father's hands holding the seat of her bicycle as he taught her to ride; of the silly faces he made to cheer her up after she came home, sulking from not acing a German test; of the tears of pride he'd wiped discreetly with the back of his hand at her graduation ceremony; at the new patent leather shoes he bought for her when she announced that she was going to dances with her new beau. Of the last tight, bone-crushing embrace he'd given her before she set off to Brussels, never to see him again.

"I saved him, Zippy," she whispered through her sleep now and again, a rare smile warming her face. "I saved him after all…"

The following morning, she marched straight to Hössler's office with a handwritten report detailing everything that had transpired. The further the camp leader read, the paler he grew until his hand began to shake with righteous anger.

"That swine!" he snapped, pushing his chair away with a screech and marching out of the office.

He never brought up the subject of Moll with Mala again, even when he stopped by to have his usual coffee and chat with her. Instead, he placed a transfer letter bearing Hauptscharführer's name on Mala's desk and asked her, as nonchalantly as possible, to type three copies for him. In a few days, Moll had disappeared. The *Sonderkommando* celebrated his departure with such a feast, Mala heard their singing well into the night in her room.

Chapter 15

Wiesław's bribery skills had finally paid off. He had purchased his and Edek's temporary freedom for a few sardine tins, a couple of liquor bottles and a lemon he had received from the generous women's sickbay supervisors. Almost all of them were German Black Triangles, asocial prisoners and former prostitutes sent to Auschwitz for re-education. Enduring their affections for a chance to step outside the impenetrable Auschwitz gates was worthwhile as far as he was concerned. And so he smiled politely whenever they cornered him in their personal quarters or pinched his behind or outright smothered him with kisses, pressing their impressive bosoms against his ribs until he'd worm and apologize his way out of their suffocating embraces and promise to stop by later, when the dreaded Kapo Jupp wasn't around.

The *Kapo* threat never failed to work its magic. Wiesław narrowly escaped quite a few unwanted encounters by mentioning the name of the man who was notorious not only among the inmates but the SS as well.

Aside from mentioning it once to Edek, Wiesław kept silent until the very last day, unsure whether the bribed *Kapo* who dealt mostly with civilians would go through with the enterprise. Only after the two of them had been singled out of the entire fitters' detail and escorted by the *Kapo* first to Auschwitz and then outside its gates and straight into the pristine wintery expanse and forest looming ahead, did he explain to Edek what it was all about.

"One of the SS big shots' wives arrived from Germany recently and announced that the bathroom was not up to her standards," he announced, his eyes shining about with excitement. "Well, guess who'll be fixing it for her for the next week?"

Edek only looked at him, incredulous and fighting the desire to scoop his ingenious friend into a bear hug. Intoxicated by the sudden promise of freedom, he kept gazing about him, almost drunk with the fresh winter air that smelled of pine forest and sharply of fresh snow and not the nauseatingly sweet scent of churned flesh and unwashed bodies stuffed into airless barracks, five soon-to-be-corpses per bunk. It got to him, this sudden pristine expanse; it went straight to his head like cool wine on a sweltering summer afternoon; he swayed slightly as he walked, and this time not from hunger, but from the overwhelming sensation of being a free man once again.

"That's right," Wiesław confirmed, very pleased with himself indeed. "Us, and a certain civilian tiler from Kozy."

"Not Szymlak?"

Wiesław didn't have the chance to respond—the *Kapo* swiped his club over his head half-heartedly.

"Quit your jawing!" His face was twisted into a grimace of utter distaste, but in his eyes was a silent warning.

Only then did Edek notice an SS man strolling through the woods with his submachine gun at the ready. It had suddenly dawned on him that he had failed to notice it all before—the SS patrol, the guard towers neatly tucked away in between the trees, camouflaged so that an inexperienced eye wouldn't spot them or their hawk-eyed inhabitants with their machine guns mounted on the tables and trained on any moving target. Presently, its black muzzle followed their small procession. Stealing another glance around, Edek counted several more such installations and his heart dropped to the pit of his stomach. Black despair overcame him, far stronger than the exhilaration he'd felt not even five minutes ago.

Auschwitz didn't end with the Auschwitz gates. Just then a nightmarish thought occurred to him: the entire world was now

Auschwitz; it had swallowed the planet and there was no escape from it. Edek stumbled, as though stunned by a *Kapo's* club—full force, straight in the chest, shattering his heart and all the hopes it had been nursing in its wake.

"That's right," the *Kapo* said very quietly through his teeth, almost without moving his lips. "Don't get any ideas, lads. They're all sharpshooters, those sods in the towers, and even if they weren't, with their machinery, any idiot would make a colander out of an inmate within seconds."

His head hanging low, Edek followed the round-bellied German with the green triangle of a professional criminal on his chest, who, oddly enough, turned out to be a decent fellow.

Wiesław tried to encourage him with a friendly dig in the ribs, but Edek felt nothing but those cold, piercing eyes on his back; could think of nothing else but the muzzles of the guns trained on them from every side.

The house turned out to be a small but splendid affair. A woman in her forties with a purple triangle sewn onto her civilian cardigan opened the door to them, a wide, gentle smile on her face. Edek was aware that the role of domestics for the SS was reserved for the Jehovah's Witnesses, but he'd never come across one himself. He couldn't understand what they were doing in the camp in the first place. Unlike him, the enemy alien, they were Germans, for the most part, of good racial stock, according to their idiotic Nuremberg Laws on race and blood, non-violent and certainly far from being criminal. Their only crime was their devotion to their Lord instead of Adolf Hitler and their fierce opposition to all forms of violence. They refused to perform the obligatory Hitler salute and shied away not only from the military service itself, but from any type of work that directly or indirectly contributed to the war effort. In the eyes of the Nazi regime, such "crimes" were punishable by imprisonment in concentration camps. Former camp Kommandant Höss had made it clear that any Purple Triangle would be released at once—all they had to do was to sign a renunciation paper. *One idiotic signature*, Edek thought to himself in despair, *just one idiotic signature and they'd be free to go.* But, instead, they suffered nobly for their faith and died for it, wearing smiles on their faces.

The same kind, gentle smile this woman before them was displaying.

"Come on in," she urged in German. "Poor children! Such a long walk, through all that snow. You must be freezing. Come to the kitchen; I'll fix you tea and sandwiches at once."

"Are you mad? Tea and sandwiches are for the guests." A tall, slender woman appeared in the hallway, her platinum locks twisted into an intricate hairdo. She was dressed with great taste, in a silk pale-blue dress with a leather belt and high-heeled shoes matching the belt in color. Her cool, gray eyes observed the trio with barely veiled disgust. "These are foreigners and criminals." Her white, beautiful arm shot in the direction to her left. "The bathroom is over there. That other Pole is already working on it. I want you to stand there the entire time to make sure they don't steal anything." She gave her maid a pointed look. "Oh, and if one of them tries to use our facilities…" She let the phrase hang ominously in the air.

"I guess we'll just have to hold it till the evening," Wiesław muttered in Polish and, this time, Edek actually smiled.

Antoni Szymlak, who must have arrived earlier due to living in a village that was a twenty-minute walk from the SS settlement, was hard at work at the bathroom wall, but he lowered his spatula at once to greet the men with a warm handshake. He was an elderly man with a kind mouth hidden under a formidable white mustache and bright, lively eyes shining with quiet intelligence.

"They're all mine for the day, aren't they?" he asked the *Kapo*.

"All yours."

"It'll be a little too tight for all of us here." Szymlak gazed about the bathroom skeptically. In fact, it was a grand affair where all of them could work comfortably, but it appeared that the Polish tiler had his own agenda. "There's a laundry room right next door," he said meaningfully, addressing the *Kapo*. "It's very warm and the Frau never sets foot in there. A perfect place to rest your head for a few hours, while we work here. You ought to be exhausted after supervising the inmates every single day."

"I have been working rather hard lately, now that you brought it up." The *Kapo* obviously wasn't stupid. The old Auschwitz rule was, "one must take the good as it comes"; only a complete blockhead wouldn't make use of the local civilian's generous offer to look after the inmates while he slept soundly nearby. "As long as you promise to keep an eye on them—"

"Herr Kapo, I shall guard them with my life."

The *Kapo* knew the tiler would. If one of them decided to make a run for it, it would be Szymlak who'd be thrown into Auschwitz as a replacement, innocent civilian or not.

"And make sure they don't slack off."

"Herr Kapo, you have my word. I won't shout at them though, you know, not to disturb your rest."

"As long as the day's work is done, I don't care one way or the other."

"Magda shall wake you when lunch is ready." Szymlak was already escorting him by the elbow in the direction of the laundry room.

Edek and Wiesław exchanged incredulous glances. A job outside the camp and now this? It was all too good to be true.

When Szymlak returned, a big grin nearly split his face in two. "I'll show you what needs to be done," he said in a whisper. "As soon as your watchman is fast asleep, we shall talk business. Now, this sink needs to be taken out. There's a new porcelain one in the cellar…"

They worked in agreeable silence for the first thirty minutes. After sonorous snores reached them from behind the wall, Szymlak turned to them, suddenly all business.

"So? What is it that you need? A letter delivered to the family? Some contraband smuggled back to you?"

Wiesław looked at him gravely. "We need a place to stay."

Szymlak's eyes widened slightly but, otherwise, he didn't betray himself.

"A place to stay and civilian clothes," Edek added.

For a time, Szymlak considered their request. "It's a big risk," he said eventually.

"My sister lives in Zakopane," Wiesław said. "It's very close to where you live."

"If you're a civilian." Szymlak looked at him pointedly. "Not a camp inmate hunted by the entire local SS."

"We'll go through the forest and mountains and avoid all roads," Edek explained at once. His expression didn't waver, but his eyes trained on Szymlak were desperate, searching.

Szymlak looked at the partially tiled wall, behind which the *Kapo* was presently napping, and then back at the two men. "What will they do to you if they catch you?"

"They'll hang us," Wiesław admitted the bitter truth. "But they won't catch us."

"Most certainly they'll beat the names of your accomplices out of you first," Szymlak mused aloud in the same detached tone.

"We won't betray anyone, you included," Edek promised. Auschwitz had toughened his skin with beatings and abuse. The camp Gestapo tortures wouldn't mean much to him; that much he knew.

Moving his lips under his mustache, as though chewing on something invisible, Szymlak worked things out in his mind.

"One night," he announced his verdict at last. "Only one night I shall give you under my roof, but you shall stay in the cellar. It can be accessed from the outside, so if they catch you, I'll deny everything and tell them you stole your way inside and I had not the faintest suspicion anyone was hiding in there."

For Edek and Wiesław, it was more than enough. They grasped the man's hand one after the other and gave it a thorough shake.

"We'll pay you for your troubles after the war is over—" Edek began, but his compatriot only waved him into silence.

"I don't want your money. That's not why I'm helping you."

Edek nodded. He understood, just like Wiesław did. No, it had nothing to do with the profit. Szymlak simply wanted to be able to look at himself in the mirror every morning and know that he saw a decent man looking back at him—a man who did the right thing even though he risked his own life while doing so. Money could buy a lot of things but not human decency. That wasn't something that could be purchased. It was something earned and carried later as a badge of honor; something that would never be lost or stolen.

The only thing that Edek regretted was that there were so few Antoni Szymlaks around. Perhaps, if there were more men who did the right thing instead of doing the profitable thing, who chose compassion and selflessness over power and greed, there wouldn't be any camps in existence.

Chapter 16

Sunday, the inmates' only day off, dawned tender pink and shimmering with snow. Her collar turned up against the wind, Mala was braving her way across the frost-bitten compound. In the distance, the Sauna loomed white against the greasy-gray smoke from the chimneys.

"You're actually planning to grace us with your presence tomorrow?" Zippy had asked in an exaggeratingly astounded tone just the day before. Mala had completely recovered from her recent ordeal with Moll; but her spirits soared even higher once her bribes purchased the man she'd saved a kosher place in the inmates' kitchen. She visited him from time to time, the dreamt-up substitution for her father, and he gladly played the role, slipping her potatoes or onions when he could and asking her, with a fatherly concern, how her day was. Even if Zippy thought it to be odd or unhealthy, she never said a single word of discouragement. Whatever got an inmate through their day. "I'm afraid to believe it. You've been promising me for months now."

She'd almost abandoned the idea of ever seeing Mala at one of the women's orchestra's concerts after receiving one evasive excuse or the other in response to her countless invitations. It pained Mala to disappoint her friend time after time, but she simply couldn't bring herself to listen to the beautiful music interrupted by the metallic clanking of the crematorium furnaces that operated within walking distance from the Sauna. Whoever invented the idea to use it as a concert hall certainly had a warped sense of humor, Mala thought, forcing one foot in front of the other.

"Why the sudden change of mind?" Zippy had asked.

Indeed, why? She should have stayed in her room, read a book smuggled from the *Kanada* and pretended for a few hours that the camp around her didn't exist; could have visited her make-believe Papa or enjoyed a few hours of self-imposed oblivion to get her through another week in this inferno; could have forgotten herself in a fitful sleep where voices of the dead and the dying couldn't reach her, at least for a few stolen moments of peace. Instead, she was dragging herself toward the dreaded destination, reluctance in every step, and wondered how the *Sonderkommando* felt shoving humanity into the ovens to the sounds of the Viennese waltz.

She was going because she'd told Edek that she would be there. Because she pretended to be brave and unconcerned because he was those very things; one had to be fearless to plan what he was planning, and she wanted him to see in her a comrade in arms, someone to trust above all, with his very life.

Because she simply wanted to see him.

As the realization dawned on her, Mala came to an abrupt halt as though stunned by a physical blow.

She wanted to see him because he was the only person who could still make her laugh in a spiritless place that belonged to the dead. She needed him to be near because his strength gave her strength, made her believe in the impossible, promised her that nothing yet was lost, that there was a chance for a new life somewhere beyond the outer cordons of the barbed wire-wrapped hell.

"Just want to see if Frau Alma indeed made a passable mandolinist out of you and your two left hands," Mala had said, concealing her intimate thoughts behind jest instead and grinning in gratitude when Zippy had taken the hint and didn't proceed with the interrogation.

In front of the Sauna, the crowd was already gathering. From the direction of the crematorium, the soot-stained wind threw a whirlwind of ghastly ashen flurries and, for a few instants, wrapped the figures in its shroud-like embrace, dissolving into ash. A dreadful sense of danger crept over Mala, turning her own face into a mask of chalk. They would all turn into ash, she realized with blood-chilling clarity that instant. They would all perish here, in that purgatory where the sun itself appeared dimmer, tainted by the clouds of ash and lost souls.

"I don't think we'll be able to hear the music from here."

Startled by the voice, Mala turned to the man whose hand was still lying gently on her shoulder, and felt a smile blossom on her face in spite of herself. It was Edek, his cheeks fresh with frost, white teeth bared in a smile; he was life itself against that deathly picture of eternal doom and, just for that, Mala caught his hand and pressed it with endless affection.

"I'm so glad you came," she said and meant every word.

"It seems like a few more minutes and you'd have changed your mind and stood me up, judging by your stance."

It was intended as a joke, but his eyes searched hers earnestly.

"No." Mala shook her head, still holding his cold hand in hers and feeling warmer just from standing so close to him. "I would never."

He released an audible breath of relief and, as though remembering himself, shoved his hand inside his overalls, muttering apologies about being a forgetful mutton. "Here. I got this especially for you."

Mala regarded a geranium flower in his hand in frank astonishment.

"Just how did you manage to conjure it up?" With fingers that trembled imperceptibly, she took the bright pink flower from him and slowly lifted the tender petals to her nose, across her lips, eyes closed, mind lost in memories. Belgium, apple trees in bloom, the sun warm on her face, her hand encased in the hand of the young man whose features she could no longer clearly remember. Years had passed since someone had presented her with flowers. She had long lost all faith that the day someone would do so once again would ever come.

"It's a geranium." Edek's voice was tinged with embarrassment. "I'm sorry. It doesn't really smell."

"I don't care one way or the other. It smells like a rose in my mind."

Once the flower was gone from her lips, Edek saw a blissful smile playing on them.

Opening her eyes, Mala looked at him again. "Where did you get it from?"

"I stole it from the SS," he admitted with endearing honesty. "Smuggled it in my toolbox after I was done fixing a heating element in their quarters."

"They could have shot you for that stunt."

"What a cause to die for though." He was grinning roguishly again, reminding Mala of precisely what had brought them together and how bravery was a muscle that ought to be trained. Edek had certainly excelled in that—he was the bravest man she'd come across. "Shall we?" With an old, civilian-world gallantry, he offered her his elbow.

Mala put her arm though the crook of his and, somehow, the road to the Sauna lost its nightmarish quality and the thought of hearing music in a place that processed batches of people destined to die within days, or weeks if they were fortunate, somehow didn't revolt her so much.

Inside, the women's orchestra were already tuning their instruments. In the first rows of chairs placed in a semicircle, SS men and wardens sat like distinguished guests in a Viennese opera house. Behind them, *Kapos*, block elders, and other privileged inmates were seated, while the rest of the prisoners had to crowd together by the back wall. They didn't seem to mind in the slightest, as long as they could steal a few treasured moments of absorbing the music, inhaling it greedily as though coming up from under water for a precious few gulps of fresh air. They were crammed like sardines against the back wall and yet their eyes shone with excitement, their tattered attires forgotten, the pain temporarily gone from their battered bodies. The expectation of hearing Frau Alma's magnificent Mozart worked its magic. The air itself tingled with it, while the conductor, collected and cool as always, tuned her own violin for an opening solo.

"What about all of those people outside?" Edek asked once they made their way inside the makeshift concert hall. "Will they have to remain there, in the cold, the entire time?"

"They don't have much of a choice," Mala explained softly with a smile that felt guilty for some reason. Zippy had saved her a seat—'*Two seats, actually*,' the mandolinist gave Mala a wink as though she had suspected the motive behind her friend's sudden change of heart—but now Mala suddenly couldn't bring herself to sit among the privileged crowd. "Music is the only escape that they have in this place. Zippy says they'll stand in the freezing cold for hours listening to it."

"I suppose I can understand that," Edek said pensively. "It makes them forget." Seeing the expression on Mala's face, he changed the subject self-consciously. "Not much room for dancing here, is there?"

Mala chuckled, grateful for the timely distraction as they stood elbow to elbow among the crowd of prisoners. "No. It's not allowed here at any rate. Neither is applauding."

"So what, we're just supposed to stand to attention while listening like some demented tin soldiers?" Edek snorted incredulously at the outright ridiculous set of rules.

"I'm afraid that's precisely the case."

"Sod it then." Edek grasped her hand and, before she could protest, headed for the door. "I came here to dance with you. If it means that we'll dance in the freezing cold, fine by me. We'll just have to dance faster."

When Edek pushed the door open, a gust of wind hit Mala in the face; the ash blinding her momentarily, and yet, it occurred to her that she was laughing, laughing despite it all, in a place where laughter died before anything else—and it was he who made it possible.

"Thank you," Mala said as the first notes of music struck and they lost themselves in it. "I was so afraid to come here and now I'm glad I did."

"Thank you for inviting me," Edek spoke, his cheek pressed against her hair, his hand holding hers firmly as he took the lead. "I could have never imagined that it's possible to be happy in Auschwitz, but today you have proved me wrong."

For a moment, Edek pulled away and gazed deep into her eyes and Mala felt his words inside her chest where her heart beat twice as fast just because her palm was enclosed in his and, for a few instants, the camp itself ceased to exist.

He was right; it was a capital offense to feel happy in this place, but that Sunday afternoon, they simply had no choice. The music enveloped them like a warm, tender embrace, swirled them, guided them through the brilliance of the fresh, glimmering snow and they lost themselves to its power. Eyes shining with self-forgetful, reckless joy; fingers entwined and no longer freezing; lips smiling ceaselessly and, at last, laughter erupting in translucent, misty clouds—a long-forgotten sound of the carefree past—mirrored by the uncertain, wavering grins of the inmates who stood surrounding them from all sides and watched them dance like a miracle of some sort.

Without once noticing it, Mala and Edek had created a circle of life around themselves; a circle of life in the middle of the SS-run graveyard, and instilled faith into something bigger than death itself in the hungry hearts aching for a sliver of hope.

Chapter 17

The girl, who looked oddly familiar, was wearing the Music Block uniform, but demanded two plumbers for the camp administration office with all the authority of an SS warden.

"One of the faucets is leaking in one of the SS bathrooms and the noise is driving Obersturmführer Hössler mad. He said if it's not fixed within an hour, he'll send the entire fitters' *Kommando* to the gas. He doesn't want any Jews working on it though, so I'll take those two Poles." Her slender arm, with an index finger pointing, was directed straight at Edek and Wiesław.

Their new block elder must have been familiar with Hössler's methods, for he nearly knocked the food bowls from Edek and Wiesław's hands and dealt both swift kicks to their backsides in typical Auschwitz encouragement. "Get your fat behinds up right this instant!"

Edek tried to protest that it was dinner hour and surely the faucet would still be there after they were done eating, but the block elder's expression, together with the imploring faces of the rest of the fitters, made him stop mid-sentence.

The Music Block girl watched them collect their toolboxes and only spoke to them after they were well away from the fitters' barrack.

"I hope you'll forgive me for interrupting you in the middle of your meal," she spoke to them in German, the communal language of the camp; though Edek recognized a trace of the Slovakian accent in her speech. "Don't fret, Mala and I receive double rations as the camp office workers. We'll share with you." She gave them a bright smile.

"Mala?" Edek's head shot up at once.

"Naturally, Mala. Who do you think summoned you to the office? Hössler? He doesn't use the office facilities. He has his own in his personal quarters, but your *Kapo* wouldn't know about that." The girl gave him a sly look from under her long black lashes. "Besides, all the SS are already gone for the night. Only the sentry is left, but he's harmless."

She was a head shorter than Mala and thinner too but just as confident and, it was Edek's instant conviction, just as camp-savvy.

"Aren't you with the orchestra?" It was Wiesław who regarded her blue outfit, visible under her warm coat, with suspicion.

"I am," she replied, undisturbed. "Mala and I, we do several jobs around the camp."

"You're Zippy." Recognition flickered in Edek's eyes. Now, he remembered Mala's friend from the Sunday concert, the mandolinist who had saved them the seats they traded for the freedom of outside. He searched the girl's face, wondering if she knew about their escape plan.

"Yes, but keep it to yourself. I'm Spitzer from the *Schreibstube* for everyone else."

And just like that, he had his answer. She was with the "organization" too, this young Slovak girl with wry eyes and a grin to match.

Mala met them in the doors of the office. Along the entire corridor, the lights were extinguished. She stood, basking in the soft warm glow of the office lamp, her back against the doorframe, arms crossed against her chest and the usual, somewhat mocking smile on her face. "Greetings to the working class."

Edek suddenly felt inexplicable lightness in his chest at the sound of her voice. For some reason, he was sure it wasn't from hunger.

"Is the coast clear?" Zippy demanded, removing her coat and throwing it over the back of her chair.

"Perfectly," Mala confirmed, motioning both men inside and turning the key in the office door.

"They just leave you here for the night unsupervised?" Edek looked around.

In the corner of the room, a small tree stood wrapped in tinsel and decorated with glass balls. It occurred to him that he had all but forgotten it was almost Christmas.

"Technically, we're assigned to regular camp barracks, but we have our own rooms here, in the cellar," Mala explained, searching the filing cabinet for something. "As long as we're present in our barracks for the roll call, they let us sleep here."

"Here? Inside the camp office?" Edek regarded both women incredulously.

"Sometimes I spend a night with the orchestra, but yes," Zippy replied, holding out a plate with roasted potatoes and even bits of blood sausage mixed in to the men. "We both have our private rooms here. Dig in."

The two friends exchanged embarrassed looks. It went against their personal men's code to take the food away from the girls, even though the girls belonged to the privileged caste of the camp population. Only after both Mala and Zippy assured them that they had already had their dinner and had rations from the Red Cross in their rooms did Edek reach for the plate reluctantly. Edek was relieved that Wiesław was the first one to shovel a forkful of potatoes into his mouth as he wasn't sure how long he would be able to resist the tantalizing aroma. Once the first few golden potato nuggets touched his tongue, he couldn't help but close his eyes with pleasure, savoring the taste and trying to prolong it, chewing as slowly as possible.

"You in particular ought to eat, and as much as possible." Mala gave him a strange look. She was beaming, and yet, her gaze was full of some unspoken melancholy. "How do you plan to pass as an SS man if you look starved? They'll smell a rat in a split second. As a matter of fact, I'll make it my business to fatten you up in the next few months. You aren't planning to run in the middle of winter, I hope?"

Once again, the two comrades looked at each other. They did in fact plan that very thing. As soon as they got their hands on the *Ausweis* and the uniform.

"Oh, come now, you ought to have more sense than that." Mala shook her head in disapproval. She had finally uncovered the file she was looking for and laid it out on top of her desk, right under the green-shaded lamp.

"That fellow, who had just escaped—"

"Got lucky and that's all there is to it," Mala, now holding a pair of scissors, interrupted Edek with a categorical sweep of the hand. "A snowstorm was the only factor that saved him from being discovered. It swept away his footprints and made the dogs lose his scent. Say you do walk out of the camp in your disguise. You'll have to do it in the morning or the middle of the day as no guard in his right mind shall let you out with an inmate in the evening or at night. This gives you only a few hours, and that's if you're lucky, to make it to the nearest forest before they discover your disappearance in the evening roll call. I hope you weren't considering going into the nearest village or town, because *someone conscientious* would report your SS uniform and the inmate's one before you knew what hit you and then it's the gallows for you, my children."

She finished cropping something with her scissors that Edek couldn't quite make out and straightened before her desk to look both men in the eyes.

As though on cue, the friends lowered them, chewing on their unexpected feast of fried potatoes instead of holding that accusatory gaze of hers.

"You suggest we wait till summer then?" Edek's voice cracked, in spite of himself. To him, it might as well have been another ten years.

"Till May, at the very least," Mala explained patiently. "You'll have to spend a few nights in the forest if you wish to stay undetected. If you don't want to freeze to death, I would strongly advise to wait till the weather gets somewhat tolerable. Besides, May and June are particularly misty here due to the swamps. It shall play in your favor as well."

Without waiting for their reply, Mala turned back to her desk. This time, Edek approached it as well, leaving the rest of the plate for Wiesław. His eyes widened when he saw Mala glue the photo of his friend into a camp pass—the coveted *Ausweis*—and something caught in his throat at the sight of her delicate fingers holding their very fates in them, or at least so it seemed to him at that moment.

"Won't they start asking questions about the missing photo?" He regarded the opened file, from which she'd cropped the picture, doubtfully.

"You shall be long gone by then." Mala smiled at him, seemingly unconcerned.

"Yes, but you…" He looked at her tragically.

"What about me?"

Edek heard Zippy clear her throat and, having turned his head, had just caught sight of her steering Wiesław toward the locked door. Turning the key, she nearly pushed him into the corridor.

"We'll mind the hallway," Zippy threw over her shoulder, barely concealing her grin before silently shutting the door after the couple.

Now, there were just the two of them in this semi-twilight and all the right words had suddenly escaped Edek's mind.

"Won't they… question you?" he asked, wetting his lips.

"I'll worry about that when it happens," Mala replied, much too carelessly for his liking. "It's an old camp rule. Don't waste your nerves on something that hasn't happened yet."

Edek grasped her wrist before he realized what he was doing. "Run with us."

Mala pulled back, amused, but didn't bother to release her hand from his grip. "Are you mad?"

"Not in the slightest. It's too dangerous for you to stay here after helping us. Come with us. Please."

"You *are* mad," she announced her verdict with a wistful half-smile and gently pulled herself free. "Stick to your original plan. Run with Wiesław, join the partisans and fight. I promise, I'll be here when you come to liberate us all. I'll even meet you personally at the gate."

In the silence that followed, her purposely carefree, playful grin nearly broke Edek's heart.

From the top desk drawer, Mala retrieved a stamp and rolled it carefully in the inked sponge. In another instant, she held the very official-looking *Ausweis* before Edek, triumphant and impossibly beautiful just then. "Here. Your ticket to freedom. Merry Christmas."

He stood before her, infinitely grateful and touched to the marrow, but suddenly—despite everything—he couldn't bring himself to take it. Only after Mala physically closed his fingers around it did Edek whisper his thanks, in a voice that shook slightly for reasons he couldn't quite explain.

Chapter 18

Mala turned the corner of the crematorium and set off in the direction of the sickbay. It was a short walk, which, in itself, was somewhat symbolic. Birkenau inmates avoided the camp hospital barracks like the plague; for most, the crematorium was the next stop if the SS doctors didn't finish them off with a lethal shot of phenol in the heart first. People didn't go to the sickbay to recover. They went there to die.

In her pocket, medical contraband was concealed behind the double lining. Not carefully hidden enough for a thorough search by any means, but it did the trick when someone new and itching to impress their superiors demanded that Mala empty her pockets in front of them. The old hands re-educated such new recruits quickly enough; Mala was not only Mandl's favorite, but camp leader Hössler's too. A pet Jew, and upsetting her wouldn't be beneficial for one's promotion.

Feeling the roll of aspirin and sulfa drugs through the cloth, Mala stifled a grin of satisfaction. In exchange for her nails and bolts, Kostek stuffed her pockets with a veritable haul that would make any Birkenau physician delighted. Mala was well aware of the reasons for such generosity—at any given moment, an inmate, or an inmate's friend or relative, could find themselves in the camp hospital. It was important to have comrades among the doctors, who had good memories for bribes and who would make sure that the valued patient would be kept off the SS doctors' dreaded death lists, leaving the sickbay on their own two feet instead of being transported straight to the crematorium. But, that day, there was another reason for his visit.

"That's from Rita," Kostek had informed Mala, producing vials, pills, and injections from the hidden compartment inside his overalls. "The Soviet girl whose transfer to the *Kanada Kommando* you made possible."

"She stole all that?" Mala couldn't believe her eyes.

"Well, not at once." Kostek had chuckled softly. As always, he stank of burnt flesh and some atrocious pine-scented cologne which nearly everyone in the *Sonderkommando* used in an attempt to conceal the stench. "We've been collecting it for you for a week now. Rita says if you need anything, just say the word. Her boyfriend also sends his regards. He offered to get you some dental gold—he works as a dentist in the crematorium, pulls the fillings out of poor devils' mouths—but I told him, most likely you wouldn't take it."

Mala had grimaced at first—naturally, she wouldn't—but then something shifted in her expression as she thought of Edek. In the past few weeks, she had thought of him more often than she cared to admit. She found herself pretending that it was solely because of her desire to do her utmost to help him, rejecting any sentimental undertones. She did her utmost to help Kostek as well, but she never dreamt of him kissing her, never awoke, her back wet with sweat, her breath hitching in her throat, still feeling his arms roaming over her body.

Edek had asked her to run with him. Naturally, she wouldn't consider it seriously—she had far too many lives dependent on her here, in Auschwitz, to simply up and leave them all to their fate. If it weren't for her, her newly adopted Papa would have certainly perished under the muddy waters of Moll's mass grave, the very thought of which turned her stomach with dread. Who knew how many more people she would be able to pull from the clutches of death in the future, if she only stayed inside the barbed wire? But she still fantasized about it, guiltily, invariably under the cover of the night. Her cheeks hot with a mixture of shame and the most decadent pleasure, she dreamt of being free—with Edek by her side.

"In fact, I could use some gold," she had said at length, chasing unwelcome and highly untimely thoughts from her mind. "And as for Rita, ask her if she can get me a man's wristwatch. Preferably expensive, but not overly. Something with a golden face and a leather strap. Preferably German or Austrian-made."

To her great relief, Kostek didn't ask a single question, only nodded and trotted back to his grisly work detail. Walking briskly toward the sickbay, Mala was thinking of him and his comrades and the nails she'd been smuggling for them, wondering if she would ever witness the uprising they'd been dreaming about for months now.

The hospital barrack where her friend Stasia worked was more crowded than usual. Birkenau was in the middle of a typhus epidemic and, unlike the previous Kommandant Höss, the current one, Liebehenschel, refused to send all sick patients to the gas and so they lay, five people per bunk, moaning from high fever and stomach pains that the hospital recruits had no means to alleviate.

"What are you doing here?"

Mala swung round toward the voice. An inmate doctor was staring at her as though Mala was mad.

"I thought Mandl strictly prohibited any camp office personnel from coming here during the epidemic."

Lagerführerin Mandl indeed did and was more than explicit in her orders. After a few SS men had caught the disease, Mandl outright banned Mala and Zippy from setting foot anywhere near the camp sickbay.

Offering the doctor a tentative smile, Mala stepped closer to her. "I brought medicine."

The inmate doctor's expression changed at once. Her gaze was now riveted to Mala's pockets.

"I need to see Stasia first though."

"She's in the back, behind the partition."

As Mala moved to pass by her, the doctor swiftly stepped away, pressed herself against the nearest bunk so that Mala could pass.

"Lice," she explained apologetically. "I don't want you to catch it. And please, don't touch anything, and after you leave here, run a match along the seams of your clothes."

Mala promised that she would.

Finding Stasia where the doctor said she would be, the inmate physician sat on a little stool with her back to Mala. In front of her, on a makeshift operating table, lay a woman with a chalk-white face and her legs wide open. The hem of her striped dress was pulled over her stomach; it was barely swollen, and yet, Mala instantly understood what procedure Stasia was performing on her patient.

The physician straightened in her seat, looking over her shoulder in obvious alarm, but relaxed at once when she saw Mala.

"Didn't anyone tell you that it's bad taste, creeping up on people like that, and particularly here? You scared today's breakfast out of me!"

Mala grinned, in spite of herself. Stasia had quite a way with words. "I'm sorry. Bad timing?"

"Would have been, if you were SS. Just give me a few moments. I'm almost done."

Relief reflected on Stasia's patient's face at those words. She lowered her head back on the table and closed her eyes. Stasia patted her gently on her thigh.

"Don't fret, Mama. I did everything as carefully as possible, given the circumstances. You'll have plenty of babies in the future, after you come out of here."

The young woman nodded bravely. Tears were rolling down her cheeks, but she wiped them with the back of her hand.

"Your husband will understand," Stasia continued. "There was no way around it; not here, in Birkenau, at any rate. You know what SS doctors do to pregnant women here. If someone reported your pregnancy, you'd be on the first truck to the gas."

Stasia's patient nodded again. She knew. Everyone did. The Nazis only cared about their own racial stock. Everyone else's offspring could go to the devil.

"Thank you," she spoke softly. "For helping me. The doctor in the other barrack refused."

"Is it that self-righteous Hungarian bitch you're talking about?" Stasia snorted with disdain.

"Yes. She said I'd go to hell if I went through with it."

Stasia laughed cuttingly. "We're already in hell. There is nothing worse than this. Even the devil himself doesn't have an imagination like our SS friends," she scoffed, half-turning to Mala on her stool. "You know what amazes me the most about some people? They value their idiotic ideals over actual human lives. Esty—" her hand, holding a cloth on which she had just generously poured antiseptic, gestured toward her patient, "would have died, and that self-important Hungarian broad, who calls herself a physician, wouldn't give a brass tack. All she cares about is the idea of the unborn child. The mother, who is a living and breathing human being and whose life is at stake, is irrelevant to her. She would refuse to abort a child that didn't have the slightest chance in the first place and kill the mother with her inaction as long as her religious principles aren't compromised. Isn't that something amazing?"

"I'm Jewish." Mala shrugged. "In my religion, we value a mother's life over an unborn child's. Even when it's a difficult birth and there's a choice between a mother's life and the child's, we always save the mother. She's already here on earth. She has her life, family, friends, her work and her interests. She'll go on and have more children. The child hasn't begun its life yet, so the choice is obvious. That's the logic behind all this, at least."

"Precisely," Stasia agreed. "I worked as a gynecologist, back home, in Poland. I was performing abortions—illegally, of course—for all those poor souls who had been turned away from state hospitals. I had thirteen-year-old girls who were raped by their uncles and who sat there with empty eyes and explained to me very calmly that it was the choice between me helping them or them drowning themselves in the river. I had wives who wore veils over their faces to cover up their bruises, begging me to help them so that another poor soul wouldn't be born into a household where the husband did two things: got drunk, and beat up her and the children on a daily basis. My private clinic was a safe refuge for them. But in the eyes of the self-righteous public, I was this vicious child-murderer with no morals or ethics. And you know what? If helping a woman in crisis is immoral and unethical, I think I'll remain immoral and unethical rather than condemning her to a life of abuse, poverty, or literal death as in Esty's case."

"You're neither immoral nor unethical," Esty said with a soft smile. "You saved my life."

Rising from her stool, Stasia planted an unexpected kiss on the young woman's forehead.

Mala watched them, misty-eyed, and suddenly realized that was all that mattered to Stasia. Her patients' words. No one else's.

"I never asked you why you got arrested," Mala asked the Polish woman later, as the two of them were exchanging the goods in the nurses' room.

"Most of the medical personnel got arrested in my town. We were very close to the German border, you see. They replaced us all with their German doctors and nurses."

"That's all?"

"That's all."

"You're not a communist or anything?"

Stasia snorted. "Have you ever heard me quoting Marx?"

"Do you have a family?"

"A husband and two wonderful children." Stasia patted her chest, where Mala suspected the inmate doctor carried a smuggled photograph. "What about you, Mally? Are you married?"

Mala didn't answer at once. Too much time had passed. She scarcely remembered the life before Auschwitz. With each passing day, it appeared more dreamlike, almost something she had imagined. At first, just after her arrival, Mala took refuge in memories but soon realized that memories only sucked the life out of her, leaving a black, gaping hole in the place where her heart ought to have been. And so, she began padding it out, stuffing her empty, torturous life with whatever—and whoever—she could: Hanoar Hatzioni youth group with the camp resistance; Antwerp dances with Birkenau orchestra concerts; her cheerful best friend from the fashion house with sly and infinitely brave Zippy; her former boss with camp leader Hössler and Lagerführerin Mandl; her father with a French Jew she had pulled out of the corpse-filled trench with her own two hands.

Only Edek hadn't been a mere replacement for her last beau, for a date for which her Papa had bought Mala new patent shoes. Edek was something new entirely, a force that had swept into Mala's life and transformed her from a revenge-obsessed automaton running errands for the resistance into a woman who began to thaw out, to allow herself to feel once again.

To dream.

To love.

"I had a boyfriend back in Belgium," she admitted at last with great reluctance.

"Does Mandl allow you to write to him?"

"She does. But I never did."

"Why not?"

Mala shrugged. She considered explaining it all to Stasia, the fact that she had left Belgium as one person and had transformed into a completely different one, and that the new Mala no longer had anything in common with the young handsome man whose features were growing more and more blurred in her memory. The old Mala was idealistic and just a tiny bit naive; she believed in the

Zionist cause and dreamt of fighting for it and could have never imagined, in her darkest nightmares, that her fight for the cause would take place in the death camp in which survival was the biggest form of resistance. A former intellectual, who had loved debating with her comrades and had never been afraid to speak her mind was now forced to bite her tongue in front of her superiors if she didn't want to end up getting shot for her unwanted opinions. A girl who had never been afraid to love, fiercely and with an open heart, had to close it to the outside world as soon as she had realized where she had been incarcerated. Forming attachments, let alone falling in love, was a dangerous affair in Auschwitz. One could never know when a new friend or a loved one would be rounded up at the latest selection or shot by a bored SS guard using inmates as target practice.

Auschwitz had changed her to such an extent that she wouldn't be able to shrink bank to that previous Mala, who her old boyfriend had fallen in love with. How would she even explain her experience to someone who wouldn't be able to conceive it at all—the crematoriums, the SS, the death carts, the torture chambers, the gallows on the *Appellplatz* and the sickbays where medical personnel had to rely on her contraband, for the SS thought it was a waste to supply the camp hospitals with medicaments. He would never understand what she had gone through.

She considered saying it all, but only ended up saying, "It's better this way."

Oddly enough, Stasia understood. She was an Auschwitzer too. They would forever share that bond, just like they'd share the memories of this place—the nightmarish quality of it all.

Later that afternoon, Mala sat on the Sauna's floor, her hair still wet and smelling strongly of disinfectant. *Better safe than sorry,* she'd reasoned, bribing the Sauna's madam, Mutti, with a bar of milk chocolate in exchange for a thorough hot shower and whatever green disinfectant they dunked the new arrivals into. The chocolate must have been good indeed—Mutti even arranged for Mala's clothes to be disinfected while Mala waited, wrapped in a rug the Sauna's block elder passed for a towel.

"Where's your boyfriend today?" the Bavarian demanded in her booming voice, giving Mala a sly look up and down.

"Which one?" Mala threw her a purposely seductive smile.

The former madam rolled her eyes. "The one who looks at you with the gaze of a dying sheepdog. That handsome Pole of yours from the fitters' *Kommando* who comes here almost every day asking *if we have any pipes to fix.*" She snorted good-naturedly, giving Mala another meaningful look.

As though on cue, Mala heard a familiar voice cursing crudely in Polish and smiled. Edek must have just witnessed something outside that had caused an outburst of abuse directed at "the blasted SS" and their mothers described in the most derogatory terms, and all of their enablers and some "bloody sod" whom Mala couldn't see from where she was sitting.

Edek's choice of words must have offended someone's feelings for next came the almost indignant reproach: "Mind your language, young man. There are women present here."

"…And men, who were raised better than this," someone else added.

The new arrivals, Mala scoffed, shaking her head. *It's all right. The local staff shall teach them the local ways soon enough.*

She rose to her feet and approached the small group of people. Before them, Edek stood, thoroughly incensed.

"Mind *my* language?!" he shouted. "You ought to be outraged by what is happening in the *Appellplatz* presently and not by my choice of words. You ought to be outraged at the SS for herding the entire barracks outside on Sunday, their only day off, and making them do gymnastics 'to strengthen their health.' You ought to be outraged at the fact that the *Kapos* and block elders beat the ones who can't keep up with the ridiculous pace, to death," he roared. "Those people are being brutalized as we speak, but you're offended by my description of it? I suggest you go and sod yourself then. Go tell the SS to mind their language. See what they do to you."

Purposely shoving the red-faced man with his shoulder, Edek stalked off, Wiesław following closely on his heels. Mala saw Edek's friend's shoulders quivering with chuckles. She, too, found the situation almost comical. Outside, the orgy of death was unraveling, but the newly arrived inmate was more bothered by the word "bloody" than by the growing pile of corpses.

The madam, who had also gone to investigate, sailed past the new arrival and slapped him in passing, with wonderful nonchalance about her.

"Bloody idiot."

The Sauna mob joined in at once. In mere moments, everyone was shouting all sorts of curses in their native languages. They, too, had taken the man's remark as a personal insult; most of them had been beaten and verbally abused by the SS nightly and daily for a few years now. An outsider, who hadn't felt his skin splitting under the guard's lash, who hadn't felt his ribs cracking under the *Kapo*'s boot, who hadn't pissed blood for a good couple of weeks after a block elder's beating, had no moral right to preach ethics to them. The ranks were closing around him, the cacophony of abuse rising to a deafening level. Auschwitz was an animal kingdom with animal laws. There was no place for pleasantries here. The man was about to learn it on his own skin and, oddly enough, Mala felt not an ounce of sympathy toward him.

"Bloody idiot!" she shouted, her voice joining the chorus of others, not due to the contagious influence of the mob mentality but because she, too, felt it to be a personal insult. Had he lived here at least a few days, had he personally witnessed the degradation, the depravity, the savage cruelty of the SS, he would think twice before opening his mouth and chastising them for using the language he didn't quite approve of. They, the survivors, had all the right to be coarse. Only those with a toughened skin survived. The tender moralists had all long perished in the industrial furnaces.

Mala caught Edek's eyes on her. He averted them self-consciously at the sight of her threadbare semblance of a towel and looked away altogether when she approached him. Wiesław, too, was suddenly very interested in his boots.

"It's all right. You can look at me. I'm not naked. And even if I was…" Mala gave an indifferent shrug. Being naked in Auschwitz in front of hundreds of people was nothing new. The SS and their practice of mass selections, during which they made both men and women race in a circle absolutely nude, and the communal showers they took in the presence of the SS personnel, had long reduced what was left of their modesty to nothing.

Still, Edek looked thoroughly embarrassed. "I'm sorry you had to hear that. We've been working outside the camp for the past few days, and I had no way of letting you know. We came to ask about you, pass a note to you maybe… I didn't know you were here… Else I would have never—"

Mala raised her palm, stopping him. "You did absolutely nothing wrong. He *is* a bloody idiot who had no right to say anything about your choice of words."

Edek glanced up, surprised.

"Bloody. Idiot," Mala repeated, grinning darkly. "Sodding crap-bag. Brainless hog." With some malicious relish, she proceeded to produce the most elaborate curses in their native Polish that would make any sailor in Edek's former maritime academy blush. "And yes, I used to kiss my mother with this mouth and she approved of it greatly."

Both friends were now regarding her with newfound admiration.

She was smiling at them, fearless and proud, but her chin was quivering in spite of herself. This was why she would never be able to write a word to her old boyfriend. This was why no one, outside these walls, would ever understand how a young woman could produce such "gutter language." She lived in a gutter, and all that defiance and fearlessness was a product of her brutal surroundings. It seeped from her wounds like pus; it contaminated everything it had come in contact with, poisoned it all and made her crave revenge with the ravenous appetite of a vulture.

Even if she came out of here, how would she be able to stand before her former boyfriend, hold his hand and smile at him when such darkness coursed through her veins? It was best to forget his name, just like she had almost forgotten his face. It was best to do what she knew how to do best—steal, bribe, cheat the authorities, and organize escapes.

Stasia was right; in the eyes of the world, many things were unethical and immoral. But when the world itself turned unethical and immoral, perhaps such criminals as herself and Stasia, such outlaws as Edek and Wiesław and Rita and Kostek were heroes instead.

"Come to the *Schreibstube* next Sunday," she told Edek. "I'll have the gold for your escape."

Chapter 19

"A uniform? Are you mad?" Edek's former Kommandoführer Lubusch stared at him in disbelief.

To be sure, it was a gamble coming here, back to his old work detail; it was an even bigger gamble to seek out the SS man and for Edek to openly lay his cards before him, but he had no choice.

Lubusch had all reason to drag him outside and shoot him in front of the others just for suggesting such an outrageous thing—Edek wouldn't blame him one bit. He had imagined all sorts of scenarios while walking here. And yet, he hoped against all logic, that his German namesake would come through, would show once again that his conscience was above his Führer's hateful politics.

There was a long, tense pause. Edek could hear himself breathing; could see, just out of the corner of his eye, his heart beating wildly under the blue cloth of his uniform overalls. On the opposite wall, the clock was ticking, measuring the seconds until Lubusch's ultimate refusal. Yet after an entire minute had expired, the SS officer still hadn't thrown him out. When Lubusch was lighting his cigarette, Edek noticed that his *Kommandoführer's* fingers were trembling almost imperceptibly.

"Do you know what they will do to me if they find out I helped you?" he asked Edek at length. "I have already served my term in the penal camp for my big mouth and protecting you lot before the authorities. Before releasing me back to my service in Auschwitz, they warned me that the second time they wouldn't be so lenient and it would be the Eastern front for me."

Feeling the heat growing in his cheeks, Edek averted his gaze, almost sorry to have asked. He was aware of Lubusch's imprisonment in the SS penalty unit in Stutthof-Matzkau, a concentration camp some 30 kilometers east of Danzig. He knew how much there was at stake for Lubusch. He had no right to ask his superior to risk his neck for him, but he simply had no one else to turn to. In the abode of the damned called Auschwitz, Lubusch was the only one with a heart.

"Is there a label attached to the inside of the uniform with your name?" Edek probed carefully. Despite seeing plenty of SS uniforms up close and even more boots as they were administering a beating to him for one "crime" or another, he didn't know the answer to his question.

"Whatever does that have to do with anything?" Lubusch huffed, annoyed, and released two strings of smoke from his nostrils. "Taking it off wouldn't take a minute. That's not what the trouble is. The trouble is when they capture you, and it's only a matter of time before they will, and they shall give you such an interrogation that Kapo Vasek with his whip and the *Strafblock* will feel like a ride in an amusement park compared to what the Political Department is capable of. Surely, you'll tell them who supplied you with such a disguise."

Edek held his gaze. "I didn't tell who broke the machine, did I?"

Lubusch made no reply. He didn't even look at Edek, choosing to stare at the picture on the corner of his desk instead. But for Edek, this meant hope. He'd seen that photo before—it was the wedding picture, of Lubusch in his dress uniform and his Polish bride. In it, they weren't looking at the camera but at each other, their gazes full of infinite tenderness.

"Herr Unterscharführer, I'll die under torture, but I won't betray you; you have my word," he whispered once again, his mouth dry with nerves. "I'm used to pain. I can withstand anything. You saw it with your own two eyes. They can break every single bone in my body, but I shall take your secret to my grave. Herr Unterscharführer, I beg you—"

"Oh, shut it already!" Lubusch pushed his chair back and walked over to the window just to avoid Edek's pleading eyes. He proceeded to speak in the same manner, with his back turned toward the inmate. "You're in a good detail. You shall survive it. The war will be over soon. Germany will lose; it's only a matter of time. The Soviets keep beating us something savage; the African campaign is lost; the Allied troops are taking over Italy…" Suddenly, he turned to face Edek. "Could you not wait a few more months? A year, at the most? Why risk it all now, when you have the chance to come out of here alive?"

Edek took his time to respond. It was important to choose the right words. Carefully, he licked his lips and began to speak.

"Herr Unterscharführer, you're an SS man."

A shadow of distaste passed over Lubusch's face. It was obvious he didn't like being reminded of it.

"It is in no way my intention to offend you," Edek rushed to explain. "I'm only saying it because you must have had an ideological training of sorts." When Lubusch didn't protest, Edek continued, "Whether you agreed with it or not, you did hear what your commanders were saying to you. I suspect they were saying the same thing your colleagues are saying to us openly, that we're the vermin that needs to be exterminated, that we're the parasitic leeches on the German nation's body, that we're the enemies of the state."

Lubusch had nothing to say against that either; only took deep pulls on his cigarette, staring at his boots with eyes full of inner torment.

"I don't know what instructions they gave you concerning our particular camp," Edek proceeded. "I used to be in the military—well, a maritime academy, but I suspect it's all the same in its essence— and my guess is that they most likely didn't discuss the possibility of the Soviets approaching the camp, in order to avoid sowing panic among the troops. Both you and I know that what the camp administration is doing here goes against all laws of humanity and your SS commanders would go to great lengths to ensure that not a word of what is happening in Auschwitz will leave its walls. Isn't that the reason for such security measures? I mean, would Himmler or Hitler truly care for one or two escaped inmates? Not a big loss of workforce if you think of it. No; the reason for all these guard towers and electrified barbed wire several layers deep and the endlessly roaming searchlights is to ensure that we won't escape to tell our stories. That's what frightens them the most, the fact that the world shall learn of all the atrocities, all the systematic slaughter."

Lubusch's face was growing paler and paler. Now, his hand, with the cigarette in it, was visibly shaking. Only his eyes didn't move; glassy and full of horror, they stared into the void, as though just now it had dawned on him that he, himself, was a willing cog in this machine of mass extermination. The thought of it mortified him, and it was Edek's suspicion that it wasn't due to the consequences he could possibly face. It was his own conscience that he would have to deal with for the rest of his life.

"They will never let the Soviets liberate us or any other camp inmates, Herr Unterscharführer," Edek spoke gently after a pause. "You know it. I know it. They'll dig more ditches, like they did in 1942, and either shoot us and burn us all there as they did back then, or gas us and shove us into the ovens. Either way, we won't be leaving this place alive. That's why I can't wait one more year, Herr Unterscharführer. I want to see my father once again. I want to fall asleep in my own bed and wake up with the sun, by myself, instead of being roused by a block elder's club and that demented gong blaring full volume all over the camp. I want to take a girl I like to the dances and buy flowers for her and kiss her in front of everyone without fear of being shot. I want to die fighting for my life, together with partisans, but not like this; not like obedient sheep led to slaughter." He grimaced in spite of himself. "You're a man yourself. You must understand…"

Lubusch nodded gravely. Of course, he understood.

"Do you have a plan of any sort, at least?" Lubusch asked after another intolerably long pause.

"Yes." Edek nodded readily. "A place to stay, the route to take, the money—it's all organized. We've planned it all out very carefully."

"So, there's 'we' then?" Before Edek could answer, Lubusch waved his hand before his face. "Don't tell me. I don't want to know. And just how do you plan to walk through the gates?"

"I have an *Ausweis*. A real one, from the camp office. Stamp and all that business."

Lubusch looked at him with a mixture of surprise and respect and, for the first time, a small grin was reflected on his face. "I see you have worked it all out already."

Edek smiled tentatively too. "*Jawohl*, Herr Unterscharführer. Only the uniform is missing."

To that, Lubusch shook his head. Edek held his breath, sensing how close he was to persuading the guard.

"It's January," Lubusch reflected, calculating something in his mind. "They shall be outfitting us all with new uniforms within the next couple of months. You can have my old one after they issue a new one to me. You can risk waiting till March, can't you?"

"Of course, Herr Unterscharführer." Edek breathed out in relief. The date wasn't all that important; it was the uniform that mattered the most. "Someone told me that running through snow is quite a bad idea."

"That someone has more sense than you do. I strongly suggest you listen to him in the future."

"Her." Edek's voice was a mere whisper. He lowered his eyes, feeling the heat rising in his cheeks.

"That girl you were talking about?" Lubusch's smile was much bigger now.

Edek nodded.

"Is that why you said 'we' before?"

"You told me not to tell you."

"Good. Don't tell me then. And make sure you take good care of her." Once again, Lubusch's gaze returned back to the photo on his desk. "And now, get out of here. As it is, you have spent too much time here. People will start saying we're in love."

Grateful for the timely jest, Edek rose to his feet and paused in stunned amazement at the sight of Lubusch's outstretched hand. Not quite sure that this was truly happening, he grasped it carefully and nearly choked with emotion when Lubusch clapped him warmly on the shoulder.

"Come see me in March. I shall have it by then."

"Thank you, Herr Unterscharführer. You have not the faintest idea what you've just done."

"Signed my own death sentence, but oh well." He gave a careless shrug. "At least I won't die a bastard, and at least my wife shall remember me with a few good words."

Chapter 20

"Mala, you can't keep doing this to yourself!"

The feeling was gradually returning to Mala's frozen-stiff limbs thanks to Zippy's vigorous rubbing.

"First, you jump into death ditches; now, you're walking through camp half-naked in the middle of winter because you gave away all your clothes?"

"The *Kanada* girls will supply me with new ones," Mala countered, her blue lips barely moving. "Those sickbay women don't have connections like I do."

"Those women have no conscience!" Zippy snapped, reaching for the small tin of bear fat she kept under her bed. After scooping some nasty-smelling stuff from the half-empty container, she began lathering Mala's chest and back with it. "Stripping you bare in such a manner, in the middle of winter! Do they wish for you to land in the sickbay as well, with pneumonia?"

Mala made no reply, only grinned faintly as her eyelids grew heavy with sleep. She closed her eyes as the warmth spread through her skin and tuned out the rest of Zippy's chastising, which, she suspected, her friend knew fell on deaf ears at any rate.

The truth was, Mala never planned on these things. She had never planned on *jumping into death ditches* as Zippy had called it, just like she had never planned on parting with her coat when she had set off for the sickbay to carry out her duties there, matching recovered women to different work details. It was a new coat, a much warmer one than the coat she had already given as a bribe to the doctor who'd promised to look after the Frenchman, her new substitute Papa, she'd saved. But the Slovak girl broke into such gut-churning cries when Mala had announced to her that she would have to work on a farm, sobbing and pointing at her striped dress, the only thing she owned, and pleading with Mala, claiming that she would certainly die out there in such threadbare attire that Mala had no choice. The farm detail was considered to be a good unit, albeit being an outside one; food could be had there if one knew how to pinch it right from under the *Kapos'* noses and the work wasn't too backbreaking, but the girl refused to see reason. And so Mala tore the camel-wool coat off herself, gave it to her in helpless frustration and told the girl to get out.

Mala's teeth were already chattering as she left the somewhat heated sickbay and headed toward the camp office, paperwork in hand, when a woman intercepted her, clung to her sleeve and asked Mala in broken German if a vest of some sort could be found somewhere for her mother, who was sick and wouldn't survive another night in an unheated barrack. Silently, Mala had handed her the papers to hold, took her own sweater off and gave it to the stunned woman.

With her warm woolen stockings she had parted voluntarily, when an elderly inmate who resembled her grandmother shuffled across her path on stiff, blue, bare legs stuffed into wooden clogs, slipping in the snow with a resigned look about her.

Through a fitful half-a-dream, Mala still caught snatches of Zippy's grumbling, but all the resentment the Slovakian mandolin-ist and her fellow camp office colleague expressed for the inmate women was easily explained. Just like Mala, she felt powerless to help them all and so, she huffed and cursed—at the women themselves, at Mala, at the camp and the sodding SS and their blasted Führer—because she had to vent the frustration at someone, somehow, so as not to lose it altogether. But despite all of Zippy's grumbling remarks, Mala knew that Zippy would have done the very same thing if she were in Mala's place, and Mala loved her friend all the more for that.

*

The soft, velvet darkness descended upon the camp. The SS office staff, including Mandl, had left for the night; only the lone guard was strolling leisurely around the building. Every ten minutes, Mala saw his boots pass by her window in the camp administration office cellar, the snow crunching softly under his unhurried steps.

She loved her private quarters—an unheard-of privilege granted only to the so-called camp elite. The room was small, and mice visited it more often than not, but Mala didn't mind such company. She had even befriended the most curious one of the group—the one with the missing ear—and left breadcrumbs by the hole in the wall, just by the radiator, from which her little pet appeared every night without fail.

At first, the mouse would grab the crumbs and disappear into the hole at once, but with time, it had grown accustomed to the young woman and began to eat in front of Mala, still on guard, still keeping its black, beady eyes trained firmly on the human. In Mala's eyes, that was already progress. She hoped that eventually the mouse would learn to trust her enough to eat out of her open palm. Ridiculous as it sounded, that was her private dream of sorts—to have a pet in Birkenau, even such an unorthodox one. There was so much death around, Mala wanted to return to her room, after witnessing yet another mass murder, and simply sit on the floor and hold something warm and still breathing, feeling the horrors of the day fade away as she stroked the soft, gray fur with the tip of her finger.

Another ten minutes must have passed—the guard had made another circle. But Mala was on the lookout for another pair of boots. A few days earlier, she had instructed Edek how to get to her quarters undetected and which window to knock on so that she would let him in. A risky enterprise, and that was putting it mildly, but the patrolling guard was far too lazy and predictable and, unlike many of his compatriots, didn't have the habit of shooting first and asking questions later. Even if Edek got caught, she'd explain his presence near the office building easily enough: the pipe in the cellar was leaking and could only be changed at night so that by the morning the camp office's SS personnel would return to the warmth of their offices. Fortunately for Mala, the guard wasn't overly enthusiastic and made it a point of honor to never do more work than he was being paid for. Both she and Zippy had smuggled guests into their rooms before, and the SS fellow had not once made the slightest attempt to investigate anything.

The familiar scratching by the radiator caught Mala's attention. Sliding from the top of her bed to the floor, with a smile she watched a little nose appear out of the hole, its whiskers twitching slightly. A tiny pink paw followed, the other one held apprehensively in the air. Mala had ceased to breathe altogether. That night, she had added some cheese to the mouse's usual ration of gray camp bread but placed it further away from the hole, almost by the soles of her feet. At first, the rodent appeared to hesitate; however, it was an Auschwitzer too, much like the rest of them. Just like the inmates pinched food right from under the Germans' noses, the mouse strutted, with admirable insolence, toward Mala's feet, grabbed the biggest piece of cheese and scrambled back to its hiding place.

In spite of herself, Mala discovered that she was laughing. It was a ghostlike, almost soundless laughter, but it was as genuine as it got, particularly in that hell on earth. "You fearless little thing, you!"

She watched the mouse return for more. Someone had taken a chunk out of its ear, but it still persisted. It hadn't lost its spirit and Mala couldn't help but feel a kinship of sorts with the brave furry fellow.

During the days filled with relentless gore and permanent dread, it was these moments that she looked forward to. Her small, spartan room with its bed and a table at which she ate her rations and read the books Mandl generously permitted her; the stillness of the place; the soft glow of the lamp and her little companion. It was almost a sanctuary. After the mounting pressure of the day, after feeling her shoulders tensing and gradually turning to lead with never-ending stress, what immense relief it was to come down here and just breathe, just sit on the floor and not think of anything for a change.

The sense of relief was always tinged with guilt though—guilt for having personal quarters in the first place, guilt for having access to food when others went mad from starvation; a survivor's guilt, simply for being alive. But as long as she was alive, so were the others, thanks to her tireless efforts—at least, according to Zippy's logic. Deep inside, Mala knew it was true, but that useless knowledge didn't lessen her suffering one bit. The world around her was still an ugly place and she was still powerless against its injustice and cruelty.

It was Mala's profound conviction that she would have never survived in the regular block to which she had been assigned and which she visited for daily roll calls. She would have gone mad from all the people around; people who constantly cried, pleaded, died—right in front of her eyes. As it was, everyone wanted something from her. She was Mala, the camp administration's favorite, the girl with the lists who could arrange a transfer to a detail that would make the difference between life and death. She was the girl who always carried bread on herself to smuggle to others. She was the one who could move freely about the camp and pass a note to a loved one. They just had to catch her sleeve in passing, plead with their begging eyes and she would part with her bread, take the note, promise to see what she could do about the dreaded transfer.

Zippy claimed they took advantage of her. *We're not some almighty goddesses,* her camp office friend claimed. *There is only so much we can do for the poor devils.* But Mala simply couldn't say no. She listened to the inmates' troubles even when she had too much of her own on her mind; she gave the rations she'd been saving for herself; she never turned anyone away, unless there was truly nothing she could do for them. And even then, she went to Mandl or Hössler and begged for a prisoner she barely knew, explaining what an irreplaceable worker they were and how much the camp would benefit from keeping them alive.

An urgent knock on the glass brought Mala out of her reverie, sending her heart sprinting with excitement. Eyes glowing, she was instantly on her feet, motioning to Edek, who crouched by the window, to stay put. In another moment, she was running along the corridor, barefoot and silent like a cat, to open the door through which the coal *Kommando* brought the sacks to warm the quarters.

Edek's shadowy form was barely visible from here. But then it occurred to Mala that he had spent far too many years in the camp not to acquire the lifesaving skill of blending in with the environment. He slid toward her, keeping close to the wall and away from the searchlight roving the ground, as though he'd trained his entire life to become invisible at will. For the first time, Mala began to believe that he may just succeed in his daring plan. He was a good partisan already. Give him a rifle and he'd make an excellent one.

A sudden sense of longing came over her at the thought that one day he would disappear, quite possibly forever, and she would never see those shining eyes, that smile; would never get to hold his hand again. With an effort, Mala pushed the thought away, shoved it into the darkest, cobwebbed corner of her mind. He was setting off to fight for freedom. How utterly selfish it would be to prevent him from doing so just because she wanted him near.

"Cold?" Mala asked, pulling him inside and bolting the door at once.

"Not in the slightest. I ran all the way here." He was still slightly out of breath.

"You shouldn't have. Running is dangerous in Birkenau."

"I learned long ago how to avoid the searchlights." He didn't sound boastful. Dejected, if anything.

Mala, too, lowered her eyes as she led him toward her room, her bare feet padding noiselessly on the concrete floor.

"A rather swell arrangement you have here," Edek commented, changing the subject self-consciously.

"What did you expect? We're the camp elite." Mala forced joy into her voice. It rarely came naturally; all the smiles came through the tears, all gaiety was theatrical, to cheer each other up when the entire world was shattering to pieces. Gallows humor, inspired by the very real gallows always just within reach. "Wait till you see my room. You'll grow green with envy."

With a dramatic gesture, she pushed the door to her private quarters open. Edek paused on the threshold, visibly impressed, and whistled his approval.

"No wonder you don't want to run with us. I wouldn't want to run either, if I lived in such an apartment!"

Mala laughed, grateful for the joke. "Now, if we were back in civilized society, I'd ask you if you were hungry before offering you anything, but since we're here, in this hole, it's sort of a given. So—" she moved the only chair for him to take, "sit here; I won't be a tick."

Edek watched as she kneeled in front of her bed and pulled a box from under it. His eyes widened when he saw her produce all sorts of delicacies from it.

"Now, you can't eat all of this at once—it'll quite literally kill you," Mala said in a matter-of-fact tone, placing sardine tins, smoked salami, and jars with jam and honey on the table in front of her astounded guest, "but feel free to choose whatever few items you'd like the best and we'll save the rest for later. As I said, we ought to fatten you up, as we need you to pass for an SS man. So, dig in. We'll increase the portions little by little. By May, you shall look a regular German poster boy, glowing with health."

But instead of throwing himself on the unexpected feast in front of him, Edek only observed it in stupefied silence.

"Did you steal it all?" he asked, finally recovering from the shock.

Mala laughed. "No, of course not. We have privileges. One of them is double rations and parcels from the Red Cross that Mandl allows us to take every now and then. It's all from Switzerland." Mala turned one of the tins toward Edek, so he could read the label.

"Red Cross sends us food?"

"You would never tell, would you?" A sneer marred Mala's sharp features. "It's because most of it goes to the SS. A small portion of it ends up in the hands of the privileged inmates like us. Very few of these parcels actually reach the ones who need them the most. But, on paper, everything is dandy, of course."

Once again, Edek looked at the food, then at Mala, measuring her tall frame up and down with a skeptical look. He didn't seem able to reconcile the fact that she had all these riches this entire time and yet had remained so painfully thin.

As though guessing his thoughts, she gave him a somewhat guilty smile. "I don't eat most of it. So it'll all go to you."

He was already shaking his head, pushing the food away from him and toward Mala, despite his mouth watering frightfully at the tantalizing scents invading his senses. "No, I won't take it."

"Then it'll go bad." She shrugged indifferently.

He blinked at her uncomprehendingly.

Seeing that the conversation was unavoidable and that without a proper explanation he wouldn't put a single piece in his mouth, Mala released a voluminous breath. "I don't think it'll make any sense to you, but I don't eat because life here is too chaotic."

"You're right. It makes absolutely no sense."

Mala chuckled. "Life is too chaotic, and I never know what to expect. I know I shouldn't complain because I'm not the one breaking my back in the outside detail. At Buna, hundreds die daily from hard labor. In my case, it's not about the physical toll. It's more about the emotional one. As much as I try to help as many as I can, people still die and I feel helpless. Helpless and guilty for not being able to do more. And so, I double my efforts, I try to do as much as I can, give as much as I can, but it's never enough. I simply don't have the authority over most things. Eating—or, shall I say, *not* eating—is the only thing that I can control, that I can use to feel less helpless. Usually, I give the contents away to people who need it more or bribe *Kapos* with it in exchange for favors or medicine—and I actually feel better about myself that way. Not as guilty. But these I've been saving for you specifically."

The small smile she gave him didn't reflect on Edek's face. Instead, he regarded her, almost mortified.

"Mala, you shouldn't punish yourself by refusing to eat," he said softly at last. "If anything, you ought to eat everything they give you, so you can stick around for longer, so you can help more people. They need you. What good will it do if you starve yourself to death?"

"I don't deserve to eat when the rest are starving," she objected flatly. "I shouldn't be eating more than a regular inmate."

"But it's insanity! A regular inmate survives on some soup made of rotten turnip and a piece of dry bread."

"See?" She crossed her arms over her chest. Through the gap in her uniform blouse, he could clearly see the sharp outline of her collarbone. "I'm already eating more than I should, with the rice and potatoes camp office gives us. I'll cut down on my portions even more now."

"No! That's not what I—" Edek stopped himself in exasperation.

What have they done to you? She could read the silent question clearly in the tragic look he gave her. They both knew that this was in no way normal, rational thinking. Mala had always prided herself on concealing just how broken inside she was under a carefully constructed, impenetrable façade. But he had seen right through it and, for the first time, she didn't mind revealing her weakness to someone who would never take advantage of it but would offer her the support and understanding she so desperately needed in this place where each person was out for themselves.

"I won't eat unless you eat with me," he said, setting aside a head of yellow cheese and a pretzel. "For each bite I take, you have to take one."

Mala stared at him with accusation in her gaze, but, in spite of herself, she couldn't help but feel warmth spread through her chest like a gentle caress as she looked into the eyes of the man who actually cared whether she lived or died.

"Or, it simply won't be fair," he continued, breaking the pretzel in pieces. "I have a conscience too. I'll also feel guilty if I eat and you go starving. No, Mally, this won't do."

Mally. She glanced up, surprised and touched to the marrow at the pet name only her closest friends and family called her.

"Either we both eat or we both don't. Your call." Edek held out a piece of pretzel to her.

In the golden glow of the lamp, the grains of salt on its brown crust shimmered like diamonds. No, Mala thought, these were far more valuable, for they could be eaten. She saw Edek swallow instinctively a few times; she knew he could almost taste them in his mouth, and yet, he waited for Mala to make her move.

With great reluctance, she took a piece from him and brought it to her lips.

Grinning with anticipation, he mirrored her gesture.

"Ready? Set," he said and smiled wider, for she had finally relented. "Go!"

*

"Kommandoführer Lubusch has agreed to supply me with a uniform," Edek said, after they finished their modest feast.

Mala glanced up sharply. "You told him about the plan then?"

"I had to." Edek shrugged, licking his fingers clean. The scent of cheese and pretzel bread still clinging to his skin was too tantalizing to mind one's manners. "There was no way around it."

"And you're quite certain he can be trusted?"

"If he wasn't, I expect the camp Gestapo would be beating the names of my accomplices out of me as we speak." Edek smiled briefly and then suddenly remembered himself. "I wouldn't tell them anything, of course. Even if I do get caught, you have my word—"

"I don't care one way or the other," Mala interrupted him with an astonishing indifference about her. "I'm sick to my stomach of this place. The only reason why I haven't gone to the wire yet is that there are people I can still help. If they appoint some collaborator to my position, everything will be lost for them for good. So, if someone decides to string me up on the *Appellplatz* for aiding you, they'll do me a favor, if I'm entirely honest with you."

Edek pulled forward, reaching for her hand, but stopped short of taking it into his. More than anything, he wished to touch her, but the setting was much too intimate, the light much too dim. It frightened him for some reason. He felt himself balancing on the edge of the metaphorical abyss from which there was no return, for once he had tied himself to her, there wouldn't be any turning back. It would be only her or nothing at all. All else would simply cease to exist, lose its meaning without her by his side. "Run with us then. This place is destroying you, both physically and mentally. Run with us. We have already secured the aid of a civilian man who will shelter us and provide us with civilian clothes."

"Your plan is only good for two men." Mala grinned crookedly. "How are you planning to take a woman out of the camp without causing major suspicion?"

"I'll think of something," Edek promised with certainty he didn't feel. "Just say yes and I'll invent something."

Shaking her head, Mala stood up. While she was searching for something in her pillowcase, Edek heard her mutter something about his being an insufferable idealist. He felt his breath catch in his throat when she approached him, holding a few nuggets of gold in her open palm.

"Here. I promised to secure it for you," she said, regarding the gold with an unreadable expression on her face. "It's dental gold, but I asked my friend from the *Sonderkommando* to melt it for you, so it won't cause any suspicion from the locals when you try to trade it for food. Now it's unrecognizable. They won't ask you any questions."

Edek stared at it, unable to force himself to take it. It was Mala who took his hand in hers, placing the gold into it and closing his fist around it with desolate finality.

"Rotten business, buying food with dead people's dental gold. Trust me, I know. But you two will need to survive to avenge those people who perished. They wouldn't mind. Better you two put it to good use than the Nazis."

"I suppose." Edek's words were a mere whisper. He smiled at Mala in sudden gratitude. "Thank you for being so logical about it."

"I'm always logical. That's why so many people think me to be so heartless."

"You?" Edek pulled back in amazement. "Heartless?" It was inconceivable to him. She was one of the most selfless people he'd encountered in his short life.

From Mala, another indifferent shrug. "Yes. Heartless. That's what a woman called me at the sickbay after I tried to explain it to her that I can't possibly transfer everyone to a good detail. It wasn't even the rejection itself that annoyed her; it was the way I explained my reasoning. I had just assigned a Slovak girl to a good detail, for farm work, so it was only a matter of good fortune, and fortune had it that the Slovak girl's number was the first on the list, so she got in and the woman didn't."

Mala's face turned pensive.

"I've never been an emotional person, you see. My father raised me differently. He taught me to rely on my intellect first and foremost and never act out of emotions. But that's not how women are supposed to behave in society's eyes. We're supposed to be compassionate, empathetic, helpful, caring… And it's not that I'm not any of these things; it's the fact that I don't show it on the outside. The woman in the sickbay accused me of refusing her with such a straight face. She accused me of not being sorry simply because I didn't look sorry. But I never understood the point of showing emotions just for the sake of showing them. What would really change if I began to cry along with her and lament our common fate and drop to my knees and beg for her forgiveness? Absolutely nothing."

Edek discovered that he was nodding enthusiastically while she was speaking. It made a lot of sense to him just then.

"For some reason, everyone has always assumed that I don't feel anything just because I don't express my feelings like a girl ought to. I do feel everything very deeply, but I simply don't demonstrate my feelings to the entire world. If a problem arises, instead of crying and tearing my hair out, I sit down and try to come up with a viable solution."

"Like you came up with a solution to mine." Edek's grin grew even wider.

Mala looked at him, somewhat surprised, but then the corners of her mouth turned upwards as well. "Yes. Like I came up with a solution to yours. I'm glad you see it that way. Many people hate a cold, logical mind in a woman."

"Well, I think you have a wonderful mind. I wouldn't love you as much if you were any different," he blurted out and immediately stopped in horror, realizing what it was precisely that he'd just confessed to.

At first, Mala made no reply; simply regarding Edek with a mysterious smile growing slowly on her face. In the twilight of the room, her amber eyes looked almost black.

"No need to grow so deathly pale," she commented at last. "I like you too."

Even though she didn't say "love," Edek stared at her, grinning like an idiot, the forgotten gold lying in his open palm atop the tabletop. It mattered not what word she'd used; the emotion was in her eyes. An Auschwitz veteran, Mala expressed with her gaze all the words she was too fearful to utter. Forming attachments was a dangerous business in the grim world of the camp. It was best to distance oneself from the others... until one couldn't fight one's heart any longer, just like they couldn't now.

"Do you have a friend waiting for you at home?" he probed carefully, holding his breath and not quite noticing it.

"A friend?" Mala arched her brow, amused. "I have a lot of friends waiting for me at home."

"A boyfriend," Edek was forced to clarify.

She was laughing softly now and he discovered that so was he.

"Why? Wondering if there are any vacancies?" Mala teased again, suddenly all playfulness. "Even if there is a position available, what's the point? You'll just run out on me in a few months."

"If you just say the word, I'll stay," he said, surprising himself with the determination in his voice and realizing that he actually meant it.

Mala slowly shook her head. "I would never keep you from freedom."

Rising from his seat, Edek stepped toward her. "But don't you understand?" With utmost gentleness, he placed his hands atop her arms. "Since I met you, I haven't been free. And you know what? It's the best non-freedom one can ask for."

He leaned in and kissed her gently on her cheek, but as soon as he was about to tear himself away, Mala wrapped her arm around his neck and pulled him close, pressing her mouth against his. He tasted every unspoken word in that kiss, every hidden emotion trapped under the silk of her skin, every promise she'd made without uttering a single word. Intoxicated by the honey of her lips, the room spinning around him, he drank from her greedily, without restraint, and for the first time in years felt hope stir in him that nothing was yet lost as long as he had her to come back to.

Chapter 21

As soon as Edek had learned that Antoni Szymlak, their civilian Polish connection, would be working on the women's camp hospital's new bathhouse, he immediately bribed the *Kapo* to get himself and Wiesław into the bathhouse fitters' *Kommando*.

The old man appeared genuinely glad to find both comrades alive and well, greeting them with a cordial handshake. For the first half of the day, they didn't have a chance to talk, aside from exchanging work-related remarks—the proximity of the *Kapos* and their fellow inmates made it impossible—but when the sound of the gong announced lunch hour, Edek promptly took his food bowl to the corner where the old man was eating his homemade ham sandwich. Upon seeing him approach, Szymlak broke the sandwich in two and handed the second half to Edek without another word. In turn, Edek divided it in two as well and shared his half with Wiesław, who had followed him to Szymlak's corner, carefully balancing his own soup bowl in his hands.

No one paid them any heed; Poles were known to congregate together, civilian workers and inmates alike, not raising suspicions as Jews making contact with Poles normally would. Making use of such lax discipline, Edek almost instantly broke into urgent whispers.

"We have an *Ausweis* and, soon, we'll have a uniform as well. Is your offer still open?"

Before answering, the old man, who had finished his half of the sandwich by then, produced a tin of tobacco and proceeded to roll three cigarettes.

"When are you planning to go through with the enterprise?" he asked at length.

"In May or June." Edek nodded his gratitude for the cigarette but didn't light it, sticking it behind his ear instead.

Wiesław did the same and proceeded to polish off his soup bowl with what was left of the bread.

The Polish tiler nodded sagely as he twirled his thick mustache. "That's wise. The forests are much thicker in summer. Plenty of places to hide."

Something in that remark caused Edek to glance up at him in alarm. "Yes, naturally... We've already discussed it. We'll avoid all major roads and will stick to the forests after we leave your place."

He searched Szymlak's face as the old man smoked, staring pensively into space. Edek suddenly found it disturbing that the tiler was avoiding meeting his eyes.

"You'll still help us the very first night, won't you?" Edek ceased to breathe altogether as he awaited the old Pole's verdict. "You said we may stay in your cellar and use your clothes. You haven't changed your mind, have you?"

Szymlak shook his head absently. "No, of course not. May or June then." He appeared to be working things out in his mind as he chewed on his lip under his mustache. Suddenly, as though remembering himself, he looked at the two friends brightly. "In the meantime, is there anything else I can do for you? Smuggle a letter to your families perhaps? Or would you like some more of this?" He pointed at the empty newspaper, which still bore the faint tantalizing smell of the ham sandwich and homemade bread. "My daughter makes them for me."

The blood suddenly drained from Edek's face. "Your daughter?" he repeated, his head ringing as though in some bad dream. "I thought you said you lived alone."

"I did, back when we had that conversation." Szymlak smiled uneasily. "Now that the Soviets are pushing closer and closer, she and her children came to stay with me. It wasn't safe where she was."

Dazed, as though from the sharp, physical blow, Edek tried to process the news and what it could mean for their plan... but couldn't.

Feeling himself on the verge of some terrible emotional collapse, Edek sought out Mala first thing after the evening roll call was finished. The night had descended upon the camp, spiritless and deathly still, enveloping the barracks in its dark shroud. Even the lights appeared dimmer to Edek. Or, perhaps, it was his hope that was dimming before his eyes, dissolving slowly, melting into the night just like the snow under his feet.

He even left his own dinner portion to Wiesław; the food didn't interest him any longer after Szymlak had broken the news about the arrival of his daughter and grandchildren. Edek didn't mind accepting help from a sympathetic Pole living by himself and willing to do his utmost to help the inmates. Szymlak had made it understood that he had lived a long and good life and didn't mind dying a good death for the cause. But how could Edek possibly, in good conscience, risk the lives of Szymlak's daughter and her small children? If the Gestapo uncovered the fact that it was Szymlak's family that aided him and Wiesław, they'd throw them into Auschwitz without any further ceremony, and Edek knew far too well where children ended up upon arrival—the gas chambers or Dr. Mengele's experimental block, where they'd be measured and prodded and injected with all sorts of poisons until their young bodies succumbed to one of Herr Doktor's pseudoscientific experiments. He couldn't possibly have their deaths on his conscience.

Running his hand over his shaved head for the umpteenth time, he marched forward in exasperation, unsure of what to do. He desperately needed to talk to someone, to hear much-needed words of comfort, meaningless promises that everything would turn out just fine. But when he found Mala near the *Schreibstube* building where the lights were still on and two other runners waited with her, when he saw her drawn, pale face and the dark half-moons under lusterless eyes, he suddenly couldn't bring himself to burden her with his troubles.

"Are you still working?" he asked softly, throwing a concerned look at the two girls who were watching the couple with natural curiosity.

"They have begun the construction of a new ramp," Mala explained. Even her voice was dull, utterly devoid of all emotion. "It'll be round-the-clock production. They have some deadline they have to meet and for a reason which I can't even bring myself to consider. We runners will be working in day and night shifts from now on. The SS really do want this one done as soon as possible."

As though on cue, the door flew open and a warden appeared on its threshold holding a paper of some sort. "Mala! Get it delivered to the chief engineer."

"*Jawohl.*" Mala saluted the SS woman.

The warden was staring at Edek like a hawk. He felt heat coming from the opened door mixing with the heat rising in his cheeks at the possibility of being discovered. It was fortunate that he had thought of taking his toolbox with him.

"What do you want?" the warden barked, narrowing her gaze.

"Kapo Jupp sent me." Edek swiftly produced a credible lie. "In case I was wanted on the new ramp."

"A fitter, on the ramp?" the warden snorted with disdain. "Has he completely drunk himself blind?"

"I'm also a carpenter," Edek supplied yet another explanation, his face betraying nothing. "I can work on the ramp. That's why he sent me. I have several qualifications." Out of the corner of his eye, he saw Mala's tense face relax with relief at his swift response and quick thinking.

"Oh." After measuring him from head to toe, the warden finally shrugged. "Well, doesn't concern me one way or another. If Jupp wishes to be so helpful, go to the ramp and inquire if they can use you. Mala shall take you. She's going there herself anyway."

For some time, they walked silently side by side, their hands brushing as though by accident every now and then, sending a rush of excitement running through them. Only when the office building disappeared from view completely and in front of them lay only the vast expanse of the camp did Edek catch Mala's hand in his, kissing it ardently.

Reluctantly, as though not wishing to offend, she pulled it away. "Not now. The guard towers…"

Edek nodded. Of course. The blasted guard towers, sweeping the compound with their searchlights like demented lighthouses, seeking out lost ships just to obliterate them with their machine guns.

"Now, tell me what's wrong," Mala demanded, her voice suddenly full of strength.

Edek looked at her and, in the wavering light of the overhead lamps, saw her steely determination to help. At once, his heart swelled in his chest. Utterly exhausted and pale with worry, she still thought of others before herself. His Mala.

He had just opened his mouth to recount his troubles with Szymlak and the unexpected reappearance of the Pole's daughter, but ended up shaking his head instead. "Nothing. Just wanted to take a walk with you under the moon."

Mala scowled faintly; she looked as though she didn't quite believe him. Then, it was her who caught his fingers in her cold and slender ones. "I'm glad you're here," she said.

"I wouldn't want to be any place else."

"Not even outside?"

"Not even outside. Here, with you is where I belong."

Mala looked at him and something shifted in her gaze. "Come to the *Schreibstube* on Sunday, like last time. Germans don't work on weekends, deadline or not. But this time, stay, will you?"

Edek nodded very slowly as the meaning of the words hit him full force. There was some unspoken promise hanging in the frosty air between them just then, invisible and yet almost tangible, and at that moment, Edek swore to himself that he would never part with her; not against his will at any rate.

Every Sunday for the next two months, Edek began sneaking into Mala's quarters. Wiesław had long given up on trying to persuade his best friend to stop it with their amorous excursions—it was not the place or the time—and turned his concerns into a joke.

"Are you staying out again then? Good; I'll be sleeping by myself again. Like a king. No obnoxious tossing and turning of yours."

The block elder didn't ask any questions; simply took his bribe—a lemon or a piece of salami—and looked the other way when Edek slipped outside under the cover of the night. As long as Edek was back for the morning roll call, he cared not on whose pillow "the blasted Romeo" was resting his head.

And Edek didn't rest his head at all. He ate his dinner and tried not to cringe when Mala would slip more molten dental gold nuggets into his palm. He sat next to her on the floor beside the bed for the next few hours, laying out breadcrumbs for the mouse that was growing more and more comfortable with the oddly generous humans. And he spoke to Mala about things that no longer were and things that would hopefully, one day, be once again.

With unmistakable longing in her voice, Mala told him all about her first job at the major Antwerp fashion house Maison Lilian, where silk cascaded in waves around the measuring tables and where she sometimes stood for hours on end while designers pinned and stitched the material on her slender frame whenever one of the models called in sick and needed a replacement. Her eyes grew wistful when she recalled the camaraderie among her colleagues at her second job as a linguist-secretary in a small company in the diamond trade and how they did anything possible and impossible to shield her from the Nazis when the German troops had marched into Belgium and having a Jew working in one's company was suddenly a crime.

In exchange, Edek told her about his maritime school in Pińsk and the pranks they played on their superiors and the size of the dormitory's bathrooms they had to polish with toothbrushes in punishment for those very pranks. He shared his past with her the same way she shared her food with him, without holding anything back and soon, somehow, his memories became hers and hers became his and he discovered that he knew Belgium without once traveling there and loved Mala's father without once meeting him, just like he'd grown to love Mala's adopted Auschwitz Papa of whom she often spoke with great fondness.

"Do you think he would approve of me? Your real father, that is?" he asked her once, only half in jest. According to Mala, Auschwitz Papa approved of him already, solely because Edek made his adopted daughter smile in a place where tears were a much more common occurrence.

"I strongly suggest you ask him that yourself."

"Just how would I go about that?"

"Well, I assume, you'll have to get out of here first, obtain a white stallion, then ride back into this camp with the Soviet Army and save this damsel in distress." She pointed at herself, keeping her poker face intact throughout the entire exchange. "And then deliver me, in the same manner, to my familial house, where you may request my hand in marriage from the patriarch of the family directly."

Edek couldn't help himself. His shoulders began to quiver with laughter. "With all due respect, milady, you're the furthest thing from a damsel in distress I've ever come across."

"I'll take that as a compliment."

"And from what you've told me, your household was the furthest from a typical patriarchal household."

"You're quite right there as well. My father raised me to be a self-reliant harlot who thinks for herself and whose tongue is too long for most people's liking."

"I like your long tongue. I only have one question: does the stallion have to be white?"

"Only white, or the marriage is off."

"What if it's a brown mare but it has a rope attached to it, from which one Nazi or the other dangles?"

Mala pretended to consider. "Make it two Nazis and it's a deal."

"As a wedding present?"

"Yes, as a wedding present."

"How about I make it three Nazis and you kiss me right now, to seal our engagement?"

"I don't know; I haven't seen the Nazis yet."

But she kissed him all the same, breaking her act at last. It began slow but soon grew into something wild and desperate, leaving both of them gasping for breath but refusing to let go of one another all the same. Skin tingling, hearts beating one hundred beats per second, fingers in hair—sheer madness and eternal salvation all blended into a night to be remembered and cherished, in which the death camp itself had no power over them for a few heavenly hours. It had been the beginning of January when she had asked him to stay the night for the first time. By the end of February, he didn't want to wake up anywhere else but in Mala's arms.

Chapter 22

"I'm being transferred."

Lost in his dreams of Mala, still feeling her lips on his, her caramel-colored hair in his hands, Edek didn't quite grasp the meaning of the very distressed-looking Wiesław's words.

"What did you say?" He stared at his friend in astonishment.

The morning had dawned gray, shrouded with mist. He had just made it in time for the morning roll call to discover Wiesław staring blankly into space as he stood outside the block, waiting to be counted.

"I said, I'm being transferred," Wiesław repeated, his trembling lips scarcely moving. He appeared stunned, as though he, himself, couldn't quite believe it. "You were already gone last night when the SS came with the inspection."

Edek frowned in confusion. They had stowed the *Ausweis* together with their gold under the board next to Edek's bunk. Each time, after hiding another portion of goods under it, Edek personally nailed it back. There wasn't a chance in the world it could be discovered, even during one of the thorough SS searches.

The block elder came out of the barracks, his *Schreiber* in tow, holding the list of the inmates assigned to the block in his hand.

"We ought to tell them it's a mistake," Edek whispered. "You didn't have anything illegal on you."

He felt himself grow cold with suspicion when Wiesław didn't reply at once. For some time, the only sound was the block elder's hoarse voice and their fellow fitters shouting *Jawohl* back at him whenever he called their respective numbers.

"Remember Szymlak offered to smuggle something edible for us?" Wiesław's words emerged as a whisper.

Slowly, Edek shut his eyes, refusing to believe such stupidity.

"Well, long story short, just yesterday he smuggled an entire parcel for me," Wiesław proceeded, his voice betraying him with a slight tremor. When Edek stole a glance at his friend, he saw guilty tears ready to spill from his eyes. "I opened it but didn't touch it; I was saving it until you came back, so we could share it. Needless to say, the SS pounced on it at once. 'What?! Eating like a king when our soldiers are starving on the front, you Polish swine!' And just my misfortune, I had silk underwear stored under my pallet as well…" He glanced at Edek tragically. "You know it's not out of vanity or anything; lice don't cling to it as much as they cling to cotton underthings…"

Edek knew. Only, he couldn't quite talk just then. He would say something driven by anger, something that would be impossible to take back and break the friendship that had seen them through the most brutal of times.

Why would Wiesław ask Szymlak for food? Edek left him his own dinner each time he went to see Mala; he smuggled whatever goods she gave him and split them evenly in half with his best friend. They didn't starve by Auschwitz measures, and besides, the women in the sickbay where he occasionally worked supplied him with all sorts of extravagant treats and even booze. Why? Risking it all for a few homemade sandwiches? He felt like raging, screaming into the fog but could only stand to attention and wait for his name to be called.

"Where are you being transferred to?" he asked at last, after the block elder ticked his name off the list. His voice was robbed of all force. "Not the punishment *Kommando*?"

"No. Well… almost." Wiesław let out a sad, ghostlike chuckle. "To Block 8. Where Soviet prisoners of war are."

Almost, indeed, Edek thought grimly. The Soviets were infamous among the camp population for openly snubbing authority and even earning the respect of Lagerführer Schwarzhuber himself, however they managed that. Birkenau men's camp leader Schwarzhuber, who was in charge of selections, took great pleasure in "ridding the Reich of the subhuman vermin," as he called them. To everyone's astonishment, the Soviet prisoners of war no longer fell under such a category in Schwarzhuber's eyes. On multiple occasions, he was seen bantering with them through a translator about battlefields they'd marched through and weapons they carried and strategic points they'd fought over—all the things he dreamt of and didn't have a chance to fulfill.

"What's worse—" Wiesław began and bit his tongue at Edek's look, who appeared positively homicidal just then.

"There's *worse?*" he hissed.

At the accusation in his best friend's voice, Wiesław hung his head entirely. "They're making me into a block clerk there. So I won't be with the fitters' *Kommando* any longer. At first, I didn't understand what sort of punishment it was, turning a guilty inmate into a block clerk, but then I realized what it meant. The Soviets are notorious for their tempers. They kill whoever they don't fancy. I suppose that's precisely the fate the SS have in mind for me."

Edek stared with unseeing eyes into the breaking day that couldn't possibly get any worse and, finally, released a heavy breath. "They won't kill you. At least, they'll have to get through me first."

When Wiesław blinked at him uncomprehendingly, Edek dealt him a friendly blow in the ribs.

"Don't fret. I'll bribe someone to get into Block 8 with you. I won't abandon you, I promise."

First thing in the evening, Edek went to see the same *Arbeitsdienst*— the inmate functionary in charge of assigning prisoners to different blocks and work details—who had transferred Wiesław. Rather to Edek's surprise, the old Pole, who spoke with a distinctive Silesian accent and introduced himself as Jozek, spread out his arms regretfully and explained that he had nothing to do with the transfer, that he had merely followed orders and that Edek's friend ought to be grateful that the SS hadn't assigned him to the actual punishment *Kommando*, where he wouldn't last longer than a few days.

"Is it possible for me to transfer to his block?" Edek asked, already pulling a bottle of spirits from under his overalls.

Jozek stopped him with a gentle, apologetic smile. "Keep your bribe. I can't help you with the transfer at any rate. Here, in Birkenau, all transfers are sanctioned either by Lagerführer Schwarzhuber and his underlings or camp Kapo Jupp. Are you friendly with either one?"

Needless to say, the question was rhetorical. Anyone who could avoid Schwarzhuber did so as much as possible; as for Kapo Jupp, he rivaled his SS counterpart in brutality. An old criminal who delighted in pouncing on anyone displaying weakness just for the thrill of it, he had climbed his way to the top of the camp hierarchy by killing and brutalizing the inmates under his charge. The SS valued such servants; they helped them save the gas by slaughtering the prisoners with their bare hands.

"Tell you what." Jozek's voice pulled Edek from his unhappy musings. "You go see your friend tonight—as a block clerk, he's entitled to his own room in the barracks—and have a chat with him in private. Explain to him that he ought to make friends with the Russians. It won't be easy; they aren't particularly famous for listening to orders coming from our lot, but if he establishes himself as their ally, he'll be in one of the most kosher positions in the entire camp."

"How so?" Edek scowled uncomprehendingly.

From his own experience, Edek remembered the brutal attitude of the SS to the Soviet prisoners of war. When they had just arrived

at the camp, the Nazis made it their business to turn their lives
into virtual hell. Where a Pole might have received a beating for
a slight misdemeanor, a Russian was shot. The worst camp jobs
were reserved for the Soviets. It was them who were gassed among
the first in Block 11. It was them who were constantly tortured,
abused, lashed, starved, and subjected to the most horrific medical
experiments. Some camp old numbers speculated that only the
Jews had it worse. After what he'd witnessed in Auschwitz, Edek
begged to disagree.

"Things changed after the Germans lost Stalingrad," Jozek
explained ponderously. "Now, they consider it better business to
keep the surviving Russians safe."

Edek was just about to interject when the old Pole raised his
hand, stopping him with the same soft smile. "I know, I know.
I arrived at Auschwitz with one of the first transports too. I
remember very well what they did to the poor devils there. But
here, in Birkenau, the ones who survived are treated like privileged
inmates now. Lagerführer Schwarzhuber has his own sentimental
feelings toward them, something to do with a soldier's honor or
some such, but the fact remains: he assigns them to the kitchen
detail and different depots, where they occupy more than decent
posts. Some of them chose to work in the Mexico *Kommando*, you
know the one I'm talking about—the breakers' yard that's presently
being built next to the men's camp."

After Edek nodded his acknowledgement, Jozek proceeded.

"I haven't the faintest clue as to why they'd choose such a
doubtful *Kommando* as the work in the Mexico is hard. Rumor
has it, it has something to do with either ethyl or methyl they
extract from downed airplane parts they disassemble, which they
purify somehow and turn into drinkable alcohol. I personally
doubt that's their primary reason, but the true one is best known
to themselves. At any rate, tell your friend to leave the Russians to
their devices and keep to himself, at least in the beginning. They

have their own hierarchy, leaders, and justice system there and sort all problems among themselves. If he manages to earn the friendship and respect of the men in charge, he'll fare just fine. Kapo Jupp himself fears them as they've murdered a few of his inferiors who made a mistake of putting their nose in the Soviets' business. Now, he steers clear of them. So, I'd say, if your comrade plays his cards right, he can turn his punishment into quite a favorable position. As long as he doesn't antagonize anyone… dangerous," he finished somewhat ominously.

After thanking the man profusely, Edek burst into a run and didn't slow down until he reached Block 8. However, despite his haste, he appeared to be too late. The fight was already in progress.

In horror, Edek watched his best friend locked in a deadly embrace with his Soviet opponent, who towered over Wiesław with his powerful build, muscles bulging on his neck and shoulders. Cheered on by the rest of the block, they struggled right near the entrance of the barracks, punching and kicking each other in earnest. Their faces bloodied and torn, they were breathing heavily as they circled one another before tearing at each other's throats with almost suicidal determination.

As though under some demented spell, Edek saw a semicircle of faces surrounding them, their eyes trained greedily at the fighting men, hearing them shout encouragement in their strange language, as he dreaded the outcome of the entire rotten affair. No matter who won the fight, Wiesław would have it. Either his opponent would kill him with a well-aimed blow to the temple or they would all pounce on him and murder him, the new, green-horned block clerk, right there and then.

A gasping, pale-faced block elder ran out of his room and pushed his way toward the two fighters. But his attempt to separate them failed as the Russians yanked him back by the scruff of his neck, demanding he let the pair sort their business themselves. No authority except their own martial law existed for these savage, battle-hardened men, it suddenly dawned on Edek as he watched the helpless block elder implore them to do something, only to be told to piss off with great disdain.

Dazed, his nerves strained to the utmost, Edek glanced around the block in the hope of finding something, anything, to stop the brawl. His gaze landed on a bucket of water that stood by the block entrance. At once, he grasped its metal handle, elbowed his way toward Wiesław and the Russian and doused them both with ice-cold water.

The effect was immediate. Sputtering and gasping, they cleared their eyes and looked around, suddenly confused. Quickly, Edek pulled Wiesław toward him, shielding him with his body. In his eyes was an open challenge to all four hundred Russians who occupied the barracks and whose sharp, hawkish gazes were directed at him from the depths of the dimly lit block.

A tense stillness enveloped the barracks. Not a single person moved. For some time, they appeared to be contemplating something as the silent standoff continued. His breath hot and shallow in his throat, Edek was afraid to blink, not wanting to miss a sudden movement, an attack that could come from anywhere, a sharp blade stuck into his ribs in a split moment of negligence.

Wiesław's adversary slowly turned his head, seeking someone in the thick, still crowd. As though on signal, it parted like a sea, and a rather nondescript man stepped forward. He wasn't tall or powerfully built like the fighter himself, but he bore an air of that silent authority that only revered leaders who had earned it carried about themselves.

He said something in Russian to Wiesław's opponent and, at once, the man obediently nodded and went inside the block, accompanied by the quiet cheers and back claps of his comrades.

The strange Russian remained standing before Edek and Wiesław, his spectacles reflecting the light in such a way that it was almost impossible to see his eyes behind them.

"That was rather foolish of you, making enemies on the first day," he finally uttered in very good German. "We shall write it off as the hotheaded stupidity some of us are prone to whenever they're appointed to a position of even the most insignificant power. However, I would strongly recommend curbing your enthusiasm as a servant to the Nazis. The second time, I won't order them to stand down." With those last words he left hanging ominously in the air, he turned to take his leave, the rest of the Soviets following him closely like a king's entourage.

As soon as they were left alone, Wiesław allowed Edek to lead him back to his room—the only privilege that came with such a rotten appointment. It was small and scarcely furnished, very much like Mala's, but there was a lock on the door, flimsy but at least offering some protection, and that was something.

"What happened?" Edek demanded, tending to his friend's split lip that was swelling in front of his eyes.

"A curfew was announced for our few blocks for whatever reason earlier today, just after the roll call." Wiesław sniffled and wiped the blood that was still dripping from his nose with his sleeve. "The block elder posted me at the door with explicit instructions not to let anyone out and retired to his room to put some papers in order. And then that bastard, Kolya I think his name is, he's some big shot in the kitchen, decided that the rules didn't apply to him and went right past me. I tried to stop him, but he shoved me roughly—you saw that bull's size—and proceeded to the exit. Well, I grasped him by the collar of his shirt. He swung round and dealt me one on the cheek. I reciprocated by blackening his eye. The rest you probably witnessed yourself."

That was putting it mildly. Edek rubbed his eyes. It was all too much for one day. And now, he couldn't leave this poor sod alone with those beasts. They'd eat him for dinner, throw his body outside and report, with the smirks he'd seen on their faces, that the new block clerk had suffered an unfortunate fall from his bunk and broken his neck. How sad. They had just begun to genuinely like him.

No. That just wouldn't do.

Edek placed both palms on Wiesław's shoulders, looking him in the eyes. "Wiesław, you ought to go there and apologize."

For a few moments, his friend appeared to be at a loss for words, staring at Edek in stunned amazement.

"Did you not hear what I have just told you?" he cried at last, his face twisting into a mask of indignation.

"I did. I heard everything." Edek's voice was grave. "And if it was a Pole you were fighting, I'd swipe him a couple on his snout myself. But these are Russians. Actual soldiers, who fought the Nazis while we were still building our own barracks here in Auschwitz. They're warriors and survivors—one has to be to make it through the several years of annihilation the SS have been putting them through. These ones are the toughest of the lot. We can't afford to have them as enemies. It's much smarter to have them as allies. And that's why you'll take this bottle—" Edek produced the same liquor with which he'd attempted to bribe Arbeitsdienst Jozek, "and give it to Kolya as a peace offering. You'll apologize to him and promise that the entire business will never repeat itself."

Something in his tone must have influenced Wiesław better than the words themselves. Slowly, he nodded and took the bottle from Edek's hands. "Will you come with me? In case…"

"Of course." Edek clapped him on the shoulder, rising from the bed. "Do you need to ask?"

Together, they emerged from Wiesław's room and, followed by rows of unblinking eyes, made their way to Kolya's bunk. Hostility no longer marring his broad features, the Russian took the cold compress away from his swollen eye and regarded the two men with interest.

Silently, Wiesław held a bottle in front of him, his hand betraying him with a tremor. The Russian surprised them both greatly by bursting into laughter and patting the spot on his bunk, inviting his guests to share it.

"You—fool, me—fool," he explained amiably in his bad Polish, opening the bottle and handing it to Wiesław first, a gesture that Edek understood sealed their friendship. "Nazis—bad. You—comrade. I fight Nazis, not comrades."

"Yes," Wiesław agreed readily and grasped the bottle by the neck, pumping the Russian's hand with a feeling of kinship that only two men who had just been slaughtering each other could share. "No more fighting among friends."

Chapter 23

"Transferred?"

Mala didn't conceal her alarm at the news Edek had broken. It wasn't Sunday, their agreed-upon "date day"; he'd simply headed to the new ramp under construction masked by the cover of night as he'd done once before. Highlighted by the pale-yellow glare of the overhead lamps, the tracks were cutting further and further between the men's and women's camps—an ugly black scar on the pristine white surface of freshly fallen snow. He'd caught Mala just in time—after delivering written orders to the *Kapo*, she was about to head back to carry out the rest of the night shift along with two other runners.

"What are you going to do about it?" she asked, searching Edek's face with concern. "You can't smuggle a block clerk out of the camp. Wiesław has to belong to an actual *Kommando*."

"There's still time till summer," Edek said, injecting a note of nonchalance into his voice that he didn't truly feel. "More than enough time for the camp authorities to realize that he makes a lousy clerk and dismiss him back to an ordinary work gang."

Mala smiled weakly at him and gave his hand an encouraging pressure.

"Are my eyes playing tricks on me or do the tracks indeed seem to creep closer and closer to the—" Edek stopped himself abruptly, mentally tracing the ominous direction the railway was leading toward.

The crematorium chimneys loomed ahead of them, slumbering deceivingly against the bright arch of temporary overhead lights. The route that took them a good forty minutes just a few weeks ago had turned into a short trek of scarcely fifteen. The banging of the heavy instruments hammering the tracks into the frozen ground echoed eerily around the camp like a ghastly clock measuring time till something mortifying and inevitable. The workers were building the new ramp in double shifts, with deadly efficiency.

"No. Your eyes aren't deceiving you. The new ramp shall be constructed right here." Mala pointed at the still-empty plot of land that separated the men's and women's camp. She paused before speaking in a voice that sent a tremor down Edek's spine, ".I've seen the plans in the camp office. I deliver the orders, too."

Edek felt his ears ringing. The stillness had suddenly turned into a shrill cry of sheer terror. Something was being readied, new ultimate extermination procedures were being laid in place, concealed under the guise of darkness. The skull of the moon grinned down at him with its bare jaws from the indifferent sky. He could swear, if Mala didn't hold his hand just then, he would fall over from that dreadful realization. In his already troubled mind, the words of the Auschwitz historian who used to share his barrack with Edek, materialized: "They'll slaughter us all; mark my words. No one wants us to walk out of here and start telling our stories."

"It's not for us." As though sensing his horrible dread, Mala pressed her hand over his in a reassuring gesture. "Not yet, at any rate. What do we need the ramp for? The ramp is for the new arrivals. We're already here. It's for the Hungarian Jews. The Hungarians thought it to be good business to switch sides in the war but miscalculated. Now Hitler will take his revenge in his favorite manner—obliterating their entire Jewish population. As for us, the Nazis still need us. Who else shall aid them with that mass murder, if not us?"

In the darkness, her pained smile was the only beacon of light that gave him hope. It suddenly occurred to Edek that he couldn't bear parting with her, not just yet.

How will you say goodbye when the time comes? Another thought crept into the corner of his mind, coiling there silently like a snake ready to strike at the moment of vulnerability. Edek let it rest there—for now.

Sunday couldn't come fast enough. Edek counted days and suffered through the sleepless nights, but when it finally arrived, he had suddenly discovered that he wasn't the only guest in Mala's private quarters that evening.

"Forgive me for not warning you in advance," Mala said, pecking him swiftly on his lips. "There was no time. It's an emergency meeting."

Mala's small room appeared even more crowded and thick with cigarette smoke that hung in the air in hazy, gray ringlets. Edek recognized Zippy, who presently sat on Mala's bed; exchanged handshakes with several people he'd never met before. Their faces were grave; their voices subdued. At first glance, it was obvious they belonged to the camp elite. The man sitting on the floor with his legs crossed was clearly from the *Sonderkommando*. The stench of burnt flesh clung to his well-tailored clothes despite the rest of his appearance being well-groomed and neat. Mala introduced him as Konstantinos.

"Kostek."

The hulky man hesitated before offering Edek his hand. Not because it went against his principles to shake hands with a maintenance worker but because so many inmates were disgusted at the prospect of having to shake the gas chamber attendant's palm.

Edek grasped it firmly and offered his name.

A physician from the camp hospital sat on Mala's bed next to Zippy, her off-white gown sporting fresh blood on its sleeve. Mala introduced her as Stasia. He grinned—the inmate doctor was Polish as well.

Two other men sitting by the radiator belonged to the carpenters' crew, judging by their distinctive uniforms. One of them looked familiar. Only when Edek looked closer did he recognize Pavol, the Slovak who had put him in contact with Mala.

Mala herself sat on the only chair like a president of the small assembly. She offered Edek to sit on the bed as well, but he preferred to remain standing by the door, not wanting to crowd the women on Mala's much-too-small cot.

The second carpenter regarded Edek with suspicion at first, but Mala eased his concern with a simple sweep of the hand. "He's one of us. He can be trusted."

Her words appeared to be good enough for everyone present, as the tension on their faces eased.

"Something is brewing with the Family Camp," Mala filled Edek in without any unnecessary preamble.

"The Theresienstadt Jews?" Edek blinked.

Since they had been first brought from the Czechoslovakian Theresienstadt ghetto to Birkenau last September, the Family Camp inmates were considered a curiosity of sorts. Unlike the rest of the new arrivals, they weren't chased through the Reception Block with blows and shouts and abuse; weren't shorn like sheep before being tattooed and hounded through the Sauna's disinfection facility before being herded outside completely naked, shivering with terror and cold. On the contrary, they were escorted inside their new barracks almost cordially by the suddenly soft-spoken SS, treated like welcome guests, allowed to keep their civilian clothes and even suitcases—something unheard of in Auschwitz-Birkenau. Ever since, they lived just as they had arrived, all the families together, while the rest of the camp population, torn from their loved ones, stared at them from behind the barbed wire and scratched their heads uncomprehendingly at such unexpected favoritism.

Only later did the local resistance learn that it was all a sham. That the only reason why the SS tiptoed around their poster Jews was propaganda they kept feeding to the international press, claiming that the Jews were well cared for and provided with everything they needed. The most unfortunate part was that the Red Cross, which sometimes visited German camps with their inspections, swallowed the Nazis' stories without suspecting any malice on their part and ended each visit with offers to provide more humanitarian help to the Jews. The camp administration agreed with great enthusiasm and rubbed their hands in glee behind the Red Cross inspectors' backs, imagining the feast they would organize for themselves with Swiss-supplied goods.

"I said from the very beginning that something was not right with that camp." Zippy was the first one to break the silence. "It was far too good to be true. All those angelic-looking children with their toys, all those women in stockings and high heels, all those former war veterans strolling about as though on parade, with all their regalia in full display. Not in Auschwitz. No," she finished with a categorical shake of her head. "It didn't come to me as a surprise when their local underground confirmed my suspicions that it was all a show for the Swiss."

"The SS made them write postcards to their families and postdate them by one month." Mala's eyes stared at the opposite wall as she spoke. A sharp crease sat between her eyebrows. "Zippy and I were sorting them in the camp office. When I asked Mandl if there was a mistake of some sort with all those incorrect dates, she became very vague and claimed it had something to do with the delay at the censorship office in Berlin."

"Horseshit," Kostek commented at once.

Edek snorted softly at such endearing bluntness. He began to like the *Sonderkommando* fellow more and more.

"They're planning the extermination *Aktion*," Kostek continued. "You can take it from me. I've seen plenty of similar business before. Censorship office, my foot," he scoffed, shaking his head in disgust.

"That's precisely what Zippy and I thought." Mala looked at Kostek. "Hence the meeting. We ought to tell them."

"Suppose we do tell them," Pavol spoke, rolling a cigarette after stubbing out the one he'd just finished in an empty sardine can. "And then what? I've been there countless times. They're the most insufferable, stuck-up herd I've ever seen. They think that Auschwitz rules don't apply to them. Only very few of them suspect that something is cooking. The rest prefer to remain blissfully ignorant and rely on the SS's good graces." He rolled his eyes emphatically.

"But there are underground members among them," Mala insisted.

"Yes, thirty-three out of five thousand," Stasia commented, obviously not impressed by such numbers. "How do you plan to create an uprising out of those measly thirty-plus people?"

"They can act as leaders," Mala persisted, but the physician only waved her off.

"If people don't believe that they're about to be killed, no leader will move them to a revolt," Kostek's tone turned unexpectedly wistful. "Back in 1942, when those monstrosities next to the *Kanada* hadn't been built yet, I was driving a truck full of freshly gassed people back to the old crematorium in Auschwitz. The road we were supposed to take went along the ramp, so we had to go very slowly in order for the bodies not to fall off as we were always overloaded and the road was bumpy. At any rate, as we were crawling forward, I witnessed the following scene: a well-dressed woman, not from a ghetto but some well to-do Jewess from wherever they'd picked her up, was marching toward an SS man on the ramp, her little son in tow. So, she walks up to him and points at one of the *Kanada* men who was taking care of the luggage on the ramp. The poor sod must have tried to warn her that she should let go of her child if she wanted to live… Whatever the case was, she didn't believe him and stormed toward the SS guard instead, almost screaming her accusations about the poor *Kanada* lad. 'Herr

Offizier, that vile criminal has just told me that if I don't let go of my child, we shall both be killed!' The officer looked at her almost apologetically—he knew the deal, no panic on the ramp under any circumstances—and smiled at her in the most benevolent manner. 'Madam, he's criminally insane. His kind, they invent all sorts of wild fantasies. Do you truly think German people are barbarians who kill women and children?' And what do you know? The crowd believed the SS man and not *the criminally insane* inmate."

Kostek patted himself for a packet of cigarettes and lit one absentmindedly. "When she turned to face the *Kanada* lad in triumph, he wasn't there any longer. She couldn't see it from where she was, but I could. Two guards had already dispatched him behind the stocked luggage, so he wouldn't wag his tongue next time. They motioned for me to stop and told me to wait so I could pick up one more body after everyone was gone from the ramp."

Edek watched Mala's reaction as Kostek recounted his story and saw that there was not a trace of surprise in her gaze, only dark melancholy of someone who'd seen it all before.

"They shall see that we were right," the second carpenter said. "Only, it'll be too late."

"Still, it's our duty to try." Mala refused to surrender. She turned to Kostek. "Do you have enough supplies to support the uprising, if they decide to go through with it?"

He pulled on his cigarette, calculating things in his mind. "We have some makeshift bombs and a few guns. The idea is to overpower at least a couple of SS manning the machine guns; then we're in business, ladies and gentlemen."

From his position on the floor, Pavol's fellow carpenter with a Red Triangle on his chest was shaking his head vehemently. "You'll only get us all killed. The plan was start an uprising when the Soviets are nearby so we can run toward them once we break away. Where are you planning to run now? Back into the Nazis' hands? We ought to wait."

"You commies have always had trouble acting on your own initiative." Kostek shook his head in disgust.

"Us commies prefer to think with our heads before we act," the carpenter bared his teeth in a snarl. "If it weren't for us commies," he continued mockingly, "you would have been chased through the chimney instead of stocking it. Forgot who put you in your kosher spot already? The blasted Red Triangles!"

"Enough!" Mala's shout quickly put an end to the discussion. "We ought to work together instead of bickering among each other. I understand that the general population of the Family Camp have trouble believing us. But what if we give them actual proof? Perhaps then they shall act."

"What sort of proof? A signed paper from the camp office?" Zippy chuckled grimly. "Fat chance Mandl will permit us to take that home."

"No." Mala turned to Kostek. "You said your SS supervisors always tell you exactly how many people you should stoke the furnaces for, so you don't waste any… whatever you call that special coal you're using for the ovens?" She snapped her fingers, groping for the needed word that kept escaping her.

"Coke," Kostek supplied, suddenly all attention.

"Well, if the SS tell you to stock the ovens for five thousand people, won't it be proof enough?"

For a long time, Kostek remained silent. At last, he sighed. "Perhaps." His half-shrug didn't deceive anyone. He had not an ounce of faith in such an idea.

After all of them left—one by one, through the same back door leading to the cellar that Edek always used—Edek crouched at Mala's feet and held her hands in his. "Is there anything I can do, Mally?"

For a few moments, it seemed as though she didn't hear him. But then her fingers curled around his and some wild force appeared in her eyes.

"Yes. Yes, you can. Get out of here with as much proof as you have and warn anyone who shall listen of what's going on in Auschwitz, so they don't come here in the first place. So that they get a chance to fight on their own territory. So that, even if they die, they at least take a couple of Nazis with them."

She was fierce, full of hate, and even slightly terrifying as she spoke those words. And it suddenly dawned on Edek that he had never loved anyone as much as he loved her, this new underground leader who had taken up the position no one else wanted to even contemplate out of fear of repercussions, this Amazonian warrior with fire in her blood and ice in her gaze.

Chapter 24

March 1944

After the last snowstorm that had left the camp shrouded in white, the spring crept up and washed off the muddy roads, leaving the barracks roofs dripping with moisture and smelling faintly of wet wood. By the time Edek had reached his former work detail, his heart was pounding against his ribcage with force that rivaled Kapo Vasek's expert blows. His former Kommandoführer Lubusch was his only hope. But what if that hope decided that his own skin was more important than Edek's freedom? What if he laughed at Edek's naiveté and pretended that their conversation never happened? What if he'd gone on leave to his wife and now, after his return, he refused to leave her a widow?

In front of the door leading to Lubusch's office, he took a deep breath in a futile attempt to calm his nerves. He'd worked himself up into such a state that his hand was trembling as he was raising it to rap on the familiar door. He was swaying on his feet, woozy, ashen, damp with sweat under his blue overalls; and he winced imperceptibly at the familiar soft voice issuing permission to come in. Much too soon, he hadn't recollected himself yet—but his hand was already pushing the door open of its own accord. His legs carried him inside; Edek had a vague, out-of-body sensation of clicking his heels and pulling his striped cap off in the practiced gesture. The camp was a ruthless teacher. It had trained them to obey any SS man's order—even half-alive, even shivering with dread, they did what they were ordered to.

"Galiński!" Lubusch rose from his chair, visibly pleased to see his former worker. "You're still alive, old dog?"

Ordinarily, both the SS and the *Kapos* followed up such a rhetorical question with "it's all right, we'll fix that quickly enough" before setting off to work on the unexpectedly resilient inmate with their whips and batons. Yet there was genuine joy in Lubusch's tone. Edek's lips quivered with the oddest mixture of emotions.

"*Jawohl*, Herr Unterscharführer."

He must have stared at the SS man with such wild desperation, Lubusch took pity on him and decided not to torment Edek with the empty exchange of pleasantries.

"I have it." Lubusch said three very simple words, but all at once, Edek felt as though he'd grown wings.

His body almost weightless with a surge of exhilaration, he followed Lubusch's hand with his gaze as the SS officer turned the key in the door with a look of a conspirator about him. His face nearly split in two when his namesake crossed the office, motioning Edek after himself, and extracted a neatly folded SS uniform from the bottom drawer of his desk.

"It's just uniform and a belt; no gun or holster yet. I'll get you those separately. And don't fret. It's been thoroughly deloused."

The joke was not lost on Edek—it was usually the SS who were terrified to catch lice from the inmates, not the other way round—but Lubusch's jest wasn't the reason for the laughter of pure elation that Edek was presently desperately trying to suppress. His fingertips were reaching for the coarse material, skirting the very edge of it. He didn't dare touch the brass buttons that gleamed seductively in the warm light of the room; not yet. It would turn a vague dream into a very real plan and, suddenly, Edek was petrified and excited about the possibility of such a miracle. He'd dreaded it and prayed for it, and now, Lubusch held it before him like some religious, sacrificial offering and, all at once, Edek couldn't catch his breath.

"Well?" Lubusch had to nudge him into action. "Are you planning to stare at it or will you try it on?"

Edek didn't hear him at first. He was still much too lost in his contemplation of the coveted garments.

"Try it on?" Edek blinked, the SS man's words finally reaching him in the depth of his reverie. "Here?"

"Naturally. Or did you wish to parade in it on the *Appellplatz*?" Lubusch was laughing. "Put it on. The door is locked; no one will see you. Except for me, and I have to see how you carry yourself in it. I was thinking about it, you see." He had dropped his jesting at last—it was also from nerves, Edek realized just then—and looked at Edek confidentially. "They can uncover you at once if you do something idiotic while wearing. So I must see how exactly you're planning to go about this."

He stepped away and motioned for Edek to get dressed. Edek took the uniform from his hands with a mixture of revulsion and awe, once again cursing the camp instinct that made him obey authority without allowing any time for hesitation or consideration.

Edek was buttoning the tunic when he caught sight of his own reflection in a mirror that hung on the opposite wall. At once, he was paralyzed with shock. An inmate just a minute ago and now—a master of the world, arrogant and powerful, was glaring back at him from under the uniform cap with a skull and two crossbones.

"After you're done admiring yourself—" Lubusch's voice once again brought him back to himself, "walk over to me and present yourself as you would." He took position by the opposite wall. "Let's imagine I'm the guard who minds the gates. Walk toward me and salute me and report, or whatever it is you've planned to do."

He hadn't quite planned that far, but Edek was famous for thinking on his feet. Pulling his tunic down sharply to make the creases under the belt even more pronounced, he squared his shoulders and walked toward Lubusch, not quite in a rush but with purpose.

Lubusch nodded his approval at the sharp click of his heels and aimed an imaginary rifle at Edek's belly. "I regret to inform you, but you're quite dead at this point."

Edek could only stare at him uncomprehendingly. "But… why? I saluted you just like you asked…"

Releasing a sigh, Lubusch looked like a kind teacher apprehending a failing student. "And that's precisely why you're dead."

Edek followed Lubusch's gaze that had stopped on Edek's right hand in which the SS uniform cap was clasped; at once, he closed his eyes against his own stupidity. No SS officer would tear his hat off. Only the prisoners, trained into the position of slaves, were ordered, under the threat of death, to do so. "Forgive me, Herr Unterscharführer. Camp instinct."

"Exactly what I've been afraid of. Now, salute me as an SS man would."

Edek slammed his heels together and straightened his right arm out. "Heil Hitler!" The words tasted vile on his tongue, but there was no way around them.

Lubusch adjusted his arm slightly. "A bit higher and slightly more to the right. And look me in the eyes when you salute me. You're not an inmate reporting to an officer; you're my equal now. Not even; your rank shall be higher than whoever minds the gate, so look as arrogant as possible."

This time, Edek strolled toward Lubusch, slower than before and with an expression of disdain painted on his face. "Heil Hitler," he said almost conversationally as he clicked his heels, staring straight into the SS man's eyes. The latter nodded appreciatively.

"You're a quick learner, Galiński."

"I have to be, Herr Unterscharführer."

In Auschwitz, only the ones who could adapt survived.

"That much is true." Lubusch's tone turned wistful. He tossed his head, shaking off the melancholy and assuming his role once again. "Heil Hitler, Herr Unterscharführer." He stopped, looking at Edek expectantly.

"Allow me to report—"

"No," Lubusch stopped him abruptly. "You don't report, and you certainly don't ask for a permission to do so. He's only a lowly guard, your subordinate."

"Open the blasted thing—" Edek had picked up on Lubusch's correction at once. "I'm late as it is. This stupid shit's block elder," he motioned to where Wiesław would stand, just by his side, "took his sweet time counting those bloody shits this morning."

Lubusch began to grin. Edek's acting was very convincing indeed. "I apologize, Herr Unterscharführer, but I will need to see accompanying papers. You know the rules…" He spread his arms in a defenseless gesture, smiling apologetically.

Rolling his eyes emphatically, Edek made a big show out of extracting an invisible piece of paper—the *Ausweis* that Mala had gotten for them—out of his breast pocket.

"Happy?" He regarded Lubusch with a thoroughly sour look. "Can I go now, or shall you come up with more bureaucracy?"

That last comment earned him a clap on his shoulder. Lubusch was nearly beaming now. "That'll do," he kept repeating, visibly relieved. "That'll do splendidly."

Edek was looking at him, at the young man's face before him, and thinking what rotten business it was, this war-imposed division, this racial hatred that forced them into opposite camps. In different circumstances, they could have been friends.

"Herr Unterscharführer," he began to say what he didn't dare to even consider before that very moment. "I feel it will be wise for you to go on leave when we—"

Lubusch was already shaking his head. "If the truth comes out, the Gestapo shall get me regardless. It matters not if I'm inside the camp or outside. They are infamous for pulling wanted people from under the ground if needed, and rogue Germans even more so. It really is all right, Edek."

Edek's head shot up. Lubusch's grip on his bicep tightened—an oddly friendly, don't-worry-your-stupid-head-about-anything gesture.

"I've already decided everything for myself. I've never been a murderer, but I have been an accomplice to murder. If this is the only right thing I do in my life, even if I have to pay with my own, that's fine with me. It's a fair enough trade."

"I would still prefer it if you didn't die, Herr Unterscharführer," Edek said, realizing that he sincerely meant it.

"I would prefer it if you made it out of here alive as well, Galiński. Do me a favor and do just that, will you?"

They shook hands, not enemies any longer, but two comrades parting before a difficult battle.

Chapter 25

It was just after lunch when camp leader Schwarzhuber marched inside the office and went straight to Mandl's private room, completely ignoring Mala and Zippy who'd leapt to their feet to greet him. Even after he shut the door behind him, both women remained standing, staring at each other in tense silence. They had grown used to any irregularities in the camp routine meaning trouble for the camp's inhabitants and the officer's preoccupied look and sudden secrecy could mean only one thing: something was happening.

Subdued voices floated from behind the closed door, and abruptly it flew open, revealing a very displeased-looking Schwarzhuber and ashen-faced Mandl at her desk.

"Why am I not hearing your typewriters?" he demanded in his usual cutting manner. "Has anyone ordered you to stop working?"

Mumbling an excuse, Mala and Zippy took their seats and began typing as swiftly as possible, just meaningless words, simply so he would hear the clattering of the keys.

Satisfied, he slammed the door shut once again.

Her head turned sideways, Mala strained to catch at least some snatches of the conversation, but Schwarzhuber was no idiot. Behind the mechanical noise of the typewriters, it was nearly impossible to hear anything at all.

"Anything?" Zippy mouthed at her from across the room.

Mala only shook her head. Zippy's eyes widened when she saw Mala rising from her chair and signaling to her friend to continue to type.

"What are you doing?" Zippy hissed, not daring to raise her voice any higher. "Sit your behind down before you get us both killed!"

But there was far too much at stake to worry about such trifles as one's life. As noiselessly as possible, Mala inched toward the door, pressing her ear against it. She could hear Schwarzhuber talking and, judging by the pauses in the conversation, he was on the phone with someone.

"*Jawohl*, Herr Obersturmbannführer… No, it's no trouble at all. We'll secure the entire perimeter beforehand… Yes. The crematoriums can manage five thousand in one night."

There was obvious pride in the SS man's voice. Mala felt her extremities slowly turning to ice.

"They've already sent the postcards home. Yes. Postdated, as you ordered… We shall be ready to receive the next batch already next week. Yes, of course, you may schedule the next transport. We shall be ready by then—"

Too preoccupied with Schwarzhuber and his sinister plans, Mala entirely forgot about Mandl also being in the room and felt her shoulders jerk when the women's camp leader pulled the door open and came face to face with her. At once, Mala caught Schwarzhuber's sharp glare on her.

"I was just about to knock, Lagerführerin," Mala uttered the words she knew no one would believe. "I wanted to ask if you would like some coffee perhaps."

Mandl didn't have a chance to reply, as Schwarzhuber was already on his feet, promising to call back at once. "An emergency has occurred that needs swift dealing with."

He crossed the office in a few long strides and grasped Mala by her forearm. She thought to protest, to try to weasel her way out of it, to claim that she didn't hear anything as he was dragging her across the room. But she decided to say nothing at all. He would shoot her regardless, so why humiliate herself with begging in her last minutes on earth?

Out of the corner of her eye, Mala saw Mandl standing in the door—pale, wringing hands against her chest—and so very silent.

Mala didn't blame her for that cowardice, for the refusal to stand up for her secretaries. Under the Nazi regime, German women had been conditioned from an early age that a man's word was the law to obey, and particularly if that man was one's superior. It was the price they paid for a slightly longer leash and a measly bit of power thrown at them like a bone.

No, Mala didn't blame her. She simply despised Mandl just then.

On the threshold, Schwarzhuber abruptly came to a halt and swung round, turning to Zippy.

Mala's heart skipped a beat; *No, not Zippy!*

But it was much too late.

"You, Slovak bitch, do you need a special invitation?" He roared at Zippy, digging his fingers even deeper into Mala's arm. She didn't flinch, only watched her friend cross the room hurriedly in utter desperation.

"Herr Lagerführer, please, leave her be." She would never plead for her own life, but Zippy's was something different entirely. "She was typing the entire time, she couldn't possibly hear a single word—"

The officer backhanded her with such force, she instantly tasted blood in her mouth. "Shut your trap!" he bellowed. "Sly Jew-bitches… We appoint you to privileged positions and that's how you repay us? Dirty, scheming tramps!"

He was still raving as he dragged them both after himself down the stairs.

Mala tried to apologize to Zippy, only to receive another three slaps that left her ears ringing.

"Which part of 'shut your trap' do you not understand?!"

Mala had expected him to take them outside and dispatch them both next to the entrance, but instead, he brought them to the cellar.

"You'll stay here until I decide whether to hang you in front of the entire camp or gas you along with your friends from the Family Camp," he snarled, pulling the coal storage door open and shoving both women inside with such force that they landed on their hands and knees, scraping them.

The coal dust raised into the air by the women landing on the ground was still settling long after the SS man had slammed the door shut, bolting it from the outside. Feeling their way around in absolute darkness, Mala and Zippy crawled back toward the door and pressed their backs against it, coughing and rubbing their eyes to clear the black dust.

"Forgive me, please," Mala rasped, searching for Zippy's hand. "You warned me and I didn't listen."

"It's all right. I'm not mad. Well, a little mad, but not at you. I'm mad at myself for being a chicken and not going to that door myself."

Mala couldn't see her friend's face in the darkness, but she could tell that Zippy was smiling.

"We were right then," Mala said, wiping her busted lip with the hem of her skirt. "They *will* gas them. Only, now there's no way to warn them. God damn it," she suddenly cursed out loud and slammed her fist into the metal door.

"Did the door have it coming?"

"No, but I feel slightly better now."

Zippy laughed vacantly and then gasped as something occurred to her.

"What?" Mala tensed up as well.

"Alma's lover, Miklós, lives in the Family Camp. Technically he belongs to Laks' Music Block—Miklós is a pianist—but he specifically requested to be placed in the Family Block after they transferred him from Auschwitz. I think he has friends there, old acquaintances from the music world. He took Alma there once to see a play. She was positively glowing when she told me about it."

"Alma Rosé? Your conductor?"

"Yes." Judging by the sound, Zippy was biting her lips. "God, I hope they don't liquidate him along with the others. Alma loves him to death. She won't survive it."

"I'm sure they'll take him off the list. You said he belongs to Laks' detail. He's not part of the Family Camp."

"The trouble is, one never knows with the SS. Mandl adores his playing though. I can only pray she spares his life just for the sake of his talent. Because if she doesn't, Alma—" She receded abruptly, as though terrified of her own thoughts. "We still have the *Sonderkommando* underground," Zippy continued after a pause, nudging Mala with her shoulder. "The SS must have told them how much coke to prepare for the next *Aktion*. They'll put two and two together. Kostek will warn them in time. There's still a chance that there may be an uprising."

"Even better. There will be an uprising and we'll sit it out in this blasted basement. I wish he would have just shot us and got it over with." The sarcasm in Mala's voice was evident.

"Speak for yourself, Joan of Arc. I rather enjoy my life. And don't arch your brow at me; I know you're doing it even if I can't see your face."

"It's for the best that you can't see my face. Whether they hang us or gas us, I'll look like a right beauty for the occasion, thanks to Herr Lagerführer."

"Does it hurt?" Zippy dropped her jesting, her tone growing concerned.

"Only my heart."

Engulfed by the darkness, they both went silent, knowing what the other was suffering.

*

As soon as an SS man appeared in their block and demanded whether anyone could drive a truck, Edek knew that something was up. With a deep sinking feeling in the pit of his stomach, he volunteered for the task and was immediately driven toward the camp's garage with shouts and blows. He'd grown tender and rather spoiled in the fitters' detail; the block elder was a decent enough fellow and the *Kapos* didn't slave-drive them too much. Even the SS left them pretty much alone, but today it was Edek's profound suspicion that something major was occurring that had gotten the guards so agitated.

No one told them anything specific. The SS merely shoved them toward their respective trucks—there were sixty or even more of those altogether, according to Edek's quick calculations—and told them to follow the leader. That was the extent of the instructions.

Next came the *Kapos*. Some vicious-looking, hulky Green Triangles with the faces of murderers and heavy wooden batons clutched firmly in their great paws. Like a small, well-trained army, they hopped into the trucks and pulled the tarpaulin down as though to conceal their presence from the general camp population. Edek didn't like the sight of them at all.

The sheer amount of SS, in steel helmets, with submachine guns at the ready and dogs straining on the leashes they held wrapped around their wrists, stunned Edek as the column of trucks crawled slowly forward along the main camp street—Lagerstraße. They were virtually everywhere, grim and watchful, seemingly waiting for any sign of a revolt to exterminate at the root at once. His fingers clasping the steering wheel with such force that his knuckles turned white, Edek knew that there could be only one explanation for the gray-green mass of uniforms and steel.

The Family Camp would die that day.

He still hoped for some miracle against all reason; hoped that they would pass the Family Camp and drive forward; that there was, perhaps, some logical explanation. Perhaps, farmers needed trucks for—

Dejectedly, he released a ragged breath and shook his head. *Farmers, his foot. And the SS were there to guard the potatoes, no doubt.*

Of course, there were no farmers and no reasonable explanation.

Once the truck leading the procession turned into a muddy semblance of a road leading to the Family Camp, all of Edek's hopes were obliterated. Here, there were even more SS, even more machine gun squads, more Alsatians foaming at their mouths as they pulled on the leashes of their uniformed handlers. They were driving inside the perimeter now, pulling to a stop next to the barracks. Inside Edek's chest, his heart was thumping furiously.

Not a person was outside. For an instant, Edek was gripped by a desperate hope that the underground had warned the camp's inhabitants, that they had barricaded themselves inside, that there would be a battle, an uprising, in which he would join, even if it meant being mowed down by the steel shower of SS machine guns within seconds.

Didn't Mala say that the *Sonderkommando* were making bombs? To be sure, they would share them with the Family Camp's underground. Perhaps they'd even give their Theresienstadt counterparts their entire stash and distract the SS by sabotaging a crematorium…

But there was no uprising. The Green Triangles were already pouring out of the trucks and inside the barracks, from which they instantly began to drive out the terrified Family Camp inmates with blows and crude curses.

"*Raus, raus, raus!* Out, out, everyone, now, you bloody shits!"

They were beating everyone indiscriminately, women and the elderly and children too, herding them toward the trucks with truly horrifying efficiency. From the safety of his vehicle, Edek watched the tragedy unfold in real time. For an instant, the sheer inhumanity of it made it appear almost unreal.

In front of Edek's truck's hood, an elderly musician was cradling his violin case against his chest like a child; trying to explain something to one of the German murderers in a polite tone. The *Kapo* listened for exactly five seconds, then yanked the case out of the old man's hands, hurled it to the ground and began stomping on it with savage force. Not a muscle moved on the musician's face, but from under his rimless glasses, heavy tears rolled, collecting under his chin. He didn't have to mourn his instrument's loss for long: the same *Kapo* swung his club and dropped it precisely on top of the violinist's head. Blood pouring down his face, the man sank softly to his knees, swayed ever so slightly and keeled over, his bloodied hand landing atop his crushed instrument as though in some devastating farewell.

An SS guard stomped into the scene, his sense of order outraged. The Berlin office had ordered for the Family Camp to be gassed, so they ought to be gassed and not clubbed, according to the SS man's tirade. To Edek, it appeared almost ghastly amusing that the officer was berating his inferior not for killing the musician—some brilliant virtuoso, no doubt, whom the entire music world would mourn—but for killing him at the wrong place, at the wrong time, and in the incorrect manner. Then, both figures in front of Edek's eyes began to blur and he rubbed his eyes viciously, swallowing hard and biting his tongue when the swallowing didn't help any longer.

In the truck just in front of him, a man in a three-piece suit was helping a mother lift her child inside. The little girl with a big blue bow in her blond hair was still clutching a stuffed rabbit to her chest. Edek saw another SS man shake his head and turn away, spitting on the ground. His colleague, who was watching the mother closely, commented something to the effect of "a fine piece of tail going to waste," but the first guard didn't join in with the joke; only glared at him with hatred and told him to shut his ugly mug right that instant. It suddenly occurred to Edek that even some of the calloused SS men found the picture of such heartless annihilation unraveling before their eyes appalling. Or, perhaps, this particular one also had a blond little girl at home who this child reminded him of. Whatever the case was, the German marched off as though washing his hands of the entire bloody affair.

In the midst of all that violence and destruction, a couple caught Edek's attention. They stood, holding each other and speaking softly to one another while waves of bloodied people washed around them, without touching them, as though they were an island of love and serenity that even death had no power over. The young man clearly belonged to the camp elite with his riding breeches and tall boots; a *Kapo* or a clerk of some sort—Edek couldn't quite make out what precisely his armband said. His beloved, into whose mahogany eyes he was gazing with infinite adoration and profound sorrow, was dressed with great taste in civilian clothing. The Family Camp girl, Edek concluded to himself and rubbed his chest, the spot that was aching dully at that devastating sight before him, for he knew very well how such farewells ended in the hell of Auschwitz-Birkenau.

He tried not to think of Mala, yet he couldn't stop himself. He saw her face in place of this young girl's; he imagined having to kiss her goodbye for the last time and averted his eyes—it was too much to bear.

"Get that bitch up in the truck!" a coarse voice shouted. "There's no time for screwing!"

With tremendous effort, Edek turned back to the couple. The young man was still saying something to his beloved, completely ignoring his *Kapo* colleague and his baton, with which he was administering cracks to anyone who happened to be within reach.

"Well?" The *Kapo* stopped short from grabbing the girl by her arm, restraining himself out of respect to the fellow inmate functionary. The young block clerk's girl was about to die; the least he could do was not manhandle her roughly. "The bitch goes onto that truck this instant or you both go."

At once, the girl stepped away. Her pale hand lingered on the young man's face that was twisted with tragedy; he made a move after her, but she shook her head and jumped into the bed of the truck.

An SS man slapped the hood of Edek's lorry, signaling that it was full. With a heavy heart, Edek pulled away from the spot where the bereft man still stood, gazing after the departing vehicles, and his departing lover, with a look of someone who had been mortally wounded.

The drive was oddly, frighteningly quiet. Outside, the dusk crept over the barracks, entangling itself in the barbed wire. Rigid with horror, Edek followed the leader of the column like some demented automaton. His hands turned the wheel, his feet pressed on the gas pedal, and all the while his mind screamed in agony at the sight of the crematorium toward which they'd been creeping—accomplices in murder and future victims, all wrapped in one. Not a sound came from the bed of the truck. Only after the lorries pulled to a stop and the SS began tearing children out of mothers' arms did the blood-curdling cries break the deathly silence. Edek sat at the wheel with his eyes shut painfully tight and felt as though the entire world wept together with them.

And then, a young woman's voice tore through the fiber of the terror, clear and high, singing the Czech national anthem with fearless determination. Stunned by the sheer power of it, Edek opened his eyes and recognized the block clerk's girl—a sole motionless figure in the ocean of chaos. Soon, more voices joined in; the SS tried to club and whip them into submission, but in vain. Before long, the entire camp had picked up the notes of the resistance and carried them long and far above the land, defiant and proud, refusing to surrender even at the sight of the approaching, unavoidable death.

Edek saw the young block clerk again near the entrance of the crematorium the next morning when he inquired about Mala, who was nowhere to be found. Kostek was just in the middle of assuring Edek that he had nothing to worry about—Mala wasn't among those poor wretches they'd been cremating all night—when the same man, torn from his lover the day before, staggered on uncertain legs toward the entrance.

At first, Edek assumed that he was drunk. But when the young man stopped next to him and began to speak—tried to speak, with carefully faked nonchalance but with a voice that was hoarse and shaking in spite of it—Edek realized that he was perfectly sober.

"How did it go yesterday?" he asked.

"All right," Kostek replied, throwing a warning glance at his *Kommando* mate, who was smoking next to him. Filip, if Edek remembered correctly. He was too preoccupied with Mala's whereabouts and forgot the lad's name right after they'd been introduced to each other. "It was a dry night. They didn't suffer."

The *Sonderkommando* were specialists in Zyklon-B now. They knew exactly in which conditions it performed most efficiently.

Kostek spat on the ground in disgust.

"Three girls tried to fight—" Filip began.

The young clerk's head shot up. But Filip had already clammed up after receiving a sharp blow in his ribs from his Greek mate.

"No one suffered," Kostek said evenly once again. "Everyone went very quickly and as painlessly as possible."

"Go back to your barracks and sleep it off, Rudek." Filip regarded the young clerk with genuine sympathy and offered him a cigarette. Rudek took it with trembling fingers. "And don't torture yourself over it. What good would it have been if you both went into that truck?"

Edek watched Rudek nod and suddenly realized that he would have jumped without a second thought into the back of that blasted lorry just to hold Mala's hand for a few minutes, to be with her till the last dying breath, to hold her in his embrace just so she wouldn't feel alone and terrified, among strangers. He didn't judge this young man in the slightest, but deep inside, he'd already come to a decision. He would live with Mala or he would die with her. For him, there was no other option.

Chapter 26

The door to the coal room swung open. The light in the cellar's corridor was dim and yet Mala and Zippy felt momentarily blinded. In the door stood the same inmate who had brought them two buckets the previous evening—one with water and one to use for their needs. Only this time, instead of a warden, Mandl herself stood behind the prisoner functionary's shoulder.

"Don't touch them," Mandl said when she saw Mala reach for one of the buckets. Her voice sounded oddly tired. "Lena will take care of those." She nudged the inmate from the maintenance *Kommando* forward. "Out with you two. You're lucky I managed to persuade Schwarzhuber that it'll be impossible to find suitable replacements for you two. He had worked himself up into such a state, he was ready to send you both to the gas along with the Czechs."

Mala considered thanking their benefactress for her intervention, but with the best will in the world, she couldn't force the words out of herself. She too had worked herself into quite a state, while being locked in that dusty, dark cellar. Her loathing for Mandl, for the SS in general, had increased tenfold and now there was no going back to her previous compliant self.

"Go to the Sauna and put yourself into a presentable state," Mandl continued. "You two look like chimney sweeps; I can't have you in the office in this condition."

"Lagerführerin, may I check on the orchestra?" Zippy searched Mandl's face.

Mala saw the SS woman cringe ever so slightly, as though that was precisely the matter she wished to avoid.

"Yes," the women's camp leader said at last after a long pause, averting her gaze. Her discomfort was audible in her voice. "I was planning to send you there at any rate. Fetch Alma Rosé. Tell her I want to see her in my office."

Zippy stopped in her tracks, her hand clasping her mouth.

Mandl turned to face her, annoyed. "What?"

"You killed him," Zippy whispered with barely suppressed emotion. "You didn't take Miklós off the list. You knew how much she loved him and you killed him."

"It was an accident!" Mandl's shout reverberated along the cellar's walls. Her cheeks were blotched in red patches—either from shame or indignation or a mixture of both. "If I wasn't so preoccupied with saving your sorry lives, I would have remembered to take him off the list. Whatever was he doing in the Family Camp at any rate? He was a pianist; he was supposed to live in Laks' block. It's not my fault… I can't remember every single inmate…"

She was still going on and Mala stood, staring at her and wondering how she could live with herself and justify her actions.

Hypocrite.

Murderer.

Mala's expression must have been much too eloquent, for Mandl shouted at her, visibly unnerved: "Quit your staring! You ought to be grateful for what I did for you. Off to the Sauna, now! And report to the office in thirty minutes precisely."

She stormed off, leaving Zippy crying softly and Mala enveloped in cold, hateful silence.

Alma Rosé, the celebrated violinist virtuoso and women's Music Block conductor, came into the office precisely at ten. She sat across Mandl's desk, deathly pale and silent, and stoically bore all of Mandl's fussing and explanations that mattered little and helped even less.

"Ach, what a frightful night for all of us." Mandl's tutting and incessant head-shaking and sorrowful, guilty looks she threw Alma's way—truly pitiful attempts at displaying sympathy—made Mala cringe inwardly with disgust. "Mala, go. No need to loiter here. No, actually, wait! Bring us coffee, will you? There's a good girl. A frightful night indeed. I, myself, haven't slept a wink. Those liquidation orders came out of nowhere..."

Heavy silence followed, drowning Mandl's hypocrisy, her pretense at pity and compassion Mala knew the women's camp leader was simply incapable of. Mala purposely took her time fixing the coffee tray in the neighboring room just to torment the chief warden with that nerve-grating stillness, interrupted only by the squeaking of Mandl's chair.

Let the bitch squirm. Let her deal with the consequences of her actions at least once. Let her look in her favorite mascot's eyes and choke on her excuses for murdering the only person who still kept the violinist alive in this hell.

When the pregnant pause had grown intolerable, Mala lifted the tray off the table, pushed the door open with her shoulder and could scarcely suppress a sneer at the visible relief on Mandl's face.

"Ah, there you are! I had begun to think that you had lost your way."

Mala didn't deem the jab worthy of a reply. Alma's suffering occupied all of her thoughts. The haunted look in the violinist's eyes nearly tore at Mala's heart. She felt Alma's pain sharply in her own chest as she was pouring coffee for the camp leader and her distinguished guest.

As though sensing the silent comradery between the two women inmates, Mandl pushed Mala's hands away. "Just put it down and go. Go! I can do everything myself. No need to loiter here."

Lagerführerin Mandl serving coffee to a prisoner? With a tremendous effort, Mala restrained herself from arching a sardonic brow. She was truly growing despondent, the Birkenau Beast.

They always fussed over the celebrated Frau Rosé; the countless privileges afforded to the Music Block testified to that. But now, Mandl's fussing had notes of desperation to it.

Alma hardly reacted to the camp leader's words; it was as if she had already decided that she didn't belong to the camp any longer and, suddenly, Mandl was terrified at the prospect of losing her favorite pet whose playing she so enjoyed.

Before taking her reluctant leave, Mala stood just by Alma's shoulder in silent solidarity and thought of Edek. She suddenly realized that she, too, wouldn't want to live without him; that she, too, would follow him wherever he went—to hell, if that's what it meant. As long as they were together, even hell would be a fine place. This camp had already proved it to be true.

When Mala saw Edek shifting from one foot to the other in the door of the office—he had smuggled himself through all of the SS officials somehow—a beaming smile warmed her face at once.

"Inmate number 531 reporting," he said, clicking his heels smartly at the SS officer who regarded him with displeasure. "Kapo Jupp told me you need some pipes to be checked in the cellar?"

"I'll take care of it." Mala was already on her feet, sailing past the SS man and toward Edek.

It took him great effort not to scoop her into his embrace right there and then.

As soon as they were alone in the cellar, he dropped his fitter's toolbox and took Mala's face in his hands, regarding it tragically: the red, angry slash cutting across her swollen mouth—the Nazi punishment for opening it when she shouldn't have; the slightly faded, purplish imprint of a heavy SS palm on the marble of her cheek. "Mally, my dear, dear Mally! What have they done to you?"

"Freshened up my principles for listening at the door to my superiors' private conversations." Mala laughed in spite of herself.

"Considering what I overheard, I expected Schwarzhuber to shoot me. He satisfied himself with giving my curious mug a couple of slaps. I ought to consider myself fortunate. Don't just stand there, kiss me. I've lived through such torture for these past few hours, I need to reassure myself that love still exists in this world."

As though he'd been waiting for that invitation, Edek rushed to cover her face with kisses. She laughed softly and winced when his mouth brushed her broken lip and the skin on her cheek that was slightly discolored from Schwarzhuber's slaps, but not once did she pull away.

"I have decided everything," Edek breathed. "I'm not going anywhere. I'm staying here with you."

"I have decided everything too." Mala grinned, stroking his unshaven cheek. "I'll go with you if you want me to."

For an instant, Edek had lost all faculty of speech. "You will?" he asked at last.

Mala only nodded, offering him her bruised face again.

Thoughts swarming in his mind like a disturbed beehive, Edek hammered absently at the roof in the new Mexico compound, next to the Russians from Wiesław's block.

"Where your head today, comrade?" Kolya called to him jokingly in his bad Polish after Edek hissed in pain and brought his finger, throbbing, to his mouth. "Try get yourself in sickbay with broken hand? Hammer for roof, not fingers!"

After spending nearly every evening in Wiesław's block, Edek had grown friendly with the Soviet prisoners of war. They were strange men, secretive and slightly frightening still. What appeared to be lack of discipline and snubbing of authority to an outsider was, in fact, the strictest set of rules that guided all of their decision-making. After befriending the one they'd addressed as the Professor, the man who had brokered peace between Wiesław and Kolya (it was Edek's most profound conviction that the Professor was a senior officer who had only survived because his men had remained silent and thus saved his life), Edek realized that they had their own system of justice as well. If they suspected an informant within their ranks, they court-martialed him on the spot and submitted an official report to their new block clerk Wiesław—*number so-and-so fell off his bunk and broke his neck, make sure you take him off your list for this morning's roll call*—with unemotional, still faces. Wiesław shuddered each time he recounted the affair to Edek.

But their cold-blooded sense of justice rivaled only their hot-hearted sense of brotherhood and loyalty that Edek had never encountered among the other nationalities inside the camp. Either it was their political ideology that held them together like glue—the worst offense he'd heard from the Soviets was that something was not a behavior worthy of a good communist, which invariably sent the offender hanging his head in shame—or their military code, but they stuck by each other with the tightness of a wolf pack and snapped their teeth at outsiders who threatened their members.

What amazed Edek the most was how organized and well-informed the Russians were. The Professor and Kolya, his adjutant of sorts who followed on his heels and watched after his master with the loyalty of a guard dog, brought newspapers into Wiesław's private room and shared the frontline news with their block clerk and Edek in exchange for some vodka and tinned sardines. To Edek's question as to where they were procuring such dangerous contraband—anyone found in possession of a newspaper was automatically sentenced to several weeks in a *Strafblock,* the dreaded prison barracks with their standing cells, which few could brag about surviving—the Professor had only grinned slyly.

"There are many civilians working in the Mexico compound, where the breakers' yard is and where we disassemble the downed airplanes," he'd explained in his impeccable German, his language of choice. "Some of them are sincere sympathizers. Some are savvy enough to know what's good for them in view of the Red Army approaching. They consider it good business to aid us with whatever we need."

And suddenly, the words uttered by Jozek, the inmate in charge of assigning prisoners to different blocks and work details, about why the Russians worked in such a difficult unit began to make a whole lot of sense. They had their civilian connections there. The war was still going on and they were already plotting for the future. However, as Edek had recently discovered, there was another reason.

"Summer is coming," the Professor had declared during one of their evening meetings, his eyes once again concealed behind his spectacles reflecting the light at an odd angle. "Perfect timing for joining the partisans in the forests."

So, contrary to their belief, Edek and Wiesław weren't the only ones entertaining the idea of an escape. The Russians had their own plans and their own escape route they were presently preparing somewhere in the Mexico compound—at least such was Edek's personal conviction.

Pulling himself out of his musings with difficulty, Edek moved closer to Kolya. "Comrade," he began in a very soft voice. "Do you think it's possible to smuggle a woman out of here?"

Even if Kolya was surprised, his broad face betrayed nothing. "A woman?" he considered, positioning a plank into its place. "Possible. You just have to dress her like man."

At first, Edek turned away, annoyed by the dismissive attitude. But a moment later, when it struck him that Kolya was very much serious and the simplicity of such a plan could be just the solution he had been searching for, he grasped the Russian's great hand and shook it with great emotion. "Thank you, comrade. You have just saved my life!"

"Not if you get caught with your lady friend," Kolya joked in his usual grim way, but nothing could dampen Edek's spirits.

A warm spring breeze caressed his face and he closed his eyes against it. For the first time in years, he smelled freedom in the air—his and Mala's.

Chapter 27

Mala was alone in the camp office that gray, dreary afternoon. Drafts howled in the deserted hallways; the heavy dome of the sky pressed down upon the camp like a coffin lid and the chill clung to Mala's ankles; death was in the air.

Just a night ago, Zippy's worst fears had materialized: her dear friend and mentor, the beloved Birkenau orchestra conductor Alma Rosé had taken her last breath at the camp sickbay and even the infamous Dr. Mengele who'd been summoned to her deathbed wasn't able to save the celebrated violinist. He'd been visibly upset, Zippy had announced, her eyes wet with unshed tears. It appeared that the one whom they rightfully called the Angel of Death had been genuinely fond of Frau Alma's playing.

Mandl was also openly mourning her favorite mascot's death. When Zippy asked if a memorial service could have been arranged for Alma, the women's camp leader displayed a surprising degree of enthusiasm and even went as far as permitting Zippy to organize funeral wreaths for the Music Block and the sickbay, where the late conductor's body was presently lying—washed, dressed, and mourned by both inmates and SS personnel.

Mandl herself kept blowing her nose in her private office and powdering her face deathly white, but Mala still noticed her puffy skin and red-rimmed eyes. Though, to the SS woman, Alma Rosé's death was a personal inconvenience more than anything. The camp leader wept for her with the injured look of a spoiled child who'd just broken their favorite toy.

"How could she do that to me?" That was the question she repeated with sincerest self-pity in front of stony-faced Zippy, vainly searching for sympathy in the inmate's face. "I always treated her exceptionally well... Granted her all the privileges she asked for."

Except for the most important one—saving Alma's beloved pianist's life.

No one said anything officially, but Zippy confided in Mala that it was poison.

"Poor Almschi just couldn't take it anymore. After Miklós died, something died in her also. She went through the motions like a ghost, but the light was gone out of her eyes; the entire orchestra could see it." A single tear rolled down Zippy's drawn cheek. Under her eyes, devastated by such a personal loss, dark shadows lay. "He was the only person who gave her hope in this hell. Without him, life itself lost all meaning."

Now, left alone in the office after Zippy and Mandl had gone to bid their farewells to Alma at the sickbay, Mala found herself replaying Zippy's last words in her mind. She felt them deep in the pit of her stomach that kept contracting painfully with every breath.

He was the only person who gave her hope in this hell. Without him, life itself lost all meaning.

She understood Alma's decision perfectly well just then. If she lost Edek to this camp, she wouldn't want to prolong her senseless suffering either.

Before her, on the unusually cluttered desk, an order for a transfer lay addressed to camp leader Hössler. From its yellowish page, Hauptscharführer Moll's name stared back at her in Gothic script as though mocking her with its foul presence.

With a moan, Mala wiped her hands down her face.

He was the only person who gave her hope in this hell.

"Edek, I'll run with you," she whispered under her breath, "just take me away from here, for if I stay, I shall end up just like Alma."

Just then, familiar navy-blue overalls appeared in the periphery of her vision. Exhilarated, she was about to leap to her feet but ended up slumping back into her chair, disappointed.

"Sorry." The bear of a man, who was shifting from one leg to another in the doorway, grinned at her in apparent embarrassment. "I take it you were expecting someone else?"

"No, Jerzy." Swiftly recovering herself, Mala greeted the Polish giant with an artificial, bright smile. "Come in. Can I help you with something?"

Just like Edek, Jerzy Sadczykow also belonged to the fitters' Kommando. He was built like a professional boxer and had a face that intimidated even the infamous camp Kapo Jupp, but Mala was well aware that behind that threatening exterior beat the most loyal, kindest heart of pure gold. Also a camp underground member, Jerzy was held in high regard by Kostek and his mates from the *Sonderkommando* for procuring countless contraband for their cause from the main camp Auschwitz, where the Pole mostly worked.

"Are you all by yourself?" Jerzy asked in an undertone, maneuvering his giant frame between Mala's desk and the radiator—a convincing disguise of a typical fitter at work, in case one SS or the other decided to stick their curious mugs into the office.

"Yes. Mandl and Zippy are at the sickbay, saying their goodbyes to Frau Alma."

"That poor lady." Jerzy shook his head, genuinely upset. "I heard her play several times. Such talent. Such a shame."

A sad smile tugged at the corners of Mala's lips. Jerzy was a man of few words, but somehow, he always managed to express precisely what everyone was feeling.

"So what was it that you needed?" Mala inquired, all business once again. She knew that his visits meant only one thing: some resistance affair was presently in planning.

"A razor or a hunting knife," he replied in his usual conversational manner, as though listing products for the grocer from his shopping list. "Preferably two, but one will do. The sharper the better."

Mala couldn't help but arch her brow. "How many necks are you thinking to slit?"

"It's not for me," Jerzy explained, poking at the radiator half-heartedly with his wrench. "The *Sonderkommando* are organizing an escape for a couple of fellows. From what they told me, one of the men will be carrying certain compromising documents on his person. In case he gets caught, he'll slash his own throat, just like his comrade, so that the Political Department won't be able to get the names of their accomplices out of them."

Silent and forlorn, Mala rubbed at her chest discreetly. All at once, a tightness gripped it, making it difficult to breathe. It overcame her just then, all these deaths, these voluntary deaths, so very avoidable and devastating.

"Do I know them?" she asked weakly.

Jerzy didn't reply at once, working things out in his mind. "I don't think so," he replied at last. Mala wasn't quite sure whether he truly meant it or said it just to ease the burden for her, the person who procured the weapons that would ultimately spill friendly blood.

Releasing a difficult breath, she nodded, determination once again entering her voice. "I have a Soviet girl, Rita, whom I personally assigned to the *Kanada* detail. She'll get you the goods. Come and see me tomorrow, same time. I'll have them ready for you."

Comforted by the promise and visibly relieved, Jerzy grasped Mala's narrow palm in his bear paw and gave it a gentle but thorough shake. "You're a good comrade, Mala. I hope I'll be able to reciprocate someday."

Mala watched him go with a pensive look about her, a wild mixture of melancholy and the most desperate hope alight in her eyes.

Perhaps.

Someday.

*

"I visited Lubusch again. He promised to give me an SS holster and gun tomorrow," Edek informed Wiesław as soon as the two exchanged warm handshakes. A week had passed since his conversation with Kolya which prompted Edek to renew his plotting with even more enthusiasm. "I suppose your recent appointment as a block clerk was a blessing in disguise after all. I'll pass it to you during lunch break and you can hide it in your room. Everyone will be out working, so no one shall see."

"My room is subject to periodic searches by the SS, since, you know, I have history." Wiesław grinned crookedly. "But I made a special hiding place under the floorboards in the bread store, pushing a cupboard to cover the spot."

"Even better." Edek clapped him amicably on his back. "I'll send someone with the message when the goods are ready. We'll have to pass it through the wire. Lubusch will give it to me in his office; I can't risk going through any checkpoints with a hidden SS holster and gun."

"Of course not," Wiesław agreed emphatically.

"Watch for Kapo Jupp though. You know how he's famous for patrolling the area."

Edek's suspicions turned out to be justified. The *Kapo* was stalking the area near the ramp with a vigilance that would make any SS man proud. Only, his interest in the wire was purely self-serving: he simply confiscated his "share" and let the inmate go with a blessing in the form of a kick to the backside.

The afternoon descended upon the camp. A warm spring breeze, gentle and fresh, caressed his skin. Change was in the air; it smelled of hope and new beginnings and Edek inhaled it greedily, filled his lungs until he grew lightheaded and just a little bit drunk on the promise of it. Edek had very little time to spare—he was supposed to report back to his *Kommando* in fifteen minutes and, instead, he smoked and pretended to chat nonchalantly with Wiesław through the wire while Jupp watched them both with his hawk's eyes.

"Will he never leave off?" Edek grumbled through his teeth. He felt nervous, sweat dampening his back. The hidden gun singed through his clothes like a red-hot poker. "Lunch break is almost over. I can't go back to my *Kommando* with a blasted gun on me."

"Just wait a little more." Wiesław was smoking in agitation too. "He'll lose interest in us soon."

At last, Jupp spotted new victims a little further away and descended upon them with truly impressive speed.

As swiftly as possible, Edek unbuttoned his jacket and shoved the gun with its holster under the wire and straight into Wiesław's awaiting hands. His eyes never leaving the *Kapo*, Wiesław pulled all of his clothes up and quickly fastened the belt atop his bare skin, pushing the holster against his shoulder. By the time Jupp turned to face them, already pocketing some commandeered contraband, Wiesław had adjusted his clothes and was walking away from the wire in the opposite direction from Edek.

"Hey, you! *Schreiber!*"

Edek's breath caught. He had nothing to fear—Jupp was on Wiesław's side, but his stomach plummeted all the same. Not risking openly stopping, Edek threw a glance over his shoulder.

"What have you got there, *Schreiber?*" Jupp was already poking Wiesław in his stomach with his *Kapo*'s stick.

In utmost horror, his heart beating wildly in his throat, Edek watched his friend hang his head and unbutton his jacket.

Dead. Both of us.

"The real stuff?" Jupp demanded, tossing his head at Wiesław's belly.

Only then did Edek see the neck of a bottle poking from under the belt of his comrade's breeches. Edek nearly laughed in relief. *The old fox,* he thought, shaking his head at Wiesław's ingenuity for smuggling the bottle which Edek suspected was Soviet-supplied vodka as bait.

Kapo Jupp, meanwhile, was passing the parcel he'd commandeered from another inmate to Wiesław.

"Take it to the block and wait for me before you open that bottle, hear me?"

Wiesław dutifully clicked his heels.

"Run along, *Schreiber*." Jupp laughed. "Today the Camp Kapo shall have a feast."

That evening, while Jupp was drinking himself unconscious, Edek and Wiesław sat near the cupboard under which their ticket to freedom was buried and toasted the *Kapo* with broad smiles. Without uttering a word, exchanging conspirators' looks, they toasted to Lubusch and Szymlak and the Polish partisans they planned to join. If Jupp was drinking to his own health, they were drinking to freedom.

Chapter 28

April 9, 1944

There had been another escape. Two days later, the SS were still stalking about the camp with their Alsatians in tow, staring everyone down suspiciously. The culprits had miraculously avoided capture so far and, with each passing day, Edek's hopes soared higher and higher. He didn't even mind being stopped a few times on his way to Crematorium V, near which Mala and he had agreed to meet; fortunately, his innocent look and his toolbox, which pretty much explained his presence anywhere in the camp, saved him from further harassment.

When he finally made it to the crematorium, he saw that Mala wasn't alone. Hands jammed in the pockets of her coat, she was talking animatedly with Kostek and his *Sonderkommando* mate, Filip.

Much to his astonishment, Edek recognized another familiar face in a group of conspirators. Jerzy Sadczykow, one of the fitters who shared the same block with him, smoked a cigarette with his gaze trained on the Mexico compound looming in the distance. Astonishment reflected on his face when he noticed Edek approaching his group.

"Are you…?" Sadczykow managed only two words, a look of disbelief creasing his brow.

"Yes." It was Mala who replied to his unfinished question with a wry grin. "Edek's with us as well."

"I'll be." Laconic as always, Jerzy only replaced his cigarette into the corner of his mouth and shook Edek's hand with emotion.

They'd never shared any semblance of close friendship, but at that moment, they sensed that something had shifted. Without knowing it, both belonged to the Auschwitz underground and such bonds were stronger than blood in that purgatory.

"Of course, I shall bring them food," Mala already returned to the matter she had apparently been discussing with the *Sonderkommando* men before Edek arrived.

"Jerzy will take you there and point you to the right spot," Kostek said, passing a small pouch to her, which Mala immediately concealed in her pocket. Edek caught a strong whiff of some Russian tobacco the prisoners of war from Wiesław's block smoked and which made his own eyes water. "Jerzy will be your lookout. When he tells you that the coast is clear, remove the planks, drop the food in between them, put everything back in order and sprinkle this Soviet makhorka all around it so the dogs can't sniff them out. For some reason, only this potent tobacco works."

Jerzy measured Mala doubtfully. "Are you sure you'll be able to move those planks all by yourself?" He turned to Kostek, concern written on his face. "Perhaps it would be better if Mala stands as a lookout and I move the planks?"

Kostek tossed his head. "We need someone with a very slight build. The construction of the dugout is very flimsy. A rhinoceros like you will fall right through and then we can say goodbye to the entire enterprise."

Filip guffawed while Jerzy grinned, not appearing offended in the slightest.

It was then that the meaning of their words finally dawned on Edek. His eyes flew wide open as he gaped at them, stunned with sudden realization.

"They haven't escaped, have they?" he asked in the softest of whispers despite their location being quite secure—no one could approach their group without being noticed. "They're still inside the camp."

"My child, you're a quick learner." Kostek dealt him a friendly clap on his back, chuckling. "The Russians invented the idea after studying failed escapes for years. That was why they installed themselves in the Mexico—it's the closest to the forest work detail that is presently under construction, swamped with building materials."

"Among which it is perfectly convenient to hide," Filip added, nudging his friend in the ribs.

"The Germans are very efficient, but our Russki friends are much savvier," Kostek continued. "The Germans rely on logic, whereas the Soviets rely on their... I don't know what to call it, but I admire their inventiveness."

"The reason why so many escapes have failed is that the outer cordon is so well-guarded," Mala said, motioning her head toward the Mexico, behind which the cordon lay. "SS dogs would sniff out the escapees within hours. If they don't discover their trace within a few days, the SS will decide that the inmates are long gone. They'll send telegrams to local authorities to be on the lookout for them, but they'll abandon the search inside the camp."

"So, after a few days of lying low, it'll be perfectly safe for them to leave," Edek concluded, his voice thick with a mixture of disbelief and admiration. Kostek was right. The plan was truly genius and crafty as hell.

"Will you come with me tomorrow?" Mala asked him, looking into his eyes searchingly. "As my lookout."

"Of course. Do you truly have to ask?"

She beamed at him in gratitude.

"Do I know them?" Edek asked, addressing no one in particular. "Their names didn't ring a bell when the SS announced them."

It was Filip who nodded at once. "You met at least one of them. Rudek. He was the fellow who came to the crematorium the morning after that rotten business with the Family Camp, asking about his girlfriend."

"Not the block clerk? The young fellow?"

"The very same," Filip confirmed. "He couldn't bear losing her. Swore revenge and said he'd do anything to stop the Nazis from murdering more. Well, we took him up on his word, stuffed his pockets with blueprints of the crematoriums, wrote the names of the SS men who work here, numbers of transports and people gassed, added a Zyklon-B label I personally tore off from one of the containers, and sent him on his way. If he lucks out and reaches the Jewish leaders in time with all those documents, perhaps they'll do something to prevent the Hungarian Jews from being sent here to die in the gas chambers."

Edek felt the blood draining from his face at those words. "The SS will slaughter him properly if they discover all those papers on him."

"And that's why it's in his best interests not to get captured." Filip shrugged, but a ragged breath he released betrayed his true feelings.

"We armed him and a friend who's accompanying him with hunting knives." Mala's voice had a strange undertone to it. She didn't look at Edek when she spoke, staring vacantly past him instead. "In case the Nazis discover them, they'll kill themselves so as not to betray anyone."

"Rudek is our only chance," Kostek announced, contemplating the finished ramp with eyes full of unspoken torment. Still empty and silent, it would soon be swarming with innocent souls who would perish forever in this very crematorium, burned with Kostek's own hands. He stared at his palms with sudden hatred before burying them in his pockets. "Mala says there's a rumor that the Old Man shall soon return to replace Kommandant Liebehenschel."

At the mention of the camp nickname for Kommandant Höss who'd been shipped away just last fall on corruption charges, Edek leaned against the wall, his head turning light with a sense of approaching terror. Unlike the soft Liebehenschel who had been fighting with Berlin about every transport and never sanctioned any gassings on his own initiative, Höss was a perfect bureaucratic murderer who had turned Auschwitz into a veritable annihilation machine. Unlike Liebehenschel, Höss wasn't burdened by any sentimental principles that at least women and children didn't belong in gas chambers. He'd personally shove the last batch in there and lock the door, his face as impassive as a Teutonic Knight's statue—stone-cold and devoid of feeling.

"I've seen papers mentioning Moll's name as well," Mala added. The dark shadow that passed over her face didn't escape Edek's attention. He sensed with his gut that there had been some history between Moll-the-brutal-SS-killer and his beloved and, whatever it was, it sent a cold chill down his spine. "Berlin officials proposed to appoint him as head of the Hungarian *Aktion,* virtually placing him in charge of all crematoria."

"Moll? The glass-eyed Moll?" Kostek turned to her, instantly alarmed. "The one who locked us inside the crematorium and gave me a beating for trying to warn him that you were among us?"

"The very same," Mala confirmed his worst fears, softening the words with a crooked grin.

"Just what I needed to hear today." Filip wiped his hands down his face with a moan. "Cyclops as my immediate boss."

"Don't shoot the messenger," Mala quipped grimly.

No one laughed, a tense silence hanging around them like gray mist. The faint scent of some terrible approaching danger tainted the air they breathed.

Edek was reluctant to leave her. He longed to speak with her in private—no, that wasn't quite the truth, he wanted to hold her against him for a few precious moments at least, to feel her warm lips open to his, to inhale the heady scent of her hair—but Mandl was already waiting for her at the camp office and he had to head back to the men's camp with Jerzy in tow.

"Jerzy?"

"Yes?"

Edek hesitated before opening up to the man whom he didn't know all that well, but suddenly, he didn't have a choice. "I also have an escape plan."

"Oh yes?" For some reason, Jerzy didn't appear surprised. It occurred to Edek that after the Family Camp liquidation, every other inmate began considering such an idea.

"You work mostly in Auschwitz, right?" Edek probed once again.

Jerzy grunted in response and looked at him with his big, kind eyes, the gentle giant who looked like a grizzly bear but had a heart of gold, as Edek would soon discover. "Just tell me what you need and I'll do it," he said simply and grinned.

"I'm going to need you to help me with Mala."

"Done."

One simple word, a proffered palm and the deal was sealed. They made the rest of the way back in companionable silence. No words were needed between two newfound resistance brothers. Everything was understood.

Chapter 29

Two weeks had passed since then; two weeks thick with fog and tension and eerie stillness. The night had enveloped Birkenau and the men's camp was still being confined in *Stehappell*—the standing roll call. The men were tired, but no one dared to complain: after all, a standing roll call as a punishment was quite an improvement after the summary executions in which all escapes had ended just a year ago.

The liquidation of the Family Camp reverberated through the camp and resulted in a series of escapes, spurring the men on. Rudek and his friend were the first ones to run; Soviet prisoners of war from Block 8 followed them by way of the same "Russian route" through the Mexico, and more of their comrades had joined them. Some were caught, some remained blissfully at large, but the communal feeling was there: it was now or never.

The SS had made their plans for the camp inhabitants' account known after they gassed the Theresienstadt inmates directly under the protection of the international Red Cross. If the world's biggest humanitarian organization meant nothing to them, the organization for the sake of which they had established the Family Camp in the first place, all bets were off. There would be no more pretending that the Jews were well cared for in Nazi concentration camps. The propaganda films made in the Theresienstadt ghetto to feed to the world leaders were all that was left of the Theresienstadt Jews. There would be no more Red Cross delegations inspecting the inmates, scrubbed off and dressed up for the occasion; no more pretense as to what the Nazis' goals concerning them were. By mid-April, everyone who could, decided to make a run for it. At least this way they had a chance to survive.

"I'm not liking this present state of affairs," Edek commented to Wiesław after yet another escape. As was their habit, they sat at the table in Wiesław's room, drinking the fiery Soviet-made vodka. Making use of his position as clerk, Wiesław had procured neatly made civilian clothes for himself. Edek began to grow out his hair, which the barracks' barber was cutting for him in exchange for cigarettes. Both friends could have passed for civilians now, if it weren't for Edek's overalls. "More and more of them bolt," Edek carried on, "and half of the escapees are from your block."

"And?"

"Do you not think the Political Department will take special interest in your barracks?"

Perfectly unfazed, Wiesław waved him off. Edek watched his friend stir his goulash soup—a special favor bestowed upon all clerks, which Wiesław had split with his friend—and lowered his own spoon, unable to force a single bite down. It wasn't only the possibility of the camp Gestapo descending on the block with a search that was gnawing at him. It was the only secret he'd kept from his best friend that made him hide his guilty eyes from Wiesław's searching ones and mumble something incoherent in reply to Wiesław's question if anything was the matter.

Edek couldn't explain, even to himself, why he still hadn't said anything to Wiesław about Mala joining them. Was it his reaction that he feared? Inwardly, Edek scoffed at the idea. Wiesław was the kind of a friend who would give his own life for a comrade. It was ridiculous to imagine that he would suddenly begin to protest Mala's involvement with their daring plan.

As though reading his mind, Wiesław nudged him gently with his elbow. "Eat before it gets cold."

The understanding in Wiesław's kind eyes nearly tore at Edek's heart. He felt himself a traitor, a pitiful traitor, with a very guilty conscience.

Putting away his own spoon, Wiesław folded his hands atop the table. "Edek. Are you afraid? Is that it?"

Seeing that he was smiling, Edek also broke into laughter, but it came out uneasy and hollow. And then it occurred to him that his friend saw right through Edek's own heart, guessing instinctively what was in it before Edek himself could.

He *was* afraid. Only not of the gallows; he was terrified to put the final plan into words, terrified to make it real and thus somehow jinx them all.

But then Wiesław patted his hand with his, which was reassuring and steady unlike Edek's, and the terror melted away.

"Wiesław?"

"Yes?"

"What would you say if I told you that I want to take Mala with us?"

Wiesław didn't answer at once. When Edek risked a glance at him, he saw mirth dancing in Wiesław's eyes.

"I'd say, I thought you would never ask."

Edek laughed, but this time with immense relief. The pressure fell away from his chest. The steaming plate before him suddenly looked appetizing. "Your Soviet friend, Kolya, gave me an idea for a disguise. We'll dress her up as a fitter as well, so I can lead you both out of the gates dressed as your SS escort." He paused for effect. "And as for concealing her face, the credit for that idea goes to you."

Curious, Wiesław arched a lively brow.

"Remember how you carried a sink to the Music Block, on your shoulders, with your head concealed completely inside?" After getting a nod of acknowledgement, Edek continued, "If we put a sink on top of her shoulders in the same manner, no one shall know she's a woman."

"That is a brilliant idea!" Wiesław exclaimed in approval and raised his mug with vodka. "And here's to yours truly who'd conceived such a brilliant plan without realizing it."

There was no arguing the point. Laughing at such shameless self-praise, even though he knew Wiesław was only jesting, Edek toasted him and downed his vodka in a few fiery gulps.

"There's an issue with an *Ausweis* for her though…" Edek mused out loud, shoveling the goulash into his mouth to kill the burning aftertaste.

Before his friend could work himself into a nervous state again, Wiesław dismissed that new concern of his with another wave of the hand. "You'll figure something out. You always do."

"Are you working on bribing someone to get you into a work *Kommando*? I can only escort a regular inmate out of the camp; not a block clerk. And particularly not one attired as fancily as you are now."

"Edek." His head tilted to one side, Wiesław gave his friend a look of faint reproach. "Stop fretting over everything and eat. There's still time. We aren't going anywhere till June, are we? I'll get myself a position in a regular *Kommando* a couple of weeks in advance. There's no reason to rush things now. Look how nice of a room we've got ourselves here. And the hiding place for the goods—that, too."

To be sure, Wiesław had a point, and so, Edek tucked away his concern into the darkest corner of his conscience and patted his friend's hand instead. "You just keep watch over that hiding place, will you? It would be idiotic to lose all that hard-earned stuff to some stupid block search."

"Don't panic. They won't search the bread store. Not under the floorboards at any rate."

For a couple of weeks, it appeared that Edek was worrying for nothing. More men escaped and, this time, annoyed with having to stay up every other night minding the inmates, the SS didn't even summon the prisoners for the *Stehappell* punishment.

"See?" Wiesław beamed at Edek. "They don't care anymore. The Soviets worry them much more than our sorry lot. By the time we run, they probably won't even search for us."

Edek wanted to believe him, yet something was still nagging him.

On Sunday evening, he went to see Mala. On his way, he had to pass right by the gallows, from which three recently captured men were swinging, with mocking signs "We're back!" hanging off their necks. For a few instants, he stared as though hypnotized at their protruding, black tongues, their swollen faces around which the swarms of flies were buzzing, their sightless eyes looking fixedly at their feet that had failed to carry them far enough away from the camp. Swiftly, Edek averted his gaze, a superstitious fear threatening to seize him once more.

It was best not to think of it just then.

It was best to believe that Mala, Wiesław, and he had a chance to escape that inferno alive.

Mala met him by their usual cellar door, sun-tanned and smelling faintly of lavender. After the suffocating stench of thousands of unwashed bodies, rotting flesh, and incinerated humanity that burst from the chimneys and contaminated the very air they breathed, it was as if Edek was inhaling heaven itself.

"Your hair has grown even longer," she said to Edek, brushing it neatly to one side.

"Do I look like an SS man yet?" He tried to hide a grin and couldn't.

Mala made a face. "You'll get there."

Still smiling, he followed her into her room. For some reason, Mala almost danced on the way there, replying with a mysterious, "you shall see, all good things for those who wait," to all of Edek's questions.

Once inside, she produced a plate with cheese and breadcrumbs scattered on it and gestured excitedly to Edek to join her as she settled herself in front of the radiator.

"Look!" she whispered with a triumphant look, gathering a palmful of crumbs and holding it to the hole in the wall.

After only a few short moments, a familiar rodent with a missing ear poked its face out and sniffed the air, its shiny black eyes trained on the generous offering. With a look of utter concentration, Mala held her hand, palm up, as steadily as possible. It occurred to Edek that she was scarcely breathing at all. It was then that he realized that neither was he, much too self-conscious so as not to frighten Mala's tiny pet.

To his great astonishment, the mouse hesitated for just a fraction and then leapt straight into Mala's open hand, grabbing a tiny fistful of crumbs and stuffing them at once into its cheeks that were growing rounder and rounder as Edek watched on. He felt his shoulders quivering with silent chuckles which soon grew louder and louder, joined by Mala's.

"Look at the little fellow, not afraid in the slightest," he declared, obviously impressed.

"No wonder. This little man is an Auschwitzer. He's a tough old prisoner."

"He's a survivor." Edek nodded, his voice weighted with unexpected emotion. "Just like we shall be."

Mala's eyes met his gaze, full of golden specks. "You haven't given up on your idea to smuggle me out of here, have you?"

"Never in my life. I go where you go and if you stay, I stay. That was our deal, was it not?"

"There's logistical trouble is all I'm saying."

"No more logistical trouble." With utmost gentleness, Edek took a pinch of crumbs and carefully dropped them into Mala's palm in which the mouse was still feasting. "One of my new Soviet friends gave me an idea and Jerzy agreed to help. We'll dress you as a male inmate in fitters' blue overalls, cut your hair and cover your head with a sink or some such to conceal your face. All you'll have to do is to put another name inside that *Ausweis,* so that there are two of you I'll be supposedly escorting. And as for the picture, I'll just say there was a shortage in printing paper or some such—the war is going on. Some lowly guard at the gate won't doubt an officer's word."

"I see your Lubusch has taught you well."

"He did," Edek confirmed with a warm grin and nuzzled Mala's hair. "Just think of it, Mally. A couple more months and we shall be free. Perhaps, one more year and the war shall be over."

"What do you want to do after the war? Go back to your maritime academy?" Mala looked up at him, genuinely curious.

"No." Edek shook his head categorically. "Never in my life shall I ever wear a uniform again. I've had enough of this war rot to last me a lifetime."

"What then?"

"I considered becoming a carpenter—I'm certain anyone will employ me with my extensive experience." He burst into grim chuckles. "But then I realized that you will probably be an interpreter again and it'll be unseemly for you to have a husband who's a simple carpenter. So, I've decided to become an architect instead. The studies shall take a few years, but it'll be worth it in the end."

"An architect?" Mala arched a brow, impressed. They had joked about getting married before and despite never discussing it in all seriousness—making plans was much too laughable an affair in an extermination camp where an inmate's life could have been cut short by any SS person's whim—it had been somehow assumed that this was precisely what would happen, if they ever made it outside Auschwitz's walls.

Edek tried to laugh, but his smile slipped off his face in spite of himself, and a wistful look veiled his eyes. "I thought the world could use more architects instead of more soldiers. So that we can rebuild whatever we have destroyed."

"I think it's a wonderful plan." Mala took his hand with her free one and clasped it tightly.

"And what is yours?" he asked.

"To be with you."

"That's not what I meant."

"I know precisely what you meant." She nodded a few times. "My plan is to be with you. That's all I want. It doesn't matter what I do or where I work. If I have you to come home to every evening, I shall be happy."

In the meadow behind Crematorium V, Hauptscharführer Moll was raging.

"You bloody lot of idiots, are you blind?!" the newly appointed head of the *Sonderkommando* bellowed, pointing with his swagger stick at the taut marking string. "Do you have enough mental abilities to understand that you are to dig inside the mark and not around it? One more mistake like that and I'll dispatch you personally where you stand. Stinking, brainless carcasses!"

He had arrived a few days ago with the former Kommandant Höss, who once again had replaced the "humane Kommandant" Liebehenschel. At once, Moll threw himself into his favorite pastime—the organization of the extermination site on the scale of mass annihilation. From Mala, Edek had learned that Moll had once been in charge of extermination, long before the four Birkenau crematoriums were built and Hössler took up that position. It was Moll who had invented the idea to bury the corpses, with which the only crematorium in Auschwitz couldn't cope, in mass graves in that very meadow where Edek was presently standing. It was also Moll who supervised the exhumation and cremation of the decomposed corpses after they began to rise to the earth's surface, contaminating the water in the vicinity with the black poison seeping from their mass graves. It was Moll who had later liquidated the entire *Sonderkommando* as soon as they finished their morbid task of exhuming and burning the bodies. And it was Moll who nearly killed Mala as well, shoving her into a death ditch filled with bodies.

Aware of Moll's gruesome résumé by now and observing him at work, Edek had no difficulty in concluding what precisely the one-eyed beast was organizing in a formerly emerald meadow that had been broken into sections, sliced and dug up by the somber *Sonderkommando* men. Their faces were sweat-streaked and smudged with dirt, they shoved their spades into sticky clay; already doomed; painfully aware that they were digging their own graves into which they would perish right after Moll was done with his intended victims, the Hungarian Jews.

Steering as far away from Moll and his pristine white summer uniform as possible, Edek inched his way toward Kostek, Mala's resistance friend from the *Sonderkommando*. Shirtless and bronze from the sun exposure, the Greek freedom fighter stood waist-deep inside the fresh pit, busy wrapping his bleeding palms with bandages crudely made out of his own torn undershirt. He must have just paused; his chest was still rising and falling with visible difficulty, yet his face immediately split into a huge grin as soon as he noticed Edek squatting on the edge of his trench.

"Greetings to the fitters' *Kommando*." Kostek raised his torn palm in a mock salute. Only his green eyes didn't smile, full of unspoken suffering. Edek regarded him with sympathy and felt it all in his own soul—the immense burden of being forced into an accomplice in the Nazi mass murder. At least Edek only fixed the pipes for them. Kostek was digging the pits which soon would swallow countless families, entire communities, without a trace. "Whatever you need, make it snappy. We have a new administration here, as you can see," Kostek said. "If Moll sees you loitering about, he'll test his new method of extermination on you."

In spite of himself, Edek's eyes widened with growing concern. "After everything they've already done to us, he's managed to invent something new?"

Kostek only waved him off, as if he was saying, *you don't want to imagine something of the sort.*

"So, what is it?" Kostek asked.

"Mala said you were holding a wristwatch for me?" Edek asked, lowering his voice to a whisper. "A German one? Something an SS man would wear?"

Before Edek could finish his explanation, Kostek had dug out something small wrapped in a grubby handkerchief from his pocket and threw it into Edek's awaiting hands. "I hope this watch brings you luck. Hide it well before the actual day when you have to wear it. Use the admissions block as a hiding place if you need one; it stands empty most of the time and the SS never search it. We store some of our own contraband there. The fellow in charge of it is called Jurek."

Edek nodded readily. "I know him. Superficially, but still. I once helped fix a radiator in his personal room."

"Even better, the fact that you know each other. He'll hide a suitcase of goods for you as long as you pay. And now scram before the Cyclops sees you."

As Edek trotted back in the direction of the crematorium, he surveyed the meadow cut into the ugly wounds of the future mass graves, its flowers upturned and discarded, slashed by the sharp spades. In the distance, SS men were crawling on top of two former gas chambers that hadn't seen action due to the new Birkenau constructions for over two years, probing at the hatches in the roof and dusting off two inconspicuous former farmhouses turned extermination facilities. In the rays of the fiery sunset, the Little Red House and the Little White House were stirring back to life. Shuddering with dread, Edek hastened his steps as though Satan himself was chasing him.

The next evening, Edek returned to Wiesław's barracks just in time to see blocks 4 and 6 being turned virtually upside down by the Political Department. It appeared that their thorough search produced no results apart from a few bits of food and a few bottles of spirits which the SS didn't even bother to requisition. Annoyed, the SS officer in charge stalked off, accompanied by his entourage.

At once, Edek nudged Wiesław with his elbow. "We've got to move the goods," he whispered to his comrade almost without moving his lips. "Today it's blocks 4 and 6, tomorrow it shall be 5 and 8."

"Seven," Wiesław tried to argue unconvincingly. "They're Germans. They love order."

"Yes, but more than order they like surprising us with searches we don't expect." Edek stared at him hard. "Tonight, we're moving it. A fellow from the *Sonderkommando* has just told me about a perfect place—the admissions block. It's only busy during the day, when the new arrivals go through it. No one lives there. It's perfectly empty at night. The SS never search it. Jurek, the admissions clerk, is all by himself and Kostek says he'll help us in exchange for a couple of gold nuggets and the promise of his own freedom."

"I can't go out at night. I'm the block clerk."

Edek cursed under his breath, patting himself for a cigarette. His nerves were strained to the utmost. Smoking was the only thing that calmed him. Smoking and feeling the weight of Mala's head on his arm as she slept soundly, her breathing deep and undisturbed. "I'll go by myself then."

"If you just wait till tomorrow, I'll move the goods myself, during the day. No one will be here in the afternoon—"

"Tomorrow may be too late," Edek interrupted him abruptly. "I'm moving them tonight. You worry about getting yourself into a working *Kommando* and quit delaying it till the last moment and blaming it on our 'fine arrangement' here." Seeing an expression of profound hurt on his friend's face, Edek softened his tone at once. "Forgive me, please. I didn't mean anything by it. It's just… the nerves; surely, you understand?"

Wiesław nodded, and walked toward the block without waiting for Edek. Cursing under his breath, Edek threw his unfinished cigarette on the ground and wiped his hands down his face.

"Lovers' quarrel?" Kolya mocked him good-naturedly as he passed him by.

"Piss off, Bolshevik," Edek grumbled back. "All the trouble is because of you. If you Reds didn't bolt a dozen a day, the Political Department would have never showed their noses here."

"At least we have the balls to run," Kolya replied lightheartedly, aware that Edek wasn't blaming him in earnest. After a fight with one's best friend, one ought to have taken out his frustration on someone. "Don't fret; we'll come to liberate you, gentle Polaks, soon enough!"

Laughing, Kolya and his comrades went inside, leaving Edek alone with his uneasy thoughts.

At night, when the rest of the camp was dozing peacefully, Edek crept across the compound and into the bread store of Wiesław's block. In the uncertain light of the moon, throwing one nervous glance over his shoulder after the other, he pried the floorboards open as silently as he could. He didn't know what possessed him, whether it was Kolya's teasing or his former *Kommandoführer*'s acting lessons, but before he knew what he was doing, he was pulling on Lubusch's uniform over his own.

It was a reckless and utterly idiotic idea, but before long he was strolling along the camp, whistling a tune, hands in pockets—a typical master of the world who had the right to be where he wanted to be and do as he pleased. His stomach somersaulted each time a guard passed him by, but even then he discovered that he had nothing to fear. Recognizing officers' markings, they jumped out of his way, slammed their heels together, saluted him, and waited at attention for Edek to stroll by, his arm bent lazily at the elbow.

"Heil Hitler," he barely bothered to reply in response, the words tasting vile in his mouth.

Jurek, the admissions block clerk, had quite a fright after Edek strode into his quarters.

"Stand to attention! Eyes right! Heels together!" Edek bellowed in his best German.

Instantly scrambling off his bunk where he was reading a book, Jurek tripped on his own boots and nearly fell face down at the sight of authority. It took him a few more moments to recognize Edek in the laughing SS man.

"Edek, is that you, you miserable sod? I nearly pissed my pants! What in the blue hell are you doing, wandering around in such get-up?"

"Practicing," Edek answered evasively.

"For what? Your own execution at the *Appellplatz*?"

"No. For walking around like a free man again."

Jurek looked at him. "Oh no. You too, then?"

"Me too, then. And it shall be you who will help me."

Jurek was already shaking his head, holding up his hands in the air. "I don't want any part of it. I have enough troubles with the *Sonderkommando* and whatever it is they're stuffing all over the place."

"Oh, you don't? Have you seen those pits Moll is constructing behind the crematoriums? Have you seen the SS readying the two former gas chambers? Little Red House and the Little White House are being prepped as we speak. What do you think they're doing?" He pretended to ponder. "Spring cleaning, perhaps? Simply dusting off the old gas chambers? Or perhaps it's because the second ramp is now completed and soon trains full of Hungarian Jews shall start arriving here in such quantities they're sending you helpers from other details?"

"I didn't hear about any helpers."

"The official order hasn't come out yet. It's still in the administration office."

"Please don't tell me you saw it after you strode in there looking like that."

"No. I have my own people working there." There was no need to mention Mala's name. He stepped closer to Jurek, who now looked thoroughly frightened. "If you help me hide this uniform and gun, you can use it for your own escape after I'm gone. I'll send it back through a civilian who works here."

For a very long time, Jurek paced the room, considering the offer. He smoked two cigarettes in a row while Edek waited patiently in the corner. At last, he motioned Edek to follow him into the block itself.

"There, under the roof of the landing." He pointed to the place he had in mind. "There's a double layer of boards that form the ceiling. Wedge it between them. No one will ever think of looking there."

Chapter 30

May 1944

Mala stood on the newly constructed ramp and watched the train pulling up, her gaze full of sorrow. It was the very first one of many that were scheduled to arrive in the next couple of months—she had personally typed and copied the schedule that was later distributed among the SS chiefs. Next to her, camp leader Hössler stood, his hands clasping his swagger stick behind his back. Only, his usual benevolent grin was absent from his face that day. Wistfully, he searched the spot where Alma Rosé used to conduct her orchestra. Instead of the violinist, the head of the male orchestra now waited the order to begin, and Hössler turned away in disgust.

"Laks is a very good conductor," Mala tried to smile, but Hössler only glared at her.

"He's not Frau Alma."

It had been over a month since the violinist's death—suicide, according to Zippy—but he still suffered. Silently, perhaps, refusing to acknowledge it even to himself, but he did. Hössler had summoned Mala here supposedly as an interpreter, but it was her suspicion that he just wanted to have someone near. Someone who wasn't wearing the same uniform. Someone with whom he sometimes shared his memories and could speak of things which his colleagues at best wouldn't understand and, at worst, would report him for. Someone, who reminded him of his Alma—the only woman whom he'd loved innocently and selflessly and whom he'd lost to the very camp he was in charge of.

Mala pitied him. Loathed him just like she loathed all SS—but pitied him all the same. It couldn't have been an easy burden to carry, this realization that he, himself, was complicit in the death of someone who meant so much to him. Served him right, and still…

With a groan, the train had pulled to a stop. At once, the *Kapos* charged at the doors, undid the heavy locks swiftly and expertly, and began herding the frightened crowds onto the platform. Both the inmates and the SS operated in a much different style than usual. Instead of the dogs straining themselves on the leashes, barking at the new inmates, officers calmly directed the arrivals into two columns. Polite requests replaced the usual curses and blows.

Her heart as heavy as a rock in her chest, Mala watched the SS with cold hatred in her eyes, knowing all too well what they had in store for the new arrivals. The gas and furnaces right after. With a shudder of anguish, she swiftly averted her gaze, feeling utterly helpless and loathing the Nazis even more for making her feel so.

"Please, leave your luggage right here on the platform. We have a special *Kommando* who shall carry them into the camp."

When someone tried to protest that his luggage wasn't marked, an SS guard went to pains to write the gentleman's name on it with a piece of chalk. Pacified, the elderly man raised his hat and took his place in the column where men stood. Mala saw him give someone in the women's column an encouraging smile—*Don't fret, these Germans seem to be very correct*—and felt her heart sinking to some unimaginable depth of despair. Poor man. If only he knew the reason for all this "correctness."

Just two days ago, Hössler was giving instructions to his underlings on the parade ground before the camp office. "The Hungarians never lived in the ghettos. They have never seen any violence. It is of paramount importance to instill peace in them and reassure them that they have nothing to fear from us. In the next couple of months, we shall be getting transports daily. It means thousands and thousands of people will need to go through all six gas chambers, the Little Red House and the Little White House included, every single day. To ensure the smoothness of the operation, we need to do our utmost to assure the new arrivals that they shall be completely safe in our hands. There must be absolutely no cursing, no shouting, and definitely no physical action against the Hungarians. If they ask for water, tell them they shall have it after their shower. If they want to drink from the hose, allow them to go to the hose. If they want to sit on the grass before the crematorium while we're gassing the first batch, let them sit, as long as they believe they're about to have an innocent shower. I don't think I need to explain to you what's going to happen if one of you idiots says anything about them going to the gas like some of you love to taunt them. If that crowd of several thousand people starts a riot, we're in big trouble. So it's in your best interests to act as politely as possible. Joke around with their men. Comfort the women. Play with their children, like you did with the Family Camp. Be as accommodating as possible…"

Hössler's words were still playing on Mala's mind when a woman signaled for her to come over. Behind her, two girls of about twelve stood wearing matching velvet dresses and shiny, polished shoes. It stunned Mala how many families here looked as though they were dressed for some special occasion. She could only guess what lies their local leaders had told them about their destination.

"Is that gentleman on the podium a medical doctor?" the woman asked.

Mala traced her gaze to the small platform on which Dr. Mengele stood, picture-perfect and immaculately dressed as always. To the new arrivals, he appeared thoroughly reassuring with his handsome face, polite manner of address, welcoming smile and the insignia of the medical staff on his shoulder boards. Behind the kind Herr Doktor's deceiving façade, they failed to see the predator's nature; didn't recognize the maniacal gleam of the mad scientist in his dark, impenetrable eyes; didn't find anything distressing about his interest in anything that came in identical pairs, pregnant, or physically deformed. They weren't humans to him, but objects, something to be tested, prodded, measured, experimented and, eventually, cut open to see precisely how the experiment went. Painfully aware of what those experiments entailed, for it was her who shipped preserved body parts and eyes swimming in different solutions to Dr. Mengele's superiors in Berlin, Mala grew cold each time someone mentioned his name, let alone when Herr Doktor himself made an appearance in the camp administration office. It was from his unhealthy interest that Mala's physician friend Stasia saved many pregnant women by performing abortions on them, for the alternative in Dr. Mengele's hands was much too shudder-inducing and invariably lethal.

"Why?" Mala replied to the woman. She knew that the order was to nod and smile and generally lull them into temporary peace, but with the best will in the world, she couldn't force herself to.

"He was just saying something about twins. My girls are twins. Is that good?"

Mala thought of Mengele's barracks full of such twins on whom he experimented like on guinea pigs, purposely injecting them with all sorts of deadly serums or viruses and then cutting them open to compare the differences between the infected and healthy twin. She stepped closer to the woman.

"Take off your cardigan and put it on one of your daughters," she began to whisper in the woman's ear. "Separate them, so that they stand in different parts of the column. Tell one of them to unbraid her hair and when your girls approach him—separately, you hear me? It is of utmost importance—tell them to reply 'fifteen' when he asks how old they are."

When Mala pulled back, she saw that all the blood had drained from the woman's face. It took her a few moments to compose herself, a few moments during which Mala feared the lady would start shouting and accuse her of being a vile criminal spreading dirty rumors, but in the end, she collected herself and began to remove her cardigan with unsteady hands.

"Here, take it," she whispered, passing it to her daughter.

Mala stepped away, breathing a sigh of relief.

For the next few days, she proceeded to do the very same thing. Using her position as an interpreter, she approached one person after another, whispering softly into their ears, "Tell him you're forty-five, if he asks your age… Tell them your son is sixteen… Drop that instrument case, tell them you're a carpenter, not a flautist…"

A highly risky enterprise, but so far, she'd been successful: nearly all of the people she'd managed to warn in this manner were sent by Mengele to the column, which led to the Sauna and not to the gas chamber, thus saving them from imminent death. The rest of that never-ending stream of humanity were *very correctly* escorted by the SS along the ramp toward the grove where two other "Saunas" stood, their chimneys belching clouds of a sickly-sweet, nauseating smell. The rest were led along the Lagerstraße and into the peaceful Birkenau woods, in which two other "Saunas" were concealed. In front of those two, the *Sonderkommando* had even planted some flowerbeds on Hössler's orders, according to Kostek's latest report.

"Those poor devils have not the faintest clue where they're going," he said, shaking his head in disgust while Mala was transferring a few folding knives from her pocket into his. It was another dangerous enterprise, rummaging in the discarded luggage right on the ramp while the SS were distracted with their new charges, but Mala risked it all the same. "Look at them. Lying on the grass, newspapers atop their heads, without a care in the world—a veritable beach." He spat on the ground.

Due to the backlog, crowds of new arrivals had to wait for their turn outside the crematoriums. Blissfully oblivious to the fate awaiting them within the walls of these constructions, they positioned themselves in front of the doors, atop the dewy grass, and waited apathetically for the water promised by the SS. Elderly relatives hid in the shadows provided by prams; the young children ran around them in circles, their innocent laughter sending chills down the spines of the *Sonderkommando* men returning from the inferno raging just behind the tall protective screens, a mere twenty or so meters from the crematoriums' backyards. Sweat running down their faces, they observed the children tragically, knowing all too well that within the next hour, it would be those very children's bodies they would be throwing into Moll's hellish pits.

"Hössler promised them iced tea and coffee after their shower," Mala replied hollowly.

There was no one to warn in this crowd, their fates had been sealed; there was simply no place to run anywhere from here. The crematoriums had been surrounded by an outer cordon of electrified barbed wire and guard towers. The only reason why she came here in the first place was to pass her contraband as quickly as possible before the *Kanada Kommando* got their hands on it. The underground had their people in the sorting detail, but it was anyone's guess if they could get to the possible weapons concealed among the possessions before some crook who'd later sell them to the SS or civilians working in the camp for a bottle of spirits and a smoked sausage.

"Moshe Liar." Kostek shook his head.

Mala didn't argue. That, Hössler certainly was.

"We even give them cotton towels and individual pieces of soap now," Kostek continued.

"No one gets suspicious?" Mala regarded the smoking chimney doubtfully. Its infernal orange glow obscured the sky itself, turning it ashen-gray. All around them, the ghastly snowflakes gently floated in the middle of June; the snowflakes that didn't melt when they touched one's skin. Only smeared and left an oily film of terror and death, impossible to wash off.

"Very few. The SS take them quietly outside and fire at them with their air pistols, so that no one hears the shot. Then, they drop the body behind the crematorium. We have a small gang working there since our ovens can't manage the amount. Moll has set up quite a production line behind Crematorium V. Twenty pits, forty or fifty meters long, two meters deep, about eight meters wide, where he burns the bodies that don't fit into the four crematoriums."

He was still saying something, and Mala was already calculating the numbers. *Crematoriums II and III had five ovens in each, each with three chambers. That's ten ovens, thirty chambers. On each gurney, four bodies fit at the same time. Crematoriums IV and V had two ovens each, with four incineration chambers in each one. Twenty pits, two meters deep, fifty meters long...* Mala felt lightheaded.

"How many people..." she swallowed with difficulty before continuing, "how many people have you cremated so far?"

Kostek screwed up his face, calculating the approximate numbers.

"About two hundred thousand now," he announced in the tone of a banker stating the latest stock market report. "They say we're to expect three hundred thousand more in June."

"That'll make half a million people," Mala whispered, wiping her forehead with her palm where a film of sweat had broken. "Half a million people in two months."

"It's Auschwitz." Kostek spread his arm in a terrifyingly ghoulish gesture.

Mala looked into his eyes and saw that they were completely dead. One would never recover from something of that sort. He seemed like he knew it as well.

Chapter 31

June 1944

The SS "celebrated" D-Day by gassing the next three full transports without holding any selections. They were rabid this time,
punishing the Jews for the Allied landings in Normandy, for the
war that could no longer be won; clubbing people on the ramp,
smashing children's skulls on the sides of the cattle cars, drunk on
schnapps and their hatred. There were not enough *Kapos* to mind
the order. Edek's fitters' *Kommando* had been transferred from their
work on the road construction in women's camp to the ramp as
temporary enforcers.

White-hot June sun was also without mercy, singeing through
the uniforms of camp veterans and burning to painful blisters the
freshly shaved heads of the new arrivals. In the quivering waves of
rising heat, the uncertain shapes of the Hungarian Jews disembark-
ing from the trains had a specter-like quality to them, disappearing
into the boiling air before anyone could remember their names,
dissolved into ashes just as a new transport was pulling up to a
ramp that was never left empty these days to spill a new load of
humanity to be slaughtered by Moll's henchmen.

Edek tried to stay close to Mala at all times, only wielding his
stick at the unfortunates who were near when the SS happened
to be watching. He cursed a lot at the top of his lungs and swung
the club ferociously but not once did he hit anyone.

"Soon," he would mouth to Mala whenever their eyes met.

"Soon," she invariably mouthed back.

They had already agreed on the day—only a couple of weeks from now—and spent countless clandestine meetings discussing the details. The best place to hide an SS uniform so that Edek could change into it, unseen—the potato storage bunker, a solitary, unguarded building in Auschwitz; the best place to conceal Mala's disguise—the toilet of the guardhouse, which provided not only the perfect place to hide fitter's overalls for Mala to change into, but a place to store a sink that she would use to conceal herself. The accomplices who would aid the couple—Jerzy who would help escort Mala to Edek, and Jurek, who would help Edek with his uniform.

But all that would come later. Now, Mala discreetly asked for the new arrivals' documents and shoved them under her clothes, committing the names to her memory. Those now-useless papers would be burned in the *Kanada* at any rate, but if she smuggled them out of the camp, she would have proof of their fates. It was too late for the Hungarians, but at least they could tell the rest of the world what was happening right under their noses and perhaps save a few lives with their action.

When Mala was sent to Moll's ghastly detail, Edek invented an excuse to accompany her as though he was afraid to even let her out of his sight in the midst of that orgy of death.

Behind the tall screens, concealing the nightmarish sight from the Hungarians' eyes, lay the ninth circle of hell, with Moll presiding. In twenty deep pits, hundreds and hundreds of bodies were burning simultaneously, their flesh popping and sizzling as the *Sonderkommando* men prodded them with long iron sticks, their faces grim and running with sweat—or tears; Mala couldn't quite tell in the waves of rising heat that distorted their features.

Attired in a white summer uniform, an Iron Cross gleaming on his chest—his newest decoration for "excellent service" from his demented Führer, no doubt—Moll was explaining his invention to a small delegation of officers Mala had never seen before.

"To incinerate as many bodies as possible at once, we have invented a special system that uses human fat as fuel." With a look of a lecturer about him, he pointed his swagger stick at the nearest pit. "Inside, there is a wide strip that runs down the middle from one end to the other. Following my precise directions, the *Sonderkommando* dug a drain channel that slopes to either side from the center and thus catches the fat that burning bodies produce in two collecting pens that I ordered them to place at either end of the channel. In this manner, it is possible to burn virtually countless numbers of bodies without using any outside source of fuel." The pride from his diabolical invention was visible on his freckled face. Only his glass eye remained dead, just as soulless as the man to whom it belonged.

The invited officers nodded with knowing looks. "We could organize a similar operation in our camp."

"Oh, most certainly. I shall give you the precise instructions later."

Moll noticed Mala, who stood in the waves of infernal heat with her fists tightly clenched, pale and trembling with inhuman hatred for them all.

"Ah, Mally, old girl. You're still alive? Don't fret; I'll save you a warm spot after we're done with these Hungarian shits." He motioned his head in the direction of the nearest pit with a terrible smile on his face. "If you ask really nicely, maybe I'll shoot you first before throwing you in there."

Mala realized that he too hadn't forgotten that occasion with Hössler nor his transfer, but her face betrayed nothing. "Obersturmführer Hössler is holding up a new transport on the ramp. All crematoriums are already at full capacity and he was asking if you can take another thousand people. That is, if he should start processing them," she said, keeping her voice as flat as possible.

"Of course, I can. The more, the merrier, eh?" At the sound of his laughter, both Mala and Edek shivered with dread. "Tell Hössler he doesn't even have to gas them first; we'll just throw them here as is." The gaze of his only good eye stopped on Edek. "And what do you want, Bolshevist pig?"

"I'm Polish."

"Same shit. Did Hössler send you as well?"

"No. Hans, the *Kanada Kapo*, was asking if he should send more dentists for the golden crowns or if you have enough?"

"We have enough. Tell him we'll send all the golden crowns later, together with the ash gold."

"Ash gold?" Edek scowled uncomprehendingly.

"After we're done pulverizing these stiffs, we sift through the ashes to see if those sly apes were hiding something in their asses. You'll be surprised how much we find at the end of the day."

From the direction of the crematorium, two *Sonderkommando* inmates were already pushing a cart stacked with freshly gassed corpses.

"Make it snappy, you filthy pigs!" Moll bellowed. "You're not on a blasted stroll in a park! Shall I help you find your legs?"

Unable to remain in the middle of that raging hell any longer, Edek grasped Mala's wrist and pulled her away—away from the flames consuming human flesh with truly mortifying speed, away from the SS who observed it with self-satisfaction, away from the fate they would undoubtedly share if they didn't go through with their plan. Just then did it dawn on him what precisely was at stake.

"I'm not dying in one of those pits," Mala spoke, her voice thick with ash and, oddly, steely determination.

"No," Edek agreed, narrowing his eyes at the horizon. "Neither of us will. I'll see to it. I swear."

Later, in Mala's room, Edek handed Kostek Lubusch's gun. From the shadows, the sightless eyes of the dead watched them closely, mutely asking for vengeance in the deafening stillness. After what they had witnessed that day, after what they had to take part in—unwillingly, but still—there was no turning back, no negotiations with the enemy, no hope for the humanity of the SS beasts. Their only option was to fight; till the last breath, till the last drop of blood, till the last ounce of courage.

"You're not taking it with you?" Kostek regarded the weapon in his hand in disbelief.

"No one will check an *Unterscharführer*'s holster to see if he has a gun in it." Edek gave an absent shrug. "And you'll need it more than I will."

Somber, ominous silence filled the room after those last words of his. The Family Camp was the first to die; now, it was the Hungarians. No one had illusions as to whose turn it would be next. The *Sonderkommando*, so that they wouldn't spill their secrets to the approaching Soviet army.

Kostek shoved the gun into the waistband of his trousers, concealed it under his shirt and clasped Edek's hand firmly.

"Take at least a few of those SS swine with you," Edek said, his voice thick with emotion.

Kostek nodded. He swore that he would.

Inside the crematoriums, the *Sonderkommando* on the night shift were still burning the remaining bodies. Inside the storage depot, the fitters' *Kommando* were holding a celebration. It was a grim date—four years exactly since their transport had pulled up to the infamous Auschwitz ramp. In any other circumstances, it would have never occurred to them to celebrate in the midst of that Dante's inferno. Just outside the doors, the chimneys were belching foul-smelling smoke, and yet, they laid the tables with cloths and organized a whole bucket of schnapps for the occasion.

Four years. For four intolerably long years, the Nazis had tried to slaughter them in different manners—by starving them, beating them, harassing them, exposing them to extreme cold and heat, refusing them medical help and sanitary conditions, but they were still here, still alive and very much breathing, and such an act of ultimate rebellion was worth celebrating.

Jerzy, the gentle giant who had sworn to Edek that he would do anything in his powers to help him and Mala with their escape, rose unsteadily to his feet. It was the very first toast of the evening, but he swayed slightly with emotion as though he was already drunk.

"May I please…" He made an effort to collect himself. In his great paw, an aluminum mug filled with vodka appeared no bigger than a thimble. "Just a minute of everyone's attention."

When the room quieted down, he wetted his lips.

"I know we're celebrating today, but I consider it appropriate to raise this very first glass—"

"Mug!" someone interrupted him, causing the room to break into guffaws.

"Yes, a mug—" Jerzy grinned feebly, "to our comrades who aren't with us any longer. There were seven hundred and twenty-eight of us on that train. And how many are left?" His eye roved the room, swimming with tears. "Thirty? Thirty-five? How many lives—"

"Shut it, Jerzy!" one of the Polish fitters shouted.

But Jerzy stared straight ahead, pale and trembling, as though he didn't even hear him. "There was Djunio. Romek. Tadek—"

"Quit it with that roll call!" It was Edek this time, visibly unnerved. "If you start enumerating all the comrades we've lost, we'll be sitting here for two days. We shall mourn them all later. Not now. Everyone's guts are churning as it is with those poor Hungarian bastards and here you start as well. Let's just be silent for a few moments." He stood up and lifted his mug in the air, inviting everyone to stand with him. For a minute, not a sound could be heard. "Thank you. To our fallen comrades. Let them rest in eternal peace. And let us avenge them the first chance we get."

Kolya, the Professor's adjutant who had managed to get himself into the kitchen *Kommando* that was ordinarily only reserved for the German Green Triangles, marched in and raised two buckets in the air.

"Anyone place an order for goulash and potatoes?"

"Kolya, you Bolshevist profiteer! Wherever did you organize it from?" The inmates stared at the buckets in amazement.

"Two guesses." Kolya barked out laughter, placing the buckets, full to the brim, next to the tables. All at once, the mouthwatering smell of fresh meat and potatoes enveloped the stuffy room, almost intoxicating and going straight to one's head. With eyes full of infinite gratitude and wonder, men watched the Russian distribute the goods into the dishes with a generous hand and a broad smile on his face. "The SS will have to go on a diet for the next couple of days, but we shall eat our fill today."

"Soon, we shall eat all we want," Edek proclaimed, dipping his mug into a bucket of schnapps again.

Several men exchanged knowing glances.

"So, you too then?" the Professor asked, his spectacles gleaming in the dim light with unexpected conspiratorial joy. "When?"

"In a couple of weeks," Edek replied, his eyes crinkling above the rim of his mug.

"Us, too."

"Hey, not everyone at the same time, comrades!" Kolya held up his hand in mock protest. "We're getting out as well, so let's make a schedule or some such."

"Let's agree where we meet once we get outside as well," Wiesław proposed, a wide grin splitting his face.

"I'm calling dibs on being in charge of the brigade!" Edek's enthusiasm knew no restraint.

"Kolya will be in charge of the field kitchen," someone suggested.

Outside, the chimneys continued to relentlessly belch smoke. Inside the storage depot, an island of life in the midst of death toasted its near-freedom.

"I hid your SS uniform and the holster in the potato bunker in Auschwitz," Jurek reported in an undertone a few days after. The admissions block clerk seemed to be more fidgety than usual, his beady eyes shifting nervously behind his glasses. The *Sonderkommando* with Kostek as their leader had just brought more contraband into his always-empty barracks, making Jurek frantically search for more hiding places under its thatched roof and under the floorboards. *He was already risking his neck for their cause and now Edek with his escape plans was making him run around the camp with an SS uniform hidden under his own clothes,* his pained expression seemed to say. Though, the promise of freedom made even cowards commit heroic acts, and Jurek was no coward. A profiteer only, who knew where his bread was buttered, but essentially a man with a good enough heart, at least as far as Edek was concerned. "And I'll pick up your fitter's uniform right after you change and walk out of there," Jurek said.

The processing block stood silent once again. Only a few papers scattered on the floor, bearing the footprints of the *Kanada Kommando*, were evidence of the people who had passed through its door mere hours ago.

"Thank you." Edek grasped his hand and shook it with gratitude.

"Do you have anyone picking up your lady friend's clothes after she changes into a fitter's attire?"

"Yes. Jerzy will take care of it. He'll be the one escorting her."

"Do I know Jerzy?"

"He's from my *Kommando*, also a fitter. A Pole; political; bald; over two meters tall; looks like a grizzly bear; can bend a crowbar with his bare hands," Edek supplied only half in jest.

"Ah!" Recognition reflected instantly on Jurek's face. "He's the one who even camp Kapo Jupp steers clear of."

"That would be Jerzy," Edek confirmed with certain pride in his voice; pride for being able to call him a friend. The only thing he regretted was not befriending him earlier. But who knew that appearances could be so deceiving and that such a menacing façade could hide such a selfless, gentle soul?

"He doesn't say much, does he?" Jurek asked.

"No. But he does a lot. For the cause."

"Naturally, for the cause." Jurek sighed, turning a gold nugget Edek had supplied him with as a payment in his pale fingers. After a few more moments of hesitation, he pushed it into Edek's palm and only shrugged, appearing slightly embarrassed, in response to Edek's questioning look. "For the cause. You'll need it there, in the outside."

"What about you?" Edek asked quietly, regarding the nugget in his hand in disbelief.

"Don't worry about me." Jurek waved him off. "The *Sonderkommando* fellows take good care of me for my troubles."

Edek thanked him again, but this time pressed his hand with genuine emotion. His chest swelled with it, his eyes began to sting. Wiping them discreetly with the back of his hand, he took a deep breath to recollect himself and switch the subject that was growing much too emotional for both men's liking: "As we have agreed, as soon as Mala, Wiesław and I get to Szymlak, the civilian tiler who works in the camp, we'll leave the uniform and the pass with him. He'll smuggle it back to you when he comes to work the following day. Then, Jerzy shall lead you out of the camp the same way I'll lead out Mala and Wiesław. Due to our disguise, the SS won't realize how we escaped. They'll assume we took the Russians' route, so you'll be safe to repeat our performance with no trouble at all."

Jurek nodded, his eyes shining in excitement. The plan was good, almost foolproof; even such a veteran as he knew it.

"Perhaps, we'll meet outside someday," Jurek said, seeing Edek off at the door.

"I'd like that." Edek smiled warmly, grasping the admissions block clerk's hand for the last time.

Edek was in excellent spirits that day. He had managed to worm himself into Kapo Jupp's good graces by bribing him with alcohol nearly every day for the past two weeks. As a result, Jupp permitted Wiesław to also join the temporary ramp *Kommando* which would mean he'd be with ordinary inmates once again.

However, when Edek excitedly broke the news to his friend, Wiesław only sat, silent and subdued, running his nervous fingers through his long hair.

"Are you not happy?" Edek regarded him in wonder, feeling faintly hurt. "Everything's settled with Jupp. Jurek from the admissions block shall get you a regular inmate's uniform tomorrow. On the appointed day, you'll walk straight to the potato bunker, where I'll be waiting for you, dressed as your SS escort. After Jerzy brings Mala to us, we'll leave this place forever. What I don't understand is why you aren't covering my face with kisses as we speak?"

Wiesław made an effort to laugh, but then only looked at Edek wistfully.

"Edek, thank you for everything, truly…" Another tremendous breath, full of the unspoken. "But… I can't… I won't go."

"Are you mad?" Edek asked very quietly and sternly. "We have a chance to be out of here, once and for all."

"I know. It's just…" A gentle smile warmed Wiesław's features. "It'll be much more difficult to get two inmates out. The plan was good only for one—one inmate escorted by one SS man—"

"I'm not listening to this nonsense," Edek cut him off with a categorical shake of the head. "We'll make it through, all three of us, and that's that."

"And when we're outside? Two can still hide; three is a crowd. We'll never be able to go unnoticed. And besides, a couple—a man and his wife or lady friend traveling alone—raise much less suspicion than two men and a girl. If I were a German patrolman, I'd think them to be partisans for sure."

"Szymlak will supply us with civilian clothes," Edek pressed, refusing to surrender. "Perhaps, we'll beg a couple of farming tools out of him, in exchange for gold? Then we'll pass for Polish farmers with ease. All three of us are Poles after all; we speak the language perfectly and know the land. German patrolmen won't even have a reason to stop us for a paper check—"

"They won't have a reason to stop *a couple* for a paper check," Wiesław interrupted him. "A farmer and his wife look natural. Two farmers and a girl with them look like they have just stepped from their Nazi anti-partisan poster."

"Rot," Edek grumbled stubbornly and was about to argue further when it occurred to him that there was nothing he could possibly interject against Wiesław's more than sound argument. The realization came like a punch in the gut, making him pained and breathless at the prospect of leaving his best friend behind. He tossed his head, disgusted with himself for even considering it. "Then I won't go either."

"Now you're talking rubbish," Wiesław admonished him with a sad grin. "What about Mala? Should she also stay and continue to suffer in this abattoir, solely because of your brotherly feelings for me?"

With an anguished moan at the seemingly impossible choice, Edek dropped his head on his arms folded atop the table. How was he supposed to decide who was more important: the woman he loved more than life or his friend who had saved his on several occasions?

Fortunately for him and his infinitely guilty conscience, Wiesław made the choice for him. "You go with Mala and I'll follow you two with Jerzy or Jurek a few days later." Edek nearly choked at the warmth of his comrade's palm on his shoulder. "And then we'll all meet in the forests and fight shoulder to shoulder, just like we planned. It's the most sensible solution. You can argue till you're blue in the face, but you know I'm right."

A grim, lopsided grin appeared on Edek's face when he lifted it off his arms to look at Wiesław. "I hate it when you get all logical."

Wiesław snorted softly. "I know. I'll help you and Mala with whatever I can though. I would never back out of that."

"Thank you. I know you wouldn't." He looked at his best friend long and hard, as though memorizing Wiesław's features for years—or days—to come. No one could tell when, or if, they would ever meet again. "There's only one thing I need you to promise me."

"Anything." In a rush of emotion, Wiesław clasped his friend's hand.

"Remember we spoke of you writing a book about our experiences here?"

"Yes?"

"If you're the one who survives it, write it for both of us, will you?"

Wiesław looked at Edek for a long time before finally giving him his solemn oath, not because he hesitated giving it, but because he had a sudden premonition that he would be the only one alive to tell the tale.

The sun was scorching the earth and Edek was messing about with the lock on the guardhouse toilet. Even the wooden planks of the guardhouse radiated heat; the metal of the lock was outright burning to the touch. Rivulets of sweat pouring down his face and back, he cursed the blasted thing for the thousandth time. He'd been poking at it for over twenty minutes now and it still refused to budge.

Exasperated, he threw a glance over his shoulder. Wiesław, his lookout, signed to him to go on—the coast was clear. The camp lay deserted in the sweltering afternoon. The outside gangs and the *Kapos* guarding them were all outside the perimeter and the SS, including the ones in the guard towers, were busy napping after consuming a recently doubled ration of cold beer and schnapps. Sensing their SS Teutonic warriors' shifting attitudes at the news of the allied victories, their commanders pacified them into submission by supplying them with almost unlimited quantities of alcohol, much like they did with the frontline troops.

To a drunk infantryman, even a roaring Soviet commissar with a hand grenade didn't appear all that terrifying. To a drunk SS man, tens of thousands of Hungarians blurred into a faceless mass, making killing them much easier. Rumor had it, after the Hungarians were all dealt with, the rest of the Auschwitzers would share their fate, veterans or not. The clock was ticking, menacing and unrelenting, measuring what remained of their pitiful lives.

With renewed vigor, Edek threw himself at the task. He needed to break the lock so that Jerzy would have a reason to be here the next day. Edek had already concealed the blue overalls inside the facility, behind the water tank attached to one of the toilets—a perfectly safe place as not a single SS man would lower himself to poking behind such unsanitary items. Tomorrow, Mala would change into them and walk out of here accompanied by Jerzy, a porcelain washbasin on her head. She had already taken care of her hair the day before, cutting it off in front of Edek's stunned eyes without even wincing at the sight of the long golden locks falling all around her onto the concrete floor.

"It'll grow back," she had shrugged, smiling and undisturbed, at the devastated look on his face. "It already has once before."

At last, the lock gave way. Barely restraining himself from releasing a triumphant cry, Edek shoved his uniform inside, picked up his toolbox and began making his way along the sunlit road, his eyes half-closed with pleasure against the golden rays. For the first time in Auschwitz, he was overcome with an overpowering desire to break into whistling.

He was almost free.

He was almost free, with Mala.

Chapter 32

June 24, 1944

Today was the day—the day that would either seal her fate or set her free, together with Edek. The plan was genius in its simplicity: she was supposed to walk into the guardhouse's toilet, change into a fitter's clothes, conceal her face and hair under the porcelain washbasin Jerzy had prepared beforehand, and walk out of there, accompanied by Jerzy as escort. From there, Edek, dressed as an SS man—he had assured her already that Jurek, the admissions block clerk, had successfully hidden the uniform in the potato bunker for him to change into—would escort her through the gates and… to freedom. It was both infinitely exciting and too terrifying to even contemplate it. It was unfortunate that Wiesław wouldn't be joining them, but she had understood his reasoning all too well when Edek had explained it to her. Still, she felt infinitely guilty for upsetting the best friends' initial arrangement.

"Because of me, he'll be stuck here," Mala had groaned, hiding her face in her palms, unable to face Edek just then.

"He won't be stuck." Gently, Edek had removed her hands from her face and kissed them both tenderly. "He'll follow us right after. As soon as Szymlak passes the uniform back to him, he'll go with Jerzy or Jurek, or maybe both at once."

Nodding, Mala had thought how wonderful it was that Edek could always comfort her whenever she needed it the most.

But now, Mala's throat was entirely dry, as though someone had wiped it with sandpaper. She was heading in the direction of the guardhouse, praying to all the gods she didn't believe in that no curious SS would be loitering around. Before setting off, she had glimpsed the guards' schedule in the camp office. Much to her luck, only Blockführer Perschel was supposed to be on duty that day—the carefree youth who enjoyed riding his motorcycle much more than minding his immediate duties. If fortune was on her side, that's precisely what he would be doing.

Just to appease one deity or the other, Mala quickly uttered a generic prayer, unsure if she had gotten it right and crossed her fingers on both hands. The sun was in her eyes; she could barely see where she was going. Above the main camp road, waves of heat rose. The air quivered and distorted reality, swimming like a mirage before her eyes.

Only, it wasn't a dream. It was happening.

The main guardhouse came into view. Mala could already make out its sturdy gray walls, the fresh white paint on the window frames, almost blinding in the bright sunlight, and even the bright-pink potted geraniums in its windows. Her heartbeat turned frantic.

"Mala!"

She didn't hear her name at once, her gaze concentrated solely on the guardhouse door.

"Mala! Do you have a minute?"

Only when a woman came running along the fence that separated the sickbay from the road, waving her frail arms to attract Mala's attention, did she notice her. Noticed, and cursed under her breath. The woman, who looked vaguely familiar but not enough for Mala to recognize her, was flapping her arms like a windmill, attracting everyone's attention. That was the last thing she needed.

"Are you coming to the sickbay later?"

Without slowing her steps, Mala shook her head. "No. Not today. Sorry."

"Tomorrow?" The woman would not stop running. Her sunken eyes were searching Mala's face in desperation. "I'm being discharged tomorrow. I know that sometimes you assign women to good details… Could you perhaps—"

"I really am in a terrible rush," Mala interrupted her. But, seeing the woman's face fall, she released a sigh and, after checking her surroundings, took off her wristwatch and threw it over the fence. It landed precisely at the woman's feet. "Go to Anni, the sickbay *Kapo*, and give it to her as a bribe. That German bitch won't move a finger otherwise. Tell her to fetch Zippy from the *Schreibstube* and, when you speak to her, tell her Mala has sent you. She'll arrange your transfer to a good detail."

The woman snatched the watch from the dusty ground and clasped both hands in front of her chest. "Thank you, Mally! You're an angel. Oh, thank you so much! You have just saved my life."

Now, if only someone saved hers.

As she expected, Blockführer Perschel was exiting the guard-house, limping heavily on one leg. Coming to an abrupt halt, Mala watched him maneuver his bicycle as she feverishly considered her options. She had no business to be here; should she turn around and—

It was too late. Perschel had already spotted her and was motioning to her to come over. Not feeling her own legs, Mala walked toward the SS man, her head growing dangerously light with every step.

With a tremendous effort, she forced herself to smile. "Can I help you with that, Herr Blockführer?"

"Yes, if you could just hold the handles of this blasted thing for me," he replied, somewhat embarrassed. "I had a little accident with my motorcycle yesterday…"

"Of course, Herr Blockführer." Discreetly wiping her sweaty palms on her skirt, Mala dutifully grasped the handles. "How's your leg? It's not broken, is it?" She forced as much concern as possible into her voice.

"I'll live and won't even limp, according to the doctor, but I wish I was lying by the river somewhere instead of riding this embarrassment around this sodding place." He grinned, swinging his bad leg over the bike.

"They should have given you a few days' convalescent leave, Herr Blockführer. You're working too much. And you ought to rest your leg. These boots aren't good for you just now; too much pressure."

"I wish you were the main SS physician!" Oddly good-natured, Perschel laughed and pedaled away, forgetting to ask her what she was doing in the guardhouse in the first place.

When he was gone, Mala released a breath she didn't realize she'd been holding.

The pleasant coolness of the guardhouse enveloped her as soon as she stepped inside. Jerzy, who must have been waiting by the door, caught her by the elbow at once and steered her toward the toilet. As it always was with SS facilities, it was spotless and smelling faintly of lye after the daily scrubbing performed by the inmates. Porcelain washbasins reflected the bright light of the fluorescent overhead lights just like the white tiles on the walls, giving the simple lavatory an air of a sterile operation theater, no less. While their victims lived in filth, the SS made it a point of honor to ensure that everything that their Aryan hands touched squeaked with cleanliness.

"Thank God, Mala!" Jerzy's voice was hoarse with nerves. "I nearly had a heart attack when I heard him talk to you. In this stall, quick. Change into these overalls and give me your clothes after you're done. I'll dispose of them."

She barely remembered how she made it into the stall. For a short while, she stood there, with her forehead pressed against the cold tiles, trying to calm her breath. For the first time, doubts began to gnaw in her mind. It was a bad idea. An utterly idiotic idea if you took everything into account. It would only take one vigilant guard lifting the washbasin off her head—she had already seen it lying right there, by the opposite wall, just outside the stall—and it would be all over for them.

Just then, there was an urgent knock on the door.

"Mala?" It was Jerzy's voice, dimmed somehow, as though she was underwater. There was a distant ringing in her ears, mixed with blood pulsing in them much too wildly as she panicked. Mala felt as though she would faint any moment now—faint for the first time in her life. "Are you dressed? Mala?" came his voice, more urgent.

With the best will in the world, she couldn't move. The next few moments were a blur. She was faintly aware of Jerzy bursting inside and cursing softly under his breath. She was so paralyzed with sudden, chilling fear, Jerzy's swift actions scarcely registered with her as he tore the clothes off her limp body and pulled the overalls right on top of her slip, taking charge when she needed it most. The entire time, he stared anywhere but her half-undressed body, even though she was too panic-stricken to feel anything close to embarrassment.

Mala nodded to some of his instructions without comprehending what it was precisely that he was saying as he forced her to move outside the bathroom stall, shoving her clothes inside his overalls at the same time. She felt the pressure on her shoulders when Edek's comrade lowered the sink onto them.

"Mala? I'm asking if that's all right? Will you be able to carry it all the way outside the outer cordon?"

It was dark and oddly safe inside and Jerzy's voice sounded clearer now. It occurred to Mala that she was all right. Everything was all right. Everything was possible.

"Yes. I'll be fine," she replied finally after clearing her throat. "I'm sorry for—"

"Don't apologize, old girl." He dealt her a light and friendly clap on her back. "Everyone's nerves would snap. I'll be in your shoes in a few days. I can already imagine how my teeth will chatter."

*

Receiving a signal from Wiesław that Mala and Jerzy were on their way, Edek emerged from the potato bunker, squinting against the blinding sunlight. His heart was frantically pounding, but, on the outside, he remained perfectly calm. Lighting his cigarette, he strode toward the side of the dusty road sprinkled with sparse patches of grass and only then turned his head in the direction from which Jerzy was leading Mala. Jerzy's towering frame was a perfect façade for her slight figure, contrary to what Edek had feared. Anyone appeared to be short and almost antlike next to the giant Pole, even the tallest SS leaders; with her face hidden and her body concealed by the shapeless blue overalls, Mala was indistinguishable from any other inmate, even to Edek's eye.

His stomach contracted with almost physical pain when he saw the heavy washbasin on Mala's shoulders. It was a miracle she could lift it in the first place; how was she to carry it for such a long distance? Inside of him, a veritable war was raging, and yet, his face remained impassive. He only pulled on his cigarette harder as Jerzy stopped in front of him at regulation distance and reported the arrival of the inmate.

"Good luck, Edek," Jerzy whispered before performing an exemplary about-face and marching off.

Edek couldn't thank him out loud, but his eyes had said it all: *If we're fortunate, we'll all fight for our freedom shoulder to shoulder.*

"Mally, are you all right?" Edek whispered to Mala, barely moving his lips.

A strained "mhm" came from under the washbasin. He took it as a sign to shut his trap—it was bad enough for her to carry that load and here was he, trying to make conversation—and leveled his steps with her so she could set a comfortable pace.

The heat turned outright unbearable as they exited the camp, a guard saluting Edek and not even bothering to ask for papers, rather to his relief. Now, just the outside cordon was left.

The sun kept scorching the earth.

They walked.

At last, the final checkpoint. Just a bar blocking the road in the middle of a field and a sole SS guard manning it, but to Edek it could have very well been the entrance to heaven itself. The ultimate gate, behind which was death or freedom. Was it truly possible that a single wooden bar painted in black and white stripes could hold so much power over a person's life? An idiotic piece of wood and, behind it, the entire world ready to embrace them if only they made it past it.

Down from the sky, golden sunlight poured its warmth upon their faces, but it wasn't the reason for the rivulets of sweat snaking down Edek's back under the stiff material of his uniform. Such perfect stillness in the air; only Mala's labored breathing and the wild sprint of his own heart interrupting it. It would all be decided in mere moments, whether they were to live or to die. Edek stilled his breathing and tried to look as nonchalant as possible as they approached the guard.

"Heil Hitler, Herr Unterscharführer!" The guard clicked his heels and froze to attention.

Edek barely bent his arm in the elbow.

"Blasted heat, eh?" He shook his head, extracting the *Ausweis*. Oddly enough, his hand didn't shake in the slightest.

"To be sure, Herr Unterscharführer," the guard replied sympathetically and took the pass. As he was studying it thoroughly, Edek was overcome with an overpowering desire to swallow a nervous lump that had lodged itself in his throat. Instead, he cleared it intentionally loudly, indicating that he was in a great rush and didn't fancy spending another moment on such unnecessary bureaucracy. The guard mumbled an apology, but his brows still drew to a confused scowl. "It says here you're supposed to be escorting two inmates?" He looked at Edek questioningly, tilting his head slightly to one side like a dog.

Edek gave an indifferent shrug. "I shot one on the way here. He was annoying me."

The young guard paled visibly and handed Edek his *Ausweis* before snapping to attention once again. It was clear that bothering Herr Unterscharführer with any further questions was utterly beyond his desire.

"At ease," Edek smirked, passing him by.

All at once, his heart was in his throat. They were walking on a dusty road and toward a cornfield. In front of them, stiff corn leaves whispered gently in the warm breeze. With each step, the emerald forest looming ahead was growing closer and closer. The hideous gray guard towers had long disappeared from view, replaced by pines and birches—white, clean, with lime-green leaves cascading down around their slender trunks like waterfalls. Behind were the Auschwitz gates. In front of them, was freedom.

*

Head pounding from the weight of the porcelain sink, Mala trooped forward beside Edek, chest heaving, sweat pouring down her face and back from the nerves and overpowering heat. The black SS boots and a dusty, uneven road was all she could see, still too apprehensive to glance over her shoulder, too fearful to believe that the camp was left behind. In front of them, the afternoon unfolded, golden and without end and Mala squared her shoulders as though spreading wings for the first time in years, her load growing suddenly weightless.

The road bent sharply, walls of corn leveling their heads now.

"Here," Edek called, stepping off the road and parting the corn with his hands for Mala. "Follow me closely. Just a few more steps and you can throw it down. Just away enough from the road so that the SS don't notice it."

Brown earth welcomed them, unraveling its soft carpet before the travelers' feet. Stiff green leaves reached out to pat them on their shoulders and backs for the bravery that went beyond any comprehension. Gently, Edek lifted the sink off Mala's shoulders and she felt momentarily blinded by the wide blue expanse over her head, by the platinum disk of the sun pouring down its light on her, melting away layers of despondency, terror, and death.

An uncertain, ghostlike chuckle escaped from her throat and soon grew in power and volume, purging her lungs of the crematoriums' ash and smoke. Mala laughed, rebellious and free, as though taking revenge at the SS for robbing her of all the reasons to smile... or perhaps just to prove to herself that she could laugh after everything that had been done to her, that she didn't lose the habit for it.

After regarding her quizzically for some time, Edek joined her in her laughter at last, as though realizing the reason for it.

"Give it to me." Her entire face glowing with some inner radiance, Mala took the sink from his hands and, with an effort, hurled it into the corn, feeling as though the last chains had fallen off her limbs with that last defiant gesture. "Thank you," she said, her voice thick with emotion, as she wrapped her arms tightly around Edek's neck.

"For what?" he asked, head tilted to one side, genuinely puzzled.

"For giving me the most precious thing there is," Mala whispered against his parted lips. "My freedom. *Our* freedom."

She kissed him, ravenously and without restraint, tasting life itself open its petals on his lips, intoxicating and painfully sweet. For several precious minutes, the entire world belonged to them and to them only.

Chapter 33

In the serene stillness of the evening, the sound carried long distances. With his back against the pine, Edek sat and listened, his ears strained to the utmost. From the edge of the wood, he could discern the border of Szymlak's village. The twilight had colored the forest indigo blue. As soon as the last of the light had faded out of the sky, they would make a dash for Szymlak's house; not earlier than that. It was imperative to stay unnoticed, to become shadows themselves, to blend with the night and disappear along with it back into the woods.

For the umpteenth time, he consulted his wristwatch—Kostek's parting gift. It was barely discernable now, but he still made out that the minute hand had only moved a few pitiful notches since he had last checked. It was damnable business, this intolerable wait. He desperately wished to leap to his feet and pace just to shed this nervous energy, the adrenaline coursing through him, just to give himself something to occupy him, but Mala was sleeping with her head resting on his lap, exhausted from their trek of several seemingly endless hours and the heavy washbasin she had to carry until they found a suitable ditch far enough from the camp to throw it into. So Edek remained as still as possible, guarding her peaceful sleep, caressing her serene features with his loving gaze—his fearless Amazonian warrior, his comrade in arms, his future wife, the love of his life.

In the camp, the roll call was well under way. It was only a matter of time until the block elders discovered the disappearance of two prisoners. Then they would recount everyone again, following the protocol in case it was a mistake, which would prolong the roll call for another hour—another hour gained by Edek and Mala. His lips all bitten to blood from the nerves, Edek prayed like he'd never prayed before for the camp siren to remain silent until they were in the safety of Szymlak's house.

"Quit your fidgeting," Mala said with her eyes still closed. "They won't report us missing until they double- and triple-check everything. Me in particular. I'm a runner. I can be anywhere on Mandl's orders."

"I thought you were sleeping."

"I am sleeping. Camp has taught me how to sleep and still be aware of everything happening around me. That's the only reason I survived for so long. I taught myself how to become an animal. And animals hear everything even in their sleep; else, the predators will snatch them before they know it." Her face suddenly twitched and pulled to a wistful smile. "Amusing, isn't it? I feel more at peace in the woods with actual predators lurking around than in the camp with gray-clad human ones. I trust wolves better than I trust the SS."

"You have all the reason to. At least wolves kill to survive. The SS kill because they enjoy it."

Silver shadows glided along the moss, but they bore no threat any longer, only shelter and comfort. Through the web of the trees, village lights mirrored the first stars in the darkening sky slowly growing in number. A faint trace of smoke tinged the air and, for the first time, Edek's nostrils twitched with excitement as he inhaled it greedily. This smoke was clean, domestic, familiar, without the nauseating stench of death in it. It bore with itself the memories of home, of a black pot in the oven, of the homemade bread baking to a golden crust, of the dog's warm fur as it lay outstretched in front of the stove, paws twitching as it chased a rabbit in its sleep. Edek tried to resist it, but with the best will in the world, he couldn't. Before long, he was shaking Mala's shoulder gently but with unmistakable urgency.

"Come, Mala. It's time."

She didn't argue. She recognized the smell of home too.

On the edge of the wood, they paused and waited. In the distance, the bleating of the goats mixed with the chorus of crickets. And through the guttural croaking of frogs, children's laughter broke occasionally—a long-forgotten, carefree sound that clenched at Edek's heart until tears sprang to his eyes as the realization dawned on him that he hadn't heard it in years. In Auschwitz, the only surviving children belonged to Dr. Mengele. It wasn't all that surprising that they not only never smiled, but never cried either. Upsetting Herr Doktor meant an instant shot of phenol in one's heart. Even the five-year-olds knew it.

Tugging at the tight SS collar—it was suddenly difficult to breathe—Edek grasped Mala's hand and searched her face in the darkness. Perfectly calm, she reassured him with a nod, her smile serene and fearless.

"I'm ready, Edek. Don't fret."

"Stay close to the ground and drop as soon as you see anyone," he instructed, his voice betraying him with a slight tremor.

"I said, don't fret. I was in a Zionist camp for Jewish youth. We had a sort of army training. I was the best at ducking."

Even in the dark, he could see her eyes crinkling mischievously in the corners despite her deadpan tone. Grateful for the moment of lightness, he took her face, so pale and beautiful in the moonlight, into his hands and kissed her with all the passion of a soldier going into battle. In another instant, they were gliding forward, eyes alert and constantly searching the unfamiliar terrain; jawlines set; all muscles strained with animalistic agility as they navigated the patch of the meadow that lay between the wood and Szymlak's house—their personal no-man's-land between life and death itself.

Halting by the wooden fence, crooked and disassembled in places, used for firewood no doubt, they dropped to their stomachs and pressed themselves flat against the dewy, sweet-smelling grass. In a neighboring house, a dog broke into frantic, hoarse barking. Tensing at the risk of being discovered, Edek made a move to leap up, but Mala pulled him forcefully down, surprising him with the steely strength of her slender hands.

"It's chained; can't you hear the metal clanking?"

He recognized a hint of a grin on her face and laughed soundlessly at his own stupidity. "Forgive me, please. It's the nerves."

She regarded him with faint reproach. "Would you be just as nervous if Wiesław was by your side and not me?"

Edek was about to argue the point, but at the last moment stopped himself and lowered his gaze, feeling guilty for some vague reason. As though sensing his inner torment, Mala placed her warm palm in between his shoulder blades and all at once, the tension began to fade. He could breathe again.

"I appreciate that you worry about me, Edek. I know that you feel responsible for me, that you'll blame yourself and yourself only if something goes wrong. But you ought to stop. It's not helping. I'm strong. Just as strong as you are. I won't break. Treat me as your comrade, not as a girl you ought to protect. I've been working with the resistance for years; I dug my Papa out of the death trench; I assisted Rudek with escape; I carried the blasted porcelain sink on my head for what felt like hours under scorching heat—I think I have proved myself capable enough. We'll have much more of a chance if we work as a team."

Her voice was hushed but full of force and, suddenly, it struck Edek how fortunate he was to have a fearless warrior by his side.

"Thank you," he whispered at last.

"For what?"

"For being so calm when I was about to fall entirely apart."

"Well, one of us has to." Mala arched a brow in mock reproach and Edek nearly suffocated from the power of his feeling for her just then.

He was about to say something else but decided to leave it for later. After all, he would have his entire life to tell her just how much he loved her—her cool, logical mind, her steady hand in his, and her spirit that instilled even him with confidence that everything would turn out just fine as long as they were together.

"I'll go fetch Szymlak," he told her instead, letting go of her hand with great reluctance.

*

From her hideout by the fence, Mala watched as Edek approached the house and knocked on the window by the porch. After a brief wait, a curtain twitched, revealing a woman's face. Her eyes widened in fear as she recognized the SS uniform on the stranger, but she didn't dare close the curtain in his face.

Soon, the door pulled open, but it wasn't the woman who came out onto the porch; it was an elderly man whom Mala assumed to be Antoni Szymlak, the Auschwitz civilian tiler. Mala had only a moment to make out his gray, thick mustache and lined face in the pool of light that came from the house. In great haste, Szymlak pulled the door closed, obscuring Edek and himself almost entirely from curious eyes.

For some time, they were talking, their voices inaudible; only wild gesticulation betraying the urgency of the subject. From the corner of her eye, Mala saw the curtain move again, revealing the round, curious faces of two young boys, their eyes riveted in fascination to the mysterious SS man. Noticing them, Edek raised his hand and gave them a friendly wave, but they didn't get the chance to respond; their mother, her face white with horror, snatched them away from the window, pulling the curtain tightly closed once again.

And then, distant, but bloodcurdling nevertheless, the camp siren finally began its wailing, instantly turning Mala to ice.

The men heard it too; they froze where they stood and peered into the darkness as though expecting the search party to pour out of the woods with their beastly dogs any moment now. Alarm written all over his creased face, Szymlak turned his gaze slowly to the window, behind which his family sheltered. Edek followed his gaze and clearly understood everything without a single word being uttered. He clapped the old man on the shoulder and said a few words that only made the old man shake his head in obvious despair and lament his fate—their common fate, the oppressed, persecuted people—and apologize profusely for making promises he could no longer keep. Mala couldn't make out the words, but she saw every emotion painted as clear as day on the men's faces; she felt it all too—their sorrow, agony, and the soul-tearing manner in which they had to part, two countrymen separated by the war.

Not wishing to endanger the tiler with his presence any longer, Edek thanked him all the same and turned to take his leave, when Szymlak reached out and grasped him by the sleeve, saying something urgently and pointing in the direction of the meadow which they had just crossed. In the uncertain light from the window, Edek's face brightened visibly. A second later, he turned on his heel and trotted toward Mala's hideout, keeping to the shadows out of precaution.

"We can't stay in his house for obvious reasons," he informed her as soon as he reached her, his breath short. Yet Mala was relieved there was a note of excitement in his voice as he confirmed, "But he said we can spend the night in the barn that belongs to him, where he keeps the hay. It's a perfect hideout, even if the Nazis come here at night, which is highly improbable. Most escapes are from Birkenau and they all take the opposite route, so it's a safe bet that they won't disturb us tonight. He said he'll bring us food and milk later."

"And what about clothes?" Mala asked, raising her voice in spite of herself. The blaring of the siren, no matter how distant, seemed to drown everything else. Only the wild pounding of Mala's heart against her ribcage, forceful like a fist against the bones, overpowered it.

Edek's face fell. "No clothes, unfortunately. He owns only two different shirts just like his daughter, who came here with her sons and whatever clothes she had on her back. If he gives us his clothes and we get caught, the village people will recognize them instantly when interrogated. He doesn't want to risk it."

Mala nodded—yes, that was perfectly understandable—and rose to her feet, the dew glistening in her hair like diamonds. She narrowed her eyes as they stopped on the two lightning bolts on his collar. "You know, I hate that uniform on you."

Without another word, Edek removed his belt and began to unbutton his tunic. Before long, he stood before her only in Lubusch's old breeches which bore no insignia for her to disapprove of.

"Better?"

Her eyes almost black against the satin of the night, she slowly shook her head. "No. The jodhpurs have to go too."

"Do I at least have permission to keep them on until we reach the barn?"

Mala made no reply, only laughed in that way that made his blood turn to molten lava and set off in the direction of the barn, the creature of the night he'd give his life and soul for.

Later that night, they lay atop the roof to which they had migrated from the stuffy confines of the barn and gazed at the stars dotting the inky sky. The scent of fresh hay clung to their hair; on their lips glistened the remnants of rich and sweet goat's milk supplied by Szymlak's daughter a couple of hours ago. The jug of it was still half-full and warm, standing next to a basket with bread, potatoes, and smoked meat also delivered by the farmer's daughter, along with apologies they refused to listen to.

"You risked enough for us as it is," Mala had assured her, accepting the jug from the woman. "We couldn't be more grateful, truly."

A gentle breeze caressed their bare bodies, still hot and wet with sweat after their lovemaking. From their vantage point, the entire world appeared to be sprawled before them, ripe for taking, brimming with possibilities. That night, death had ceased to exist. The air itself was full of life and, for a few stolen instants, they breathed pure freedom.

"Even if we get caught—" Mala began in her still-husky voice, with which she had whispered the most impossible things to Edek just minutes ago.

"Don't!" he interrupted her, his arm stiffening under her neck at once. "You'll jinx us."

"Even if we get caught," she repeated, lifting herself on one elbow so he would see her eyes that were bright and clear without the haunted look in them that she had carried in their amber depths for far too long. "It was worth it. Just to have this one night with you, free, on this roof—it was worth dying for."

"We won't die," Edek said with certainty he didn't feel.

"Everyone dies, my love." She smiled serenely at him. "What's important is how you die. And I'm determined to die a hero, not a coward."

"You're already a hero." Edek reached for her fingers and pressed his lips against their tips. "My hero. You made this night possible."

"No, love." She shook her head and tenderly brushed a lock of hair away from his forehead. "*We* made it possible. Together, we're indestructible. In spirit, if not in flesh."

That night, for the first time in years, they both slept deeply, without any dreams. Their most important one had come true, and now, there was nothing else to dream of.

Chapter 34

In the dusty, golden-red rays of the setting sun, the water in the small lake shimmered as though infused with a thousand precious gemstones. Having scrubbed themselves raw with the fine, yellow sand from its bottom, Mala and Edek reclined on the bank, soaking up the tender warmth of the day that was balancing on the brink of the approaching twilight. An opened map before her, Mala traced their progress with her finger, measuring the distance not in kilometers but in days they spent away from the camp and nights they spent in each other's embrace.

"How far away from Szymlak's village?" Edek asked, caressing her bare thigh absentmindedly.

"Seven days precisely. Last Saturday, we waited in the forest for the dusk to settle in."

"How many more till the mountains?"

"If we take the roads, only two weeks."

"But we're not taking the roads."

Mischievously, Mala glanced over her shoulder. "That would be an incredibly idiotic thing to do."

"You're a commanding officer here; I'm your loyal infantryman." Edek grinned in response. "Out of us two, you spent years preparing to become a soldier in your Jewish army. I'm only a useless naval cadet, who got arrested by the Gestapo before I could make use of my new uniform. You know how to read the map. You know how to avoid them the best."

A teasing smile slipped off Mala's face, as though a mask from which someone had cut off the strings. "Two thousand years of persecution are in my people's blood, I suppose." Heaving a sigh, she concentrated on the map again. "Might as well make some use of it."

The shadows were already settling all around them, drawing mysterious designs on their bodies. With his finger, Edek traced them along Mala's skin that had acquired a healthy golden tan after all the days they spent sunbathing naked by the streams, concealed on all sides by the thick woods. On her expert advice, they moved only at night, invisible as shadows, blending with the environment and stopping at hearing any suspicious sound that travelled long distances in the dark.

Shivering with pleasure against his touch, Mala felt him counting her ribs that stood out even sharper under her skin now that they had to rely only on mushrooms and berries and an occasional fish instead of smoked sausage from the Red Cross parcels and whatever else privileged inmates like Mala could secure on the Auschwitz black market.

"After this war is over," Edek said, "the first thing I'll do is fatten you up."

Sitting up, Mala tossed her head with unexpected resolution. "No. Leave all my bones to me. I want to wear them proudly as proof of what they failed to break. And leave all my muscles to me, so I'm ready to fight at the first sign of this fascist filth spreading through the world again. Even after Germany falls, it will go nowhere. It will lie in wait until some fanatic comes and stirs all this baseness and hatred in his followers once again and reminds them of how their ancestors loathed and annihilated everything foreign and how immigrants were always the enemy and how anyone who differs from them in any way deserves to be persecuted and exterminated without mercy. I don't want to soften up and forget it all like a bad dream. I want to remember every person who died on my watch and I want to stay sharp as a knife, so I can cut out this cancer as soon as I recognize it spreading through the body of whatever nation I shall belong to."

In the descending twilight, her eyes shone like two fiery coals. Bare-skinned, savage creature of the night, of the forests they crossed, of the lakes they bathed in, she watched Edek regard her with pure reverence in his gaze and heard him say quietly: "No. You're not just my commander. You're my goddess," breath catching in his throat, he reached for her face and traced the sharp outline of her jaw with his fingertips with an awe-like fascination, "and I shall worship you all my life, no matter how long or short it shall be."

Zywiek Mountains, Poland. July 6, 1944

The road before them stretched long and empty in the early-morning sunlight. Under the dome of the pale blue sky, the air was fresh with the promise of freedom in it. Her blue overalls dusty and wrinkled after yet another night spent in a forest, Mala chewed contentedly on the blade of sweet grass, unbothered in the slightest by the rumbling of her stomach. Next to her, Edek was whistling a joyful tune, his arm draped around her shoulders, his SS tunic unbuttoned and smelling faintly of moss and smoke.

In the distance, the mountains rose, hiding in their shadows the coveted land of freedom, of partisans, of glorious fights to come. Just the last barrier to cross to forever shed the title of the Nazis' slaves and turn into fearless fighters instead, to avenge the ones who had perished and protect the ones who were destined to die.

Alone and unchallenged, they traveled during the day now, the map forgotten in the pocket of Mala's overalls. After poring over the map for weeks, she had memorized the local terrain like the back of her hand. She knew precisely where they were heading.

It was because of that unshakable certainty of their success, of her faith in their glorious future together, that the blow came like a physical one, straight into her gut, forcing the air out of her lungs—a doomed half-a-gasp cracking with horror.

"Edek."

Halted in her tracks, Mala stared in despair and horror at the two uniformed figures walking purposely and deliberately toward them. Her blood turning to ice, she recognized the uniforms instantly.

The border patrol.

The *German* border patrol.

Edek hadn't spotted them yet, only turned to her, smiling— *What it is, my love?*—but then his smile faltered as he slowly followed Mala's gaze.

They must have appeared from behind the bend of the road, heavens only knew why, as they knew that the Germans hardly ever patrolled this area.

Already doomed, already half-dead with anguish—so very close to freedom!—Mala saw Edek look with infinite longing at the forest looming to their right, then shift his gaze back to the approaching German border patrol. The muzzles of their submachine guns shone brightly in the golden rays of July sun. He stared at the weapons with bitter disappointment, angry tears pricking his eyes just like they were pricking hers.

So very close and so infinitely far…

Mala picked up his hand and pressed it tightly, shaking her head with a small smile. *No, Edek, my love. We shall never make it into the forest. Let's die with dignity instead; not like two cowards, shot in the backs at the attempted escape.*

He had always been a dreamer. She had always been the voice of reality, and now, that reality stared into her soul with those black muzzles and there was suddenly no escape from it all.

"Forgive me, please, Mala… I love you."

The very last words he uttered before the Germans leveled with them, saluted crisply and politely demanded, "Your papers, please, Herr Unterscharführer."

Of course, Edek didn't have any, only a useless camp *Ausweis.*

Of course, they instantly recognized the telling Auschwitz tattoo just below Mala's rolled-up sleeve.

Of course, the border patrol agents had a paper on them with two recent escapees' names, descriptions, and numbers and, of course, after exchanging knowing glances, they swiftly put two and two together.

"No, you forgive me, Edek," Mala whispered just before the Germans took them into official custody and prohibited them to talk altogether. "I may die, but my love for you never will."

Chapter 35

Auschwitz. July 1944

"It was good while it lasted." Edek released a dejected breath and handed Jakub, the Block 11 bunker *Kapo*, a note for Wiesław. "Thank you for letting me write it. It explains everything: how we got arrested and, what's more important, why I couldn't get the uniform back to the others from Szymlak. He wouldn't take it from me. He suddenly realized it was too much of a risk for him and his family."

"So, you just kept wearing it?"

"I had no choice. He was too afraid to give us his clothes in case someone from his village recognized them." He shook his head. "Blast it, I should have foreseen it. I shouldn't have had such blind trust in people. There's a war going on; I should have known. I should have taken clothes out of the camp myself, so we could change into them. If we wore civilian clothing, that border patrol wouldn't have given us a second glance. But an SS man without documents? I knew we were done for as soon as they stopped us and asked me for papers." He sighed. "Again, thank you for allowing me to write to Wiesław. Tell him, please, to stay put and not try anything. The war shall be over soon. I want at least one of us to come out of here and tell the world what happened."

Jakub concealed the note in a seam of his sleeve and gave Edek a sympathetic look. *Hey, that's what comrades are for.* He felt for Edek and Mala. He was from the underground too, despite being an inmate functionary in charge of the most dreaded punishment block in the entire camp complex. "I'm sorry about how it all turned out. People are cowards for the most part. Only few rare ones…" He broke off.

Edek only smiled sadly. "I have no hard feelings for Szymlak. He made a promise he thought he could keep, but when it came to reality… Many people think they're braver than they are until they're faced with a decision that will show them what they are or aren't capable of. He had a family; he'd explained it all to me. If it was just him, it would have been an entirely different matter. But you know how the Nazis retaliate."

"Is there anything else I can do for you?" Jakub asked.

Edek regarded him for a moment. "Is it possible for me to see Mala one last time? Just for a few minutes."

Jakub considered the request. "I'm not promising anything, but I'll see what I can do."

"How are they…" Edek's voice betrayed him, trailed off. "How is she holding up?"

For a few moments, Jakub seemed to search for the right words. It was Block 11, the personal kingdom of the Political Department butchers, built with the sole purpose to torture information out of its prisoners, to bleed the words out of them, to break them into betraying their accomplices. It was a prison within a prison, an extermination facility within an extermination facility—how could Mala possibly be treated by the Gestapo sadists in one of its dingy cells? "She's a very brave and a very strong young woman," he announced at last in a still and grave voice. "She told them she would die before they'd get a word out of her."

Edek's lips quivered. He tried so desperately to hold it together, but at the last moment his face twisted into a painful grimace and he broke down in tears. "All because of me." He sobbed. "Because of me and my stupidity. I should have never risked her life in such a reckless manner. I had no right."

Jakub lowered his palm on Edek's shoulder and squeezed it lightly. "You didn't force her into anything. That was a choice she made herself."

"I wish she had never met me."

A sad smile appeared on Jakub's face. "Last night, I smuggled coffee and cake into her cell. You know what she told me? That meeting you was the best thing that has happened to her and that she regretted nothing. Not a damned thing, you hear me?"

Edek nodded, weeping harder.

*

Hauptscharführer Moll, acting as a temporary aide to Political Department interrogator Boger, leaned over Mala, boring his gaze into her. The wire holding her wrists together behind the chair was cutting painfully into her skin but, oddly enough, she found the pain almost empowering. The more they hit her, the more resilient she was growing, baring her bloodied teeth at them in a snarl and almost challenging them to hit her harder.

"Make no mistake, I have made the toughest *Sonderkommando* men under my charge cry like little babies," Moll hissed his threat. "And I specifically asked to be assigned as one of your interrogators. Burning stiffs gets boring after a while. They don't react much, as one should expect. But you, Mally, I shall make sing. Even your protector Hössler won't save your sorry behind this time."

Mala's broken lips twisted into a vicious grin. What started like a ghostly quiet chuckling soon transformed into full-blown laughter. Witches must have laughed in their inquisitors' faces centuries ago, Mala realized, as the sound was wrenched from her. In spite of himself, Moll pulled slightly back.

"I somehow doubt that boastful claim. You can't even make a tiny slip of a girl like me talk!" Mala's hysterical laughter echoed around the walls. "A girl, who is tied to a chair, no less. Tell me this: does it make you feel more like a man when you hit a woman? Do you feel strong and powerful when you strike someone who can't strike back? Do you feel proud of yourself? Do you go home to your wife and boast to her how big of a man you are after you spent your day slapping about a girl tied to a chair? Or do you hit her too, just to teach her who's in charge of the house?"

Moll straightened completely and took a step back, pale and visibly unnerved.

"Tell me, why aren't you on the front? Why aren't you fighting someone who can fight back?" Mala narrowed her eyes. "I'll tell you exactly why. Because you're a coward. Men like you never challenge anyone who is even remotely strong enough to fight back. You're a school bully, who only picks on small defenseless children. You're a wife-beater, who can only feel like a man if his entire family is in fear of him. You're a member of the troop that doesn't even fight real wars, but burns corpses behind the gas chambers and beats helpless inmates tied to chairs and who can't hit you back. You're a coward. You're a pathetic, quivering nothing and I despise you and all of your comrades who hide behind political slogans and fight political wars simply because they don't have the balls to pick up a real weapon and step onto a real battlefield. I'll slap you still, Herr Hauptscharführer. You mark my words, I'll slap you in front of the entire camp and that's how they shall remember me."

Breathing heavily, teeth still bared, she slumped back into the chair, exhausted with effort but pleased with the effect it had produced.

Much to Mala's satisfaction, she saw that Moll's entire body was shaking, either in indignation or something quite different. *Fear.* She could almost smell it on him, just like she smelled the copper scent of her own blood that had filled the interrogation cell many hours ago.

"Take that insolent bitch back to her cell!" he roared at his subordinates. "No water and no food! I want her to starve until the day she hangs." He stared at Mala with his only good eye that rolled wildly with rage. The glass one was dead, as Moll's soul must have been. "I will personally put that noose on your neck, Jew-bitch."

"I promised that I would slap you in front of the entire camp." Mala smiled viciously at him. "It would simply break my heart if you missed our date and delegated the responsibility to someone else."

*

Curled in the corner of his cell, Edek tried to forget himself in a fitful sleep when the door to his cell opened. It was Jakub.

"Pick up your tail, lad, and put yourself into a presentable state. Your lady friend is waiting."

The SS had been hitting his bare soles with a metal rod for several hours that day in the hope of untying his tongue, just to fail miserably, but at once Edek leapt up, forgetting all about the pain. "Jakub, if you're joking…"

"I don't jest with such holy things." The *Kapo* dunked a rag he'd brought into a bucket filled with water that stood in the cell and began to clean Edek's wounds with utmost gentleness. "Those SS bastards are having a little party upstairs. Our friends from the underground managed to bribe one of them with a whole case of brandy, which he, naturally, decided to share with his comrades. Kostek, I think he said his name was, the fellow who brought it here. He's from the *Sonderkommando*, he said."

"Yes." Edek smiled warmly.

"Well, you can thank him for his efforts and all others for donating to the good cause. It was them who arranged your date."

Not quite believing his luck, his head swimming with nerves and excitement, Edek followed Jakub along the dimly lit corridor that smelled of mold and damp earth.

When the *Kapo* unlocked Mala's cell, just as musty and dark, his heart exploded with joy. She threw herself on his neck and covered his face with kisses. Her cheeks were bruised and swollen;

her lips were torn; blood was caked in the corners of her mouth and yet she was beaming at him with those broken lips as though the mere sight of him had wiped away her pain once and for all.

"Mala—"

"Shh, not a word about it." She was smiling radiantly at him and brushing his hair with infinite tenderness. "I'm so happy to see you."

"Mala, I don't know if you will ever forgive me—"

"I said, not a word about it. I have nothing to forgive you for."

He shook his head. "Because of me, you will now…"

Die.

What a terrible thought; what a terrible word—he couldn't force himself to utter it out loud.

Still, Mala understood and smiled gently at him. In the pallid, yellowish light, her eyes shone like two precious gemstones—hard, golden, full of life despite the death sentence hanging over their heads. "You gave me something to die for. You gave me hope. We gave everyone hope. Didn't you hear? Kapo Jakub says the entire camp is talking about us. The entire camp will continue our battle, long after we're gone."

"Mala, no…" A sob of pure torment tore from his chest. All of a sudden, the very thought of a world in which Mala's brave heart was no longer beating was too much to bear. Silent, impotent tears spilled down his unshaven cheeks as he cradled her in his arms, burying his face in her hair, inhaling the scent of her skin, trying to clutch at something precious that would soon perish, robbing humankind of its light. Without uttering a word, he wept—desperate, helpless, slowly dying on the inside with every breath he took. "I should have never asked you to run; I had no right to risk your life in such a reckless manner—"

She tossed her head impatiently at that. "Quit it this instant. You didn't force me into anything. My entire life I have decided everything for myself. This was my decision also. Mine and mine alone. And besides, what are you asking my forgiveness for? For the nights we spent under the sky full of stars? For the roads we traveled together? For the dreams we shared at least for a few weeks? For making me believe that a future with you was possible? Would you really rather leave me here alone and rob me of sharing all of those precious moments with you?" She shook her head with mock-reproach, her fingers warm and loving around the back of his neck, caressing him gently, tangling themselves in his hair matted with blood. "What we had, I would not trade for anything. Even my safety, my life—it's simply not worth it without you in it; you understand?"

He nodded, pressing his forehead against hers. He could barely see through the film of tears.

"I regret nothing," Mala repeated with a smile that tore at Edek's heart. "I lived a good life and I'll die a good death. I'm happy, Edek. Look into my eyes. I am. And it's all thanks to you."

He covered her mouth with his and for a few short instants, the entire world stood still. The earth itself had come to a halt to make way for their kiss.

Chapter 36

Birkenau. Two weeks later

The verdict was out. He was to be hanged tomorrow. Edek had already seen the solitary gallows—crude but deathly effective—erected next to the inmates' kitchen block, close to where the large water tank stood. He had no illusions concerning his fate. The SS weren't known for granting pardons at the last moment.

Alone in a small room next to the kitchen block, for Birkenau didn't have a punishment block, Edek sat and contemplated his very short yet very eventful life. The bitterness and anger at the unfairness of it all had passed. His breathing was no longer shallow and frantic, like that of a cornered animal. With his head against the stone wall, Edek sat and stared at the only barred window, at the stars that would still be there long after he was gone, at the soft velvet night, at the slice of moon that bathed his last residence in cool silver light.

Just a month ago, he and Mala had lain in the field near the barn, her head on his shoulder, her hair smelling sweetly of hay. He'd promised her the entire world that night and, for a few hours, he had kept his promise; Mala had told him that much during their last meeting at the punishment bunker.

Mala.

With a nail he'd discovered on the floor of his cell in Block 11, he'd inscribed her name and number and his own right next to it. *Mala Zimetbaum 19880 + Galiński Edward 531 + 6.VII.44.* Edek wished he had something sharp to scratch her name into the wall of this little room as well, but the floor had been swept clean and so, he whispered it instead—*Mala, Mala, Mala*—fervently, almost religiously, his very last prayer to the only goddess he'd ever worshipped.

*

Alone in the cellar of the camp administration building, Mala was studying a piece of razor blade in her hand. Jakub was kind enough to give it to them during their last meeting. That way, they could cut off locks of their hair and pass that sad memento to Wiesław in a note that bore their names and numbers, so that Wiesław would pass it to Edek's or Mala's father—whoever was alive. Overcome with emotion, Jakub didn't notice that the blade she had returned to him had been broken in two, its second half hidden carefully in the seam of Mala's skirt.

She sat by the wall, a soon-to-be-martyr surrounded by a pool of silver moonlight, and contemplated her much-too-short life and inevitable death. Its dark shape slumbered in the darkest corner, but Mala had no fear of its ghostly breath. Hers was a good, honorable death; a noble warrior's death—the death of a freedom fighter who lived and loved fearlessly and would die the same way.

Looking back at the years of her youth—eternal youth, for she would never mature, never grow older and wiser—Mala smiled serenely at the pictures of the past, her eyes without tears in them, clear and bright. Yes, she only had hours left to live, but she was infinitely soothed by the thought that she had no regrets whatsoever and no desire to change a single thing about the choices she'd made, the paths she had traveled, the beliefs she'd stood up for... the people she'd loved.

Edek.

A gentle smile appeared on her face when she thought back to the day when she first met him.

He'd brought her nails.

She gave him her heart in return.

That was her only regret—being robbed of the time they could have shared, the battles they could have fought, the celebration of honesty, human decency, and universal love that would undoubtedly triumph over hatred, nationalism, and bigotry. But even that regret failed to dim the light in Mala's gaze. She'd lived; she'd loved; she'd fought side by side with her loved ones. In her eyes, it was more than enough.

*

The day dawned mercilessly beautiful, with a mother-of-pearl sky tinted blue and a warm breeze, soft and tender like a woman's last caress. Inside Edek's holding cell, camp Kapo Jupp finished binding Edek's wrists with a wire.

"Not too tight, is it?" he inquired, looking oddly funereal that day.

"No," Edek lied. "It's just fine."

Jupp brought him outside, to the sunlit square where the entire men's camp appeared to have been assembled. Desperate eyes full of grief followed his every step. Old comrades stood in the very first rows. Like an honorary guard, the *Sonderkommando* men formed the vanguard, shoulder to shoulder, chins up, eyes right, with Kostek as their leader saluting Edek, the resistance martyr, with his gaze. In the next row, Jurek from the admissions block stood pale and trembling, crushing his inmate's striped cap in his nervous fingers. Recognizing Jerzy-the-giant, Edek nodded to him, thanking him silently for his help and friendship and wishing him better luck in escaping death. Not a single muscle moved on the Pole's face; only tears rolled down his cheeks, endless streams of profound grief. Among the Russians, Wiesław stood, ashen-faced and sobbing without shame, without restraint.

Edek ascended the gallows, tall and proud, and himself climbed the stool that was positioned under the noose. He felt rough rope touching his cheek and looked straight ahead.

"Attention!" an SS man bellowed.

The second one began reading out the sentence, but Edek wasn't planning on listening to that circus. Making use of both guards' turned backs, he pulled his head through the noose and kicked the stool from under himself.

One by one, the inmates removed their hats, pressing them against their chests. The SS scrambled to pull Edek out, shouted at the prisoners to put their blasted caps on, there was no such order, they'd make them all stand *Stehappell* for that, they should just wait and see…

Yet no one budged. The SS raged in their powerless ire, threatened with retributions and beatings, but no one listened. Edek showed them something that day. He showed them that the resistance was very much an option and that dying as a free man was better than living as an animal.

Their eyes were riveted to the gallows.

The powers had shifted.

The end was near.

The end of the Nazis.

*

A gentle wind caressed Mala's hair. Fearless and proud, she faced the crowd of women—the entire women's camp, it seemed—some of them weeping openly. Her dark hair shifting in the breeze, Zippy stood in the front row with her kerchief pressed against her mouth to silence her sobs. At the sight of her quivering shoulders, Mala smiled at her tenderly, apologetically. *Forgive me for leaving you just like Alma had left you… Neither of us had a choice. But you're strong; you'll survive; you'll leave this place and tell the stories of the ones who didn't.*

In front of Mala, Mandl was reading out her sentence, her voice oddly soft and shaking slightly, as though tinged with guilt for being an accomplice in her former favorite secretary's execution.

A dark smile on her face, Mala was secretly cutting the ties on her wrists behind her back and then, as soon as she was free at last, her wrists themselves. She felt no pain, only a rush of strange, triumphant exhilaration at the thought of sticking it to the Nazis when they least expected it—perhaps her last act as a free person, but the act of someone who resisted them to the very end.

A few moments later, blood ran freely onto the gallows. In the crowd, someone gasped. The warden that stood on the ground just by the gallows noticed it first and shrieked, calling Moll's attention.

He turned to Mala, stunned. Her grin transforming into a vicious snarl, she slapped him hard across the face, leaving a bloodied print on his immaculately shaven cheek.

"You shall never wash it off!" Her voice roared, carried far above the parade ground, sending chills down everyone's spine. "I'm going today, but you'll be standing in my place soon enough. Just like I promised that I would slap you, I now promise you this." Another resounding slap, this time with her left hand.

Recovering himself at last, Moll grasped her arms and threw her off the gallows, to the ground. Jumping down, he began kicking at her body with his steel-lined boots, sweating and panting with effort. And she was still laughing, laughing at him in front of the entire camp, laughing at ghostly pale Mandl who stared at the unraveling scene of sheer brutality with her mouth agape and the official document with Mala's sentence hanging limply from her shaking hand. And Mala didn't feel pain any longer, only some gleeful, lightheaded joy, and the harder Moll kicked, the louder her howling laughter echoed around the compound, eerie and sending chills down everyone's spine.

At last, Moll couldn't take it any longer.

"Get that witch out of here!" he bellowed at his underlings. "Take her to the crematorium and burn her alive!"

An audible gasp traveled through the ranks. Even the wardens exchanged bewildered glances; surely, it was too much.

Through a bloody film in her eyes, Mala stared at the painfully blue sky above, as if her fate was of no concern for her any longer.

She had done her part. She had given the people hope. Now, it was up to them to use it against the men who had sentenced her and Edek to death.

For whatever odd reason, Zippy's words about Joan of Arc resurfaced in her memory and Mala smiled blissfully through overwhelming pain. If she were to die in the flames like the French warrior and saint, so be it. At that instant, Mala found such an end inexplicably befitting.

Some Slovak girls gently lifted her body off the ground so that the SS wouldn't defile her with their touch. They put her on the death cart and pulled it in the direction of the crematorium, thousands of eyes following their grim funeral procession. As soon as the cart was out of their sight, all those eyes turned to the SS and, for the first time, the SS felt unnerved by those hateful stares.

A girl had slapped the most feared SS commander in front of the entire camp.

Suddenly, the SS didn't seem so invincible anymore.

*

Inside the crematorium, Kostek and his friends gently took Mala's body off the cart and laid it onto the table, where Edek's body was already lying. She had died of blood loss and her injuries on the way there, robbing Moll of his final death wish. Kostek was cleaning her face with a handkerchief, just like she had cleaned his in some other lifetime, as it now seemed.

"Shall we cremate them together?" Filip asked.

Kostek nodded. "Yes. Only together." He looked at the man. "Could you go outside and cut all the flowers from the flowerbeds? The Hungarians are all dead. No one needs to be deceived anymore."

"What of the SS—"

"Screw the SS," Kostek declared dangerously loudly.

The entire room stared at him in stunned amazement; then, someone else repeated, "That's right. Screw the SS."

"Kill them all."

"Burn them in these very furnaces like they've been burning us for years."

"Burn it all down!"

The soft grumble turned to shouts. Surrounding two dead heroes, the *Sonderkommando* were planning the revolt.

Chapter 37

October 7, 1944

The day dawned pale-blue and pleasantly warm, and yet, some vague, invisible threat seeped into the air, poisoning it and shielding the disk of the rising sun like a dark cloud. In the yard in front of Crematorium IV, the *Sonderkommando* exchanged subdued whispers as they eyed the SS with suspicion. Two days ago, Moll had demanded a list with three hundred names on it—supposedly, for a rubble clearance team somewhere in Upper Silesia, where the food would be plentiful and the barracks warm and clean. Only, the *Sonderkommando* had burned enough men whose names had also been put on similar "rubble-clearing teams" to put two and two together.

For the past forty-eight hours, they'd been stuffing rags soaked with oil under their bunks, in between the crematorium roof rafters, and in the coke store as well.

For the past forty-eight hours, they'd been carrying their hidden contraband from Jurek's admissions block into their own, pulling the planks of the floor open and distributing whatever makeshift bombs and weapons they had managed to gather among themselves.

For the past forty-eight hours, they solemnly shook hands and thanked one another for being a good comrade and swore to give their lives in the name of freedom and take as many Nazis with them as they could.

Now, as they stood assembled in the yard, Kostek felt the cool metal of Edek's gun tucked in the back of his trousers and felt a dark grin twisting his features into a grimace of pure, cold hatred.

Unsuspecting and sure of himself, Moll began to call out the names. Seeing that no one had budged, he raised his voice, his brows knitting together. In another minute, he was outright screaming, his good eye rolling wildly in rage, just to be met with the defiant, deafening silence from the *Sonderkommando* ranks.

"Do you not understand German all of a sudden, you ugly stinkers?!" Moll bellowed, sweat breaking under his collar. Nervous sweat, for—for the first time in his glorious SS career—he had realized that they didn't fear him any longer; him, the man who used to instill mortal terror into anyone who wore an Auschwitz prison uniform.

A young woman had slapped him in front of the Auschwitz crowd and now, they saw him for what he was—the pitiful, short, one-eyed coward. If he couldn't frighten Mala, how could grown men possibly be terrified of him?

Laughter broke from the back of the ranks, as though they found him, the SS commander, incredibly amusing just then with his red, sweaty face and all of his senseless shouting.

"Piss off, German swine!" someone cried from the back.

Moll swayed when a stone, hurled by one of the prisoners, struck him in the head. Slowly passing his hand over his forehead, he regarded the blood on his hand in great astonishment, as though he couldn't quite comprehend the fact that he, the invincible Aryan warrior, could bleed like the Jews he had personally shot.

It wasn't Mala's blood that marked his face this time; it was his own and they smelled it, the former prey turning predators at the tantalizing metallic scent of it. Wild fire ignited in their eyes. A savage cry for revenge broke through, slashed the air like a whip, and from all sides, a hail of stones flew like projectiles at the few defenseless guards.

The SS drew weapons, began shooting in the general direction of the *Sonderkommando* crowd that had already scattered, occupying strategic positions behind the crematorium walls—their former prison turned into a fortified bastion in mere minutes.

"Kill the oppressors! Burn it all down! Raze this blasted camp to the ground!" a hoarse cry broke from Kostek's throat. He didn't recognize his own voice, his own hands that were pulling the gun out; the sheer power coursing through his veins to finally defend himself and his fellow sufferers against evil.

The acrid, black smoke poured from the roof of the crematorium, the alcohol-soaked piece of felt igniting within moments from someone hurling a Molotov cocktail atop it. The air grew thick with the victorious screams of the inmates and the petrified cries of the retreating SS. From the darkening sky, the camp siren's wails came crushing down, but even they couldn't suppress the calls for an uprising.

Fascinated and mortified, from behind the barbed wire, the rest of the camp inmates watched the *Sonderkommando* successfully fend off the SS, arriving in great numbers, in steel helmets and with machine guns at the ready, for a few glorious minutes.

To be sure, it could never last long, this unfathomable revolt, this awe-inspiring revolution of the free men against their enslavers. But even though the fearless heroes were being mowed down by the hail of machine-gun fire and steel, they didn't fall in vain. For on the blood-soaked ground, the dead SS men lay next to their former victims. Just two months ago, two martyrs died simply to prove that the SS were mortal. Now, the camp resistance died following their suit, just to show their fellow inmates that the SS also bled, that they could be overpowered and killed, that the crematorium could be burned down—one just had to find courage in themselves to fight.

"Raze this blasted camp… to the ground…" His stomach riddled with bullets, Kostek raised himself on his elbow, gathered all of his powers, aimed Edek's gun at the nearest SS man and shot him, with his last bullet, clean in the forehead.

Epilogue

The man looked about fifty, with a mane of dark hair streaked with gray and anxious dark eyes under the knitted brows and a somewhat haunted look about his lined, yet still-handsome face. He was dressed formally in a navy suit and a tie under his unbuttoned camel-wool coat, as though for an official reception. The staff kept regarding him quizzically as he paced the grounds of the former concentration camp in visible agitation, shoulders stooped, eyes scanning the empty guard towers as if he expected to see dark specters of the SS men materialize out of thin air.

Two days had passed since the twenty-third anniversary of the camp liberation. Most of the invited speakers and survivors were gone. In the distance, the voice of a tour guide explaining the structure of the camp compound to a group of schoolchildren echoed around the red-brick walls.

The man squeezed his eyes shut and pressed his fingers against tightly closed eyelids in a futile effort to make the nightmare fade away. But when he opened them, the past was still there, unavoidable and frighteningly real. Seeing that there was no escape from it, he took the deepest of breaths and forced himself to ascend the stairs, each step heavy with dread.

Pale as death, beads of sweat above his lip, he approached one of the museum workers and muttered something indistinctly as he fumbled with the contents of his pocket.

"Is there anything I can help you with?" the young woman asked. It was her third week working here. An idealistic historian, she wished to be as helpful as she possibly could. "Would you like a private tour perhaps?"

"No." The man released an odd, ghostly chuckle and shook his head without meeting her eye. "No, I'd rather not. I've had enough of those back in my day."

He stopped abruptly and, driven by some inward impulse, looked at the young woman sharply before yanking the layers of his overcoat, jacket, and shirt up to his elbow. On his forearm, the number 290 was stamped in fading blue ink.

The museum worker's breath caught in her throat. It was rare that they saw such low numbers here. It was rare, because most of the low prisoner numbers—the veterans of the camp—didn't survive all five years of Auschwitz hell.

"Could you wait here just a few moments, please?" she whispered hoarsely, her hand hovering with reverence over his arm, not quite daring to touch his sleeve. "I shall fetch the person in charge—"

"No, no!" the man cried, his gaze turning pleading. "I'm not here for myself. I don't want any attention. I'm here because… it's time. I gave my oath to him and I haven't kept my word. It was too painful, all too fresh in my memory. I couldn't bring myself to… He was always braver than me, you see. He was a true hero. Just like she was…" His voice trailed off, thick with memories and tears.

He wiped them discreetly with the back of his hand and extracted an envelope out of his breast pocket. With tremendous effort, he opened it and produced a small piece of paper, which he held out to the museum worker in his open palm. With a trembling finger, he pulled its ends open to reveal two locks of hair—one very short and brown, and the other, longish and golden—interwoven together.

The young historian's hand flew to her mouth when she recognized the names scribbled with pencil on the edges of what appeared to be an old German newspaper.

Mally Zimetbaum 19880, Edward Galiński 531.

"I would like to donate these two locks of hair to the museum. It is an inscription made by Galiński. It's his hair and that of Mala Zimetbaum. The camp Kapo Jupp, who was forced to hang Edek, gave me the hair and the note an hour after his death, stating that it was the last request of the condemned that I should give it to his father or Mala's. But, as I later discovered, Mala's father perished in Auschwitz without her knowing and Edek's father was shot in reprisal for some Nazi big shot being killed by the partisans. And so, this tragic memento went with me through all the camps through which we were moved at the end of the war as the Allies drew near—Oranienburg, Sachsenhausen, Neuengamme, Schandelach, and I kept it to this day." After releasing a ragged breath, the man added in a voice that was barely a whisper, "Edek was my best friend. He and Mala, they became Auschwitz legends after their deaths. In part, it was their heroic last words and refusal to submit that inspired the *Sonderkommando* rebellion in October 1944. They died, but they became the symbol of the resistance. The *Sonderkommando* men picked up arms inspired by their example. I should have told their story a long time ago, but…"

"You're Wiesław Kielar, aren't you?" the young woman asked, recognition flickering in her eyes.

"Yes," he confirmed softly. "I am. I promised Edek I'd write a book about Auschwitz, to tell the truth of how we lived and died. I've been avoiding my memories for far too long. It took me years to force myself to face the past again. I had to come here and see it all once again to realize that the memories, they aren't just mine to guard. I owe it to the dead to release them." When he looked at the historian, his eyes were clear once more, filled with steely determination. "I think it's time I finally pick up my pen. So that the world learns, and never forgets."

A letter from Ellie

Dear Reader,

I want to say a huge thank you for choosing to read *The Girl Who Escaped from Auschwitz*. If you did enjoy it, and want to keep up to date with all my latest releases, just sign up at the following link. Your email address will never be shared and you can unsubscribe at any time.

www.bookouture.com/ellie-midwood

Thank you for reading the story of this truly remarkable woman. I hope you loved *The Girl Who Escaped from Auschwitz* and, if you did, I would be very grateful if you could write a review. I'd love to hear what you think, and it makes such a difference helping new readers to discover one of my books for the first time.

I love hearing from my readers—you can get in touch on my Facebook page, through Goodreads or my website.

Thanks,
Ellie

EllieMidwood
elliemidwood.com

A Note on the History

Thank you so much for reading *The Girl Who Escaped from Auschwitz*. Even though it's a work of fiction, it's based on a true story and, while writing it, I tried to keep as close to historical fact as possible, only taking creative license to enhance the reading experience. The circumstances of Mala's and Edek's arrival at the camp, their pasts, the development of their relationship, their eventual escape, capture and execution are all true to fact.

Edek Galiński indeed arrived with the same transport as Wiesław Kielar in June 1940 and worked in a locksmith shop under Edward Lubusch's command. Edward Lubusch was one of the rare sympathetic SS guards who did everything in his powers to make life in Auschwitz somewhat bearable for the inmates under his charge. For his lenient attitude and his constant clashes with the camp authorities, Lubusch was sent to a penal camp for the SS in Stutthof-Matzkau which was focused on "re-education" of such kindhearted guards; however, according to Wiesław Kielar's testimony, "the result was… exactly the opposite. Not only his attitude towards prisoners had not changed, but he actually treated them more leniently still."

Edward Lubusch indeed agreed to provide Edek Galiński with an SS uniform and a gun and thus made Edek and Mala's escape possible. Even though Edek and Mala didn't betray a single person to the SS interrogators and Lubusch remained safe from the prosecution, he deserted shortly after the couple's execution. As he tried to contact the Polish Home Army—*Armia Krajowa*—he was captured by the German forces and sentenced to death. As the German army desperately needed manpower to protect itself from the Allies, instead of executing Lubusch, they sent him, along with other such "criminals," to the defense of Berlin from the Soviet Army. But even then Lubusch managed to desert after obtaining false papers and escaped to Poland, where he lived until his death in 1984.

Wiesław Kielar, who became a filmmaker and an author, indeed wrote a book about his experiences in Auschwitz and about Edek's and Mala's escape, which was titled *Anus Mundi*. While writing this story, I relied mostly on his account of events as it provides an insider's look into what was truly going on in the hellish world of Auschwitz-Birkenau. I strongly recommend everyone read this first-person account if you wish to see the story unveiled through Wiesław's eyes. Wiesław indeed donated Edek's and Mala's locks of hair, which he'd kept for years, to the State Museum Auschwitz-Birkenau, where the sad memento remains on display to this day, just like the inscription that Edek had made in his holding cell in Block 11 while awaiting his verdict. If you ever visit Auschwitz, make sure to ask your guide to show it to you.

The *Sonderkommando* did revolt against the SS in October 1944, managing to destroy Crematorium IV and kill and injure several SS men. The revolt was suppressed, but the gassings soon stopped and the remaining *Sonderkommando* men, who were fortunate to escape the execution, survived the camp. You can read more about their ghastly experiences and the revolt itself in Filip Müller's account, *Eyewitness Auschwitz*. The character of the fictional Filip, Kostek's friend, is based on the very real Filip Müller.

The story of a successful escape of a block clerk known to the reader simply as Rudek is also based on a true story. The character of Rudek is based on a real Auschwitz survivor Rudolf Vrba, who escaped from Auschwitz in April 1944 after losing his beloved from the Family Camp to the gas chambers (the scene with their farewell is based on his memories) and managed to smuggle countless documents Filip Müller had given him to Jewish leaders in the hope of preventing the Hungarian Jews from being deported. However, partly due to the bureaucracy and partly due to the public's disbelief that such atrocities could have been taking place in Auschwitz, no significant action was taken and most of the Hungarian Jews still perished in Auschwitz's gas chambers. You can read more about Vrba's personal experiences and his escape in his memoir, *I Escaped from Auschwitz*.

The character of Stasia, the Polish doctor and a camp resistance member, is based on a real Auschwitz survivor, Gisella Perl. A Romanian-Jewish gynecologist, she was deported to Auschwitz and saved many lives by performing abortions on female prisoners as pregnancy was virtually a death sentence in Auschwitz-Birkenau. As pregnant women were either subjected to horrific experiments and later murdered or gassed upon arrival, Gisella Perl did everything in her powers to save those expectant mothers' lives even though the conditions of the camp hospital barracks were far from sanitary and she lacked the bare necessities she'd ordinarily use for work. She survived the camp and described her experiences in her memoir, *I Was a Doctor in Auschwitz*, which was published in 1948.

All of the other historical figures that feature in the story, such as Lagerführerin Mandl, Obersturmführer Hössler, Lagerführer Schwarzhuber, Kapo Jupp, Otto Moll, Antoni Szymlak, Alma Rosé, and Mala's friend and colleague Zippy are based on their descriptions provided by camp survivors. You can read more about them in H. Langbein's study *People in Auschwitz*.

Mala's past, upbringing, and the history of her deportation are also all true to fact. Upon her arrival in Auschwitz, she was indeed appointed as a *Läuferin* (runner) and an interpreter and worked for the camp administration. Her resistance activities are also based on survivors' recollections, just like her selflessness and desire to help anyone she could. According to survivor Anna Palarczyk, "resistance in Birkenau was to help each other survive. And Mala was eager to help; that was deeply rooted in her ethics."

Unlike most privileged prisoners who only cared about their own well-being and survival, Mala did everything in her powers to improve other inmates' situations. Lorenz Sichelschmidt reports in his study, *Mala—a Fragment of a Life*, that Mala fed starving prisoners: "Now and then Mala brought me some bread, a little honey, a carrot. Without that, I would have died" (testimony of R. Liwschitz); Mala helped lift the prisoners' morale by supplying them with vital information: "She supplied us with newspaper clippings which we read before passing them on" (testimony of R. Liwschitz); but, most importantly, Mala helped procure much-needed medicine for sick inmates, which was quite often a matter of life and death in Auschwitz-Birkenau: "I hurried to the lavatory, the usual place for secret meetings. Mala was waiting there. 'Greetings from your friend,' she said. 'She is ill; she needs medicine, Digitalis or Cardiazol.'—'I don't have any,' I said desperately. 'I shall try and get some but no one dares to smuggle anything into Birkenau…'—'I will,' Mala interrupted me with a handwave, and she did" (testimony of R. Kagan).

When Mala managed to persuade Maria Mandl to allow her to work as an inmate functionary who assigned recovered inmates to different work details, she saved many more lives with her action, according to multiple survivors. "It did not matter whether they were Jews or Poles or whatever. Whenever possible, she sent the weaker ones to a place where the guards were not that strict or work was not that heavy, so that these people had at least a small chance to survive" (testimony of Anna Palarczyk). Another survivor, Margita Švalbová, also testified to Mala's courageous actions and her belonging to the camp resistance: "In order to save human lives, to caution against dangers such as selections or roll calls, and to thwart particular directions of the SS, we had confidantes in almost every block. That is why Mala could act in such a highly courageous way—which means that she must have ranked high with the resistance."

But I think it's Giza Weisblum's, another survivor's, assessment that summarizes Mala's character most perfectly: "Mala was known as a person ready to help. She used to act in the way she regarded as appropriate, and, regardless of nationality or political affiliation, helped everyone as best as she could."

Thank you so much for reading the story of this courageous young woman and a brave young man who defied fate itself and inspired many others to open resistance with their brave action. Let us never forget their heroism.

Acknowledgements

First and foremost, I want to thank the wonderful Bookouture family for helping me bring Mala and Edek's story to light. It wouldn't be possible without the help and guidance of my incredible editor Christina Demosthenous, whose insights truly bring my characters to life and whose support and encouragement make me strive to work even harder on my novels and become a better writer. Thank you Kim Nash, Noelle Holten, Ruth Tross, and Peta Nightingale for all your help and for making me feel welcome and at home with your amazing publishing team. It's been a true pleasure working with all of you and I already can't wait to create more projects under your guidance.

Mom, granny—thank you for always asking how my novel is doing and for cheering me up at every step. Your support and faith in me make this writing journey so much easier, knowing that you always have my back and will always be my biggest fans. Thank you for all your love. Love you both to death.

Ronnie, my love—all of this wouldn't be possible without you. Every time you meet a new person, the first thing you say about me is "my fiancée is a great novelist, you simply must check out her books!" I always grumble that you're embarrassing me with all that attention, but inwardly I'm so very grateful for you being so very proud of me. Thank you for all your support and for putting up with my deadlines and all that research information I keep dumping on you. You are my rock star.

A special thanks to my two besties, Vladlena and Anastasia, for their love and support; to all of my fellow authors whom I got to know through Facebook and who became my very close friends—you all are such an inspiration! I consider you all a family.

And, of course, huge thanks to my readers for patiently waiting for new releases, for celebrating cover reveals together with me, for reading ARCs and sending me those absolutely amazing I-stayed-up-till-3am-last-night-because-I-just-had-to-finish-your-wonderful-book messages, for your reviews that always make my day, and for falling in love with my characters just as much as I do. You are the reason why I write. Thank you so much for reading my stories.

And, finally, I owe my biggest thanks to all the brave people who continue to inspire my novels. Some of you survived the Holocaust, some of you perished, but it's your incredible courage, resilience, and self-sacrifice that will live on in our hearts. Your example will always inspire us to be better people, to stand up for what is right, to give a voice to the ones who have been silenced, to protect the ones who cannot protect themselves. You all are true heroes. Thank you.

Made in the USA
Las Vegas, NV
26 May 2021

23656507R10184